This book is dedicated to three inspirational women. Each one, despite suffering from debilitating illnesses, still makes time for others, supplies endless support, and is always there to listen.

So, Joanna Larum, Sylvia Stockwell and Barb Zavadil, my dear friends, this one is for you. With so many thanks for your wonderful, heartwarming, funny and supportive messages. You really do make writing worthwhile, because without the books, I would never have met you.

DARKNESS ON THE FENS

A gripping crime thriller with a huge twist

JOY ELLIS

Detective Nikki Galena Book 10

JOFFE BOOKS

Revised edition 2024
Joffe Books, London
www.joffebooks.com

First published in Great Britain in 2019

This paperback edition was first published
in Great Britain in 2024

Cover art by Nick Castle

ISBN: 978-1-83526-611-3

CHAPTER ONE

Jim Fortune had probably been in every one of Greenborough's sixteen pubs at some time or another, but his favourite was the Hanged Man. The beer was good, it was lively without being rowdy. Being old, it had bags of character, and the landlady was a real looker! To cap it all, it was only a ten-minute walk home, so it had quickly become his pub of choice.

The place had been buzzing tonight. Lots of incomers trickling in, being lavish with their money. Discovering he was a local, several bought him drinks and plied him with questions about the forthcoming festival. Jim was more than happy to extol the virtues of 'Dark Greenborough' in exchange for a pint of best bitter.

A kiddie's thing, it had started way back, always around Halloween, although long before trick or treat became such big business. In those days it was simply an evening where old superstitions, ghost stories and folklore were acted out on the streets. People dressed up as ghosts, or witches and warlocks, and there was music in the town square and braziers burning and stalls selling food and drinks. It had an old-fashioned fairground appeal. Lots of fun.

But that was then. Now it was a big attraction, bringing in serious money and an influx of tourism. Nowadays,

"Dark Greenborough" celebrated the darker side of life, and explored the town's mysterious, sometimes notorious, happenings. Old "haunted" houses were opened to the public, groups of "ghost walkers" trailed round the streets at night led by guides carrying lanterns. Pubs and restaurants took on otherworldly themes and old murders and terrible deeds were reenacted in makeshift street "theatres," while all manner of spookily dressed street entertainers roamed around, performing for anyone who cared to watch and throw them a few coins.

Jim welcomed it. For a few nights, everyone was your friend and you could team up with perfect strangers, dance and sing and laugh until the early hours of the morning, forgetting your own miserable existence. For someone like him, a lonely man with no close relatives, no wife or significant other, it gave a sense of belonging, of being part of something for a change.

Jim tilted back his head and drained his glass. He was beginning to feel the effects of all those free ales. He glanced at the big clock behind the bar and decided it was probably time to call it a day. The Hanged Man was open until midnight, but he rarely stayed beyond ten o'clock. He liked to watch a movie before going to bed. Still, it was Wednesday night and his temporary job had come to an end that day, which meant no work tomorrow. So maybe just one more?

'Hey, Jim! Tell us about the Black Dog of Gibbet Fen,' one of the tourists called out.

Jim looked pointedly at his empty glass.

'Get him another, miss! He tells a great yarn, doesn't he?'

Sheila Pearson raised her eyebrows. 'Oh yes, our Jim does that alright.' She shook her head and pulled another pint of ale into a straight glass. 'And after this one, my friend, it's my considered opinion that you'll have had enough.'

Jim grinned at her. 'This is my last, Sheila, I promise. Can't let these good people down, can I?' He smiled innocently and turned to the three young men on the opposite side of the table. 'Now, you see, Gibbet Fen is a remote spot, close to the sea-bank and the marsh. It's not the place to go on a moonless night, I promise you. Even so, some people venture up there, and some have been unlucky enough to come across the Barghest, the Black Dog. Not that many lived to tell the tale, because they say that if you look into its blazing eyes . . .'

They were right, he did spin a good yarn. The tale of the Gibbet Fen Black Dog had never sounded so exciting. Some of it was folklore, some he'd heard from his grandmother, and some was pure invention. The listeners were enthralled. Jim looked over the top of his glass at the eager faces, and for once in his life, he felt good. It was going to be a great weekend. Starting tomorrow, three days of drinking and being someone.

He sat back, story over, feeling pleasantly fuzzy. Sheila was right, he'd had enough — or maybe a tad too much.

He stood up a little unsteadily. 'Goodnight, friends. Goodnight, Sheila! See you tomorrow.'

'Silly sod. You take care walking home in that state,' replied Sheila. 'Keep to the pavements, and no wandering in the road, you hear me?'

'I'm fine,' he slurred. 'Perfectly fine.'

Outside, the cold October air made him catch his breath, as if he'd jumped into the North Sea. His head spun and he had to put his hand on the pub wall to steady himself. This was unusual. He drank regularly and was no lightweight. Even the few extra pints shouldn't have affected him like this.

Jim began the walk home. The road seemed different somehow, unfamiliar, and even landmarks he knew well seemed foreign. After about five minutes he stopped. He no longer knew where he was. Where was his house? Which way should he go?

'Blimey, Jim! You've had a skinful, haven't you, mate? Here, take my arm, I'm going down your way,' a man said to him.

Jim muttered a few words of thanks that didn't seem to come out straight.

'Good evening down the Hanged Man, was it?' The man laughed. 'You better pace yourself, mate, or you'll never make it through the festival!'

Jim leaned heavily on this stranger. The guy clearly knew him well, but Jim had no idea who he was.

They stopped outside a small terraced house in a narrow lane at the back of the football stadium. Did he live here? He supposed that he must, because the man had propped him up against a gatepost and was going through his pockets, looking for a key.

Then he was opening the door, but Jim was struggling to keep him in focus. His vision was blurry and darkness threatened to encroach.

'I hate to leave you like this, but my Barb'll kill me if I'm late home again. Will you be alright, Jim?'

He tried to smile and said he would be fine, he just needed to lie down.

His Good Samaritan propelled him into the lounge and sat him on the sofa. 'Get some sleep and I'll see you over the weekend.'

Then he was alone, in a room that was spinning faster and faster. With a groan, Jim sank down, closed his eyes and passed out.

* * *

Although it was many years since his days as a special operative soldier, Joseph Easter was still a light sleeper. At around four in the morning he woke to hear someone softly sobbing.

'Nikki?' he asked.

Nikki Galena turned her face to his. 'It would have been Hannah's twenty-second birthday today.'

'Oh, my darling, I'm so sorry.' There was nothing he could do but hold her tightly.

Nikki's only child had died tragically as a teenager and she always carried the heartbreak with her.

After a while the sobs subsided, and she began to talk about the early years with Hannah, the good times, the little funny details of her childhood.

Joseph let her talk, for he could only guess at the torment Nikki went through at times like this when there was nothing to distract from thoughts of Hannah. Tamsin, his own daughter, was now married to Sergeant Niall Farrow, one of their uniformed officers, and was as happy as he had ever known her to be. Even though she was now a married woman, losing her was unthinkable.

After a while, Nikki fell silent and he realised that she had gone back to sleep. Joseph continued to hold her until dawn spread its welcoming light across Cloud Fen.

* * *

They very rarely drove into work together. Few people knew that they were in a serious relationship. It would cause all manner of problems for them at work if it became known. It wasn't the most satisfactory of situations, but it helped that Joseph's home, Knot Cottage, was just a stone's throw from Nikki's lovely old farmhouse, Cloud Cottage Farm. With no other houses close by, it was natural that they should see a lot of each other. So far, none of the higher-ups had twigged that they were more than just "friends and neighbours," but they lived in fear that one day the cat would get out of the bag. If it did, their team would have to break up. They would not be allowed to work together, it was as simple as that.

Today, however, Joseph had insisted that he drive them to the station in his car. Their excuse, if one should be needed, was that her mother was having some work done on hers, so she had borrowed Nikki's car for the day. He'd already texted Eve and warned her, just in case.

Understandably, Nikki was still feeling pretty low. Ideally, she should have taken the day off but with the festival looming, that was impossible. A three-day event of that magnitude in their town meant big fun for most, and a nightmare for the police.

As he drove, Joseph encouraged her to talk about Hannah.

'When she was little, I think she loved the Dark Greenborough Festival even more than Christmas.' Nikki smiled sadly. 'And, fifteen, twenty years back, this event was such fun — harmless fun, you know? Nothing was as threatening as it seems now. The drunks were less aggressive, and I don't ever remember taking a knife from a gang of kids.'

'Selective memory? Or were things really less violent, I wonder?' Joseph said.

'No, it wasn't like it is today. The atmosphere was almost magical back then. Hannah used to love seeing the street traders all dressed up in fancy dress costumes — witches, devils, ghosts, fairies and elves. And they sold such delicious stuff. There were sticky toffee apples, big trays of parkin, marshmallow cones with hundreds and thousands on top, hot dogs, oh, and one woman always used to make these funny little cakes in the shape of pumpkins. They were covered in this bright orange icing! They were Hannah's favourite. There were probably enough E-numbers in them to keep the kids high as kites for hours!'

'Guess it's changed beyond all recognition?'

Nikki nodded. 'You're not kidding! It's like they've taken a cute Disney film and remade it into a thriller. It's advertised everywhere now, all over the country.'

'It's good for the Greenborough economy though,' Joseph said. 'The hotels and guesthouses are full, and the pubs and restaurants are packed out. And then there's all the venues, market traders and street entertainments.'

'Good for the drug dealers, the pickpockets and the muggers too,' added Nikki morosely. 'Remember last year? The cells were full to bursting.' She sighed. 'What's even worse is that it's lost its magic.'

'It's what they call progress.' Joseph pulled off the marsh lane on to the main Greenborough road. 'Not that I approve, but it has put Greenborough on the list of Great British Attractions.'

'And caused the police a whole load of extra work. Cam has had to draft in uniforms from all round the division.'

Cameron Walker had been acting superintendent, holding the fort while the new incumbent recovered from a skiing accident. Then it was realised that Greenborough needed stability, and as Cameron seemed to be supplying it by the bucket load, he was offered the post permanently. It couldn't have been better for Nikki and Joseph. Cam knew about their domestic situation and chose to ignore it. He was an old friend and a good one, plus he was a damned fine super to work for.

'It's going to be three nights of hell,' Nikki complained, 'what with drunks spewing up all over the place and picking fights, and all manner of petty crime.'

'Oh, I don't know. A lot of it is pretty good-natured fun. Niall's actually looking forward to it,' Joseph said.

Despite being a police sergeant, his son-in-law, Niall Farrow, was still young enough to enjoy the festive atmosphere, and Joseph knew that he would try to ensure that the party-goers enjoyed themselves in a trouble-free environment.

Nikki threw him an apologetic smile. 'Take no notice of me, I'm just a grumpy old woman. And right now, I'm wallowing in the past and resenting the new Dark Greenborough.'

For a few moments they were silent. 'One year,' Nikki said, 'Hannah asked for a birthday cake in the shape of a pumpkin, because she liked the little ones from the market. So, I made her one.'

Joseph stared at her, incredulous. 'Nikki Galena baked a cake?'

'Don't mock, Easter. Actually, the cake itself was okay, it was my artistic interpretation of a pumpkin that failed miserably. Luckily, Martin Durham called by and saved the day. Somehow, he managed to turn my orange disaster into a ginger cat just like the Cheshire Cat from Alice in Wonderland. Hannah absolutely loved it.'

Joseph smiled, but there was sadness there too. Martin had been the original owner of Knot Cottage and had died tragically a few years back. He had been very attached to Hannah, and Nikki had been devastated. 'Martin was a really good cook, wasn't he? He left lots of wonderful cookery books in the cottage and I've kept them all.' The smile broadened. 'But *you* actually baked a cake? I mean, really?'

'Just the once, and don't worry, it won't happen again.'

'I'm just so impressed.'

'Oh, bog off. It was a packet mix, if you must know.'

'Aha! The truth is coming out.'

By the time they reached the security gates, Nikki was smiling.

CHAPTER TWO

The meeting room was packed with people waiting for their instructions for the next couple of days. The atmosphere was light-hearted, with derogatory comments about how Greenborough had become the weirdo capital of the world, and the usual suggestions for opening a book on who could grab the most Goths in one night.

'Okay, settle down! We've got a lot to cover and I want you guys out of here and on the streets ASAP,' Niall said.

Joseph still found it a revelation to hear his son-in-law speaking in such a commanding tone. Niall Farrow had travelled a long way from young, fresh-faced "Boy's Own" adventurer to a very good uniformed sergeant.

Niall glanced down at a printout. 'First, reports of incidents from overnight.' These he listed, noting those that needed following up, then he mentioned a few suspects known to be at large in the area. That done, he drew in a long breath. 'Now, most of you know all about the Dark Greenborough Festival from previous years, so you know what to expect. For any newcomers, it starts tomorrow, Friday, and runs through to Sunday night. It's a huge attraction that brings in a lot of revenue to the town. For the most part, the people attending are out to enjoy themselves, but a venue of this nature does attract its fair share of oddballs.'

'By the bleedin' cartload!' called out one of the older constables.

Niall chose to ignore the comment. 'It's also an excuse for every kind of street crime, especially drug dealing. You all know the faces to keep your eyes on, and the ones to watch in particular. It's open season as far as the dealers are concerned, so come down hard on anything you get intel on. We are working in close partnership with the event organisers to ensure public safety and we want this festival to be as successful and enjoyable as possible. It's up to you to make this happen.' He then paired up the crews and handed over to Nikki for the CID briefing.

Nikki still looked tired, Joseph thought. After detailing progress with the ongoing investigations, fortunately not too overwhelming, she said, 'Saltern-le-Fen have warned us that there's talk of a team of dips heading our way, but they aren't just opportunist pickpockets, they work with a guy called Harrison, who specialises in getting the dips to nick wallets and handbags that might have addresses on something in them. They then turn over the owner's house while they are out at the festival. He's a real piece of work this guy, always got an alibi, and we could well do with getting him and his mates off our patch fast.'

'This kind of festival would be right up his street, boss,' said DC Cat Cullen. 'I've met Harrison before. He likes to prey on people in a club or a pub who've had a skinful. His favourite trick is to get one of his thieves to nick a handbag from a punter, see if there's an address in it, and hopefully a keyring. If there is, he takes just the door key, and puts the handbag back, apparently untouched. Half the time the victim has no idea what's happened until it's too late, especially if they're pissed.'

'And I've had dealings with some of his crew,' added DC Ben Radley. 'They work in pairs, sometimes there's three of them. It's the old distraction game. One or two keep the mark chatting while the third checks out the bag.'

Nikki grimaced. 'As I said, any hint of their presence here, and I want them gone, okay? Now, talking about presences, one of the biggest attractions of this festival is the opening of Cressy Old Hall to the public. As you probably know, the Hall is supposed to be one of the most haunted buildings in the county. Yes, I know how most of us feel about that sort of twaddle, but ticket sales are through the roof.' She paused. 'There are a lot of valuable antiques and paintings there belonging to the Cressy-Lawson family who own the Hall, so we need to keep a close eye on the place. I know it's not strictly a CID matter, but uniform is going to be stretched with the general stuff, and the Cressy-Lawsons are friends of the chief constable . . . need I say more?'

There were grunts of understanding.

'Actually, it's a very interesting place,' added Dave Harris with a big grin. 'I'd volunteer for a shift there, boss. I've been dying to see around that old house for years.'

Dave was now working with the team as a civilian after having retired from his position as a DC. Mainly functioning as an interviewing officer, he also helped man the office when the others were out in the field. In fact, he did what he had always done, and no one felt that he had ever really retired.

'In which case, my friend, Cressy Old Hall, along with its valuables and its ghosts and ghoulies, is all yours.' Nikki smiled serenely. 'So are Clive and Priscilla Cressy-Lawson, and may heaven help you.'

'I'll manage them,' Dave replied stoically. 'Can't wait.'

'Then I suggest that you ring them when the meeting's over. Drive up there and have a word with them, and do make sure they realise that even though we are going to be policing an entire festival, we are taking their precious bloody artefacts very seriously indeed.'

'Do I use the same heavy sarcasm, boss?'

'Perhaps it would be preferable to tone it down a tad,' Joseph suggested.

'My thoughts precisely, Sarge,' said Dave. 'I'll say it in my own inimitable way.'

'Just get the message over, Dave. Other than that, we are going to have to take things as they come. Needless to say, if we can handle things without putting extra strain on uniform, then we will. And one last thing.' She smiled. 'If you get the chance, try to enjoy yourselves too. It might not be the festival it was years ago, but it is very important to Greenborough. We need to get behind it and make it the best it can be.'

Joseph knew that most of the officers present actually welcomed the break from the daily grind of boring petty crime. Apart from all the hype, this kind of event had a frisson of fear about it, the possibility of something unusual happening. Seeing different faces and the party atmosphere would give everyone a lift, even if only because the arrest rate would undoubtedly rise. Apart from that, everyone would be busy, and going home tired out and buzzing is always better than a long day spent behind a desk writing up reports and drinking too much coffee.

'Right, I think that wraps it up for now. So, eyes and ears open for the Harrison gang. Let's do our best to survive the next three days and come out the other side covered in glory.' Nikki crumpled up her crib sheet and threw it into the nearest bin. The officers dispersed, amid chatter and bursts of laughter.

'Nice rallying speech for the troops, boss.' Joseph smiled at her. 'Even if you do hate the "new look" bloody festival.'

She raised her eyebrows. 'How I feel has nothing to do with it, does it? We have a job to do, that's all.' She turned towards her office. 'What have you got on your desk that needs tying up?'

'Mostly all sorted. Just a few last-minute reports on the burglary in Stanhope Gardens. After a couple of phone calls regarding that, I'm pretty well free.' Joseph held her door open for her. 'Want me to liaise with Saltern-le-Fen about Harrison and his motley crew?'

Nikki nodded. 'Sounds like a plan. It's DS Marie Evans who passed on the info, so give her a call and then maybe pass it all onto Cat and Ben to follow up. If they've both met Harrison, that could be an advantage to us.'

'Wilco, boss.'

* * *

Nikki sat in the relative quiet of her office and scanned through the itinerary for the three-day festival. When she considered what it had been, the transformation was amazing. She also had a wonderfully eerie looking brochure that the Tourist Information people and travel agents sent out. The coach trips would start arriving today, bringing people from all over the country for a dose of ghostly fun. There was also a small contingent coming across from Holland, so she'd been told.

She looked at the main attractions. Prominence had been given to the Greenborough Ghost Walks. They were the brainchild of the local history society, each walk led by an experienced guide with extensive knowledge of the town's history. Picturing some of the creepy old buildings and the narrow, cobbled alleyways, Nikki reckoned they were probably onto a winner with that one. Plus they finished up at the Drunken Miller pub which not only had a notoriously chequered past as a meeting place for gin-smugglers, but served some of the best pub grub for miles.

Cressy Old Hall spoke for itself. It was an ancient pile dating back to the late 1500s, and boasted a plethora of hauntings and ghostly sightings. It was doubly attractive because the owners rarely opened it to the public. Nikki frowned at the thought of the Cressy-Lawson family. She guessed Dave was probably one of few people who might just get a civil answer out of Clive Cressy-Lawson. He was a difficult man, whose supercilious attitude had put her back up from their first meeting. He treated the police as if they were his private army, and addressed them as such. Talk about lord of the manor! Needless to say, he was not the most popular landowner in the area. His wife Priscilla was possibly even worse than her husband, with her constant whining about

13

the hardships of living in this socially deprived backwater. Poor Priscilla, the travails of having to travel miles for her Louis Vuitton handbags and Clivey's Ralph Lauren dinner jackets!

Next in line on the list of attractions were two deserted and supposedly haunted WWII airfields, at one of which ghostly men in flying gear had been seen running towards the shadowy outlines of Lancaster bombers. The other boasted a range of apparitions, ranging from women driving ambulances, outriders on vintage motorbikes to full-on air raids. Nikki had been to both in the past, and all she'd ever seen was overgrown runways, derelict hangars and a rotting control tower. Not a long-dead airman in sight.

Another popular treat for the visitors was the Murder Most Foul exhibition at the old town Elizabethan Wool Exchange building, which told the stories of various gruesome deaths in the local area over the ages. Nikki pulled a face, grateful that they had all taken place in the long distant past.

She skimmed through the rest of the attractions, noting several deserted buildings, an old dockland warehouse and an old cinema that were being opened up for various forms of ghost-related entertainment. There were competitions for the best dressed 'Night Creature,' readings in the public library about local traditions and superstitions, fortune-tellers, and a Zombie-thon dance marathon. She shook her head. Who had dreamed up these nightmares? On Sunday night the big finale would take place, with a firework display and live concert at the Greenborough Rugby Club grounds.

Joseph poked his head round the door. 'Got a moment?'

'Come in, Joseph. I'm just going over the festival attractions. I hope you don't mind, but I'm going to give the fireworks a miss.'

'Well, that's a relief!'

She hadn't expected that. She thought most blokes liked fireworks and the bigger the better. She looked at him enquiringly.

'Like a lot of ex-soldiers, I don't hear fireworks, I hear mortars, grenades and sniper fire, and I don't see pretty displays, I see dying comrades and screaming civilians.'

Nikki could have kicked herself. 'I'm so sorry, Joseph, I never even thought.'

'Why should you? And I'm not nearly as bad as some. I just prefer to avoid them if I can. Funny, it never used to affect me, but as I get older, it seems to bother me more.' He shrugged. 'Still, as I said, some of my old mates are phobic about them, especially the ones who suffer from PTSD.' He grinned sheepishly. 'Like Vinnie. But don't tell him I told you.'

'Vinnie Silver?' Nikki was really surprised. Vinnie was a security expert and ex-special services comrade of Joseph's, who had helped them out on more than one occasion. He was tall, built like a tank and apparently fearless. Nikki always pictured him galloping across the prairie in a ten-gallon hat and high boots.

'Light a firework near Vinnie, and he'll most likely lamp you one! He spends bonfire night indoors with the curtains closed, headphones on and rock music playing at full volume and gets as drunk as he can until he crashes out.'

'They should be banned from residential areas and restricted to organised displays in specifically designated spots,' Nikki said vehemently. 'I heard one of the young PCs telling his crewmate that he'd paid over two hundred quid for something called a cake? Turns out it's a firework that lasts for about two and half minutes and has over 180 "shots" in it — whatever they are. Something like that belongs on Sydney Harbour Bridge, not nestling in Daddy's raspberry canes.'

'Well, that's settled then, we'll leave the concert to the kids, and find something better to do.' He grinned lasciviously at her.

She smiled back. 'Oh, I'm sure we'll think of something. Now back to work, Sergeant Easter.'

'If we really must, DI Galena.'

* * *

Lucas Reid crawled out of bed, trying to remember what had happened the previous night.

His head throbbed, and nausea quickly escalated to full-blown vomiting as soon as he stood up.

Three trips to the bathroom later, he sat at the kitchen table, his head in his hands. Work was out of the question today. He was on a final warning already, and this would be the final nail in the coffin.

Very funny, Reid. Lucas was a trainee undertaker. When the guys in the pub had heard that, he had been regaled with ghoulish questions about dead bodies, and bought rather a lot of drinks.

Sheila had warned him, but had he listened? No, he hadn't, and now it was going to be back down at the Job Centre again. He groaned, not just because of his headache, but because he actually liked working at the undertakers. For once, he had felt he could be good at something. The problem was, although he wasn't a regular drinker, he also liked his beer. Settled into a "night out with the boys," he didn't know when to stop.

'Never again,' he whispered to the empty kitchen. 'This time it's final.'

He'd had more hangovers than he cared to remember, but today he felt worse than usual, if that were possible. Although he knew he should try to get some liquid down him to fight the dehydration, he just couldn't face the idea of swallowing. Food would help too, but the mere thought of it sent him dashing back to the bathroom.

Somehow Lucas managed to get to the phone and leave an unconvincing message about a stomach bug on his employer's answerphone. Then he found a bucket under the sink in the kitchen and went back to bed.

Once again, the wardrobe was slowly dancing across the ceiling, and the floor was moving up and down like the one in the Crooked House in the fairground. His vision was hazy, as if he were lying in the middle of a snowstorm.

Lucas pulled the duvet around him and curled into a foetal position. This was the worst hangover he'd ever had.

CHAPTER THREE

Dave had driven past Cressy Old Hall many times over the years, but the gates had always been locked. His delight at seeing them wide open was surprising in an old-time, streetwise copper. Dave loved old English manor houses, and had been dying to get inside this one for as long as he could remember.

In the mess-room, anyone who'd had dealings with them considered the Cressy-Lawsons to be a couple of "toffee-nosed twats." Dave knew that type. They responded well to having their over-inflated egos stroked, and he was good at that. He had a talent for getting the best from difficult people. Over the years, it had helped increase his arrest rate to a pretty impressive level.

Now he'd retired from the force and become a civilian investigating officer, he felt closer to the public. People treated him more like an equal, and he found this enormously useful when interviewing them. He had tempered the aggressive manner all police seemed to acquire, the "police speak" that put people's backs up. And it worked.

He parked the car some distance from the impressive frontage of the manor house. This was partly out of politeness, and partly so he could get a better look at the magnificent facade of Cressy Old Hall.

Dave had done his homework. He knew that Cressy Old Hall was the most historic house in the Greenborough area, and unless you went to the very grand Grimsthorpe Castle, Burghley House or Doddington Hall, you'd be hard pushed to beat it. After his wife died, Dave had spent his free time touring the county, mainly to get out of the house and all its memories, but also looking for a new interest. He had joined the National Trust and English Heritage and used his days off to get away from the gritty reality of modern-day policing.

He looked in appreciation at the rows of mullioned windows, the ornate chimneys and the prominent gables. What it must be like to call this home!

He rang the bell and waited.

The door was opened by a rather austere-looking woman who was somewhere in her late forties. Her clothes looked "sensible," but smart and clearly very expensive. She had brown hair swept up in a severe plait so neat that not one stray hair escaped, and she wore narrow framed glasses.

Dave smiled. 'My name is Dave Harris. I'm here on behalf of the Fenland Constabulary regarding the event taking place here tomorrow and over the weekend. Mr Cressy-Lawson is expecting me.'

The woman stepped back and opened the door wider. 'Oh yes, he did mention it. Step inside. I'll go and see if he's free.'

Dave had never met the Cressy-Lawsons before, so he wasn't sure who he was speaking to. He suspected she was the housekeeper, but over the years he'd learned never to make assumptions. He looked around the wood-panelled hall, and then up to the rich plastered ceiling. It was beautiful.

Clive Cressy-Lawson kept him waiting for about ten minutes, but Dave didn't even notice. 'What an extraordinarily beautiful house, sir!' were his first words.

Cressy-Lawson opened his mouth, and shut it again. 'Er, yes, it is.'

Dave introduced himself, and explained what his role would be over the coming three days. Could Mr Cressy-Lawson spare some time to point out the things that were of particular value or concern to him?

Cressy-Lawson seemed about to object, but then stared thoughtfully at Dave. 'We've got a damned lot to organise before tomorrow, Mr Harris, but I suppose I can spare half an hour. We'll start at the top and work down.'

Dave took out his notebook and followed Cressy-Lawson up the sweeping staircase. 'I know something of the history of the Old Hall, sir, but nothing about the alleged hauntings. Could you fill me in on them too?' he asked.

Cressy-Lawson gave a short laugh. 'You do? A policeman with an interest in Jacobean manor houses? This is a turn up for the books. I expect you drew the short straw for this job, didn't you? My wife and I are not the most popular couple in the county.'

'Actually, I volunteered, sir.'

At this, Cressy-Lawson gave a guffaw. 'No one volunteers to come here! I've seen some of the looks your fellow officers have given us, and heard some of the snide comments.'

'Well, you won't hear any complaints from me, sir. And rest assured, I'll be here throughout the entire three days, from when you open until you close. Any suspicious activity, if it's something I can't handle myself, I'll have a crew here in no time.'

'Okay, Dave. You are clearly the exception to the rule, so I'll tell you what I can about the hauntings. We have four ghosts, which is unusual, even for an ancient pile like this. The one I've actually had a sighting of myself is the Green Lady.'

'So, the hauntings aren't just invented for the punters to marvel at? You've actually seen something yourself?'

'I'm a businessman, Dave. I deal in hard facts, much like you do, but there are phenomena here that I can't easily dismiss.' He shrugged. 'What can you expect from a house that was originally built in 1560, and added to and extended over the generations?' He paused. 'Listen, if you're really interested, there's a chap from the local history society coming here this afternoon. He's organising a group of stewards and guides to take the parties of visitors around the house and the grounds. Why don't you have a word with him? He knows the history of the hauntings better than anyone. His name is Murray Kennington. I'm sure he'll be happy to give you the potted version.'

'I'll do that, sir, if I won't be in the way.'

'I'll tell him to expect you. He's due at two o'clock. Now, let's get on with the inventory.'

'I should think there are quite a few treasures,' murmured Dave, almost reverently.

'Not as many as there were. We're a very wealthy family, Dave, but the costs of running and restoring the Old Hall are astronomical. We've had to sell off some of the paintings and antiques to help refill the old coffers. Damned shame, but there we are.'

Dave was beginning to rather like Clive Cressy-Lawson. 'Why not open up to the public on a regular basis, sir? Then you'd likely get a grant to help you with the maintenance.'

'It's my *home*, old chum. Would you want riffraff traipsing through your dining room, dropping chocolate wrappers and dragging their muddy feet and snotty-nosed offspring over the carpets? This weekend is bad enough, but it'll give us a quick financial boost, and I can't justify turning it down.'

Dave laughed. 'I wasn't going to suggest an inflatable bouncy castle in the grounds or a hot-dog stand in the formal garden. I was thinking of the more discerning visitor, like the history societies and the U3A.'

'We *are* considering opening a couple of times a year. We really should do more with the grounds, then maybe we could get on the National Garden Scheme, and combine house and garden.'

'Good idea,' said Dave, admiring a classical bronze figurine that stood on the upper landing. 'But I really don't want to hold you up, sir.'

It took an hour. Cressy-Lawson actually seemed to enjoy showing off his most precious artworks. Dave in his turn was attentive. He was starting to get the feel of the big old manor house.

'Now I've got more used to the magnificence of the Old Hall, I'm looking at it from a criminal's point of view,' he told Cressy-Lawson. 'I've identified a few vulnerable areas that I'll keep a close eye on.'

'I have two men who can assist you, if you like, Dave? My gamekeeper and one of the groundsmen. Both are trustworthy, and the gamekeeper's family have worked here forever.'

'Brilliant! That will help a lot, sir.'

Cressy-Lawson stuck out his hand. 'See you this afternoon when Kennington gets here. Feel free to wander around and get your bearings. You'll find Mrs Warden in the main office downstairs if you need anything. She's my secretary and house-manager.' He paused. 'Oh, and say hello to the Green Lady if you see her. It's mandatory to acknowledge her, or you can expect some dreadful reprisal — or so says the legend. Personally, I think it's only polite to greet a lady.'

Dave watched him go. Typical upper crust on the surface, almost a caricature with his Aran cable-knit sweater, Barbour gilet and those nice tan brogues, but Dave saw something else too, a fierce pride in the house that it was his duty to watch over, and frustration. Dave was as far from Cressy-Lawson as it was possible to be on the social scale, yet he almost felt for this acerbic landowner. Juggling the maintenance work that must be necessary with a house of this size and age, and trying to keep it as a family home — it couldn't be easy. Yes, there was something to like in Cressy-Lawson.

For the next half hour he wandered around the big old building. He certainly wouldn't be able to watch everyone. Even with assistance, it was going to be a major undertaking. Luckily, the visitors were only allowed in at stated times and taken on guided tours rather than let loose to roam at will. He decided that he would watch the groups as they set off, taking note of anyone who seemed suspicious. If he noticed a person of interest, he would get one of his two assistants to keep their eye on them as they made their way around the house.

Dave returned to his car quite excited about this unusual job. He was used to working in dark places, among the dross of society, the unfortunate victims, the frightened witnesses, and the evil people who caused them pain and distress. Acting as temporary custodian to such a beautiful property was a rare treat and a welcome change.

He grinned. Short straw? I don't think so!

* * *

Eve Anderson and Wendy Avery sat in the kitchen of their old converted chapel, Monks Lantern, and read through the brochure for Dark Greenborough.

'My goodness, the police are going to have their work cut out looking after this lot!' Wendy exclaimed. 'What does Nikki say about it?'

Eve looked up. 'Oh, I think they're pretty well prepared.'

'It should be great fun, but you always get the idiots who have too much to drink and spoil it for everyone else.' Wendy pointed at one of the attractions announced in the leaflet. 'I'd rather like to see this one, wouldn't you?'

Eve leaned across and read: '"Oleander House. Home to the late Robert Matthew Richmond, Victorian explorer, botanist and artist who mysteriously disappeared, never to be seen again, while on a trip to the Lake District."' She nodded. 'Oh yes, I've heard that there are dozens of his paintings still there in that house that the family have never allowed to be shown or sold.'

'Okay, I'll put that one on our wish list.'

Eve smiled, 'I'm not sure that a botanical art exhibition fits in with the Dark Greenborough concept.'

Wendy shrugged. 'I think they are playing up the mystery thing, Robert's strange disappearance. I believe they are laying out one area like a CID investigation room, with photos, maps, old newspaper reports, last known sightings etc. The paintings are an added extra.'

'Well, I'm in,' said Eve. 'I'd love to get a look at his artwork.' Eve was no mean artist herself and since she retired and had more time, she had begun working in soft pastels. She picked up the brochure again. 'Anything else take your fancy? The haunted airfields, maybe?'

They shook with laughter.

They were both from RAF backgrounds and had spent their entire working lives in the military and then with the MOD. Between them, they had seen more airfields than most people had seen movies.

'I'd like to go to Cressy Old Hall,' said Eve. 'Now that is really worth a visit.'

'Oh, me too,' said Wendy. 'I'll put that on the list.'

'Good, and then I must start preparing for our guests. They'll be here in a couple of hours.'

Two of their old RAF buddies were coming to spend the Dark Greenborough weekend with them. Lou Fawcett and Rene Brittain were travelling down to Beech Lacey from the north of the county, and Eve had booked a table at her favourite Italian restaurant for a reunion dinner. The four women had been through a lot together, including some extremely dangerous situations. Now they were all looking forward to having some fun at the Greenborough Festival.

'I just hope we manage to meet up with Nikki and Joseph. I know they are going to be rushed off their feet, but I'm sure Lou and Rene would love to see them again.' Wendy looked at Eve hopefully.

'I've already mentioned it to Joseph. He said they'll do their very best to make some time, and maybe we can all have a drink together.' Eve's face darkened and she looked sadly at Wendy. 'Apparently, my Nikki is very down today. If Hannah hadn't died, she would have been twenty-two today. It's my greatest sadness that I never met my only granddaughter.'

Wendy patted her hand. 'I'm so sorry, Eve. Life has a funny way of messing things up, doesn't it? You do things for the best, most selfless of reasons, but they have a nasty habit of turning round and biting you.'

Her words brought back memories of the only man Eve had truly loved, and also the only one she had been forced to leave — Nikki's father, Frank Reid. It was a long time ago now, but the pain still caught at her whenever she thought about him. She had never dared hope to find a place in her daughter's life, but for once the fates had smiled on her. Now she and Nikki were closer than many mothers and daughters who had never been apart.

'Poor Nikki,' she whispered. 'I can't imagine what it must be like to lose your only child. Surely there can be nothing worse for a mother?' She felt a tear escape and run down her cheek. She cuffed it away, hoping that Wendy hadn't noticed. Eve Anderson didn't cry. Ever.

'Nikki is a strong woman, Eve. Rather like her mother, I'd say. She'll never get over it but she's learned how to go on.' Wendy squeezed her hand. 'Come on, old girl, we've got two hungry ghost-hunters turning up soon, and a fun-filled itinerary to organise for them.'

Eve nodded. 'You are so right, Wen. Back to Dark Greenborough, then you can dust and I'll hoover, okay?'

Wendy gave a smart salute. 'Yes, ma'am!'

* * *

Sheila Pearson looked around the crowded pub with a satisfied smile. Things had been tough in recent years, but thankfully the Hanged Man had avoided going out of business, unlike so many other pubs. That would have been devastating, not only because it was her livelihood and her home, but because the old inn was steeped in history.

Sheila had been born into the trade, her father having been a publican, and she had inherited all the right attributes. She could handle all types of people, even drunk males, and was a very shrewd woman, able to think her way around setbacks and problems. She had negotiated and won battles with the big breweries. She had survived the smoking ban of 2007 by preparing for it, erecting a smoking shelter out at the back, complete with lighting and furniture. She had also taken a hard look at what made the Hanged Man work, and how she could adapt it to attract a new clientele if she lost a lot of the pint drinking, cigarette-smoking male regulars. She had turned her attention to families and her female customers, upgraded the ladies' toilets, offered a "happy hour," and started serving food, not previously a big part of her trade. She brought in a good all-round cook, and started serving wholesome, homemade pub grub. The Hanged Man was back to being the thriving business it had always been. It had cost her for sure, but it had been worth it, and soon the debts would be paid off.

A young man in a black suit and flowing cape waved for attention. Dark Greenborough gave her the biggest takings of the year, so Sheila wasn't complaining.

'Your usual pint of Blood Group A, sir?'

The young man grinned to reveal pointed artificial fangs. 'I'll just have a pint of lager, thank you, but that could all change when the sun goes down.' His eyes flashed, and he bared his teeth at her.

'Very scary, dear. I'll be sure to wear some garlic around my neck for the evening shift.'

And the party didn't officially begin until the following morning. Sheila grinned.

CHAPTER FOUR

Nikki stepped out of the lift and was about to make her way towards Superintendent Cameron Walker's office when she noticed two men standing talking in the doorway. Having a natural aversion to gold braid, she stepped back and watched them from a safe distance. They were definitely not sharing a joke. One she recognised immediately as the chief superintendent but the other, although the insignia on his shoulder epaulette told her he was an assistant chief constable, she couldn't put a name to.

From past experience, Nikki knew that visits of this sort did not bode well. Despite her curiosity, she had no wish to speak to either of these officers, so she continued to wait until they had finished their conversation.

Finally they walked off down the corridor, and Nikki was able to emerge from her hiding place and hurry to Cameron's office. She knocked and went inside.

'Hiding until they left?' he asked dryly.

'Was it that obvious?' She flopped into a chair. 'Don't answer that.' She looked at him enquiringly. 'Okay, Cam, tell me the worst. I can take it.'

'Might be nothing.' He grimaced. 'But on the other hand . . .'

This didn't sound good.

'The thing is, there's been a warning. It's to do with the festival.'

The word "terrorism" burst into Nikki's mind. 'What sort of warning?'

Cam looked at her intently. 'I know what you're thinking, Nikki, but it's not that. It's an odd one. For a start, it went directly to ACC Brakespeare, who has only just arrived in the area. And it's not your usual threat — not a phone call, or even a text or email. It came in the form of a handwritten letter.'

Well, that was not the way terrorists worked. 'What did it say exactly?' Nikki asked.

'Here. It's a copy. The ACC said that the paper was plain white — good quality but nothing special.' Cameron handed her a sheet of paper. 'See what you make of it.'

Nikki looked at the writing. Though small and neat, it was impossible to tell if the writer were male or female. It read:

It would be prudent of you to take this warning very seriously. This is no hoax, I promise you. I am in deadly earnest.

My message to you is this. Dark Greenborough will be a dangerous place this year. Be on your guard because I will be walking among you, although you will not see me.

Mors certa – hora incerta.

Nikki looked up at Cameron. 'A nutter?'

He shook his head. 'I don't think so.'

'Me neither, but I had to ask,' said Nikki glumly. She knew this was something different. 'The Latin bit?'

'*Death is certain, the hour is uncertain.* Or so I'm reliably told.' Cam gave her a worried glance. 'It has a very sinister ring to it.'

Nikki could empathise. 'It reminds me of another case, the one with the "Thieves Cant" messages. I just hope we aren't facing a similar kind of nightmare.'

Cam nodded. 'I thought the same, but I get the feeling we're dealing with a very different animal here. This is no riddle or game, it is a statement of fact. A warning of intention. I don't think we'll hear from him again.'

'And here was I thinking a bunch of dips and possible house-breakers was a serious problem. Now . . .' Nikki frowned. 'How are we going to tackle it, Cam?'

'As we always do. Initially, with caution. I think it's important not to mention this outside the station. We all need to be vigilant, but we mustn't go into panic mode. It could be a hoax.'

Nikki knew he was right. There had been idiots before who had used the festival to make bomb-threats. None had ever materialised, but they had to treat all of them as real until proven otherwise. It was time consuming and a complete waste of precious resources. 'Why the new ACC?' she murmured thoughtfully. 'Why send it directly to him, and how did the sender know who the new guy was? I'm presuming it's a man.'

'How he knew was pretty easy. You only have to access a police news internet site and there's a big article about him and his new posting. But why, I have no idea. And Brakespeare's as puzzled as anyone.'

'A little welcome gift? Or perhaps our joker only deals with the higher echelons. He doesn't associate with the lower orders like inspectors or superintendents.'

'He is certainly educated. You don't use words like prudent and quote Latin phrases if you are living in a one-bed flat on the Carborough Estate, do you?'

'None of my usual suspects who specialise in scaremongering would, that's for sure. They can barely string a sentence together.'

'I'm logging this as cause for concern, Nikki. Make sure all your officers are aware of it and that they act accordingly.'

'Absolutely. I'll make sure it's at the top of the list for the afternoon briefing.' Nikki stood up. 'I'll keep you up to speed with whatever we hear or see. Right now, I'd better get on. Things are about as well-organised as we could hope for. Oh, and Dave Harris is getting on well with Cressy-Lawson, so I've handed that particular venue over to him.'

'Excellent! One less pain in the arse to worry about.'

Nikki closed the office door behind her. At least this new development had made her forget Hannah's birthday for a few minutes. It was impossible not to try to imagine what her daughter would have been like as she grew up. What kind of career would she have picked? She smiled sadly. It certainly wouldn't have been the police! Hannah had always said just what she thought of her mother's job. What kind of boy, or girlfriend, would she have chosen? She could even have been married by now. *I might have been a grandmother . . .*

Nikki trudged back to her own office, her sad thoughts all vying for attention. It was horrible, knowing that certain things could never happen, but she was lucky in some ways. Over the last few years, she had become very close to Tamsin, Joseph's daughter, and also to Niall Farrow, Tamsin's husband. They had become her substitute kids.

'Oh dear, that's a pensive look,' Joseph said as she entered the room.

Nikki immediately fell back into work mode. 'Houston, we have a problem.'

'Oh shit.'

'Big shit. Come in and I'll tell you. Close the door.'

* * *

'Okay, son, I admit it wasn't my smartest move, but—' Reggie said to his son Tyrone.

'No buts this time, Dad. We've lost a load of money that we couldn't afford. It was daft to even think it might work.' Tyrone Fisher threw himself down on the worn and shabby sofa and glared at his father. 'Right. No more knee-jerk gambles, okay? We do this as a team, or I'm off. Got it?'

Reggie didn't remind the boy that he had no job and nowhere else to go. 'You're right. Bad Vlad sold me a pup, end of. Won't happen again.' He leaned forward in his chair and faced his angry son. 'But we *have* to find something for this weekend. It's a golden opportunity, son! A whole town full of gullible punters with dosh in their pockets! We should easily recoup that money. This could be the big one for us, boy. You're the brains, so come up with a good 'un, for heaven's sake. Put your thinking cap on.' He looked hopefully at his boy. 'What about the vodka? I mean we've still got a case or two of that left.'

'You could sell it as drain cleaner, I suppose. Jesus, Dad! Have you tasted that stuff? And you bought it off Bad Vlad, didn't you? *After* I told you to avoid that shyster like the plague.'

'Come on, Tyrone! It was a steal. I couldn't walk away from a deal like that.'

'Yeah, steal was right. He stole our money. Now it's dead stock, hidden in the cupboard under the stairs, under those fire-damaged horse-blankets — another of Vlad's not to be missed bargains.' Ty sighed in frustration. 'We have to find a *proper* scam, Dad, something clever. Something that will put some money in our pockets.'

'The festival has to be the answer,' Reggie said. 'If we let this go by without cashing in, then we really are mugs!'

Ty's look said it all. He was a prize mug already.

Reggie's gaze wandered around the shabby room. Everything in it was tired, second-hand, borrowed or knocked-off. Tyrone had lived here for most of his twenty years. The lad deserved better. He had a good head on his shoulders and was capable of far more than what he was doing, being a lookout or talking people into buying his dad's dodgy goods. Reggie knew for a fact that his sister Lily had offered Tyrone a room at her place down in the smoke, and he was pretty sure that his son was thinking of going. He loved the boy and didn't want that to happen, but all his deals seemed to turn sour. Not only did he need to get some money together, but to redeem himself in his son's eyes.

Tyrone stood up and began pacing the floor. 'Actually, for once, you are right.'

Reggie stared at his son. 'How come?'

'We *will* be mugs if we miss out on Dark Greenborough. We just need something different than flogging junk to the tourists. There are only so many "glow in the dark" skeleton masks you can foist onto them. We need something big, Dad.'

Reggie nodded, went to the kitchen and got them both a beer from the fridge. They drank in silence.

The fact was, Reggie did have an idea, but it was risky, and he'd promised Ty there'd be no more hair-brained schemes. He knew his son had reached the end of his tether. Back in London, they'd had a nice little house and a steady income from his market stall. Then he'd listened to some wide boys and got himself caught up in several really dodgy deals. He lost money hand over fist, and then started borrowing. When his lovely Peg got sick and died, apart from being devastated, he was pretty well on his uppers. The bank took most of the proceeds from the sale of the house, and all he had left was his young son and enough money for two train tickets to a fresh start in the cheapest place he could find. Their little house in the now trendy Shoreditch was now worth a mint, and here they were in a backstreet in Greenborough with a bunch of crap belongings scraped together from other people's castoffs. No wonder Ty wasn't exactly filled with admiration.

But he did have an idea.

'Son? If I throw a thought at you, will you promise not to yell at me?'

'Does it involve Bad Vlad? Because if it does, I'll yell the bloody house down.'

'No way. Not at all.'

'Then try me.' Tyrone sat back and took a long swallow of his beer. 'I'm listening.'

Reggie spoke rapidly for over five minutes. When he'd finished, Tyrone remained silent for a while, and then he brought the bottle down with a thump that made the rickety coffee table shake. 'Jesus, Dad, that's awesome! If we can pull it off, we'll be rolling in it!' He jumped up and clapped his father on the back. 'Genius! Let's start making plans right now. We don't have long to get this thing moving!'

Reggie experienced a rare flush of pleasure. His son was proud of him, for once. Now all he had to do was prove that the caper would work, and Lily could get herself a new lodger for her spare room.

* * *

Spooky took a rare afternoon off from the IT department and made her way into town to meet Bliss. They planned to grab a late lunch, and then check out the attractions that they might like to see over the next three days.

Angie Blissett, known to everyone as Bliss, was waiting for her on a seat at the entrance to the war memorial gardens. As always, seeing her gave Spooky a thrill of excitement. They had been together for several years now, but the spark never diminished.

They were as different as it was possible to be. Spooky, whose real name was Sarah Dukes, looked more like a teen-age boy than a woman in her thirties with a high-powered job coordinating the police force's civilian-run IT unit. And Bliss . . . well, Bliss with her flowing mane of auburn hair, long floral skirts and hand-knitted jumpers was the epitome of the earth mother, a warm, natural woman who kept her geeky partner's feet planted safely on the ground.

Spooky had earned her nickname due to her rather unu-sual hobby of wandering the sea-banks at night — watching the sky, tracking the stars, identifying constellations, but mainly looking for UFOs. No gullible idiot, Spooky was a well read, highly intelligent, specialised computer expert with an electronic library of information about the universe that would have impressed Stephen Hawking.

Bliss saw her and waved. From beneath her mul-ti-coloured skirts, Fox, their young black and white collie gave a little yelp of excitement and wagged his tail furiously. Seeing him still gave Spooky a pang of sadness. They had bought him after losing their beloved Scully, another collie, who had been Spooky's sidekick for thirteen years.

She hurried across to Bliss, kissed her lightly and ruffled Fox's fur.

They lived in a three storied apartment over a gift shop. The Victorian building was situated in a cobbled lane called Salem Alley. Between them, there was nothing about Greenborough town that Spooky and Bliss didn't know, something which had already proved useful to their friend, Nikki Galena. Nikki was a local herself, but living in the heart of the town gave them the edge when it came to news from the streets.

'You've got all afternoon?' asked Bliss. 'No racing back to finish off an important job?'

'I'm all yours, angel. No work this afternoon, I promise.'

They strolled through the town, looking at the shops and the preparations for the festival. Bliss produced a festival pamphlet from her tapestry shoulder bag and read out the titles of some of the events that might interest them.

'Is Gill going to make it this year?' Spooky asked. Gill Mason was an old friend of Bliss's, a big, warm, caring person, larger than life, who called herself a psychic clairvoyant or a life coach. When she travelled to venues like this, Gill advertised herself as a fortune teller. Spooky had never been able to decide if she was just a very good confidence trickster. Bliss argued that if Spooky could accept the possibility of extra-terrestrial life forms, surely she could acknowledge that some people possessed exceptional talents? Bliss had a point, she supposed, but Spooky still couldn't help feeling that Gill Mason gave people just what they wanted to hear.

'She's here already,' Bliss said. 'She rang this morning. She has a booth in the covered market. I said we'd call by tomorrow and say hello.'

Spooky grinned. 'She'll be busy. She has a client list a mile long from last year.'

'Why don't you let her do a reading for you, sweetheart?' Bliss said. 'It might resolve all your doubts about her.'

'Why would I want to know the future? I know it already. It's right here with me,' Spooky said.

'Oh, right answer! But even so.'

'Nah, not my thing. This is though.' Spooky pointed to the advert for the Cressy Old Hall open day.

Bliss looked surprised. 'Have you suddenly taken a liking for antiques?'

'Not really, but I've heard that the owner has a small observatory in one of the attic rooms at the top of that old pile. I'd dearly love to get a glimpse of it.'

Bliss peered at the blurb about the venue. 'Looks like they are concentrating on guided tours of the place's ghostly history. I bet the observatory will be out of bounds.'

'If he's really into astronomy, then he should be glad to let a fellow enthusiast get a look at it.'

'Don't get your hopes up, babe. Haven't you heard of his reputation? He's not exactly a friendly guy.'

Spooky shrugged. 'It's worth a shot. Since I'll be paying good money to get over his doorstep, he might just be on his best behaviour.'

'Well, of course we can give it a try. Now, what else? I'd rather like to listen to that old chap who gives talks on local legends. He's doing an evening one at that creepy old mill on the Westwater Drain. That's an interesting building with a pretty gruesome history.'

The rest of Bliss's words were drowned beneath the shriek of sirens.

'Oh dear, sounds like a few people have started the festivities early, and they're heading for our end of town.'

Back in the seventies, to save the expense of building a ring road, a main thoroughfare was driven through Greenborough, splitting the town in two and cutting a swathe through some of the most historic parts of the town. Some wonderful old buildings had been lost. One side of the town was still a bustling market area where most of the shops were to be found, but the other, the older part, was a jumble of alleys, old shops and even older warehouses close to the tidal river. Salem Alley was at the far end of the High Street, and that was where the blue lights were gathering.

'Hope it's not a car crash,' murmured Bliss. 'It's frightening the way people drive down the main road.'

'Most likely a few idiots have got plastered in the Hanged Man and finished up fighting in the street,' said Spooky. 'Maybe we should go and check it out, just to make sure everything is okay?'

Bliss nodded, and they headed towards their home. When they got there, they found that Salem Alley had been cordoned off.

Spooky approached a PC, whom she recognised from the station. 'Stacy? What's up? We live down there.'

'Oh, hi, Spooky.' PC Stacey Smith looked anxiously along Salem Alley. 'I'm afraid I can't let you through just yet. Someone reported a kid unconscious in a doorway. They thought he'd had a skinful, but when the ambulance crew got here, it turned out he was dead.'

'Oh no! That's awful! Just a kid, you say?'

'Around nineteen, twenty, they think. It's being treated as a suspicious death, and we are waiting on instructions at present.' She shrugged. 'Not sure how long this will take, but I'm afraid you're locked out for a bit.'

'Can't be helped,' Bliss whispered. 'Poor little tyke.'

'Does it look like it's drugs-related?' asked Spooky.

'The paramedics think it's more likely drink, but until the post-mortem's done, it's anyone's guess.'

Spooky led Bliss away. 'We're no use here. Let's go.'

Bliss started after her, then turned back to Stacey. 'Where exactly was he found?'

'In the doorway to a gift shop, I believe.'

Bliss looked at Spooky, her eyes wide. 'Right outside our own front door.' She shivered. 'That makes it even sadder.'

Actually, thought Spooky, it made it kind of personal.

CHAPTER FIVE

Rory Wilkinson stared at the report his assistant, Spike, had just prepared, then back to the body of the man on the mortuary table.

After a few moments of uncharacteristic silence, the Home Office pathologist let out a long, heartfelt sigh. 'I don't like the look of this at all.'

'What do we do?' asked Spike. 'Call the Food Standards Agency?'

Rory shook his head. 'No, not yet. I don't think it's related to food. More likely this has something to do with bootleg vodka or some other kind of dodgy alcohol.' He ran his finger down the list of names. 'I'm going to run toxicology reports on everyone on this list. At first, it looked like several cases of over-indulgence or alcohol poisoning, but I think there's more to it than that. We have had four alcohol-related deaths in three days, and I've just heard that we have another kid coming in, found in a shop doorway. This is not right.'

'Stomach contents varied with all of them, Prof,' Spike said thoughtfully, 'but each had high levels of alcohol in their blood.'

'Not enough to kill them though, unless they'd mixed the drink with drugs, and only a tox screen will tell us that.'

Rory ran his slender fingers through his hair, 'I don't like the feel of this, Spike. Do you?'

'I don't. And I like it even less when you're serious.' Spike stared at Rory suspiciously.

Rory merely stared down at the body, and the neatly stitched Y-shaped incision that ran from the shoulders to the sternum, then down through the chest. 'Take this man for example. He's no stranger to alcohol, his liver tells us that much. I'd call him a seasoned drinker. The stomach alcohol concentration wasn't fully absorbed. Yes, a considerable amount had been consumed but for a regular, not a binge drinker.' He looked across the body at Spike. 'He shouldn't be dead, old fruit. He really shouldn't.'

'And the others?' Spike pointed to the list he had compiled.

'I think we are going to have to go back to the drawing board and take a second look at our findings. If our next guest turns out to be of a similar disposition to these guys, I shall be phoning our dear friend, DI Nikki Galena.' Rory stretched. 'So, let's go and welcome our latest dearly departed soul.'

'I wonder how many of them are truly dearly departed,' mused Spike.

'It matters not, dear heart. As long as *we* think of them like that. You and I, Spike, we take care of them, every one. And that means finding answers for the dear souls. Answers that right now, I don't have.'

It was true, they did care, and the departed were dear to them. Spike felt that he had found a career that made a difference. It wasn't one that many people would be able to stomach, but he found it intensely rewarding, and never more so than on occasions like this, when Rory Wilkinson smelt a rat. Then it became truly fascinating.

* * *

At exactly two o'clock, Dave arrived back at Cressy Old Hall. This time there were more vehicles parked out front, and the door was wide open.

In the hall, he came across a small gaggle of people, all talking enthusiastically to a tall, rather imposing man wearing a long, cape-like coat. On seeing Dave, he broke away from the others and strode across to him, hand outstretched.

'Murray Kennington. You must be the policeman, Dave Harris? Mr Cressy-Lawson told me to expect you.' His grasp was slightly too firm.

'Civilian now, sir, but I've done my fair share of years with the force.'

'And you've made quite an impression on the boss-man here! You are the first copper to have ever had a civil word out of him.' Kennington laughed, showing a set of remarkably white teeth for a man of more than sixty. Somehow they went with the handshake.

'I just love this property,' said Dave. 'It's absolutely amazing, isn't it?'

'With a fascinating history too.' Kennington looked at Dave with some interest. 'Why don't you join us at the next meeting of the History Society? It's at Cartoft Village Hall, second Tuesday in the month at seven o'clock. I'm giving a talk on the history of this place. You'd be very welcome to come along.'

'I might just do that, Mr Kennington. I've been thinking about it for some time.'

'Murray, please. Now,' he looked back at the others, 'my fellow historian, Donald, is just about to give the volunteers a preview of their routes for the ghost tours. I'll just check they've got it right, and then I'm all yours for a while.'

Dave didn't have long to wait before Murray Kennington returned. 'Let's go into the library and I'll give you a brief history of the ghostly goings on at Cressy Old Hall.'

Dave followed him into a lovely old room with a fireplace set in a handsome carved wooden surround. Cast-iron fire dogs stood on either side of the grate. A fire was burning. The smell of wood-smoke immediately took Dave back to his childhood, and a time when his family was together and the worries of the world were all yet to come.

Kennington flopped down into a winged armchair and pointed to a matching one on the other side of the hearth. 'Have a pew. Clive tells me you want to know about the history of the hauntings at the Old Hall. Forgive me for saying so, but I'm not sure how that will help you with making sure no one nicks the family silver.'

Dave chuckled. 'It's just the policeman in me coming out. I like to know everything about what I'm dealing with, not just the surface stuff.'

'Sensible man.' Kennington took a breath. 'Well, there are four "ghosts," or apparitions, all inhabiting particular areas of the Hall — with the exception of the Green Lady, who has been known to manifest all over the place. We'll start with her.'

'I've been told to acknowledge her if I see her,' Dave said wryly. 'Is that right?'

'Absolutely, or something dreadful will befall you.' Kennington looked at Dave from beneath bushy greying eyebrows. '*If* you believe in such things, of course.'

'Generally, no, but as this is the most haunted house in the county, I'll hedge my bets, if it's all the same to you.'

Kennington's laugh resounded around the hushed room. 'Wise decision. I'm a man of facts myself, but even I've had the creeps wandering about this place.' He laughed again, and when the echoes died away, Kennington continued with his story. 'The Green Lady is supposed to be the ghost of the lover of one of the more roguish Cressys, Edwin Lucien. In her lifetime she was Lady Amelia Harewood, a wealthy woman from an estate not far from here. Her husband was a tyrannical landowner with a violent temper. The story goes that she was about to leave her husband and seek Edwin's protection but he refused any part of it, and dumped her. She was found hanging from an ancient oak tree on the Cressy estate, wearing the most beautiful ball gown in a vivid emerald green. She also had on emerald silk shoes and a considerable amount of emerald jewellery. A picture of her in the same outfit hung above the fireplace in her marital home, the only difference being an emerald droplet necklace. She was not wearing it when she was cut down, and it was never subsequently found.'

'Ah,' said Dave, 'did she lose it, or was it stolen from her? Did she kill herself, or was it made to look that way?'

'Exactly.'

Dave smiled. 'The perfect ghost story, isn't it? The deserted lover, the broken heart, the lost emerald.' He leaned forward. 'And the other ghosts?'

'There's a rather predictable monk — well, a priest actually — who can be seen praying at night in the deserted family chapel in the west wing. Then a strange, hunched figure that appears to be a child, up in the gallery and along the corridor that housed the nursery in years gone by. One of the ancestral children died of some horribly debilitating illness, so the ghost is thought to be her. And, finally, a rather mysterious and ethereal young man in dark clothing who roams the roof tops and the attic areas. He's never seen anywhere else and is simply referred to as the Cressy Wraith. There have been several sightings of him, even recently, but again, there is no name, nor does he look like any of the old family members.'

Dave laughed. 'Quite a collection!'

'Oh yes, you get your money's worth at the Old Hall, make no mistake!' Another resounding laugh. 'Clive hinted that Priscilla, his wife, won't set foot in certain parts of the house after dark. I get the feeling she'd like to leave and move into their apartment in London, but old Clive's having none of it. This is his family home and he's immensely proud of it.'

'I gathered that on our first meeting. And rightly so. Can you imagine actually living here?'

'I'd like to give it a try, but I'm afraid it's a bit beyond my means.' Kennington sat back, belying his words, looking very much at home in the grand room. 'Still, I do get the pleasure of visiting and working here off and on, and that's worth a lot.'

'You get on well with Clive Cressy-Lawson?' asked Dave.

'I do. We have a lot in common, if you ignore the fact that we're from different ends of the spectrum, financially speaking. Clive likes anyone who respects and loves British architecture and antiques. That's why you are here now, Dave, sitting in a very comfortable chair in the library. I've seen other coppers sent to wait outside, or only allowed into the servants' quarters.'

'I'm honoured. Now, Murray, would you have time to show me the specific areas where our ghostly friends are apparently seen? That's where the visitors will gather, and I need to be sure they are carefully watched. I've been promised the help of the gamekeeper and a groundsman.'

'Ah, that will be Arthur Keats and Den Elliott, I expect. Good men, and very loyal to Clive.' Kennington stood up. 'Much as I hate to leave the fire, we'll take a stroll right now if you like, then I'll have to get back to my band of helpers.'

'I appreciate you taking the time, Murray,' Dave said. 'Thank you.'

'We'll start up in the attic and work down to the nursery and then the chapel. Follow me.' Kennington set off.

Dave followed, unable to stop himself smiling. This was one of the best assignments he'd had for years.

* * *

Nikki told Joseph about the anonymous letter to the new ACC. He stared at the copy and shook his head. 'That Latin phrase refers to our inevitable mortality: without a doubt we will all die, but we don't know when.'

'Thanks for cheering me up, Joseph. I feel *so* much better knowing that.' Nikki rolled her eyes at him. 'So, our guy is threatening us, telling us to be vigilant, because he's going to kill someone at the festival.'

'Yep. But it's an odd, rather old-fashioned way of issuing a threat, isn't it? Do well to be prudent? What's that all about in this day and age?'

'Whatever, the intent is crystal clear. And Cam is taking it very seriously indeed.'

'He can't afford not to, can he?' Joseph said. 'He has to take every warning seriously, even the most ridiculous-seeming. We can only pray that we're dealing with a hoaxer.'

'Sergeant Optimist, do you really think that's the case?'

Joseph groaned. 'You know exactly what I think, that we could have a sinister and very dangerous mind out there somewhere, that's planning on using the festival as a killing ground.'

'Well, that's a relief!' Nikki threw him a grin. 'For a moment there I thought you were missing the big picture.'

'As if! I just don't want to even consider that we are about to go looking for another deranged killer.' He grimaced.

'I think that could be exactly what we are about to do.' Nikki bit her lip. 'And do you know what frightens me most? All the people we love will be at this festival — our friends, our relatives, our work colleagues, everyone.'

'I know.' Joseph recalled Tamsin reeling off all the attractions she wanted to see — with or without Niall — and he shivered.

'Mum has two of her coven of RAF witches arriving today. Lou and Rene are apparently ready to take the town by storm, and then there's Spooky and Bliss, who actually live right in the middle of it.'

'And Vinnie Silver's coming up tomorrow. He texted me. Eve's gang invited him. I think Lou's still a tiny bit in love with him after their escapade.'

Nikki exhaled. 'Oh, great! Another friend to add to the list.'

Joseph sighed. 'At least Eve's crowd is pretty savvy. With your mother's propensity for felling dangerous men, I'm not quite as worried about them as I am about someone like my Tamsin.'

'Oh Lord, that's true. And Bliss. She could easily attract a weirdo.'

Joseph frowned. 'The trouble is, we have no idea what kind of man we are dealing with, or what he has in mind.'

'Man *or* woman,' added Nikki. 'The writing doesn't suggest one or the other. The super has sent a copy across to forensics to get a professional opinion from a handwriting expert. We could hear any time soon.'

The desk phone rang. They looked at each other. 'Maybe?' said Nikki hopefully. 'Hi, Rory—'

Nikki's face clouded over.

'Sure, come over right now. We're both here.' She replaced the receiver. 'Rory wants to talk to us, in person. He's on his way right now.'

'No clue as to what it's about?'

'Not a dickie bird. He just said not over the phone.'

Joseph exhaled. 'Nothing to do but wait then.'

'Nothing at all, except get in some strong coffees.'

Joseph made for the coffee machine.

* * *

Tyrone bent over his father, who was phoning his way down a list of contacts. 'How goes it?'

'Good. Very good.' Reggie looked almost elated as he ticked another name off the list.

His dad might not be the brightest star on the Christmas tree, but every now and then he did come up with some stonking ideas. Tyrone thought this could be his best yet. 'I've done all these. Look.' He handed Reggie a little stack of printed leaflets. 'Can't do any more, the ink in that crappy old printer has run out and I reckon that was the end of it. Still, they should be enough.'

'We don't need too many, since we have to be careful who we give them to. They're fine, lad. Nicely done.' Reggie looked at him expectantly. 'What next?'

'Pubs. Out of all the ones in this area, which do you think will attract the most tourists?'

Reggie furrowed his brow. 'I reckon the Coach and Horses, the Drunken Miller and the Hanged Man, don't you?'

Tyrone nodded. 'Yeah, they're all pretty old with loads of history, and they all flog good grub.' He sat down. 'I'm thinking we concentrate on a small area at a time, then move on quickly. We only have a limited number of people we can accommodate at one go, and they'll all be paying top whack for the chance to have a look at our special attraction.'

His father chuckled.

'Now, your next job is to make sure we have at least four decent flashlights, and I mean *decent*. None of Bad Vlad's crap, understand?'

His dad nodded furiously. 'I've learnt my lesson there, no worries. I have two already and I'll go pick up a couple more at the indoor market.'

'Right.' Tyrone stood up. 'I'm off to check out the venue. Don't want any nasty surprises when we get there. Got the key, Dad?'

Reggie pulled a set of keys from his pocket. 'The one with the blue tag is the front door, and the other's for the side entrance down the alley.'

'Got it. When I get back, we'll go over the spiel, okay?'

'Know it like the back of me hand, kid, but yes. We want it to be a sell-out, so I'll polish up me ol' market trader's technique and give 'em a right good performance.'

'You're good at that, Dad. Just get the facts right. Everyone's got a smartphone these days. They'll be checking up on the gory details the minute we sell them a ticket.'

'No worries, son. I know the story well, and they can check it up for all they like, it's all true.'

Tyrone grinned. 'That's what makes the whole thing so sweet. It's for real.'

'Isn't it just!'

After a jubilant high five, father and son went about their business.

* * *

Rory was aware of Nikki and Joseph looking at him with an air of puzzled suspicion, reminding him of Spike earlier.

'I know, I know. This is not a side of the eminent pathologist that one usually sees, but,' he peered over the

44

top of his wire-rimmed glasses at them, 'it's my anxious — no, make that my *concerned* aspect.' He sat back, grasping his coffee in both hands. 'First. This is a completely unofficial visit. I have nothing with which to corroborate my possibly wild suppositions, but I needed to talk to you, warn you about what's on my mind.'

Nikki returned his stare. 'If you're worried, Rory, then so are we. Tell us — what is it?'

'It's a two-fold thing.' He raised a finger. 'First, fake vodka. I did an autopsy on an elderly gentleman last week and found he'd consumed "vodka" made with anti-freeze and cleaning solvents. It killed him. If it hadn't, there was good chance that he would have been left blind and suffering irreparable internal damage from the poisons.'

'We've pulled in gallons of the stuff recently,' said Joseph. 'We closed down two illegal "distilleries" last month, but it's almost impossible to hunt down every bottle.'

'That was my first thought. However . . . However, I'm changing my mind.' He handed Nikki a sheet of paper. 'Four deaths over the past few days. They were all intoxicated, but not one of them should have died.'

A silence fell over the small room.

'Lucas Reid, Jim Fortune, Shirley Campion and now a lad called Simon Seaforth.'

'Jim Fortune!' Nikki exclaimed. 'He's dead? My God! I hadn't heard.'

'You knew him?' asked Joseph.

Nikki's face was quite grey with shock. 'He was a paramedic, worked here for years. He had a shocking case that affected him so badly that he couldn't continue in the service. He tried tutoring for a while, but he just couldn't hack it. I know he stayed in the area, but he kind of disappeared off the scene.'

'That's sad,' Joseph said softly. 'It happens to soldiers as well, and coppers.'

'He was a really nice guy too.' Nikki looked across to Rory. 'And you suspect bootleg alcohol? Can't see Jim drinking that crap. He drank when he was off duty, but never to excess that I recall.'

'Perhaps leaving a job that he loved made him change his drinking habits,' suggested Joseph.

Nikki shrugged.

'The reason I'm here is that I don't think he *was* an alcoholic. Nor were any of the others. Lucas Reid might have been the heaviest drinker of them all, but even he was no soak. I'm suspecting that Shirley Campion rarely drank at all, just enjoyed the occasional night out with the girls. So far, I know nothing about the lad that came in today, but early indications show no regular alcohol or substance abuse.' Rory wished he could summon up some of his usual humour to lighten the heavy atmosphere, but when he contemplated the possible consequences of what he was saying, his strength failed him. 'I suspect that these poor unfortunates were deliberately harmed.'

'As in murdered?' Nikki asked grimly.

'I don't know if death was the intention, but I'm taking no chances, I'm running extensive tox screening on all of them.'

'What are you looking for?' asked Joseph.

'That's the problem. I have no idea.' His eyes narrowed. 'But I'll find it, whatever it is.'

'So, you think their drinks were spiked?' Nikki said, her face clouding over with apprehension.

Knowing what had happened to her daughter, Rory was reluctant to go on, but he had to. 'It seems reasonable to consider that, doesn't it? The problem is, in order to find something you need to know roughly what you are looking for. I'm going to have my work cut out.' He looked directly at Nikki. 'That's why I came here, because worst case scenario, dear friends, you have a poisoner loose in Greenborough.'

'Mors certa, hora incerta,' whispered Joseph, looking anxiously at Nikki.

Rory smiled for the first time. 'Oh, very apt, Joseph.'

'We've had a warning, Rory. It was sent to the new ACC. Those were the words they used. We are holding back from making it general knowledge while the festival is taking place.' Joseph raised his eyebrows. 'Widespread panic? It could just be an elaborate hoax.'

'And if it isn't, you could be hunting for a poisoner,' Rory exhaled. 'This news has just made the whole thing ten times worse.'

'You've no idea what was used to spike those drinks?'

'Not yet. However, with gas chromatography and mass spectrometry we can identify any substance, sometimes very quickly, if we have some prior information. Then of course, when we get an accurate mass identified, we need to interpret the results, and for that we need a trained technician to search our library to find possible elemental compositions that correspond with that exact mass . . .' He looked at Nikki's blank face. 'Suffice to say, I'll find it, and hopefully by this time tomorrow.'

Nikki stared at the list of names. 'I wonder if they are connected in some way.'

Rory shrugged. It wasn't his job. 'Look, I'm sorry to dump this on you on the eve of one of the busiest weekends of the year, but I needed to make you aware of what could be lurking around the corner.'

'We appreciate it, Rory. We'll be waiting with bated breath for your toxicology screening reports. Meanwhile, I'm going to see what information we can find on these four people.'

'You might want to wait until we know that I'm not having a very rare attack of overactive imagination . . . just in case it's all a terrible coincidence, or as I originally thought, lethal fake vodka. That is still a possibility, you know.'

Nikki shook her head. 'A few very quiet enquiries won't hurt, and I promise you, I'll be discreet. If you are concerned enough to come here, believe me, Joseph and I won't be dismissing your fears out of hand.'

'I never considered that for one moment, dear heart.'

'Before I forget, we sent the warning note over to the lab for a handwriting expert to take a look at. I don't suppose you know the outcome?' Nikki asked.

'No one mentioned it to me, but I'll check for you as soon as I get back.' He stood up. 'Better return to my Necropolis. I have a mystery to address.'

'Ring me if you find anything out, no matter what time it is.'

'You have my word.'

Rory made his way back down to his car, consumed with dread. If a warning had been issued, then it was even more likely that his fears were about to become reality.

CHAPTER SIX

Eve and her old friends were delighted to meet up again. They had been through a lot together, and were now very close.

'You look great, Rene!' Eve exclaimed. 'Different hair and . . . well, you look years younger than when we last met up.' Rene's blonde hair had always been worn in a boyish, close-cropped cut. Now it was still blonde, but full on top and layered into a casual pixie style.

Lou laughed. 'That's because she's not being hounded by some murdering bastard who wants to top the lot of us!'

'And having put a good few months between me and my erstwhile partner, I'm starting to feel like a human being again.' Rene gave a little bow. 'Thank you for noticing, Eve darling. Makes me feel even better.'

Soon all the women were sitting in the lounge of the old chapel.

'So, what ghostly delights can we expect to see this week-end?' asked Lou, sipping her chilled rosé appreciatively.

Wendy listed the events they had thought their friends might enjoy, then Eve added another.

'It's not in the brochure, but I heard that a man called Amos Fuller is giving a talk about his somewhat dubious ancestors, who were resurrectionists.'

'Oh, a Burke and Hare kind of thing, you mean?' asked Lou. 'Body-snatchers?'

'Apparently. I'm not sure if they turned to murder, like your Burke and Hare, or just stuck to grave robbing. Oh, and he's doing the talk in the old part of Greenborough Cemetery, the creepy bit with that interesting columbarium.'

'Nice touch,' said Rene dryly. 'A peaceful, relaxed atmosphere makes all the difference.'

Eve laughed then looked around at the others. 'In any case, I think it could be an interesting talk, don't you?'

'Count me in,' said Wendy. 'The Resurrection Men have always interested me.'

Lou put her hand up. 'Me too.'

'Why not? Standing around in a graveyard on a freezing cold day sounds just the thing.' Rene pulled a face.

Eve smiled wickedly. 'Actually it'll be a freezing cold *evening*. Didn't I mention that it's candlelit?'

'Oh, better and better.' Rene said.

Half an hour later, they had organised their "programme of events" for the weekend, starting that evening with a reunion dinner at Mario's in Greenborough. Eve had ordered a taxi so they could all relax and enjoy a glass or two of wine.

They were a very unusual group of women. Each had possessed some particular talent that had singled them out and given them a vital role to play in the military. None of them had found retirement easy. Two of the group, Anne Castledine and Jenny Foxwell, had been murdered and the rest of them had been involved in hunting down the killer. The whole affair had been traumatic, yet they missed being in action.

'How are we all doing?' asked Wendy. 'And please give us an honest answer.'

Lou was the first to speak up. She was a stocky woman with iron-grey hair and sharp grey eyes, but her somewhat headmistressy appearance hid considerable emotional intelligence. 'Initially I was on a high after everything calmed down. I felt so relieved, no, elated, that we'd succeeded in our mission. I was also mighty happy that the four of us had survived more or less unscathed. Then—'

Rene continued. 'Then the enormity of what had happened hit home, and we realised that Jenny and Anne were gone for ever. It hurt, and it still does.'

Eve nodded. 'Wendy and I feel the same. So, you two see quite a bit of each other?'

Rene laughed. 'I more or less live at Lou's place. She was a rock when I split from Adrienne.' She looked fondly at her friend.

'Rubbish!' scoffed Lou. 'I just supplied a few crates of wine and a place to drink it in. You did everything yourself, and you've come through triumphant.'

Rene smiled at her. 'You haven't convinced anyone.' Her smile faded. 'And you two? Has living here in Jenny's old home turned out okay? Are you happy here?'

Jenny Foxwell had left her beautiful home to Eve in her will, and Eve had asked Wendy to join her. The old chapel was too big for one person living alone.

'We love it,' Eve replied immediately. 'We aim to do all the things that Jenny had planned for it, and make it just as she would have wanted. So yes,' she glanced across to Wendy, 'now we have been accepted into the village, we *are* very happy here.'

'It's given us purpose and a direction.' Wendy grinned at Eve. 'And we haven't fallen out once! Well, not too badly!'

'I'm not sure what will happen when we run out of projects, but we'll cross that bridge when we come to it.' Eve laughed. 'Anyhow, this weekend is all about fun, so let's enjoy ourselves.'

'And don't forget the gorgeous Vinnie Silver will be here in the morning!' added Lou, with a mischievous glint in her eye.

'Just don't drool all over him,' said Rene. 'Remember, you're old enough to be his granny!'

'Never heard of toy boys?' Lou smiled. 'And what's twenty-five years or so? Nothing.'

After a little more talk, Rene and Lou went up to their rooms to get ready for the evening.

Eve watched them go. For once, possibly for the first time, they were going to spend time together free of conflict and danger — act foolish, have fun. 'About time,' she whispered to herself.

* * *

Before they went home, Nikki wanted to take a short walk through the town. 'To get a feel for the atmosphere,' she said. 'Is that okay with you?'

Joseph nodded. She was right. Out on the streets you could pick up the undercurrents.

They strolled along the brightly lit High Street, down a few of the lanes, and made their way back towards the market square.

'Mario's is busy tonight,' said Nikki as they approached their favourite Italian restaurant. 'Bet he's welcoming the coming weekend's trade with open arms.'

'Look!' Joseph nodded towards the front window of the restaurant. 'It's Eve! And all her friends! Shall we stick our heads in and say hello?'

Nikki tugged on his sleeve. 'No. Look at them, they are really enjoying themselves. Let's allow them some time to catch up, shall we? We'll see them over the weekend. I think they deserve some time together without a police presence.'

He smiled at her. 'You're right. Although I doubt Eve would consider her only daughter a "police presence."'

'You know what I mean.'

A white-faced girl dressed in what was evidently supposed to be a shroud drifted towards them, uttering a mournful wail as she passed.

'They really are starting early!' Nikki shook her head. 'It gets worse every year.'

He smiled. 'Or better, depending on how you feel about it.'

'Well, knowing what we know now, I can't wait until it's over.' Nikki looked at him anxiously. 'Do you think we have a poisoner here in Greenborough, Joseph?'

'I'm reserving my judgement until Rory gets those tox reports back. Right now, my money is on fake booze. If it's really bad bootleg vodka, it could have all manner of toxic substances in it. People die all the time from drinking that stuff.'

'I hope that's what it is. Not that I want anyone to die from it, but at least it won't be deliberate, premeditated murder. I can't stop thinking about what a spiked drink did to my Hannah.'

They made their way back towards the station.

'So, what's your feeling about the atmosphere, Nikki?' Joseph asked.

'So far, so good. It's building up, but in a fun way. Let's just hope it stays like that.' She glanced up at him. 'I've never seen Rory so anxious, have you?'

Joseph puffed out his cheeks. 'I haven't. I've seen him angry, but he always manages to lighten the atmosphere. Today, he looked worried sick.'

'Which leaves me dreading those tox reports even more. He would never have mentioned a poisoner if he didn't consider it a distinct possibility.'

'So, let's leave it at that, shall we? A possibility . . . until we get confirmation. Which brings me to my next subject — dinner.'

Nikki's eyes lit up. 'Shall we go home now?'

'Didn't you want to see what Cat and Ben have found out about Rory's four deaths?' Joseph reminded her.

'Oh yes. Then we go home, right?'

'Exactly.'

They found Cat and Ben closing down their computers.

'Got as far as we can tonight, boss,' said Cat, handing Nikki a printout. 'This is what we have, but they have nothing in common, apart from a few overlaps which I'd expect from people living in the same town.'

'Well, thanks for staying on, you two, I appreciate it.' Nikki indicated towards the door. 'Now get off home, or wherever you are heading tonight.'

Ben gave a sheepish smile. 'Actually, we're going to visit that fortune teller in the covered market. Gill someone or other. A mate of mine went to see her last year and the things she told him really blew him away, so he asked if I'd go along and see what I thought about her.'

'He doesn't like to think she might really have some kind of weird gift,' added Cat, 'so he wants us to try to see beyond the smoke and mirrors.'

'Shouldn't be difficult. Load of tosh, if you ask me.' Nikki sounded her usual acerbic self again.

After Cat and Ben had left, they skimmed through the report.

'Much as Cat said,' Nikki murmured. 'Nothing obvious that connects them.'

Joseph stared at the list. 'Two things stand out to me. One, both Jim Fortune and Lucas Reid were both drinking in the Hanged Man on the night they died, and all were pretty much loners. That's the kind of person who could become a target, isn't it? No one at home to worry about them, and no one to ask questions.'

'Half of Greenborough drinks in the Hanged Man,' Nikki countered. 'And a lot of people live alone nowadays.' She paused. 'Like you and I were.'

'Just saying.'

'We need those tox reports, badly,' Nikki said grimly.

'Don't we just. But in the meantime — food.'

Nikki rubbed her eyes. 'Then let's not keep it waiting.'

Joseph drove home, still pondering the report on the four dead revellers. There were only flimsy connections, but even so, he couldn't dismiss the thought that somehow, something linked those people together.

* * *

By nine that evening, Reggie had acquired a couple of half decent flashlights and completed all his calls. This was going to be a short but very sweet scam. Time was limited. They had only three nights to carry it out, and it was most certainly not something that could be attempted in daylight. If it went well, it would be more lucrative than anything they'd ever done before. He reckoned that they could take at least six people at a time, and each "guided tour" would last no longer than three quarters of an hour. If the punters were up for it and happy to go late into the night, they could notch up eight trips a night. That would mean forty-eight tourists a night, one hundred and forty-four in total. If they'd been charging peanuts, it wouldn't have been worth the hassle, but for something like this, a true one-off, they could charge high prices for the tickets. If the kid and him worked it well, they could close up business with maybe five grand in their pockets.

This was something Reggie could do well. He had the gift of the gab, learned in the markets of London, and he intended to give the performance of his life. He had to. His son was going to look up to him again, and remain here in Greenborough where he belonged. It was by far the best scam he'd ever come up with, and one hell of a lot smarter than trying to offload bottles of Bad Vlad's hooch vodka. Fallen off the back of a lorry indeed. How had he fallen for that one? When the weekend was over, he would pour the remaining bottles down the toilet. If nothing else, they'd kill any germs.

Reggie resumed his reading, using a few old newspapers that he had stashed away at the time of the crime, and Tyrone's laptop for additional information. He knew the story off by heart, but even so, it wouldn't hurt to freshen up the details. It would ensure his patter ran smoothly. This would be one Dark Greenborough experience that the punters would not forget in a hurry.

CHAPTER SEVEN

The call from Rory came through to Nikki's office before she'd even had time to take off her coat.

'It's cost me, I'll have you know! Believe me, the promises I've made to that young technician . . .' Rory said.

Nikki almost cheered. The pathologist sounded more like his old self.

'She worked all night, bless her heart, and we have a result,' he said.

'Yes? And?' Nikki asked.

'Methanol.'

She frowned. 'Windscreen-washer fluid?'

'It is used for that, true, along with a plethora of other industrial uses. However, the most famous thing it's found in is moonshine, white lightning, fake booze.'

'So, not a poisoner?' Nikki's heart sang with relief. There was a long silence. 'Er, Rory?'

She heard him breath in. 'Let me explain a little more before we make any assumptions. Methanol is wood alcohol, much favoured by the illegal bootleggers in the poorer areas of the deep South in the United States, because they could produce a mash from wood chippings. It's pretty lethal stuff that can destroy the optic nerve, but it's cheap to make. The same thing happens here with illegal distilleries turning out fake vodka and whisky, and now we are discovering it in white cider.'

White cider, Nikki knew, was becoming the drink of choice among the alcoholics and street dwellers, as it was strong but cheap. 'White cider's made of apples and corn syrup, isn't it?'

'The legal stuff, yes, which is bad enough because of the high alcohol content, but recently we processed some counterfeit stuff that contained chloroform, and some more with isopropanol — solvent cleaning fluid to you. Toxic chemicals like that can have serious health implications. Even in small doses, they can be fatal.'

'Where are we going with this, Rory?' Nikki said shakily.

'What we found in all the victims was something new to us. It's methanol alright, but my young assistant's belief is that someone has either intentionally, or possibly accidentally, "refined" it in order to make it more potent but taste less bitter. All fiery alcohol gives you a kick at the back of the throat, and this would have seemed no different to swallowing a slightly rough whisky.'

'And presumably if they'd had quite a bit to drink already, they wouldn't notice a change of quality?' Nikki said.

'Wouldn't notice, or wouldn't care. Alcohol impairs your brain functions. Your thinking and your decision making go right down the drain, as I recall from my heady days at university — but we shan't go there now.'

'Let's not.' Nikki was trying to think. 'But surely this all points to a more sophisticated kind of bootleg liquor industry, rather than deliberate poisoning?'

'I pray that's the case, but the distribution just doesn't seem right, does it? There were just four separate, isolated cases. If you had made a batch of designer fake booze and, say, sold it to some unscrupulous landlord, he would perhaps sell on a whole load of measures during one day. He certainly wouldn't sell the stuff to a single customer. Hence, we'd have more cases and all from the same source. Sorry, Nikki, but to me this sounds like deliberate spiking.'

'But maybe not an actual poisoner?'

'It doesn't matter how you label him, someone introduced toxic chemicals into another person's drink. In my book, that is poisoning, and like it or not, that makes him a killer, dear heart.'

Nikki sat down slowly. Somehow, she had not imagined the person who sent the warning to have meant this kind of thing. Then again, he had suggested that Greenborough would be a very dangerous place to be, and spiking people's drinks was bloody dangerous. She sighed. 'You're right, Rory.'

'And with infuriating regularity, I'd say.'

'Mmm, as you say, infuriating, but thank you anyway, and pass on our thanks to your assistant. I'd better get my head around this and go make some enquiries.'

'Over to you, dear Inspector! And I'll get the prelim report on our last young victim to you as soon as possible. Ta-ta for now.'

Nikki was left staring at the phone. Oh well, at least now a proper action plan could be put into place. 'Joseph!' she called out of the door. 'Get yourself in here, pronto! We have work to do before daily orders.'

* * *

Nikki stood in front of a large whiteboard that covered most of one wall. On it were four names, accompanied by their photographs: Jim Fortune, Lucas Reid, Shirley Campion and Simon Seaforth.

To look at they were about as different as it was possible to be, but someone had taken their lives in an identical manner.

'The question is, were these unfortunate people targeted specifically, or were they random victims? And also, is this just the result of a new and very toxic fake alcoholic drink on the black market, or is someone deliberately killing people? To find the answers to these questions, we need to know everything we can about all of them, then we need to see if they are connected in any way.'

Nikki's gaze lingered a little on the photo of Jim Fortune. She had always felt extremely sorry for the paramedic. She knew why he'd left the career he adored. That kind of horror could strike any one of them at any time — the one job that pushed them over the edge.

She blinked, bringing herself back to the present. 'Get out there and talk to the people who knew them best. Ask where they usually drank or where they went to enjoy themselves. Who did they mix with? What were their interests?' She looked back at the faces on the board. 'What do we have so far?' She glanced across to Joseph, who took over.

'First, Jim Fortune. Some of you may know him. He was a paramedic here in Greenborough up until two years ago, when he suffered a breakdown and left the service. He was forty-two, well-built and pretty strong, around five foot ten. He was a local man, unmarried, and had lived here all his life. Last we heard, he was doing temporary jobs around the local farms and on some of the trading estates.' Joseph looked back to Nikki. 'That's all we have so far, other than that he was seen drinking in the Hanged Man just before he died.'

'You and I will take this one, Joseph. We'll go and talk to Sheila, the landlady at the Hanged Man. I don't suspect her of serving bootleg drink, but we need to know who he was drinking with, or whether she noticed anything out of the ordinary going on.'

Joseph nodded. 'Then we have Lucas Reid, a trainee undertaker, also a Greenborough local. He had been drinking in one of the village pubs, and finished up at the Hanged Man later in the evening. He was twenty-eight and a bit of a drifter, although he seemed to have settled down at Arthur Bevans and Son, the funeral directors on South Drive. We have very little on him yet, other than that he lived alone in a rented flat not far from the Carborough Estate.'

Nikki looked around. 'Cat? Will you take him, please? Get as much as you can from his employers and his work colleagues, and check with his neighbours.'

'Yes, boss.' Cat wrote down his name and work address.

Joseph pointed to the next picture. 'Shirley Campion, fifty-four, lived in Carlton village, just outside town, in a bungalow on a small council estate. She was a wages clerk for a food processing company. She'd been widowed some time ago, and had no immediate family. She was drinking with some of her workmates. They ate at the Indian in West Road, then went to the Coach and Horses for the rest of the evening.' He glanced down at his notes. 'So far, I have pretty well nothing on Simon Seaforth, the last young man to die. All we know is that he was nineteen, and a student at the art college. He lived with his divorced mother in a terraced house on the outskirts of town.' He looked up at Nikki. 'And I've just heard from uniform that he died in the doorway of a gift shop in Salem Street.'

Nikki's eyes widened. 'Spooky's place?'

''Fraid so.'

'Oh hell! Bliss will be well upset. She's such a kind-hearted, caring person.' Nikki reminded herself to contact Spooky immediately after the meeting. 'Nothing else on him?'

'Nothing, ma'am. We have no idea about his movements, or where he was drinking.'

'Right. Ben? Perhaps you'd make enquiries about Shirley Campion, and we'll hold up on the Seaforth boy until we get something more from forensics and a report from uniform.' She looked around. 'We are without Dave for the duration of the festival, since he's on duty at Cressy Old Hall. That means we're a man down. If this turns out to be more than a new and lethal form of moonshine, he'll be relieved of his post at the hall and brought back here. As it is, he's getting on better with Cressy-Lawson than anyone ever has before, so rather than upset his lordship, we'll leave things as they are for the present. Okay, folks, get out there and bring me back some answers.'

As the others moved out, Nikki held Joseph back. 'I need to go have a quick word with Spooky. Would you see that everyone has all the info they need? Then as soon as I'm back we'll head off to the Hanged Man.'

'Sure, see you in ten.'

Nikki hurried off to the IT unit.

Spooky was in charge of a civilian-run specialised technology unit, fortunately based right here in the station, though they took in work from the whole county. Usually, Spooky was one of the busiest operatives in the whole building, but today Nikki found her at her desk, clutching a mug of black coffee and looking thoroughly miserable.

Nikki marched right in. 'Why didn't you ring me? I had no idea until uniform told us. How did Bliss take it?'

Spooky indicated an empty chair. 'As you'd imagine, really. She's very quiet. We were kept out of our flat for hours. Of course, we were both sorry for the poor guy, but it still beats me why they want to drink so much. I mean, I was a bit of a tearaway when I was young, wasn't I? But my sole aim in life certainly wasn't to spend every weekend getting hammered.'

Nikki lowered her voice. 'We don't think it's a straight-forward case of too much booze, Spooks. He could have had his drink spiked, or maybe even have been slipped some new kind of homemade hooch.'

'Jeez! That's awful! I was reading an article about some of the shit they put into fake booze, like anti-freeze. Apparently the body can't process it properly and it turns into formaldehyde!' She gave a shudder. 'That poor kid!'

'Maybe don't tell Bliss about this until we know more, huh?' suggested Nikki.

'No way! She'd be devastated.' Spooky grimaced. 'I'll keep that to myself for the time being.'

'Back to the original question . . . Why didn't you ring me?'

Spooky gave a dry laugh. 'You have enough on your plate with this festival. And we just thought he'd been binge drinking and died as a result of that. Really sad, but not unheard of, and certainly not a CID matter.'

'You could have rung just to speak to a friend, Spooks. We've always got time for you two, you know that.'

Spooky grinned warmly. 'Thanks, Nik, and I do know. But you guys really do have your work cut out this weekend. We'll be fine. We are still going to some of the attractions, especially Cressy Old Hall. The rich bloke that owns it has an observatory in the attic, and I'm going to do all I can to get to see it.'

'Well, in that case speak to Dave Harris. He's up there all weekend, and by all accounts, is now best buddies with Cressy-Lawson, although heaven knows how he managed that. The man is a real prick!'

'I gather you've met him then?' laughed Spooky.

'Once, and that was enough.'

'Well, I'm going to creep as low as I have to, and if good old Dave can help, so much the better.'

'Then good luck.' Nikki stood up. 'I have to get off. Give Bliss my love. You know where I am if you need me, okay? Any time.'

Spooky winked at her. 'Ditto.'

Nikki hurried back to her office and found Joseph ready to go.

'I've just checked what we have on the Hanged Man. You were right about Sheila Pearson — no trouble from her and very little from her patrons either.'

'I've known her for years, Joseph. If any fake booze has found its way into her pub, it won't have been Sheila's doing. If we find she's responsible, I'll wear a feather boa for the rest of the month!'

Joseph's face lit up. 'Such a picture that conjures up!'

'And it tells you how likely a scenario we are talking about.'

'Damn.'

Nikki opened the door. 'Shut up, Joseph, and go and find us a car.'

He hurried past her, a broad grin still on his face. 'Feather boa . . .'

* * *

The back room of Arthur Bevans and Son, Funeral Directors, wasn't exactly what Cat had been expecting, but then she'd never spent much time at an undertakers.

The first thing she noticed was the cheerful atmosphere. Men and women were chatting comfortably, all busy, screwing handles or engraved plaques onto caskets, or working on satin liners. The room had quite a low ceiling, and she was later told that they kept plain stock coffins in the storage area above. When required, these were brought down by opening a trap door and sliding them down a ramp. Seeing the dartboard fixed to the hatch flap, Cat almost laughed aloud. Clearly these guys were happy in their work.

She was met by a dark-suited man called Terry Bevans whom she gathered was the "and Son" part of the business. He took her into his tiny office just off the main workroom and offered her a coffee, which Cat declined. Death was still death, however conducive the work atmosphere.

Until her call, they hadn't been aware that Lucas Reid had died, and Terry Bevans was understandably shocked. 'I haven't told the others yet, Detective. I thought I'd wait and hear exactly what happened.'

'Our enquiry has only just begun, sir, so I can't tell you much at this stage, but I can say that his death is being treated as suspicious.'

Bevans gasped. 'Murder?'

'As I said, sir, it's early days, and it could just have been a tragic misadventure. I really can't say yet.' She leaned forward. 'Please keep this to yourself for the time being.'

'Of course.' Bevan's face was a mask of bewilderment. 'I can't believe it. Lucas was a bit of a lad. He liked a drink, sadly to the point of getting a warning, but he was actually getting on really well here. Dad only gave him the warning to pull him up short, like. He was good at what he did, and if he'd managed to curb his weekend socialising, we had high hopes for him.'

'I'm sorry, sir. What can you tell me about him as a person? Did he have a close friend here, someone who might be able to give me some background?' Cat opened her notebook.

Terry Bevan exhaled. 'Not really. He was a bit of a dark horse. I know he lived alone, and to my knowledge he never mentioned his family. The only person I actually saw him talk to on a regular basis was Sophie Bannon. She's one of our most experienced funeral service workers, and she's a kind of mother hen to some of the newer lads and lasses.'

'Can I talk to her, sir?'

'Certainly. I'll see if she's free.' Bevan stood up. 'I know we deal with death every day, but this has come as a shock. I honestly liked that kid. I always felt he'd had a raw deal in life, and with us he'd finally found somewhere he fitted in. It's a real shame.'

Sophie Bannon didn't look anything like a mother hen. In fact, she was rather glamorous, with glossy black hair and perfect make-up, and Cat felt like a stick insect standing beside her shapely figure. However, as soon as she started to speak, Cat realised that Terry Bevan's description had been correct.

On hearing the news, tears formed in Sophie's eyes. Cat gave her a few moments to compose herself, and then asked her what she knew about Lucas.

'Not very much, I'm afraid.' Sophie dabbed carefully at her eyes. 'He told me that he'd had a terrible childhood but never went into any detail. He was brought up by his grand-parents, that I do know, and he felt that they resented having him foisted upon them. He left as soon as he could. He said he'd never been able to settle anywhere for long. He was trying his best here, and he would have done well.' Sophie sniffed. 'I've been in this trade a long time, DC Cullen. It takes a special kind of person to do what we do, and Lucas would have made a first-class undertaker. He understood grief, if you know what I mean?'

Cat nodded. 'I do. Did he ever mention any close friends, Sophie?'

'Never. I think we were his friends and family, end of.'

'But he drank regularly, so he must have had mates?'

'The people he drank with weren't friends, just a group of heavy drinkers who were happy enough to let him buy a round.'

'Do you know where this was?'

'A village pub, I believe. Probably the Kings Head at Norby. Oh, and he did go to the Hanged Man sometimes, but I think the publican there was a bit too ready to refuse to serve anyone who'd had too much.'

Cat nodded. 'Sensible woman.'.

'I'm afraid I can't tell you much more than that,' Sophie said.

Indeed, there was little more to say. Life had dealt cruelly with poor Lucas Reid.

* * *

It was a similar story with Shirley Campion. No one at her office could believe she was dead. After a while, Ben managed to track down her closest workmate, a woman called Denise Sparks.

'She'd had a few, Officer, but we all had. Shirley was drinking cocktails, I think. But not nearly enough to make her really ill,' Denise blew her nose loudly into a handful of tissues, 'or to . . . to kill her!'

'Why were you all out that night, Mrs Sparks?'

'It was a birthday celebration, Officer. We had a meal and then went to the Coach and Horses.'

'Did anything out of the ordinary happen there?'

Denise looked blank. 'Not that I can recall, but it was really rowdy, and much busier than usual — probably people arriving early for the festival.'

'How was Shirley planning on getting home? She lived in Carlton village, didn't she?' Ben asked.

'She'd booked a taxi. She was sharing it with girl who lives out the same way.'

'Did she leave in the taxi, as planned?'

'Yes, just after ten thirty. That was two nights ago.'

Ben calculated that it must have been the night before Jim and Lucas died. So, was someone practising their deadly art? Or was it just bad luck that fake vodka had found its way into a random drinker's cocktail? 'Can you give me the name of the girl she shared a taxi with, please?' he asked.

'She's here, Officer. Her name is Ginnie Harper, I'll call her,' Denise said.

'Before you do that, is there anything you can tell me about Shirley herself? About her life? Her family? Things she enjoyed doing?'

Denise talked for around ten minutes while Ben made copious notes, none of which were of much help, then Denise went and found Ginnie.

Ginnie Harper, clearly very upset, said that Shirley had said several times that she wished she hadn't drunk so much. Now Ginnie was feeling terrible for leaving her on her own.

'Honestly, DC Radley, she seemed quite disorientated, but it was odd because I didn't think she'd drunk that much. In fact I only saw her have three drinks all evening.'

'Did you go into her house with her?' asked Ben.

'I did,' Ginnie said. 'But she said she'd be fine, she just felt sick and she'd rather I left her to it.' She pulled a face. 'I'm not good with things like that, so I did. Now I wish to God I'd stayed.' She sniffed. 'She might be alive now if I hadn't been such a wimp!'

The poor woman's guilt would probably haunt her for the rest of her life. Ben tried to find some words of comfort. 'I think she would have died no matter what you did. The alcohol poisoned her system.'

That was the best he could do without telling her that some bastard had killed her friend and that it could just as easily have been any of the girls at the party.

Afterwards, Ben sat in the car and went over what he had learned, which was precious little. Shirley was a widow with few interests outside her home. Her only friends were her workmates and an elderly neighbour, who was too upset by the death to be of much help. He suspected that she knew little about the real Shirley Campion, other than that she liked growing geraniums, enjoyed home cooking and cleaned her own windows, but probably nothing about her private life, if indeed she had one.

Ben drove back to the station feeling that he'd spent two and half poxy hours there and come up with sweet FA. As far as he could see, Shirley Campion had no connection whatsoever to Jim Fortune or Lucas Reid.

CHAPTER EIGHT

'It's painful, isn't it?' murmured Nikki. 'I mean, having known Jim before he had his breakdown. He had a rough time. It just seems so unfair that he died in such a horrible way.'

Joseph parked the car outside Jim Fortune's favourite pub, the Hanged Man. He turned off the engine but didn't get out immediately. 'Tell me what happened to make him give up the job.'

'A burns case.'

Joseph shivered. Always sickening, no burns case ever had a peaceful end.

'Jim said he couldn't forget the smell of burnt flesh. It haunted him. Then, every time they got a shout, he was afraid it would be another one. He finished up unable to leave the ambulance station.' Nikki sounded terribly sad. 'He had been one of the bravest paramedics I've ever met. Once, I saw him crawl under a car at an RTC. It was already burning and there was a good chance the whole thing would go up. Somehow he managed to free the trapped driver and get him out. I always thought of him as a kind of superhero in a dark green uniform. It was unthinkable that he of all people should break down.'

'We all have our breaking point.' Joseph hoped he didn't sound too off-hand, but he'd been a soldier. The whole thing was a little too close to home for him.

'I'm sorry, Joseph. Maybe it's time to change the subject.' Nikki gently squeezed his arm.

He smiled at her gratefully. 'Let's go talk to Sheila, shall we?'

The pub was open, but fortunately still quiet. Sheila greeted them without her usual smile. 'I'm devastated. I've known Jim for years and this is beyond belief.'

'Could we talk to you somewhere a bit more private, Sheila?' asked Nikki.

'Of course.' She led them through the back of the bar, up a flight of stairs and into a comfortable lounge.

Joseph looked around, a bit surprised at how tastefully decorated it was. For some reason he had expected her home to reflect the pub's "olde worlde" atmosphere, but instead it was simple and elegant, done out in natural shades.

'I never realised he was that drunk, Officers, or I would have refused to serve him much earlier,' Sheila said.

'That's not why we're here,' Joseph told her. 'The thing is, we are treating Jim's death as suspicious.'

'And we need your help, Sheila,' Nikki added. 'We suspect he consumed some contaminated alcohol.'

A look of horror crossed Sheila's face. 'What? Not from here, I assure you!'

Nikki smiled. 'It's alright. We aren't thinking along those lines. We suspect his drink was spiked in some way.'

'Oh no! Poor Jim. But . . .' She paused, frowning. 'No one disliked him that much. In fact no one disliked him at all. He was one of my nicest customers.' The frown deepened. 'It was really busy last night, and Jim was doing his local yokel act, giving the incomers all manner of spooky stories and old wives' tales. They were lapping it up.'

'And buying him drinks?' Joseph asked.

'A few did, certainly.'

'Sheila?' Nikki asked. 'You are a very astute woman. Was there anyone in here last night, even after Jim left, that gave you cause for concern? Even just slightly. Someone you just felt a bit uneasy about?'

Sheila exhaled loudly. 'Oh dear! We were packed out. And they were nearly all tourists in for the festival. There were more incomers than locals and they all seemed pretty well-behaved and good-natured.'

'Can you think about it? And please keep your eyes peeled for anyone who comes in from now on who arouses your suspicions.' Nikki lowered her voice, even though there was no one to hear. 'There was a second death last night. We think it was linked to Jim's. And rather unfortunately, he was seen in here pretty late in the evening, maybe near closing time.'

Sheila's lips formed a thin line. 'Then I need to check all the barrels and the pumps, and the bottles too. I need to close down, at least for a short time. Do you have any officers who are trained to spot counterfeit labels or spirit bottles? I can do it, but not alone. I need help.'

Joseph nodded. 'We've just tied up a big crackdown on fake booze distilleries, and we all know what to look for. But, Sheila, we aren't thinking that the contaminant actually came from here.'

'You run a tight ship, we know that,' Nikki added. 'Do you trust your staff, even the extra help that you've brought in for the festival?'

'Without a doubt. I don't have a big staff, but the ones that work regularly I trust completely. The extras, well, I've used them before and I know them all personally.' She nodded as if agreeing with herself. 'You'll want to talk to them, presumably?'

'Please. In private.'

'You can use this place. Two are in already, preparing for tonight's onslaught, and the rest will arrive in two shifts, one quite shortly and the other later shift at six.' She sighed. 'Not that I think you'll learn much. If anyone bothers them, they tell me, and last night went very well, or so we thought.'

'Has anyone ever shown any antipathy towards Jim, Sheila? Even slightly?'

Sheila responded at once. 'Never. We all knew his story, Detectives, and we liked and respected him. In the years before his breakdown, he had helped a whole lot of my patrons and their relatives. Jim was a good man. He will be sadly missed.' She suddenly sat up straight. 'Heavens! I never even asked who the other one was. The other person who died last night.'

'A younger man called Lucas Reid. He was a trainee undertaker.'

Sheila frowned. 'Not one of my regulars, but I think I know who you mean. If it's the lad I'm thinking of, I've turned him away a few times because he'd had enough before he even got here. He was never nasty or rude, just a bit worse for wear. He wasn't very old either, maybe in his late twenties? That's terrible.'

Nikki nodded. 'Twenty-eight. No age at all.'

'And his drink was spiked too?'

'That's the avenue we are pursuing at present,' said Joseph.

'Even so, to cover my own back, and for my customers' safety, I'm going to check the stock. As soon as you've finished with my bar staff, I'm going through everything we touched last night, mainly the spirits. I know that vodka and whisky are the easiest to distil illegally. If someone found a way of introducing a fake bottle onto my shelves, I'll find it. And I'll start with the empties. I've handled enough genuine bottles in my time that a rogue will stand out like a sore thumb.'

Joseph threw Nikki an enquiring glance. 'If you want to talk to the staff, I'll give Sheila a hand for a while. I know fake labels and dodgy best before dates and bar codes too.'

Nikki nodded. 'Do that.'

Sheila stood up. 'I'll send them up. One by one?'

Nikki nodded. 'Please.'

Joseph followed Sheila out of the room, knowing before they even started, that they would find nothing. He was certain that whoever doctored those drinks hadn't planted a contaminated bottle for all and sundry to consume, and maybe for them to find and analyse. But what had happened? And why?

* * *

By midday, the festival was well underway, and the whole town had come alive. Niall had made quite sure that he had plenty of officers out. They were to keep their presence low-key and be seen to be enjoying the atmosphere along with the revellers.

Someone wandering into the town who hadn't been forewarned would believe they'd found themselves in the midst of some strange dream. The streets were crowded with all manner of the undead, ranging from ethereal wraiths to highwaymen, from grinning vampires to zombies.

Niall himself was out there with them, keeping a keen eye on everything, blown away by some of the younger people's amazing make-up and inventive costumes.

PC Yvonne Collins patrolled, laughing, beside him. 'I bet most of them will wake up tomorrow feeling as if they really *are* the living dead. There are going to be some memorable hangovers before this lot finishes.'

'As long as we get no more casualties from the methanol alcohol,' added Niall.

Yvonne's laughter died away. 'What does the guv'nor think is really going on, Niall?'

'Frankly, Vonnie, they're shit-scared that these alcohol-related deaths are the work of the man who sent that letter to the ACC.'

'What do you think, Sarge?' she asked.

Niall looked at her in surprise. Was Yvonne asking him his opinion? It felt weird, and a little bit sad. Time was passing too quickly for all of them. Soon she would have to retire because of her age, and he, who now had the responsibility of a wife and a home, would need to step up and stand on his own two feet without her to support him.

'I think they are right to worry, Vonnie. Those deaths were intentional, I'm sure of it.'

'I agree. We've had fake booze on the streets for years, but nothing as lethal as this stuff.' She stopped to allow a couple of werewolves and a corpse access to one of the venues, a talk on the history of the infamous Black Dogs of the Fens. 'I just hope the public don't get wind of it and we have a mass panic. Apart from being bloody dangerous, a whole load of time, energy and money have been sunk into this festival. For the town's sake, we can't let it fail.'

'I'm with you there, Vonnie. We really need to get this creep before someone else succumbs to one of his toxic cocktails.'

'All our guys and girls are on high alert for anything dodgy going on. We can only keep on our toes and make sure we don't miss something.' She gave an exasperated laugh. 'Which of course is not being made easy by having a town full of strangers, all dressed up in fantastic disguises, getting rat-arsed and acting like complete idiots!'

As if to corroborate her words, a tall Jekyll and Hyde character loomed up beside them with a wide, mad-eyed grin, before scuttling off down an alley.

She raised an eyebrow. 'If you catch my drift?'

'Perfectly,' sighed Niall.

This was going to be one hell of a weekend.

* * *

As Joseph had predicted, there was no sign of any doctored alcohol at the Hanged Man. He and Sheila checked bottles for counterfeit labels, unusual corkage and any form of tampering, but found nothing. The next thing was the CCTV, and knowing how busy the day was going to become, Nikki decided that with Sheila's agreement, they would get their IT department to monitor the whole thing from the police station. Luckily, Sheila had recently updated her security and was now using a digital video recorder that could be viewed and operated remotely.

Three areas of the main bar were covered, and now one officer and two civilians were scanning through every moment of the night Jim Fortune died. It wasn't easy. The whole place had been packed out. Nikki had watched for a few minutes and soon realised that to spot someone spiking a drink in that melée was going to be just about impossible.

'We've isolated Jim and are trying to pay special attention to anyone he's drinking with or talking to, ma'am, but the place is heaving and he was there for hours.' The female constable who'd been unlucky enough to get this brain-numbing task gave a sigh. 'It's like trying to find a needle in a haystack.'

'Keep at it, Brenda. Anyone who looks the slightest bit suspicious, make a note and check with Sheila as to whether she knows them, or if they are visitors. You never know, we might find someone who shows up both here and in the restaurant and the pub that Shirley Campion went to. That's what we're looking for, a common denominator.'

'Will do, ma'am.' Brenda Kirk returned to her screen. 'We could get lucky.'

Nikki admired her optimism. She wasn't too sure what the expected footfall was over the weekend, but she did know it was massive. The odds were not in their favour.

'Ma'am!' An anxious-looking uniformed officer appeared in the doorway. 'Sergeant Farrow has just rung in. He's made a worrying discovery. He asked would you be able to attend? It's urgent.'

Nikki nodded. 'Give me the location.'

The PC handed her a memo. She grabbed it and hurried back to CID to get Joseph. In no time at all, they were heading for a small alley that ran along the back of some of the outlying shops close to the bridge over the River Westland.

They arrived to find the blue lights of an ambulance and two squad cars at the scene. Nikki's heart sank. 'Another one?'

'Looks that way,' said Joseph softly.

They saw Niall deep in conversation with two other officers, and then Yvonne Collins was hurrying towards them. 'Ma'am? Sarge? Niall noticed him first. We thought he had just had too much booze too early, but . . .' Her face was grey with shock. 'I've never seen anything quite like it. He was simply dying in agony, right in front of us, and there was nothing we could do. Nothing.'

Joseph squeezed her shoulder. 'I'm so sorry, Vonnie. Are you okay?'

'I'm okay, yes, but it just made me feel so totally helpless. It was horrible.'

'So, not another alcohol-related incident?' asked Nikki.

'It didn't seem that way, ma'am, but who knows? It could have been some massive internal bleed or organ failure due to alcohol, I don't know.'

Nikki frowned. 'Sorry, Yvonne, it was a stupid question to ask. I'm just paranoid about this stuff. It's killed four people already.'

'That's exactly what we thought, until we took a good look at him.' She stared at the ambulance. 'The paramedics did their best, but I think he was already gone by the time they got here. They have no idea what happened either.' She shrugged. 'I suppose it will be down to the post-mortem.'

'Did he have any ID on him, Vonnie?' Joseph asked.

'Yes.' She took out her notebook. 'His name is Peter Cash. He had a wallet with credit cards and a driving licence. Niall has bagged and tagged it. He's a local, Sarge. The family lives in one of those old terraced houses that flank the river where the fishing boats moor up. His father was a shrimp fisherman. I knew him slightly, but I'm not sure what Peter did for a living.'

'How old was he?' asked Joseph.

'Around forty, I think. Unmarried, still lives with his father. The mother died a few years back.'

Nikki frowned. Yet another solitary kind of person. Maybe not a complete loner like Jim, Lucas or Shirley but still no social butterfly. Though it was a very different kind of death, she was already wondering about a connection. Those words, *Greenborough will be a very dangerous place!* echoed through her mind.

Nikki pulled out her phone and rang Rory Wilkinson on his mobile. There was no answer but she hadn't really expected one. He'd see her call. He was working his socks off at present. She left a message asking for his help — again! 'We need a cause of death on this one, Rory, and fast! This is not looking good.'

She pushed her phone back into her pocket. 'Niall is setting up a crime scene?'

Yvonne nodded. 'He was on it straightaway. He's doing well, that lad. I'm so proud and so pleased for him.'

Nikki saw how Joseph inflated with pleasure at her words. He already loved his son-in-law. In marrying Tamsin, Niall had brought his sometimes hostile daughter closer to him. Joseph had a lot to thank him for.

'Then we'll leave it in his capable hands,' said Nikki, watching the ambulance pull slowly out of the alley and onto the main road. 'Who has gone with the deceased?'

'PC Stacey Smith, ma'am. She knows the procedure.'

'Excellent. We'll meet her at the hospital.' She looked at Joseph. 'Let's get over there straightaway and see if we can find out anything from the medics.' She thanked Yvonne and they hurried off.

'It's connected, isn't it?' murmured Joseph as they climbed into the car.

'That's my opinion,' Nikki replied gravely. 'But it's something very different this time.'

'Maybe not. Maybe he ingested the same stuff, but for some reason had a massive bad reaction to it. He could already have been suffering from some internal problem and the methanol finished him off.' Joseph turned the key in the ignition. 'Anyway, we could keep guessing till kingdom come. We need a proper medical report on what killed him.'

'Then I suggest you put your foot down instead of driving like a seventy-year-old learner! Let's get to the bloody hospital and ask some flaming questions!'

CHAPTER NINE

Dave was thoroughly enjoying his weekend job at Cressy Old Hall. His two new assistants, Arthur Keats and Den Elliott, were helpful, and he soon saw in what high regard they both held their employer. Once again, the man who might seem a rude, pompous prig had managed to win the loyalty of those who got to know him.

Four o'clock was closing time, and that meant just one more guided tour before they shut the doors. Dave was relieved that the day had passed without incident. He wasn't actually expecting trouble, but he knew there were rich pickings in this old manor house.

'Action stations, lads!' called out Arthur, an ex-naval man. 'Here comes the last shower!'

Dave saw a large group of men and women coming up the drive.

The practice was to split them into four small groups of around six to eight people and take each to one of the four different "haunted" locations in turn, before all meeting up again in the main hall for tea.

To his surprise, Dave saw a hand waving frantically from the first group to come in.

'Spooky! Bliss! Didn't know you two were into old buildings.' He laughed.

'I'm into this one,' Spooky said, moving closer to him. 'Dave, I need your help.' And she told him about the observatory.

'I've not seen it, Spooks, and he never mentioned one to me. Are you sure about that?'

Arthur interrupted. 'Excuse me, Dave. The young lady is right. It's his hobby. But I'm afraid he never lets anyone up there.'

Spooky grinned broadly, maybe at being referred to as a "young lady." 'I suppose I couldn't speak to Mr Cressy-Lawson, could I? I'm studying astrophysics and astronomy, and I'd be really interested to meet him.'

Dave looked hopefully at Arthur. 'I can vouch for her, if that helps.'

'Well, I suppose we could ask,' said Arthur dubiously, 'but don't get your hopes up, miss, it's never happened before.' He looked around. 'I think he's in the office. I'll have a word with him, if the boss here doesn't mind me leaving my post?'

Dave smiled. 'We'll keep an eye open until you get back.'

After Arthur had left, Dave asked, 'Astrophysics, eh. Since when is that part of the IT department?'

'Sounded good though, didn't it?' Bliss grinned at him. 'You can tell how desperate she is to see this fabled observatory.'

Dave looked towards the office. 'Well, Arthur is well in with Cressy-Lawson, so if anyone can get you up there, he will. Mind you, if you don't get into your groups soon, you'll miss the guided ghost tour. This is the last one of the day.'

'You stay and wait,' said Bliss. 'I know it's the telescope that you're here for, not the ghosts. Apparently this is the best time to do this tour, as it'll soon be getting dark. You can catch me up later, okay?'

Spooky nodded and Bliss moved off to join one of the parties.

Dave eyed the four groups with interest. They were the usual mix of ghost-hunter tourists and nosey locals wanting a look around their rich neighbour's big drum. Fortunately, no one stood out as being particularly suspicious.

'Is that him?' whispered Spooky, digging Dave in the ribs.

'Yep. The man himself.'

Clive Cressy-Lawson was following Arthur out of the office towards them. He didn't look exactly friendly, but then he rarely did.

'Arthur says a friend of yours is a fellow astronomer, Dave?' His eyes fell on Spooky. 'And you are she?'

If the well-worn rugby shirt and Doc Martens didn't impress him, Spooky's smile certainly did.

'Sarah Dukes, sir. It's a pleasure to meet you.' She gave her real name and shot out a hand. Dave almost laughed as Cressy-Lawson automatically took it and stared down in apparent surprise. 'You are so lucky living here, sir. Not just the amazing house, but the absence of light pollution. It's perfect for sky watching. Do you take astro-photos? Gosh, they'd be amazing from a dark sky location like this. What kind of telescope do you have? I bet it's a Dobsonian, oh, yes, and—'

'Whoa!' Smiling, Cressy-Lawson held up his hands. 'You win! Just because you are a friend of Dave's, who is doing a sterling job here, I'll let you see my little observatory. And, yes, I do have a Dobsonian.'

'A LightBridge? Oh my! Don't tell me you have a LightBridge? Twelve inch?'

'Sixteen, actually.'

'Jeez! That's awesome!' Spooky gasped.

Dave stared at the two of them. He hadn't a clue what they were talking about, but whatever it was, they were enjoying the conversation. Spooky was going to get her trip to the observatory, and Cressy-Lawson was wearing a very uncharacteristic smile that rather suited him.

'Time for me to go back to work. I'll leave you to it.'

Dave wasn't sure that either of them noticed that he'd left. By that time, they were heading for the main staircase, deep in a discussion about magnification and optics. He shook his head. What it was to have an obsession!

Obsession. The word brought him up short.

It came in a lot of different forms, including murder. Dave thought of the poisoned drinks. They made Dobsonian telescopes, whatever they were, seem very innocent.

Dave and his two cohorts spent the next hour shadowing the visiting guests at Cressy Old Hall. Finally, they all came together in the main hall, where two local women were serving tea. Amid the hum of chatter and the clatter of tea cups, Dave saw Spooky and Cressy-Lawson coming back down the stairs.

Cressy-Lawson had his hand resting lightly on Spooky's shoulder, and was listening intently as she chattered away to him. Spooky, lost in her animated story, seemed completely oblivious to the hall full of people.

'Incredible! Quite incredible!' Dave heard him say. Then Cressy-Lawson looked around and blinked, obviously suddenly aware of the house full of visitors. 'Ring me. You've got my number. Next big meteor shower, the scope is all yours.' He shook her hand, and hurried off towards his office.

'Well, aren't you the special one!' Bliss appeared, carrying two cups of tea. 'Old Crusty Crutch actually smiled!'

'He's actually *very* nice,' countered Spooky, 'and you should see his telescope!'

'No thanks! We'll keep it clean if you don't mind.' Bliss sipped her tea. 'And what's this about meteor showers?'

'I have an invite to come and use the telescope to take some photos. So there!'

'That's a first, miss.' Arthur Keats appeared beside them. 'It makes a change to see him looking happy about something. You really must have made an impression.'

Spooky shrugged. 'He loves astronomy, and so do I. Simple as that.'

'I still say it's a miracle,' said Arthur adamantly. 'He's not the easiest man to get along with.'

Arthur went to talk to one of the guides, while Den accepted a mug of tea from one of the ladies helping with the catering. Dave beckoned them over and took them aside. 'Anything look suspicious on this last walk round, lads?'

Both men shook their heads. 'Nothing at all,' said Den, 'and I knew a good few of them from the town.'

'Me too,' added Arthur. 'Lots of the locals are keen to get a chance to see what's behind our gates.'

'And the tourists? Anyone there raise any concerns?'

'They all seemed perfectly happy to look and listen to the guides,' Den said. 'A lot of them were knocking on a bit. Couldn't see them shinning up a drainpipe after a Turner seascape.'

They all laughed. 'I guess not,' said Dave, 'but you'd be surprised what those Women's Institute types are capable of.' He was thinking, of course, of Eve Anderson and her friends. He was pretty sure that any of them would be more than capable of pulling off an art heist if they put their minds to it. If they ever decided to cross the line into the criminal world, they would be a force to be reckoned with.

A sudden scream broke into his thoughts.

In the ensuing silence, all eyes turned to one of the women visitors.

The woman, not a local person, was standing at a window that looked out over the drive and the grounds. 'I thought . . . I thought I saw something out there . . . something horrible!'

Instantly, Dave went to her and found Spooky by his side.

'What did you see?' he asked. She seemed genuinely afraid.

'A woman, I think, all hunched and sort of writhing, and she seemed to sort of glow.' She put her hands to her face. 'Then she was gone. Could she have been the Green Lady?'

Dave called to Den and Arthur, telling Spooky to look after the traumatised sightseer.

Outside, the temperature had dropped as the sun retreated. Shivering, Dave scanned the grounds before him, seeing nothing.

'This way!' Arthur was already running down the drive towards a copse of tall trees that flanked the entrance. 'I think I saw something over there.'

'Where?' panted Dave.

'Over here! Oh my God!' Arthur stopped short.

In the failing light, it was hard to comprehend exactly what they were looking at. Then Dave broke the stunned silence. 'Den! Get an ambulance, fast! Tell them Code Blue, medical emergency!' He turned to Arthur. 'Get buckets and bowls of water! I've seen this before, but never so bad! And get someone — er, Spooky — to make sure everyone stays in that hall! No one leaves, understand.'

He pulled out his phone and asked Control for immediate assistance, then he turned to the hapless woman.

He knew he shouldn't touch her, but every human instinct in him made him want to do just that, to comfort her. All he could do was drop to his knees a few metres from where she lay, and talk as reassuringly as he could.

'Help is on its way, love. Try not to touch your face. I know you are in pain, but, please, just try to breathe and lie still. I'm right here. I won't leave you.' He knew she didn't hear his words. It wasn't just pain she was feeling. It was agony.

He felt a hand on his shoulder.

'What on earth . . . ?' Clive Cressy-Lawson stared in horror at the terrified and contorted figure in front of them.

'Don't touch her, Clive! Help's coming.'

'For God's sake, what is it?' His voice was shaking.

'Phosphorous. I saw it once in an industrial accident. Just don't get any closer.'

The strange luminescence had been the giveaway, that and the suffering the woman was experiencing. Dave knew that unless expert help was administered almost immediately, there was little chance that she would survive. He also knew that applying copious quantities of water was the only thing they could do until that help arrived.

Den thrust his phone at Dave. 'They want details.'

Dave barked out what he knew, and that a team of specialists was required. He looked up and saw Arthur, followed by Bliss and several others, approaching with a collection of water containers. 'Keep them back,' he told Clive. 'Get them to leave the water and return to the hall. This is going to be tricky. Arthur! I need your help.'

Arthur was at his side immediately. 'What can I do?'

'We need to pour water over her face, gently but constantly. Phosphorus isn't soluble in water, so it will help to wash it off her.' Dave knew it was probably far too late, but he had to do something.

As Arthur got closer to her, Dave heard him gasp. 'Dave! It's Mrs Warden! Clive's housekeeper!'

He hadn't even recognised the woman. 'What's her first name?'

'Norma. Norma Warden,' Arthur replied shakily. 'What on earth has happened to her?'

'I have no idea, but come on, let's do all we can.' Dave did have an idea, but he wasn't sharing it with anyone.

It seemed an eternity before help arrived, though it was probably only around fifteen minutes. Now delirious, Norma was having seizures, and her wild flailing caused them to retreat and stop bathing her. As Dave told Arthur, phosphorus was unstable and highly toxic. If it got on their skin it could result in second or third degree burns.

Finally, it was all over. Dave watched as Norma Warden, wrapped up and sedated, was taken into an ambulance to be transferred to a burns unit. But it wasn't just the burns. Dave realised that she had ingested the vile stuff. She wouldn't survive that.

'Greenborough will be a dangerous place this year.' Dave wasn't aware that he had spoken aloud until he saw Arthur looking at him curiously.

'Sorry, just talking to myself. This festival causes enough problems, but you don't expect something like this to happen. It's hard to foresee everything.'

'Of course.' Arthur nodded. 'It must be a nightmare with so many people in and around the town. It's bad enough here, and we only cater for a few at a time.' He paused. 'I'm guessing that was the last tour we'll be doing this year.'

'We'll be treating this as a crime scene until we know what happened to Mrs Warden, so I'm afraid you're right. Not that I think Clive would even consider doing more after this.'

'Poor woman. I can't even begin to think what happened to her, can you?'

Dave was working on it, and he didn't like the thoughts his brain was producing. 'I can't. What can you tell me about her, Arthur?'

'Not a lot. She was a pretty private woman. Divorced. Lived alone in one of the tied cottages on the edge of the estate.' He pulled a face. 'Sad really. We worked together for years, but I know so little about her.'

Another loner, Dave thought. Then his phone rang.

'Ma'am? Sorry, it's a bad line. I'm struggling to hear you.' He walked back towards the house. 'That's better. Go ahead, boss.'

'I've just heard what happened, Dave. Are you okay?'

He gave Nikki a brief update. 'To be honest with you, it was one of the worst things I've ever seen.'

'Thank God you knew what to do. I wouldn't have had a clue.'

'I never forgot the first time I saw what phosphorus could do, and luckily I remembered what they did to help the guy involved. But it was nowhere near as serious as this. The other time was an industrial accident. This was no accident.'

He heard Nikki sigh. 'The only reason I'm not there with you is that we've had another death here in town.'

He tensed. 'Another methanol incident?'

'It's something much nastier, Dave, although as yet we have no idea what it is. We are at the hospital now, waiting on their professional opinion. All they've said so far is that it's some kind of poisoning.'

Dave puffed out his cheeks. 'This is getting serious, isn't it, boss? What the hell is he up to?'

'I dread to speculate.'

'Well, I've got things covered here, boss, and Spooky and Bliss are with me, helping to keep everyone calm. I'll let the ghost-hunters leave after we've taken all their details and contact numbers. This was a deliberate wounding with intent to kill, I'm certain of it. And we had around thirty people wandering around the house and grounds at the time. They will all have to be spoken to. I'm just on my way to talk to Clive Cressy-Lawson. He doesn't yet know that the victim was his manager.'

'Keep in touch, Dave. If you need more bodies out there, let me know and I'll organise it. Once I have an answer here, Joseph and I are going directly to the super. We are having an emergency meeting to discuss the way forward.'

'Sounds like a barrel of fun. Good luck with that, ma'am.'

Dave rang off. From his conversation with Norma Warden earlier, he understood that Clive relied heavily on her to keep the house and indeed the entire estate ticking over. Dave wasn't looking forward to being the one to tell him.

CHAPTER TEN

In flickering candlelight, Eve and her party were making their way into the Greenborough Cemetery. While Rene complained of freezing to death, Lou chuckled at the trickle of wide-eyed people winding their way through the gravestones after Amos Fuller, all clutching tacky little candle lamps.

Amos finally took up his position on the steps of the columbarium, a Gothic walled area, built in a circle. Inside, the walls were lined with niches for the storage of ashes, and one or two had heavy old doors leading to crypts that still held the coffins of long-dead families.

Wendy had seen the magnificent columbarium and the Egyptian Avenue in the Highgate Cemetery in North London. Greenborough's was a rather poor imitation. Still, on a dark and frosty night such as this, it did have atmosphere.

Amos Fuller appeared to have fully entered into the spirit of Dark Greenborough. He was wearing high boots, a long dark greatcoat with a cape and even a top hat. Wendy put him at around fifty years old. His deep voice would have delivered a perfect rendition of Dickens or Bram Stoker, and Wendy was soon immersed in the story of the men who made a living out of providing cadavers for anatomists.

'I always thought that kind of thing only went on in big cities like London and Edinburgh,' whispered Eve, 'not in rural market towns like Greenborough.'

'Me too,' said Wendy.

Amos went on to explain that the local body-snatching trade had been instigated by a wealthy and rather unstable doctor who practised at what was then the old Peace Memorial Hospital in Greenborough. He was fascinated by anatomy and had an almost fanatical following of young aspiring surgeons attending his lectures and dissections. Amos's ancestor, Caleb Fuller, had seen a profitable market opening up, and with an unscrupulous and greedy partner, one William Dyke, had taken it upon himself to provide the anatomist with a steady supply of fresh cadavers.

Amos then took the party to different parts of the old cemetery and showed them ancient graves that had been desecrated and robbed of their occupants, all in the name of medical science, but mainly to line the pockets of Caleb Fuller and William Dyke.

Apparently, the doctor began to demand more and more fresh bodies, and the local constabulary were now becoming rather too interested, so Fuller and Dyke decided to "help" a few ailing souls on their way to the afterlife. Even this became difficult after the first few "sudden" deaths, so in desperation, they took to murdering vagrants.

After the talk was over, they all repaired to the nearest pub for a warming drink.

'That was good,' Rene said, sipping her whisky mac. 'He's quite a character, that Amos.'

'I was delighted to hear that both Fuller and Dyke went to the gallows,' said Lou. 'And I particularly relished the fact that their bodies were then sent to one of the big teaching hospitals for dissection. Divine justice, I call that.'

Wendy turned to Eve. 'You are quiet tonight. Didn't you enjoy the talk?'

Eve nodded. 'Oh, I loved it. I've heard Amos talk before, although not about the Resurrection Men.' She frowned.

'I'm just rather concerned about Nikki and Joseph. I mean, I was so up for this weekend with you all, but . . .'

Wendy peered at her. 'But what?'

'I don't think I realised just what a strain an event like this puts on the emergency services, especially the police.' Eve regarded her friend pensively. 'And, Wendy, I'm afraid that something isn't right in Greenborough.'

'What makes you say that?'

'I spoke to Nikki earlier, and she's not herself. I know it's a bad time anyway, what with Hannah's birthday, but it wasn't that. She's really worried about something but she didn't say what. And, oh, I don't know, I've just got this unsettled feeling.'

Wendy knew not to dismiss Eve's "feelings." She'd been right so many times before. 'Anything tangible?'

'Not really.' Eve shook her head. 'Take no notice of me. I'm probably just being paranoid. Perhaps it's having spent the evening in a graveyard talking about murder.'

'It would take more than that to spook you, Eve Anderson.' Wendy turned to Lou and Rene who were now listening with interest. 'Either of you notice a bad atmosphere in town at the moment?'

Lou raised an eyebrow. 'Apart from all the dead people and night creatures roaming the streets you mean?'

'Actually, yes.' Rene placed her glass on the table. 'As a matter of fact, I have.'

The other three turned their eyes to Rene.

'It's the police. I noticed it earlier today. Naturally, with a festival of this nature and size in a small town, they are all geared up for trouble, but the way they looked reminded me of years ago, when we were put on high alert. I think they're expecting something, or already know about something, and are being extra vigilant.'

'That's it!' exclaimed Eve. 'That's exactly it. And it would explain Nikki's reluctance to talk to me.'

'Well, she's hardly going to be wanting us poking our noses in, is she?' said Wendy darkly. 'Not after our previous involvement.'

'I'm not so sure about that,' said Lou. 'The police stick out like sore thumbs, but who would notice a group of wrinklies? We could be a great asset.'

'Wrinklies! Speak for yourself,' Rene said, laughing. 'But you could be right. We just need to know what we are looking for.' She looked at Eve and raised her eyebrows.

Eve looked dubious. 'Hmm. I'm not sure whether Nikki would welcome us getting involved. I seem to remember promising to stick to gardening in future, and leave investigating alone.'

'Why not let her decide?' said Wendy quietly. 'Tell her we are aware that something is in the air, and we are willing to offer assistance. She only has to ask.'

'Sounds like a plan,' said Rene.

'Absolutely,' agreed Lou. 'Ball's in her court then.'

Eve pulled out her phone. 'I really hope I don't regret this, you lot. She might bite my head off.'

Wendy, Lou and Rene all smiled serenely at her.

'Make the call, Anderson,' Wendy barked.

'I'll text her. That's as far as I'm going to go.'

'That will do nicely,' Wendy said. 'Just do it.'

* * *

Nikki and Joseph were walking up the stairs to the super's office when Nikki felt her mobile buzz in her pocket.

'Message from mother.' She looked at Joseph. 'I'll just read this before we go in. We could be some time, and I don't want to be worrying about her.'

'Of course.' Joseph smiled at her, 'But don't worry too much. You know what they're like. They're probably more dangerous than half the criminals in Greenborough.'

Frowning, she read through the message and let out an exasperated sigh. 'Bloody hell! Just what I need.' She handed the phone to Joseph.

Joseph glanced through it and laughed. 'Nothing gets past them, does it?'

'It's not funny, Joseph! I have enough on my plate without worrying about my mother and the bloody Golden Girls! Again!'

'If you read it clearly, she's giving you the option. She knows what she promised you. All she's thinking is that a few more eyes on the street can't do any harm, especially as they are not wearing uniforms or equipment belts. I'd consider it carefully before dismissing it.' Joseph tapped a short reply and handed Nikki back her phone. 'There. I've bought you some time.'

The message read, *In a meeting. Contact you later.*

She smiled at him. 'She scares me, Joseph.'

'I'm not surprised. Didn't she once shoot someone right here in Greenborough?'

'It's just that we don't know what we are up against here. I don't want her, or any of the others for that matter, putting themselves in harm's way again.'

Joseph touched her arm lightly. 'I do understand, really I do, but we've been here before, haven't we? Think of the kind of work Eve and the others used to do — it was dangerous.'

'I know,' replied Nikki miserably. 'That's part of the problem. I'd do exactly the same, even if I had promised to back off.' She sighed. 'I suppose it's easiest to just say yes and know what she's up to, rather than suspect her of operating behind my back.'

'And feeling guilty about it.'

'Yes, that too.' She exhaled. 'Oh, come on, let's get this meeting over with and then I'll talk to her.' She glowered at him. 'And wipe that smile off your face, Easter. You know perfectly well that you're always bloody right.'

'As long as you know it too, that's fine.'

'Shut it, Sergeant!'

* * *

Superintendent Cameron Walker looked more anxious than Nikki had ever seen him, which was saying something, given what they'd been through in the past.

'I wanted to talk to you two privately first, before the top brass arrive.'

Nikki groaned. 'Oh, great!'

Cam shrugged. 'Unavoidable, I'm afraid.'

It was true, Nikki knew. Played wrongly, this could be disastrous for the Fenland Constabulary, at a time when all police forces were trying to build trust, while the media and others were more than happy to tear them to shreds.

'Sit down, and let's go over what we have to date.' Cameron leaned forward, elbows on his desk. 'It started with an anonymous warning letter to the ACC. By that night, three people had succumbed to methanol poisoning. I believe there was another case of poisoning today that you dealt with?'

'That's right, Cam. We are still waiting for a result on what it was. The hospital is being very cagey and no one wants to speculate, but we've heard from the head of department that they suspect some form of snake venom.'

'What?' Cam's jaw dropped. 'Snake venom? You're kidding me!'

''Fraid not. We'll know more later. Rory has volunteered to fast-track the post-mortem.'

Cam heaved in a long breath. 'And Dave Harris? I understand he was a bit of a hero this evening. But poisoning with *phosphorus*? That's almost unheard of.'

'And quite horrible,' added Joseph. 'Dave's pretty shaken, but he's still at Cressy Old Hall with a team of uniforms, going through the details of all the visitors for the day.'

'After this, get him relieved, Nikki. And do the usual with offering him counselling and post trauma support. It must have been a pretty ghastly thing to have to deal with.'

'Yes, of course.' She paused. 'Although I know exactly where he'll politely advise me to stick it.'

They were silent for a few moments.

Cam coughed. 'What I'd like to know is, are all these deaths and injuries the work of one person? And of whoever sent the warning?'

Nikki glanced at Joseph. 'We believe the answer's yes to both.'

Joseph nodded. 'Has to be. Greenborough has become a very dangerous place, just as he said. The only thing we don't know is whether it's one person carrying out these attacks, or two.'

'If it's one, he moves fast, and he's not using simple poisons either. Handling venom or phosphorus is extremely hazardous. He could have been risking death himself if he rushed things,' Nikki added.

'One dreads to think what's coming next,' Cam murmured. 'They are both very unusual ways to kill someone.'

'Even the methanol has been enhanced in some way, sir,' said Joseph. 'This killer must be a qualified chemist or a scientist.'

'And clinically insane,' Nikki said.

'What I don't get,' Cam said, 'is why use these outlandish methods of killing random people? Is he just instigating a reign of terror? Or is he exacting some sort of revenge for something? Discovering his reasoning could be vital to finding him.' He looked at Nikki. 'Any connections between the victims? Patterns of behaviour?'

'They are all rather solitary people, Cam. None was in a happy relationship or lived in a gregarious family environment.'

'Which means there's no one to give us any indication of their recent comings and goings, the people they've been mixing with, or any change in their routines,' added Joseph.

Nikki shrugged. 'It brings us to the conclusion that this killer just moves around the town targeting random loners.'

'And he could choose absolutely anyone who lives a fairly isolated life.' Joseph's expression was grave. 'That includes anyone from a street dweller to a bachelor executive. There are many reasons why people live alone.'

Cameron glanced at his watch and sighed. 'The others will be here shortly. I'm not looking forward to this meeting one bit. We have a major decision to make, and I'm really not sure which way it's going to go.'

'Does it come down to media silence or telling the public what's going on?' asked Nikki.

'In a nutshell, yes,' Cam said. 'And the final decision will rest with the chief constable. He's responsible for explaining things to the public, and that's not an easy task.'

'What's he like, Super? I haven't heard anything about him, other than that he's pretty open-minded,' Joseph asked.

'I've had very few dealings with him,' Cam said. 'He's young, compared to most CCs, and new to the job, so he's full of enthusiasm.'

Nikki sighed. 'Wonderful attributes, I'm sure, but we need someone older, who has plenty of experience.'

'Give him the benefit of the doubt, Nikki. He might surprise us,' Cam said.

'*Might* being the operative word.' Nikki hoped she'd be able to keep her mouth shut. A fool was a fool, however much gold they wore.

At the sound of footsteps outside the door, they fell silent. Slowly, they rose to their feet.

* * *

'I'm proud of you, Nikki.' Joseph beamed at her.

The gold braid had come and gone and Nikki hadn't exploded. She shook her head. 'I have no idea how I did that!'

'Nor have I, but it probably saved the day.' Cam took a deep breath, 'and the investigation. Okay, we had to make some compromises, but we are still on it.'

'And we have radio silence too — for a while.' Nikki hadn't dared hope, but it had been decided that it was not in the public interest to broadcast the full facts. Extra officers were to be drafted in, ostensibly to help with the flood of visitors, and they would include a small team of special operatives from intelligence. They were to work closely with Nikki and her team. She didn't do combined ops well, but it was a lot better than she'd expected. Right now, she welcomed whatever help she could get, even from intel, so long as the poisoner was taken off the streets and locked away.

'They'll be here at the crack of dawn tomorrow,' Cam said. 'Do you know two detectives called Flint and Hale?'

'Morgan Flint?' Joseph asked. 'Oh yes. I was seconded to work with her on a murder case before I came here. One smart lady. Not exactly friendly, a kind of closed book, but a very good detective.'

'And Hale? That's Connor Hale, I think,' Cam said.

'Met him briefly,' said Joseph.

The name was new to Nikki. She'd heard of Morgan Flint, but had never met her, and wondered if having two powerful women detectives on one case was a good thing. 'If Lucretia Borgia and Cruella de Ville can help us catch this bastard, I can work with them,' she said.

Cam smiled at Nikki's names for them. 'Good.'

She stood up. 'We need to see Rory, so if we're done here, Joseph and I will head over to the morgue. It's late, and I'd like to talk to him tonight if possible.'

'Call in when you get back,' Cam said. 'I'll still be here. There's a lot to organise, including a plausible cover story for the alcohol-related deaths.'

'Good luck with that one,' Nikki said, and headed for the door.

As soon as they were outside the office, Joseph said, 'Ring your mother while I drive us to Rory's. They'll all be on tenterhooks.'

Nikki raised her eyebrows. 'They'll probably be sitting round a cauldron throwing in eye of newt and toe of frog while they concoct their next devilish plan!'

'Bit harsh.'

'You think?'

'You make your dear mother and her pals sound like a witches' coven. Not nice, Nikki Galena!'

CHAPTER ELEVEN

Clive Cressy-Lawson poured more whisky into his glass and strode up and down his library. 'I can't get my head around this! It's despicable. Who on earth . . . ?'

In one of the chairs close to the fire, his wife Priscilla sat with her own glass of whisky, but as far as Dave could see, she hadn't touched it. She stared into the fire that was burning brightly in the grate.

Finally, Clive subsided into silence. Priscilla asked, 'Will she die, Mr Harris?'

'She was very badly hurt, Mrs Cressy-Lawson.'

'Oh, for God's sake, man, just call me Cilla. And do me the courtesy of answering the question.' The whisky glass shook.

'I'm sorry, Mrs . . . er, Cilla, but I doubt she will survive her injuries, and if she did, well . . .'

'She would be horribly disfigured?'

Dave nodded. 'I'm afraid so.'

Cilla's gaze returned to the firelight. 'She's always so particular about her looks. So smart, so neat. She would never cope with being disfigured, never.'

Dave recalled the tightly-braided hair and the crisp, well-pressed outfit. Cilla was right.

'You don't suppose it was some terrible accident, do you, Dave?' Cressy-Lawson had resumed his pacing. 'I mean, you do hear of freak accidents, people finding canisters and opening them. Had a fellow from the estate do that once, years ago.'

'Sir,' Dave said quietly, 'I'm certain that this was a deliberate attack. I need to ask you some questions about Mrs Warden.'

'Deliberate? But you met the woman, Dave! Who would want to hurt her?'

'That's what I have to find out. But before that, we have to talk to her family. Could you give me details of her nearest relatives?'

'As far as I know, Norma had none. She divorced many years ago and her philandering husband died some time after that. Her father died young and her mother was in a care home for years. I think Norma looked after her for a time before she came to work for us.' Cressy-Lawson frowned, evidently trying to recall the details.

'She worked in the same care home, Clive,' Cilla said flatly. 'When her mother died, she left and applied for this job.'

'Bit of a change of direction — care assistant to estate manager,' Dave said.

'Oh, she wasn't a care assistant, she was an administrator, and prior to that she worked in London,' Cilla said.

'Was there anyone you could think of who didn't get on with her? Someone who might have held a grudge against her for some reason?'

Husband and wife both shook their heads. Clive added, 'Norma appeared to be rather standoffish. She was very efficient, and she didn't suffer fools gladly, but she was a kind woman at heart, and I cannot imagine anyone wanting to cause her so much terrible distress and pain.' He grunted. 'God! I'm talking about her as if she were already dead!'

Dave decided that it was time to leave Cressy Hall and get back to the station. It was late, the crime scene had been established, and there was nothing more to be done here tonight. He felt tired suddenly. It had been a really good day, until that last guided tour had come to such a tragic end. Spooky and Bliss had been amazing, helping to calm and organise the visitors, quelling the rumours and assuring them that there had just been an unfortunate accident. Dave's dream job had turned into a nightmare, and the image of the formerly elegant woman writhing in agony threatened to give him nightmares for years to come.

Dave promised to return in the morning, even though the Old Hall would be closed to the public.

* * *

As the revellers flocked around the public houses, and candle-lit processions of ghost walkers clattered through the cobbled alleyways of Greenborough, there was one person moving among them who was not on the lookout for fun. He was dressed for the occasion but his purpose was different. He was hunting.

His eyes shone briefly in a stray torchlight beam, cold as those of a cat on the prowl. Crass as it was in his view, he had waited a long time for this festival, planned meticulously, and now it was time to make his move. Only one "attraction" seemed to offer more than the usual tacky thrill, promising a glimpse at the real dark side of Greenborough. Maybe he'd have a look later, when he was done with his own business.

And he felt quite safe to pursue his own business, here among the crowds. The authorities would never dare broadcast his activities to the public. Widespread panic would ensue. His planning had extended as far as throwing the police those methanol deaths in the first few hours, so that they could blame any subsequent "incidents" on bootleg booze. How clever he was!

* * *

Wendy's eyes lit up. 'Carte Blanche!'

'Observation only, mark you,' Eve said sternly.

Wendy winked at her.

'Get me in trouble with my daughter, Wendy Avery, and I'll never forgive you.'

Wendy slipped her arm through Eve's. 'You know as well as I do that your Nikki would be delighted if we managed to dig up something useful. The police are run off their feet.'

'Sorry to be a killjoy,' Rene said, 'but we're meeting Vinnie Silver in thirty minutes. The sleuthing will have to wait a while.'

'Such a shame that lovely man couldn't stay with us this time.' Lou heaved a theatrical sigh.

'Sorry, but the facilities at Monks Lantern are all maxed out at present.' Eve grinned. 'He says he'll be perfectly happy at the Premier Inn.'

'He seems to live most of his life out of a suitcase, travelling all over the place advising people about hi-tech security,' Lou said. 'What that man needs is a good woman to look out for him. Now, if I were only a couple of years younger . . .'

'A couple?' Rene rolled her eyes.

'Let her dream,' laughed Eve. 'And you have to admit, our Vinnie is a bit special.'

There was certainly no denying that the former special services soldier had charisma. He knew how to listen, and had that rare ability to make whoever he was talking to feel truly valued. To an outsider they would seem the most unlikely of friends, but Vinnie honestly enjoyed their company. Yes, they shared a military background, but Eve believed it went deeper than that. Not so long ago, they had faced a formidable enemy, all showing considerable courage. Something like that made for lasting friendships.

'Where are we meeting him?' asked Wendy.

'The car park down by the river. I've booked a table at that little café down in Mariner's Square for a late supper. Then tomorrow we can all take a closer look at the dark festival.'

* * *

'You ladies are incorrigible!' Laughing, Vinnie shook his head. 'Here's me thinking I was about to enjoy a couple of days' fun, and you tell me we're back on duty!'

'It's just a bit of surveillance, Vinnie. It came from a feeling of something being amiss, rather than anything concrete. We can still enjoy ourselves, just with our eyes wide open.'

'If you guys think something isn't right, I'm sure it isn't. So, tell me what you know.' Vinnie chewed on his fish pie and listened.

'The police are on high alert, and we're sure it's something far more serious than simply policing a big event like this,' stated Rene.

'The town grapevine tells of several alcohol-related deaths over the last few days,' added Lou, 'most likely connected to fake booze.'

'The local paper said last week that the police had made numerous arrests and closed down several illegal distilleries, but once that vile stuff finds its way into the hands of unscrupulous dealers, it can get anywhere.' Wendy frowned. 'Maybe there's an underground factory still operating and they're cashing in on the festival.'

Eve set down her knife and fork. 'But, Vinnie, here's the thing. We don't think it's that that is worrying the police.'

Vinnie looked pensive. 'Then I'll bet they've had some kind of a warning, and they don't want to make it public—'

'For fear of causing panic,' finished off Eve. 'Yes, that's how we see it.'

'Nikki? Joseph? Any clue from them?'

'Nothing, although we do have the green light to observe and take note of anything we feel suspicious about,' Wendy said.

'Not much to go on, ladies,' Vinnie said softly.

'Sweet FA, to be precise,' grumbled Rene, 'but something ain't right, that's for sure!'

'Then it's lucky the dream team is here, isn't it?' He grinned broadly.

'Hunting season just opened in Greenborough,' Wendy added.

'Whoa! What happened to my last directive? Observation only, remember?' Eve threw in.

'Sorry, got carried away.' Wendy winked at Vinnie. 'Observation only.'

'And that's exactly where we need to start. Well, this weekend looks like being a lot more exciting than I thought it was going to be.' Vinnie raised his glass of sparkling water. 'To the dream team. Back in action.'

* * *

Spooky and Bliss were sitting on the sofa, each with a glass of whisky and Fox stretched across their laps. Fox kept tilting his head to look from one to the other of them, apparently bemused by the unusually sombre atmosphere.

He blinked in the bright overhead light. Normally, they kept the room softly lit, but tonight, without putting it into words, they had agreed to banish all shadow.

'I keep seeing her face.' Bliss couldn't keep the tremor out of her voice. 'I was only carrying bowls of water so I never got close, but I saw enough.'

'Me too.' Spooky didn't elaborate. She didn't need to.

'Well, as far as I'm concerned that's the end of Dark Greenborough for this year.' Bliss sipped her drink. 'I feel like locking the door, pulling the curtains and staying put until the whole thing is over.'

'I agree, only I have to go into work for a while tomorrow.' Spooky ruffled Fox's fur and stroked his ears. 'I know it's Saturday, but there's so much going on I've had to organise extra cover for the whole department.' Still stroking Fox, she swirled the whisky in her glass and stared at the golden liquid glinting in the bright light. 'But I'd feel better if you and Fox stayed right here until I get back. We can take the lad for a walk then.'

Bliss frowned. 'It's tempting, but I hate to be intimidated, which is what this feels like.' She lowered her voice.

'Don't laugh at me, sweetheart, but there's a very bad feeling in Greenborough, and I'm not talking about anything physical.'

For her part, Spooky considered the badness totally physical. People were dying. Even so, she respected Bliss's sensitivity to atmosphere.

'I promised to visit Gill Mason tomorrow,' Bliss said, 'just to say hello and catch up. And after what happened tonight, I want to ask her whether she has sensed what might be going on.'

Gill. Try as she might, Spooky couldn't get her head around all that clairvoyant stuff. Moreover, she would have been much happier knowing that Bliss was safe behind locked doors. 'Why not wait and we'll go together. I'd like to say hello too.'

'Sorry, angel, but I know you. Though you'll have every intention of getting away on time, something urgent will come up and you'll be delayed.'

Spooky couldn't deny it. It happened all too regularly. 'Well, whatever you do, keep your mobile in your pocket, okay? You do have previous for forgetting it.'

'Guilty as charged, but don't worry. The way things are right now, I'll have it super glued to my hand.'

'And I promise to make every effort to get away on time.' Spooky drained her glass. 'I'm not sure that we'll sleep tonight, but it's time to turn in.'

Bliss eased Fox off their laps and stood up. 'I'll let the lad out. Will you make a hot drink?'

Spooky stretched. 'No, I'll take Fox. You do the drinks.'

Bliss didn't argue.

They had the use of a small courtyard garden at the back of the building, but when the gift shop was closed, it was only accessible from a narrow alley between the shops. Spooky decided to walk the dog down to the bottom of Salem Alley and along the towpath for a little way, to give him time to sort himself out for the night.

As she walked back, her jacket collar turned up against the cold wind, Spooky sensed something of the odd atmosphere

Bliss had described. The air was heavy with menace, and she found herself glancing over her shoulder and looking for movement in the shadows. There seemed to be a lot of shadows tonight.

Home again, Spooky hurried Fox through the door and locked it quickly. Even the dog had seemed edgy on their way back. Was Bliss right? Spooky hated to admit it, but perhaps logic and reason didn't have all the answers.

CHAPTER TWELVE

Reggie Fisher was used to early mornings. During his years as a street trader he'd been out before dawn, setting up his market stall as early as his licence would allow.

He and Tyrone had not got home until around three in the morning, but Reggie was up and dressed by six thirty. Now he sat at the kitchen table sipping strong tea from an oversized mug, still buzzing from the success of the previous night's hard work. It had gone like a dream, and now a big pile of banknotes was heaped on the kitchen table in front of him.

He let out a long sigh of relief. For once, a scheme of his had paid off. His son was proud of him. It was worth more than all this lovely cash. Reggie smiled.

He wasn't stupid, he knew that they couldn't sustain this particular endeavour beyond the festival's end. They had two more nights at most. Still, tonight was booked out, so as long as their luck held and there were no hitches, he could foresee another lucrative session ahead.

He sorted the cash into denominations and left it neatly stacked next to his son's breakfast plate. He owed Ty big-time, so as far as he was concerned, the boy could be the banker on this venture. He'd earned it, simply for trusting his dad, who had spent most of his life being a prize loser.

Well, all that was about to change. Reggie liked his new role. Not only that, he was determined to keep his son by his side, whatever it took.

* * *

'You do realise that I'll soon be running out of refrigerated storage cabinets?' Rory was Nikki's first caller of the day.

She smiled. 'You'll cope, my friend. What news?'

'Something you probably know already, but I am ready to confirm it in detail. And the detail is quite shocking.'

'Peter Cash? The man who died before Niall and Yvonne could save him?'

'No one on earth could have saved him, dear heart. After the hospital hinted at snake bite, I went and tapped on the expertise of some colleagues at the Centre for Snakebite Research and Intervention in Liverpool. They have identified the venom.' He paused, and Nikki heard the rustle of papers. 'Peter Cash was injected directly into an artery with venom milked from an aquatic pit-viper, which carries the inoffensive name of cottonmouth. Bit deceptive really, as there's nothing soft about this fellow. The venom kills within ten minutes. To have stood any chance of survival, he would have had to have received anti-venom within the first few minutes of being injected.'

'Deadly venom?' Nikki said.

'Oh, utterly lethal.'

'In Greenborough? How? What on . . . ?'

Rory chuckled. 'That's exactly what I said. Bootleg vodka, yes. Rare poisonous snakes, no.'

Nikki's mind was racing. At least this should help them narrow down their search for the killer. Specialist knowledge of snake venom was not a common item on most villains' CVs.

'Poor Mr Cash did not have a peaceful passing, I'm afraid. Even I was shocked. The cottonmouth venom literally dissolves any tissue it comes into contact with. The injection site was immediately apparent, as it was already gangrenous and liquefied.'

Nikki grunted. 'Too much information, Rory.'

'He actually died of internal bleeding. The poison caused multiple haemorrhages in the heart, lungs and other organs. The heart gives up, simply because there's no way it can pump effectively through all the vascular damage.'

Nikki wondered if Yvonne Collins would feel better knowing that there was no possible way she could have helped Peter Cash. Knowing Yvonne, the answer was probably not. In her eyes, she had failed a member of the public, and that was unforgivable. Nikki returned her mind to the present. 'Okay, Prof. Snakes. Talk to me about snakes.'

'Not my area of expertise, but luckily our Spike was at uni with one of the post-doctoral research assistants at the Liverpool School of Tropical Medicine. They are eagerly talking reptiles as we speak.'

'I'm just wondering what kind of person would have access to poisonous snake venom,' Nikki mused.

'A serious collector? Someone working either in a zoo or a research facility? Or maybe the venom was acquired illegally. Incidentally, there is a big market in the illegal trafficking of rare species of snake and their eggs.'

Nikki had recently read a report on the billion-dollar trade in python skins, thriving because of the worldwide demand for handbags and other fashion accessories. 'There's a black market for absolutely anything,' she said.

'Oh yes. You want something and have the cash, some unscrupulous bugger will find it for you.' Rory made a harrumphing noise. 'Been like that since time immemorial, dear heart. Supply and demand.'

There was a silence for a moment. 'Phosphorus,' Nikki said. 'Snake venom. Chemically refined methanol. What the hell will he choose next?'

'Let's not try to second guess our devious friend. He is much more inventive than us, even if it sticks in my throat to admit it.' Rory sighed. 'One thing though, he is choosing particularly insidious and extraordinarily painful poisons. Maybe I'll do a little homework into his future options? Poisons delivering extreme trauma to the victim.'

'Good idea, Rory. We need all the help we can get. Speaking of help, the legendary DI Morgan Flint and her sergeant, Connor Hale, will be here within the hour and I have to prepare.'

'Really? I've only met them the once, but they left an impression alright.'

Nikki felt her stomach sink.

'Oh, dear, what did I say? Fret not, dear Nikki, it wasn't a bad impression. I just couldn't recall ever meeting two more focused detectives. It was as if nothing else existed, other than the case they were dealing with. It was almost like they programmed themselves into the investigation at the expense of everything else.'

'And did said case come to a good conclusion?' Nikki asked.

'Textbook. Went through the CPS like a dose of salts, apparently, and then they disappeared back to Planet Zog, or wherever it was they'd been transported from.'

'They're from HQ. Part of a specialist crime unit. Intel, actually,' Nikki said.

'Believe that if you want. I'm sticking with a galaxy far, far away.'

'I'll give you my opinion when this is over. Now I'd better get myself together. Thanks, Rory, and keep me posted on all things reptilian.'

'Without fail. Oh, and I've already emailed you a jpeg of a cottonmouth viper, just in case you come across one during your investigation. Now, you'd better go and polish up your conversational Zog.'

Nikki hung up. She certainly welcomed help from Intel, but she already felt intimidated by Morgan Flint. It was not the foot she wanted to set off on. Nikki frowned. Okay, so the woman was focused. Well, she wasn't the only one. She gathered up her notes and went to find Joseph.

* * *

Superintendent Cam Walker had set aside a small conference room for the briefing. He invited Nikki and Joseph to be there fifteen minutes before the others were expected, so as to bring them the news from higher up the chain.

'I don't have to tell you the pressure they are exerting on us, do I?' Cam looked from one to the other.

Nikki shook her head. 'You certainly don't. This case is a powder keg. As far as we are concerned, hunting for a killer is bad enough, but a faceless one in a town full of masked creatures is a nightmare.'

'I appreciate that, and for once so does top brass, that's why they've thrown us Flint and Hale. We just have to see how far we can let it go before we have to let the public know what's happening.' Cam grimaced. 'Believe me, there are some very twitchy people orchestrating this one, who are well aware that someone will finish up being the fall guy if things go tits up.'

'Let's hope it doesn't come to that,' Joseph murmured, 'although we have no idea where to start looking for our killer.'

'Well, after your initial meeting here, I've mustered the troops and we'll all go down and get a strategy plan in place.' There was a knock at the door. 'Come.' He glanced at Nikki and Joseph and whispered, 'Here we go.'

Morgan Flint shook Nikki's hand. The grip was firm but not too firm.

'We are very glad to see you here,' said Nikki honestly.

'We'll do all we can, I promise you.' The voice was clipped and business-like, with just the faintest hint of a local accent. DI Flint was around five feet seven. Her rich, dark brown hair was worn shoulder length and she had very disconcerting pale blue eyes. Nikki guessed she was in her early to mid-forties, although she always found it hard to judge people's ages.

The woman was staring at Joseph. 'We've worked together before, haven't we, Sergeant Easter?'

'The Lisa Johnson case, DI Flint.'

'Of course. Good to see you again. You remember Connor Hale?'

Joseph nodded and shook the man's hand.

Probably ten years Morgan Flint's junior, Hale was one of the few black police officers in the Fenland Constabulary. Nikki discovered later that he was actually mixed race, with a white Irish father and a Jamaican mother. Whatever his ancestry, he was certainly very good looking.

After they had settled down, Morgan Flint said, 'We have been briefed at HQ, and we have a general report of what has been going on here, but could you bring us up to speed with recent developments?'

Nikki told them about the phosphorus and the snake venom, and watched Morgan Flint's pale eyes turn glacial.

'Insidious,' she murmured. 'Why the need to change methods all the time, I wonder?'

'Showing off? Proving how clever he is?' offered Joseph. 'Maybe even trying to impress us?'

'You believe the killer is male?' Connor threw in.

'A graphologist has assured us it was a man who wrote the original warning note.' Nikki frowned. 'And this has all the hallmarks of a male predator. If it turns out to be a woman, she will have to be a very strange one.'

'I agree,' said Morgan. 'Even though poison is always thought to be women's method of choice, it doesn't fit the bill in this case.'

They discussed the case for a while longer, until Cam said, 'We've arranged an office for you both, and also an officer to act as liaison since you are out of your area. Anything you need, just ask. We appreciate your help.'

'I'm not knocking your outfit here, but we do have access to some very good resources, and we can get hold of intelligence faster than most departments.' Morgan's eyes rested firmly on Nikki. 'We'll use everything available to us to help you get this killer off the streets.'

Nikki wondered where she and her team fitted in, with their barely adequate resources. She hoped the A-team here were the sharing kind. Morgan Flint didn't look like a glory grabber but looks could be deceiving.

'Our priority is intelligence gathering, DI Galena. We collect, compile and analyse. We will work hand in glove with you. You're in charge, but for heaven's sake, use us!' Morgan's eyes seemed to get paler with every word.

'But don't worry,' added Connor, 'we aren't afraid of getting our shoes dirty if we're needed out on the streets.'

'That's good to know,' said Joseph. 'Those streets are not a safe place to be right now.'

Morgan looked at Cam. 'Okay, we are ready to hit the ground running, if we're done here?'

They all stood up.

'I'll take you to your office,' Cam said, 'and introduce you to your liaison officer, and then we'll all meet in the Murder Room for daily orders. Fifteen minutes?'

Nikki and Joseph went back down the stairs. After a minute or two, Nikki said, 'I find dark hair and pale eyes rather disturbing somehow. Very attractive, but off-putting.'

'Her team called her the snow queen, I remember,' Joseph said. 'I'm kind of seeing why. Yet according to her record, she's been in some pretty spectacular scraps in the past, and definitely held her own.'

Nikki sighed. 'Well, queen or fighter, we need her and her sidekick. The clock is ticking and our poisoner is still at large.'

'You're right. Let's take her at her word and use them to the fullest.'

'I intend to.'

* * *

Gill Mason glanced at her watch. Bliss had rung and arranged to meet her before her first customer arrived at nine thirty. She had sounded odd — anxious and excited at the same time.

While she waited for her friend, Gill busied herself setting up her stall. She had erected a small three-sided gazebo around two chairs and a circular table to give her clients some privacy while she did their readings. She also had a table across the front of the little unit with a selection of crystals, runes and angel cards for sale.

When everything was ready, Gill sat down and watched the entrance of the covered market for Bliss to arrive.

Gill had already picked up an undercurrent at this year's fair — you didn't have to be clairvoyant for that. Apparently there had been several deaths locally and now the rumours were swirling round like vultures above a carcass. She'd been hearing the hushed comments all day yesterday. "He worked with my cousin . . ." "She lived a few doors away from my nan . . ." "His father used to go fishing with my dad . . ." People loved to boast of a connection with the unfortunate victim of a tragedy, no matter how tenuous. It was human nature.

Then there had been the "breaking news" report on the television. Gill had sat on the bed in her hotel room and watched as a poker-faced police superintendent had warned the public about some particularly lethal counterfeit alcohol that had already claimed several lives. He urged everyone to be on their guard at all times during the festival, and not to accept drinks from people they did not know. She had watched him closely, looking for what lay behind the practised police-speak. The tension and anxiety was much greater than was warranted by a few bottles of fake booze.

Bliss would be here soon. Gill was almost afraid to hear what her friend had to tell her.

Gill was very receptive to the different moods and vibrations people gave off. Not because of any psychic ability, she was just very sensitive to states like repressed anger and stress. It could be draining, but she had learned techniques to protect herself from all the distress, grief and anxiety that plagued her clients.

'Go placidly,' she whispered to herself.

Looking anything but placid, Bliss came hurrying through the doorway to the covered market. She made her way directly to Gill's stand without so much as a glance at the other brightly coloured stalls piled high with art and craft materials and confectionery, scented candles and giant posters of vampires and werewolves.

They hugged affectionately. They had the type of friendship that continues and flourishes, no matter how long the periods of not seeing each other, but still, Gill wished they lived nearer.

'Come into my authentic gypsy tent — I don't think, and let's talk.'

'I brought herbal tea.' Bliss placed two polystyrene beakers on the table, careful to avoid spilling any on Gill's tarot cards.

Gill gathered up the cards and sat down. 'I'm not going to ask how you are, I can see it in your eyes, so just tell me what's happened.'

'Where to begin? It's been the most awful two days ever. I just can't . . .' Bliss threw up her hands. 'I can't believe it!'

Gill sat back and listened as the whole horrible story unfolded. Finally, she said, 'Who knows about the terrible incident at Cressy Old Hall?'

'Just the family, a couple of the staff and a few of us who were there and carried water out to that poor woman. The other visitors were told there had been some sort of freak accident, and I'm certain they all believed it.'

'And just after finding that poor lad on your doorstep! Oh, Bliss, I'm so sorry! No wonder you're strung out.'

'You mustn't tell anyone what I've told you, Gill. Spooky and I promised Dave Harris we'd keep it to ourselves, but I needed to talk to you. And to ask you to keep your eyes and ears open. Something bad is happening here, and I'm frightened.'

Gill breathed deeply. Bliss had just confirmed her vague suspicion that something was awry. Whatever was stalking the streets of Greenborough, it was bad. 'I've noticed the tension. There's a real atmosphere pervading the festival this year.'

111

Gill could see that Bliss was having difficulty concentrating and changed the subject. 'Will I get to see Spooky this trip, or is she snowed under with work?'

'She's always busy, Gill, but she loves what she does, and of course she'll get to see you. She actually didn't want me coming out alone today, but,' a little of the old Bliss resurfaced, 'you can't let a situation like this rule your life, or the bad guys win, don't they?' She leaned forward. 'If you pick up on anything, or see anyone that strikes you as worrying, you will ring me, won't you? Then I can get Spooky to pass it on to DI Nikki Galena.'

'Of course, I will,' said Gill. 'Being in this kind of environment, you hear a lot.' Now she'd really keep her ears open. Bored stallholders chatted loudly, calling across to each other, or gathered together to compare sales, drink tea, and chat about the punters. 'Gossip is rife in a market, believe me. And it's a great place to people watch. I'm pretty busy, but I always leave some breathing space between readings, so I promise to keep vigilant.'

Bliss looked more relaxed. She sipped her tea. 'Excellent. Thank you so much. Is it something you might be able to tune into, er, professionally?'

'You mean as a fortune teller?' Gill smiled mischievously. 'Actually this has nothing to do with clairvoyancy or whatever people like to call it. People give off a lot of energy, good and bad. If a person is seriously disturbed, it pours out of them like poisonous gas.' Gill immediately wished she hadn't used that particular analogy. 'I don't think I'm any different to highly trained police officers when it comes to "reading" people. They just call it observational skills and copper's intuition. It comes from years of experience in dealing with people of all sorts. It's often simply understanding body language. There's nothing spooky about it.'

Bliss just gave her a knowing smile. She was a woman who accepted that some ordinary people had extraordinary talents and nothing would alter her point of view. She believed that Gill had a gift, and that was fine. There were enough people who were sceptical! She stared at her friend. 'All I can say is that if something, or someone, really disturbs me, I will contact you.'

Bliss reached across the table and squeezed Gill's hand. 'I feel better for hearing that, even if I can't wait for the next two days to be over.'

'Believe me, my friend, I'm beginning to feel the same way.'

CHAPTER THIRTEEN

Reggie stared at the TV and felt the colour drain from his face. They'd been working, so he'd missed the late night news but today the police warning about highly dangerous fake booze in Greenborough was the number one news item.

'Oh shit!' he growled. If his son saw that, and he was bound to, all his newfound admiration for his father would fly right out of the window.

He turned off the TV and hurried to the cupboard under the stairs. It pained him to do it, but the vile stuff he'd bought from Vlad had to go.

There were eight bottles left. He stared at them, as if they had done him a personal injustice, and then dragged them out into the hall. The alcohol itself was not a problem, it would go straight down the toilet, but the bottles were not so easy to dispose of. He wanted them gone, far away from here. There was no way of knowing if this stuff was part of the deadly consignment that had killed people, but they mustn't be linked to either him or his son.

Reggie decided to tell the boy before he caught the newsflash, and to ask for his opinion on where to dump the bottles.

He went along to Ty's room, sat on his bed and told him about the statement from the police. 'I've tipped the stuff away, but what about the bottles, son? Where do you think I should take them? I don't want them here, just in case the rozzers make an unscheduled visit.'

To his surprise, Tyrone frowned but didn't kick off at him. He cursed Vlad the Bad to the ends of the earth alright but, oddly, not his father.

'They say the best place to hide something is in plain sight. I reckon we shove them in a bottle bank, along with everyone else's.' Ty yawned. 'How about the big one at the recreation ground on the edge of town? There's a whole load of beer bottles in the backyard, stick them in with the vodka bottles and get shot. Those banks are full to busting in no time at all, and along with hundreds of others, those bottles'll never be traced back to us. Better wipe the bottles down and wear gloves, just to be on the safe side.'

Reggie stood up. 'Good thinking, Ty.' He'd do it immediately.

'And, Dad? Thanks for telling me.'

He flashed his son a weak smile. 'It should have been like this years ago, lad. I'm so sorry.'

Tyrone stretched and sat up in bed. 'Just bugger off and get rid, okay? We need to get our heads into planning tonight's show. We'll talk it through as soon as you're back. See if we can improve or change anything.'

Reggie paused at the door. 'Okay, son. I won't be long.'

In the hall outside he heaved a sigh of relief. Frankly, that was more than he deserved.

* * *

Vinnie Silver and his "ladies" met up at his hotel for breakfast. Rather than a bunch of school kids off an outing, they now resembled a COBRA meeting. Having thought of little else all night, Vinnie had come to the conclusion that he, along with Eve and her companions, could be a big asset to the police. He had rung Joseph, and his old army mate had agreed. They'd arranged to meet briefly later in the morning.

There were a few things Joseph wanted Vinnie to be aware of before he and his silver-haired vigilantes took to the streets.

Vinnie looked down at his full English, and thought of Joseph's parting words. 'Keep them safe, Vinnie. No risks. There's someone out there who is totally evil, and we don't want any of you guys attracting his attention, alright?'

'Loud and clear, Sarge.' What the hell was going on? Whatever it was, it certainly went deeper than a few bottles of counterfeit plonk.

Wendy set down her fork. 'Right, I'll read out our suggestions for this morning's venues. Considering what's going on, I suggest we either stick together or at least split into two groups. We should never go anywhere alone, okay?'

The others nodded.

'Choices are — here goes — a visit to the "never before opened to the public" Oleander House, the home of Robert Matthew Richmond, the Victorian botanist and artist.'

'Who unaccountably disappeared and was never seen again,' added Eve.

Wendy nodded. 'Then there's a display of historical archive material and a talk about old murders that took place in and around Greenborough.' She looked at her notes. 'Or a river trip from the Marina with a man called Trevor Layne. He's an architectural historian, and apparently you can see a whole load of interesting old buildings from the water that just aren't visible from the road. He's done some work for TV programmes and has a reputation for being a very interesting speaker. Or, we can wing it. Just pick something at random.'

'I'd dearly love to see Richmond's botanical pictures. It's a rare chance to see the originals, and in the man's old home too,' said Eve. 'But I'm not forcing everyone to come with me, as long as at least one of you does.'

'I'm in for that one too,' said Wendy.

'And I love a mysterious disappearance, so why don't we all go?' added Rene.

Vinnie pulled a face. 'Not sure flower paintings are really my thing. I'm more a Jackson Pollock kind of guy.'

Rene winced. 'You like that kind of art?'

Vinnie smiled apologetically. 'Somehow, I can relate to the chaos. I especially like his 'Black pourings.' And I love the thought of hurling and dripping paint onto a canvas. Most therapeutic, I should think.'

Rene shook her head. 'Vinnie Silver, you never cease to amaze me!'

'I'm having a short meeting with Joseph,' Vinnie said, 'so why don't you all go and I'll join you as soon as you've had enough botany.'

'Excuse me, but we've just said there's no going solo, young man,' Lou reprimanded him sternly.

'I think I'll be fairly safe with a detective sergeant, don't you? It'll be a half hour, tops, and then I'll meet you at your venue, okay?' He gave them his best bad boy smile. 'I'm going to try to wring some facts out of Joseph Easter — then we might have more of an idea of what we are looking for.'

'Well, in that case, okay, but after that, we stick to what we decided, and watch each other's backs,' said Eve. 'And no matter what we are doing, we have to remember our main directive — to spot anything that might be cause for concern.'

'Actually, I've got a bit of news for you.' Four sets of eyes stared at Vinnie expectantly. 'I've decided to sell my business. I've had a good offer from a much bigger company, and I'd be a fool not to take it.'

'Oh my! So, what will you do then?' asked Lou.

'Not sure yet. I need a new challenge every so often, or I get bored.'

He looked at the women's faces. 'You all feel the same, don't you? Must be our backgrounds.'

Eve nodded. 'If we didn't have projects to throw ourselves into, we'd finish up in the Funny Farm.'

'Speaking of projects,' Wendy said, 'I suggest we wait until Vinnie has spoken to Joseph, then we draw up a plan of action.'

'I second that,' said Eve. 'After the artist's house, maybe we should take in some of the more "sensational" attractions, those that will draw a bigger crowd.'

'Good point,' Vinnie agreed. 'Okay, ladies, let's reconvene at Oleander House.'

* * *

Nikki pushed a pile of paperwork across her desk to Joseph. 'I'm impressed — though I hate to admit it. Two hours, and they've produced all this. Lists of people and organisations in the county allowed to keep poisonous snakes and venom, including private and public collections, research establishments, zoos, wildlife parks and licensed retailers. Plus another list of people that have dealt illegally in reptiles and exotic "pets" in the last five years.'

Joseph flipped through the pages. 'I'm guessing that should we find a person of interest, this will flash up a match?'

'Absolutely. They are now working on the phosphorus, looking at chemical suppliers and manufacturers, businesses and places like labs in universities that use it legally.' She turned over a page. 'And they've found a few individuals that have been involved in "acquiring" and selling dangerous chemicals and hazardous substances. Nice commodity to trade in.' Nikki tapped the pile of papers. 'As you say, this gives us a whole database of names to draw from. We just have to find a suspect.'

Joseph put the papers into a tidy stack. 'Who is their local liaison, by the way?'

'Who would you choose? Who has an encyclopaedic knowledge of this area?'

'Ah, our Vonnie.'

'Who else?'

'Perfect. And it gets her off the streets for a while. She took it pretty badly when that lad died in her arms,' said Joseph.

'I think that was part of the plan,' confided Nikki. 'Cam was worried about her.'

Nikki's phone rang.

'Have you got a few minutes for some pearls of wisdom from your friendly Home Office pathologist?'

'For you, Rory, always.'

'Good. Well, Spike and I have been brainstorming about our poisoner, rather unsuccessfully it has to be said, but we'll come back to that in a minute. First, we've had the full report back about the original bad alcohol. Basically, whoever made the stuff would need to have pretty advanced science lab skills. Your man, and we are assuming it is a man, is of higher than average intelligence, and probably has a background in studying or working in chemistry.'

'So, he didn't pick it up in a backstreet lockup turning out counterfeit hooch?'

'This formula is highly complex, or so I'm reliably informed. This guy is smart, and not just streetwise either. He's educated.'

Nikki grimaced. 'Great. That's all a sodding festival of the occult needed — a bloody mad scientist.'

'And that's exactly what we've got. Joking apart, Nikki, psychosis coupled with an advanced knowledge of science or chemistry signals danger on a grand scale.'

'I've already got the picture, Rory.' Nikki looked at Joseph and sighed. 'And the morning had been going so well.'

Joseph, who had been listening on loudspeaker, pulled a face.

'Now, our wild and unsubstantiated theories about your killer.' Rory took a long breath. 'We've decided that he's a local. All his victims either lived alone or in rather isolated or independent environments with no spouse or other close domestic ties, so he's been observing them for a while. He could even be a fairly well-known character, a familiar face in the Greenborough community. We think he is well acquainted with the area and chooses his crime scenes carefully.'

'We agree,' said Nikki. 'Definitely a local.'

'Now, his methods,' Rory said. 'This is where we wander into the realm of speculation. We've tried to put ourselves in his shoes, even though his knowledge of poison outshines both mine and Spike's put together.'

'Very reassuring,' growled Nikki.

'Simply facing facts, dear heart.' He paused for a moment. 'Oddly, when we did so, we both felt that we were rather older men, maybe in our early fifties. I'm absolutely sure he's not young, he is far too clever, calculating and patient. We then tried to second guess what method he's likely to choose for his next killing.'

Nikki heard the chink of a teaspoon and then a slurp — Rory was drinking coffee. 'I reckon he threw in the alcohol to give you guys something to throw to the media. Normally, he favours inflicting agony and extreme distress, and he's using substances that are at toxicity rating 6 — the most lethal.'

Joseph asked, 'And you have a list of other poisons with this high rate of toxicity?'

'There are hundreds, my friend. He started his killing spree with phosphorus and snake venom, a chemical poison and an organic one. So what is he going to progress to next? I don't think he'll pick something at random, he has it all planned out, and Spike concurs.'

Nikki glanced at Joseph, who nodded. 'We are with you there, Rory. Go on.'

'Poisons. A lot of them take quite a time to finish off the victim, and we think he's going to be using a fast-acting one. I've prepared a list of possibilities which I'll email to you.'

'If it were you, as you say, inside his mind, what kind of thing would you pick, Rory?' asked Nikki.

'Me? Oh, I'd go for one of the three classics: arsenic, cyanide or strychnine. Considering his penchant for acutely painful and dramatic effects, it would have to be strychnine.' Nikki almost heard his shudder. 'A terrible agonising death producing spasms and back-arching convulsions — all while the victim is still perfectly conscious.'

'Damn,' Joseph said.

'Not nice for whoever finds them either, or for us patholo-gists, because rigor mortis sets in at the moment of death, leaving us a corpse with a contorted body, eyes still wide open and a face set in a rictus that you're not likely to forget in a hurry.'

Nikki could picture it all too clearly.

'Spike, on the other hand, favours a plant-based toxin. His first choice was Monkshood. One, because it's easily obtained and found in lots of gardens, and two, because it also causes a spectacularly horrible death. You see, what happens is—'

'Whoa!' Nikki had heard enough.

'Well, whatever kind of poison he chooses next, the effect will be ghastly.' He paused. 'I hate to say this, but if he does kill again, we might have a better chance of fathoming out how he ticks.'

More likely when, not if, thought Nikki. 'There's nothing on any of his previous victims that could point to his identity, is there?'

'Nothing at all. The phosphorus case will be coming across quite soon. She was critical earlier this morning and Spike just gave me a note to say that she's passed away. Not that I think there will be any trace evidence after such insidious chemical burns. Another poor soul that even my tender ministrations will never restore to beauty.'

'Oh dear. I'd better go tell the super.'

'Sorry to give you such a catalogue of horrors, my dear friends. I'll keep you updated as the forensic mysteries unfold.'

'If I have the stomach for it!'

'Nikki Galena, you are as tough as they come. But when you get out there and find this creature, just promise me you won't get close enough for him to touch you. I suggest Tasers, or a carefully aimed brick to the head. Anything that can be administered from a distance. God knows what he carries in his pockets! And now I'm off. *Ciao* amigos!'

Joseph glanced up at the wall clock. 'Nikki, I'm just slipping out for half an hour. I want to give Vinnie Silver some friendly advice about what to expect on the streets, and to tell him to guard those women with his life. Or is it the other way around?'

'Thanks, Joseph. It still worries me sick, knowing that my mother is out there.'

'You'd be pretty inhuman if you weren't.' He threw her an affectionate smile. 'Don't worry, I'll make our Vinnie very aware of the danger — without saying anything I shouldn't. Okay?'

* * *

Vinnie and Joseph embraced each other warmly. They were as close as brothers. You didn't fight alongside someone for years, put your life in his hands and then forget him. The bond that had been formed under fire lasted long after the guns fell silent.

'Good to see you, man,' Vinnie said. 'And I'm delighted about you and your gorgeous boss. Mind you, it took you long enough.'

Joseph grinned sheepishly. 'I know, I know. I hate to say it, but you were right.'

'Nah. I always knew it would happen one day. I'm just sorry I never got the chance to seduce the lady myself.'

Joseph steered Vinnie down a narrow, cobbled lane and into a tiny café that he often frequented. Inside, it smelt of rich ground coffee and fresh pastries, a world apart from death and hidden menace.

'I can't tell you all the details, Vinnie. 'They're being kept from the public for fear of causing panic. But since, like us, you're bound by the Official Secrets Act, I can tell you some of it.'

'Then I could make some hypothetical assumptions that you could either deny or confirm?' Vinnie said.

Joseph collected their drinks and they chose a table in the far corner of the almost empty café.

'I saw the TV news,' Vinnie said. 'Was the superintendent's statement true?'

'Absolutely. There have been four deaths that we are aware of, all involving alcohol with methanol in it.'

'But there's more to it than that.' This was not a question. 'So,' Vinnie mused, 'we have an unusual situation here.

The Dark Greenborough Festival and an influx of tourists, added to the police's state of high alert — we've noticed it in all the officers we've seen around the town — I'm surmising that some sort of threat has been issued. Terrorists, maybe?'

'Not terrorists,' said Joseph softly.

'But you've received intel, or maybe even an actual warning, about a possible incident?' Vinnie narrowed his eyes. 'Something has already happened, hasn't it?'

Joseph stared into his coffee and decided to forget protocol. 'Vinnie, there's someone bad out there, and we know next to nothing about him, other than the fact that he's intent on causing harm. He wants to take Dark Greenborough to a different level altogether.'

Vinnie sipped his drink. 'How do you mean? A serial killer of some kind?'

Joseph kept his voice low. 'There have been two bizarre deaths already. In both cases the killer used exceptionally high grade poisons.'

'And you fear this is just the beginning?'

'I'm certain of it.'

'What's his motive?' Vinnie asked.

Joseph shrugged. 'We have no idea why he's doing this. Or who he is, other than that he has a background in science, chemistry in particular. Oh, and we think he's older, partly because of the way the warning note he sent our ACC was worded.' He quoted the message.

'Yes, not how a young person would express themselves.' Vinnie frowned. 'You mentioned chemistry. So he's using chemicals to kill? What? Nerve agents? Like Novichok?'

They hadn't thought of that. Joseph grimaced. 'Snake venom and phosphorus.'

Vinnie winced. 'Ouch! But I keep coming back to why. You don't just wake up one morning and decide to unleash mayhem among the citizens of a Fenland market town. You have to have a reason.'

'I'm sure he has, but he's not shared it with us.' Joseph finished his coffee. 'Now you can appreciate Nikki's fears for

Eve and the other three warrior queens.' He gave his friend a wry smile. 'We knew we couldn't stop them, so by giving them the go-ahead, we can at least keep them on our radar.'

'Sensible move. I can say that Eve is trying very hard to get everyone to adhere to your directive of observation only — for now anyway.'

'Best we can ask for really.' Joseph gave a small smile. 'But we know what they're like, don't we? If they get the slightest whiff of a lead, they're off like a pack of bloodhounds.'

Vinnie grinned. 'You need all the help you can get, so don't knock it. And don't worry, I'll be feeding every little thing we find straight back to you.'

Joseph reached across the table and squeezed Vinnie's arm. 'Thanks, mate. I feel one hell of a lot happier with you out there with them.'

Vinnie winked. 'As if that lot needed protecting. They'll most likely be looking out for me.'

CHAPTER FOURTEEN

On hearing that Norma Warden had died, Dave decided to go back to Cressy Old Hall immediately. He found Clive Cressy-Lawson alone.

'Cilla's gone to our London flat,' he said tonelessly.

'That may be for the best, sir,' Dave said softly. 'At least you won't have to worry about her.'

'Thing is, I'm not sure if she'll be coming back.' Cressy-Lawson went through to the library, threw himself down into one of the two wing-backed chairs and pointed to the other. Dave sat down. 'She was never cut out for this place. I've always known it. What happened the other day was the final straw. Her departure was acrimonious to say the least. Harsh words were exchanged.'

Dave wasn't quite sure what to say to this. He opted for, 'I'd give her some time, sir. Let's get this horrible business over, and maybe she'll reconsider.'

'You know, I've spent my whole married life juggling between my roles as guardian of my ancestral family home and being a loving and dutiful husband. I'm not sure it should have been that way.'

Cressy-Lawson looked about as low as it was possible to get. It seemed that Norma's terrible death had thrown a shadow across his entire life.

'I think we should take this one step at a time, sir. The main thing is that your wife is safe in your London flat. Now we should do all we can to find out what happened to Mrs Warden, and when we have the answer to that, well, then you can re-evaluate your situation.' Dave tried to sound positive. 'Ring your wife. Tell her that you love her, and that you are going to move heaven and earth to help us with our enquiries. Now really isn't the time for life-changing decisions, sir.'

Cressy-Lawson was quiet for a while, obviously making an effort to pull himself together. 'You're right, of course. Stiff upper lip called for, what? Concentrate on the matter in hand.' He leaned forward. 'So, how can I help?'

'Well, sir, I'm going to need a list of everyone who works and lives on the estate and in the tied properties — workers' cottages and the like. I have to know who, apart from the groups of visitors, has a legitimate right to be here, and where everyone was at the time of the murder. We will be interviewing them all.'

The word "murder" seemed to have a galvanising effect on Cressy-Lawson. 'Yes, yes. Of course. It will all be in Norma's files.' He stood up. 'No time like the present. I'll show you her office and leave you to it, while I ring my wife. Then I'll buckle down and do what I can to help.'

Dave followed Cressy-Lawson out, relieved to note his purposeful stride, his straight back.

From the office window, he could see the cordoned-off area where Norma Warden had been attacked. Several uniformed officers were stationed at intervals around what was now a murder scene. Dave swallowed hard, trying to blank out the image of that poor woman writhing on the ground in agony.

He opened a filing cabinet and looked at the rows of folders. Each section was neatly labelled, and most contained brightly coloured plastic envelopes. Norma Warden had been very thorough.

Dave pulled out a green folder marked "Tenant Details" and began to make notes.

Cressy-Lawson returned some ten minutes later, looking much more relaxed. 'You're a wise man, Dave Harris. We are talking, and Cilla has calmed down. As you said, one step at a time.'

'I'm assuming this is all on computer, sir, as well as all these hard copies?' Dave asked.

'Yes. Norma just liked everything backed up on paper, and considering the power cuts and fluctuating broadband signal out here, she was sensible.' He shook his head. 'God knows where I'm going to find someone as good as her. She was one of the most capable people I've ever met.' He paused. 'And speaking purely selfishly, the fact that she had no dependants made her the perfect loyal employee.'

'I'm sure it cut both ways, sir,' Dave said. 'Cressy Old Hall must have given her purpose and direction.'

'I hope so. I hope she never thought I took her for granted.' Cressy-Lawson looked pensive. 'I'm not the easiest man to get along with, I know.' He threw Dave a rueful smile. 'Plenty of your colleagues will testify to that.'

'I thought she always seemed rather protective of you, to be honest,' said Dave, sidestepping his mates' opinions of Cressy-Lawson. 'I got the feeling she was proud of this place and very happy working here.'

'I'm guilty of believing that everyone who works for me should have the same passion for the Hall as I do, and that's unfair. They are only employees doing a job, and they have lives away from here — unlike me.' He paused. 'With the exception of Norma. She lived and breathed the Old Hall. It bothers me now that she might have thought I exploited her enthusiasm for this old pile.'

Dave wanted to be getting on with his work, but he felt sorry for Cressy-Lawson. With his wife gone and his manager dead, Cressy-Lawson must be feeling pretty lost right now. 'I'm certain that's not the case, sir, I—'

'For heaven's sake, man, do call me Clive. Alright?'

Dave smiled, liking this man more the longer he spent with him. Sitting amidst the opulence of his beautifully furnished house, he suddenly looked lonely and vulnerable.

'Okay,' Dave said, 'Clive, it is. Now, can you give me some background on some of your tenants?'

Clive brightened, probably as relieved as Dave to have something practical to think about. 'Fire away.'

'Well, to start with, is anyone here university educated? Do any of them have an academic background, particularly in the sciences?'

'Well, several fit part of that description, but none completely matches.' Clive drew his brows together. 'Two men immediately come to mind, and maybe three or four, although . . .'

Dave looked from him to the files. 'And they are?'

'Rufus Taylor, who rents part of the converted stable block. He doesn't work here and I've not had much to do with him, but he's certainly educated. He was a teacher, I understand.'

'But he's not staff?'

'No, he rents from us. To get some more income, we renovated a big stable block and turned it and the attached barn into flats. We have five tenants now, and their rent has made an appreciable difference.'

Dave found the name. 'You said he was a teacher. Does he work now?'

Clive shook his head. 'Oh dear. Norma would have known. I'm afraid I left all that sort of thing to her.' He stood up and went over to the old wooden filing cabinet, muttering, 'knowing Norma . . .' He rummaged around for a moment then uttered a satisfied grunt. He passed Dave a second folder, labelled "Stable Accommodation, CVs."

Norma had gone to the trouble of printing out a short resumé, with two typed character references attached. God, what a woman! '"Rufus Taylor,"' he read out, '"previously of London Road, Greenborough. Reason for moving, family home sold under compulsory purchase order to accommodate proposed estate of new-builds."' He looked across to Clive. 'I know those houses that were pulled down, and a lot of money would have changed hands for a compulsory purchase. That would explain why the next bit says, "Took early retirement from tutoring."' Tutoring what? Dave wondered.

'He looks the academic type,' Clive said. 'You know, constantly preoccupied, as if he's considering the answers to the world's greatest problems. A bit scruffy too, in that academic way — not dirty, just as if what he wears isn't a priority.' He glanced down at his own well-coordinated attire and pulled a face.

'Age forty-nine, unmarried, not much more.' Dave frowned. 'Still, well worth talking to. Now, who else have we got?'

'Anthony Laker. Another Stable tenant, but he has the rather larger apartment within the old barn conversion. Comes from money himself. I have spoken to him on several occasions, and even met him socially once or twice at county functions. Nice man, very self-assured but quietly spoken, and clearly public school. Heard he went to Harrow.'

'Age forty-five. Reason for moving, wanted more space, and peace and quiet to be able to write.'

'He's an author?'

'Most probably academic stuff — papers and articles, or some kind of reference volume. Can't see him penning a sci-fi novel or a whodunit.'

'What's his field, do you know?'

Clive shrugged. 'You'd need to ask him that, but I seem to recall someone mentioning history.'

Dave had hoped for something scientific. 'Again, I'll talk to him. And who are the others, the maybes?'

It turned out Clive was on firmer ground here. 'Our Arthur. He hasn't always been a gamekeeper, you know, although his father and his grandfather were. It took him some time to revert back to his family's old trade.' He laughed. 'But if you are looking for people that might have hurt Norma, it certainly wouldn't be him. Nothing was said, but I'm pretty sure he carried a torch for Norma.' His smile faded. 'I think he will take what happened to her rather badly. He's a deep one, Arthur. Loyal, and a solid worker, but he gives very little away.'

Cogs started to turn in Dave's mind. He liked Arthur Keats, but over the years he'd learned not to take anyone at face value. 'So, what did he do before coming here?'

'He's ex-Navy. Then he worked in research of some kind. In a laboratory, I think.'

Now that was interesting.

'And Den Elliott I suppose. He's worked here for several years now. He has a very good knowledge of woodland management and plants.' Clive spread his hands. 'That's it. As I said, no one fits your criteria exactly, but those four have some of the things you are looking for.' Clive stared at Dave for a moment. 'It can't have been anyone from Cressy Hall, Dave. Norma was a bit curt and very efficient, but she didn't make any enemies here, I swear. Everyone admired her.'

'I'm sure you're right, but we have to talk to everyone, Clive. You do understand that, don't you?'

'Absolutely. It's a police investigation. No stone unturned and all that.' Clive glanced at his watch. 'Look, I'll leave you to get on and go and do some work myself. I have to decide how on earth I'm going to find someone to take over from Norma. She'll be a hard act to follow.' He stopped in the doorway, 'You have my blessing to talk to anyone you need to. Just find who hurt that poor soul so badly.'

Dave nodded. 'Oh, we'll find him, Clive. That's a promise.'

CHAPTER FIFTEEN

Eve stared at the painting, mesmerised. It took the form of a botanical study featuring some exotic scarlet flowers against a background of vivid emerald green foliage. The juxtaposition of red and green made the flowers stand out as if rendered in 3D and the leaves looked so lush that she could almost feel the moisture coursing through the veins.

She had seen brilliant flower studies before, but Robert Matthew Richmond's work had a quality that set them apart.

'These pictures are extraordinary,' she breathed to Wendy. 'They are so vital, and considering their age, that's really surprising.'

'Shame the rest of the house isn't the same,' muttered Wendy. 'This place is so dreary it's almost creepy. The pictures are the only things that aren't drab and tired.'

To Eve, it felt almost as if the paintings had leached all the life from their surroundings, just so that they could live and flourish. She said as much to Wendy, who chuckled. 'Sounds like *The Picture of Dorian Gray*, only in reverse. Very Gothic!'

The house itself had been a big disappointment, but the pictures made up for it, and they still had the artist's studio to see. Eve had high hopes for that. 'Where are Lou and

Rene?' she asked, reluctantly dragging her eyes from another botanical masterpiece.

'In the old music room. They've set up an exhibition of stuff relating to old Richmond's mysterious disappearance in there. Lou's in her element, hunting for clues.'

Eve smiled. A mystery was much more Lou's thing than flowers. 'Ready for the trip up to the attic studio?'

Wendy grunted. 'Let's hope it's a bit more exciting than the rest of this mausoleum.'

Together they climbed the several flights of dingy stairs to Richmond's studio, which occupied the whole of the top floor of the old three-storey house. It would have been as dark and miserable as the rest of the building if it hadn't been for the three big skylights.

They stepped inside, and what they saw took Eve's breath away. It was like emerging from a time machine and landing in the 1800s.

Thick ropes of silky gold cordoned the visitors off from most of the room, but an area of about six metres had been cleared just inside the door to allow a good view of the vast studio.

'This place hasn't been touched since the artist walked out,' she whispered. 'It's bizarre!'

'Creepy,' murmured Wendy.

Eve stared at the desks, tables, easels, chairs, and all around, the canvases leaning against the walls or in stacks and untidy heaps. Some appeared to be completed works, some were partially finished, others merely preparatory sketches. The artist's materials lay scattered everywhere.

Eve saw tubes of paint, some squeezed and rolled to extract the last drop, others seemingly freshly opened, and not only tubes, but pots and pencils and pastel sticks in every colour imaginable. The paint had long since hardened, and dust clung to everything. Palettes and knives and dirty cloths covered the tables and a paint-splattered artist's apron hung stiffly over a hard-backed chair.

The place smelt musty, decay with a hint of paint and spirit. It caught in her throat and almost made her step back.

'Oh my!' she said, shaking her head in disbelief.

It seemed so wrong. She could understand the family wanting the artist's precious studio left as it had been. But in that case, surely they would have cared for it — keeping it clean and dusted, not left to fester and rot.

'Doesn't make sense,' said Wendy, clearly on the same wavelength.

Eve tore her eyes from the jumble in front of her and turned to Wendy. 'I'm going to be very interested to talk to the family, aren't you? What do we know about them?'

Wendy recited: '"After the deaths of some of the older members of the family, and having struggled with the upkeep of the old house, the younger descendants of Robert Matthew Richmond have decided to go against long tradition and allow the public to see his works." As far as I know, the present owners of Oleander House are Ralph Richmond and his wife Verna. They have two teenage children living here, and also Ralph's uncle, his father's brother. I don't recall hearing his name mentioned.'

'It's Robert, ladies. Named after the venerable artist himself.'

They had been joined by a tall, grey-haired man, standing somewhat stiffly in a check shirt and a green tweed waistcoat.

He looked down at Wendy. 'Don't fancy a job as a guide, do you? That sounded rather good. Certainly better than the one I'd prepared.' He smiled at them. 'Robert Richmond.'

'I'm Wendy Avery,' she shook the proffered hand, 'and this is Eve Anderson.'

Before she could stop herself, Eve blurted out, 'This room, Robert. It looks as though it's never been touched. Why is that?'

'Well, Eve Anderson, if you would care to follow me down to the dining room, where my nephew's wife Verna is serving tea and homemade cake, I'll tell you.'

With a final glance at the dead artist's studio, Eve and Wendy followed Robert down the stairs.

The cake wasn't exactly homemade — M&S stocked the same one, but Eve refrained from commenting. She and Wendy took their tea and a slice of cake, and joined Robert at the end of a long dining table.

'You would need to know a little about the history of the Richmond family to understand,' said Robert. He had a deep, sonorous voice, and Eve thought he would have made an excellent narrator for audio books. The tea was surprisingly good. 'Our artist ancestor's contemporaries were an odd bunch, very careful with their money. Three siblings jointly inherited this house, and each had a respectable annual allowance handed down from their father. Initially the other two brothers resented Robert spending his money on artists' materials and travel when they were forced to use theirs towards the upkeep of the home. However, when Robert started selling his paintings and receiving commissions for what they saw as big money, their attitude changed.'

'Don't tell me,' said Wendy. 'They wanted their share.'

'And more. They recognised a golden goose when they saw one, and actively encouraged him to take on more and more work, especially the lucrative commissions. Robert Matthew Richmond became the toast of the town, but being pushed to paint for financial gain ruined his work.'

'I can understand that,' said Eve. 'The pressure must have been stultifying.'

'Exactly. He didn't want to let the family down so he started accepting offers to paint in faraway places, and discovered another natural talent — he became a botanist-explorer. He would trek through unmapped jungles to find a rare species of plant that only the natives knew of.' Robert's eyes flashed. 'And his artistic fire was rekindled.'

Those vibrant paintings in the upstairs gallery came to Eve's mind, and she knew they had been painted at that point in his life. She mentioned it to Robert, who nodded vigorously. 'Astute of you, Eve Anderson. But when he brought these glorious paintings home, to his brothers' horror, he refused to sell them.'

'Bet that went down well!' said Wendy.

'They were furious. Especially as they had spent a fortune on having his dingy studio extended and improved by adding those massive skylights.'

'A sprat to catch a mackerel?' asked Wendy.

Robert beamed. 'Exactly, dear Wendy. They hoped that by providing such a wonderful working space, they would entice him to spend his time at home, beavering away, making money rather than traipsing around the world.'

'And it didn't work?' Eve asked, staring at her empty plate and wondering where the cake had gone.

'Initially, he loved his studio, and embarked on a whole series of new paintings, but as you rightly said, the urge to explore was too strong.' Robert took a drink of tea. 'Then, quite suddenly, he stopped travelling, and to his brothers' delight, began to spend long periods shut in the studio. After a while he declared that he had plans for a very special piece of work, a study of rare British wild flowers and herbs. He prepared a massive canvas and took to dashing off for days at a time, tramping moorland and meadows, searching for his tiny botanical studies. And then . . .'

Eve and Wendy looked at each other.

'On a trip to the Lake District . . .' Wendy said.

'. . . he disappeared,' concluded Eve.

'Bravo!' Robert applauded them. 'Then the troubles began. It took many years before he could finally be declared dead "in absentia" and, surprisingly, it was discovered that the normally scatter-brained artist had left a complex will. In it, his brothers could only inherit his share of Oleander House and any residual monies if they agreed to keep and not sell or give away any of his paintings or sketches, and that they shut up his studio and left it untouched. He had also added a caveat that this proviso should extend to all future generations and beneficiaries thereafter.'

Eve became so absorbed in this story that she forgot to keep a watchful eye open for suspicious goings on. She waited eagerly for the end of the tale.

'The family grew in size, and over the years they split into two warring parties, one that thought they should respect Robert Matthew's wishes, and another determined to oppose them.'

'Happy families,' murmured Wendy. 'So that explains the studio.'

'Sadly, the Richmond civil war goes on,' concluded Robert. 'Although there is only one dissenter left now — my brother, Edward.' He grunted. 'The dinosaur! He fights on, from a small basement flat in Greenborough town. It's his only aim in life — to keep this place as it was, with those wonderful pictures trapped inside, along with Robert Matthew's ghost.'

'But he doesn't live here?' asked Wendy.

'He would. It's not the house he hates, it's us, the family.'

'You would sell the paintings?' asked Eve.

'Like a shot! Sell them, donate them, give them away! They belong in galleries and collections, in halls and over fireplaces where people can see and admire them. I want people to stand and stare, with expressions like the one I saw on Eve Anderson's face earlier. They shouldn't be kept like stuffed birds, trapped under glass domes until they finally turn to dust.' He grinned at them apologetically. 'Rant over. Sorry.'

Just then, Lou and Rene arrived, and their excited chatter broke the spell.

'There you are! Well, I've solved the mystery,' Lou began. 'Robert M. Richmond met the love of his life. He feigned his death, walked away from his home and family, and lived a long and happy life with her, whoever she was, and probably lived in a tiny crofter's cottage painting away happily until he died of old age!'

Robert laughed. 'My thoughts precisely! Though since no more of his work ever turned up after that, maybe he never painted again.'

They tossed a few more hypotheses around until Eve thanked Robert for his time and reminded the others that they were due to meet Vinnie.

After they left, Eve's mind remained filled with visions of the magnificent paintings and their contrast with the desiccated husk of that attic studio. They gave her a strange sense of foreboding.

* * *

Nikki stared at the sheet of paper in front of her, and the single word she had scribbled across it: *Motive*.

Joseph had recounted what Vinnie had said. He was right. There had to be a motive.

'Have you got a moment or two, Nikki?'

She looked up to see the formidable figure of Morgan Flint standing in the doorway.

'Sure, come on in.'

Morgan sat down and looked at Nikki thoughtfully. 'We have churned out reams of facts, figures and stats that uniform and the pool detectives are chasing up, but neither Connor nor I can work out the driving force behind this unknown killer. Have you got any idea what is motivating him?'

Nikki smiled grimly and held up the sheet of paper with the single word on it. 'I hate to admit it, but not a clue. It's eating away at us too. There is no indication in his initial message to the ACC, and as we have heard nothing since, we have no idea why he wishes to make this place so dangerous.'

'I think maybe we should concentrate on that, don't you?' Morgan said. Her pale blue eyes bored into Nikki's.

'That information could lead to discovering his identity, so I'd say it's our top priority,' Nikki said.

'Excellent. We'll proceed with that avenue of enquiry. Oh, and by the way, Connor and Yvonne have gone to speak to a man who might be able to help us with that little fellow there.' She pointed to a coloured printout of a snake that lay on top of a pile of papers. 'Our cottonmouth viper. The guy's a licensed collector of reptiles, an expert of some repute, and a passionate opponent of the illegal trade in exotic pets.'

'Sounds helpful. You'll keep me up to date on that, won't you?'

Morgan stood up. 'Of course. And we'll liaise over the motive angle. By the way, thanks for lending us your Yvonne Collins. She's a real treasure, isn't she?'

Nikki smiled. 'Talking of lending, sadly she's with us on borrowed time. She was due for retirement but managed to get a stay of execution. She's one officer who will be sorely missed.'

'And part of a dying breed. The force will never see their like again,' added Morgan Flint rather bitterly. 'People who gained all their knowledge and expertise on the ground.'

After she had gone, Nikki sat trying to decide if she liked this woman or found her too hard-edged. She guessed it really didn't matter, as long as they got hold of this killer. She was sure that with every moment that passed, the next horrific death drew nearer. She had to do everything she could to prevent it.

CHAPTER SIXTEEN

As usual, the evening in the Hanged Man was going smoothly, and the punters were generally enjoying themselves. The only person who wasn't having a good time was Sheila Pearson.

Jim Fortune's death had hit her hard. She felt a lingering responsibility for it that she couldn't rationalise away. It was her pub, and so somehow she should have spotted the danger lurking on that terrible evening. She had let Jim down, the other lad too, all because of her negligence.

Now she was in danger of erring in the other direction. She had become suspicious of every stranger, and even some of her locals. She suspected everyone she served of having an ulterior motive for being there. She checked every incoming delivery twice over, making sure that everything was exactly as ordered and nothing had been tampered with or substituted. She constantly scanned the CCTV for the slightest hint of suspicious activity and never left the bar during opening hours, not even to eat or take a break.

* * *

The new assistant chief constable walked in through Cam's door, taking him by surprise. He jumped to his feet. 'Sir!'

'Relax, Superintendent Walker, this is just an informal visit.'

ACC Paul Brakespeare pulled a chair closer to Cam's desk and sat down. Cam noted the dark shadows under his eyes, and the worry lines etching his otherwise youthful face. One of the youngest ACCs ever, he had inherited a monster and Cam felt sorry for him.

'There's nothing major to report yet, sir,' Cam said. 'Everyone is working flat out.'

Paul Brakespeare shook his head. 'I'm not looking for a progress report, Superintendent Walker.' He paused 'Er, it's Cameron, isn't it?'

'Cam's fine, sir.'

'Well, Cam, I was in the vicinity so I took the opportunity to call in and have a private word with you.' He ran long, thin fingers through his neatly cut hair. 'I wanted you to be aware of something.'

Something else? thought Cam anxiously. 'You haven't had another message from the killer, have you, sir?'

'No, no, nothing like that. It's a different kind of warning.' He leaned closer. 'As you can imagine, high level meetings have been taking place ever since this case broke. We are under immense pressure. The thing is, it looks as though we, as in the police force, are going to come under heavy artillery fire from all directions over this. Every move of ours is being scrutinised and it's becoming apparent to me that we are going to be damned whatever route we take.'

This wasn't news to Cam. It was simply the way it was these days.

Brakespeare went on. 'As you know, our dilemma is whether to be transparent and make public the truth of what we suspect is going on here in Greenborough, or play up the bootleg liquor and hopefully prevent widespread panic.'

'I'm still very much in favour of keeping what we have under wraps,' said Cam. 'It's just too risky to mention the words "serial killer" or "mass poisoner."'

'I agree, and so do people like the Chamber of Commerce, who are desperately trying to protect their businesses and the prosperity of the community. But there are other factions that have a different opinion. There have been some pretty massive screw-ups in the past, so there will always be those who watch us with a critical eye, ready to pounce if we make the slightest slip.'

'So, we are damned if we do, and damned if we don't?'

'That's the bottom line. I just wanted you to know that I'm going to make sure that no one here is made the fall guy, especially you. I watched how you dealt with the media, and I was impressed.' He sat back. 'And that's why I'm here. You suspect there's going to be another death, or deaths, don't you?'

'It is very likely, sir.'

'If that happens, I want you to give another press release. Give it major coverage. Make an urgent public appeal for everyone to be extra vigilant and help us track down the distillers and retailers of this dangerous "counterfeit" alcohol. If nothing else, it will make the public suspicious of any goings on that are out of the ordinary, and hopefully report them.'

'Good point. People might then notice odd behaviour that has nothing to do with bootleg drink?'

'It could help you find your man, and if nothing else, it reinforces our cover story.'

'True.' Cam was already formulating his speech to the cameras. 'But we don't have very long, do we? Before the shit hits the fan?'

'I can't tell·you how imperative it is for you to get this killer behind bars.'

'You don't have to, sir. I know. We all do.'

Brakespeare stood up. 'Then I won't take up any more of your valuable time.' He held out his hand. 'Good luck, Superintendent.'

Cam watched him go. The new ACC was on their side — for once.

* * *

'We now know enough about cottonmouth snakes to write a book of our own, ma'am.' Connor Hale raised an eyebrow, and glanced across to Yvonne Collins. 'Don't we?'

'Yep. The main thing is that our expert thinks the only way you could get hold of that venom would be to smuggle it out of an authorised research lab, which is nigh on impossible, or get it on the black market.'

'And that's very likely the way he's done it,' added Connor. 'Unless he's an illegal collector of rare or endangered species himself.'

'Where do these particular snakes originate from?' asked Morgan.

'They're primarily found in the low marshlands of the south-eastern United States,' said Yvonne, quoting the expert word for word. 'He doesn't know of any licensed collectors locally who might own a venomous pit-viper like that.'

'So, trying to go in that direction is a waste of time, guys,' Morgan said. 'Let's assume the venom came into his hands down a black-market route. Yvonne? Do you know anyone in the area that deals in "extreme" or hazardous acquisitions?'

Yvonne shook her head. 'No, ma'am. First thing I did was get hold of my most trusted snout and sound him out. The only person who might have been prepared to handle something like that is serving a stretch in HMP Lincoln, so no luck there, I'm afraid.' She opened her mouth to continue but was interrupted by the wail of sirens.

Yvonne stiffened. She glanced at her two new colleagues and saw from their expressions that the same thing had sprung into their minds — another death. Then she exhaled. 'Not ours. That's Trumpton's sirens.'

They let out a collective sigh of relief. Not police blues and twos, but the fire service. 'Never thought I'd be happy to know there's either a fire or a serious RTC somewhere,' whispered Yvonne.

'Under the circumstances, you are forgiven,' said Morgan Flint. 'We feel exactly the same.'

A second, then a third klaxon joined the first. They stared at each other.

'Whatever's happened, it's serious,' said Connor anxiously.

'Shall I go and find out, ma'am?' Yvonne said.

'Yes, do.'

Yvonne hurried from the room and ran down the stairs to the main office. 'What's up?' she called out to the first uniform she saw.

'Fire at the sixth form college,' called back the retreating figure. 'It's all hands on deck!'

Greenborough College of Further Education was scattered across the town, split into three campus sites. From the position of the sirens she guessed the fire was in the Art and Music campus, the oldest of the buildings and set close to the river.

She strode into the office to find Niall listening to the reports coming in from the ground, and barking out orders. 'It's the college, Vonnie,' he said, 'but I think the alarm was raised in time to prevent a disaster.'

'The Art and Music Centre?'

'Yeah, in their recording studio. Not a lot of info yet, but the fire service think they have it under control.'

Thankful that it was a Saturday and most of the students would be at the festival, Yvonne asked, 'Casualties?'

'No numbers yet, but a few, mainly smoke inhalation by the sound of it.' He turned back to the radio.

'I'll let you get on.' Yvonne made her way back upstairs to Morgan Flint's temporary office, where she passed on the information.

'Let's hope they got those kids out quick. Smoke inhalation can be devastating,' said Morgan. 'And although it sounds awful to say it, at least it's not connected to the investigation.'

'I wonder . . .' murmured Yvonne. 'I just hope it's not a literal smoke-screen to distract us from some other evil deed our killer has perpetrated.'

'That's a nasty thought, PC Collins,' said Connor grimly. 'I sincerely hope you're wrong.'

Morgan and Connor weren't locals, so they hadn't heard of Yvonne's legendary "insights." But for once, she too hoped that she was wrong.

* * *

'The fire started in one of the music college buildings, apparently,' said Joseph.

'I thought for one moment . . .'

'I think the whole station felt the same.' Joseph grimaced. 'I know I did. But it's bad enough. Several students have been taken to hospital after inhaling smoke.'

Nikki hated cases that involved fire. They'd had a terrible time with one not so long ago, and she didn't want to have to face any more burnt bodies. 'That place is very old, and with all the new equipment they use these days, it's probably an electrical fault.'

'One thing worries me,' said Joseph. 'Will our killer take advantage of the mayhem caused by the fire to murder again?'

'It'd be a perfect opportunity, wouldn't it?' She exhaled loudly.

'If so, we won't have long to wait, will we?'

The awful inevitability of it.

'Motive,' Joseph said. 'Let's get back to that, shall we?'

'Start with the four "Ls:" Lust, Love, Loathing and Loot,' Nikki said.

'Okay, well, what about lust? A sexual motive? I doubt it in this case. Love doesn't come into it. Loathing? Hate, maybe. Revenge, very possibly. And loot, or financial gain? No, I don't think that applies either.' Joseph thought hard. 'That narrows it down to revenge and hate, doesn't it?'

'We forgot another "L,"' added Nikki. 'Lunacy. He could be a psycho.'

Joseph opened his mouth to speak, but Nikki's phone rang.

'DI Nikki Galena,' she said.

Joseph watched her face tighten.

'Oh hell! Right. Okay, we'll be there.' Nikki almost threw the phone down. 'The other CID team are out, damn it, and the fire chief wants someone down at the college. It looks like it was started deliberately. But considering that the killer may well take advantage of the situation, we need to be here too.'

'You stay. I'll go to the college,' Joseph offered. 'It's only five minutes away. I just saw Ben and Cat come in, so I'll take Cat with me, and you keep Ben, just in case.'

Nikki nodded. 'Deal.'

When Joseph and Cat arrived at the scene, the stench of burning immediately brought back the horrors of that last case, and particularly of a man who'd died in the final blaze. In saving Joseph's life he had lost his own. He shivered.

'You okay, Sarge?' asked Cat.

'I'm fine,' he replied. 'Just remembering our last encounter with an arsonist.'

'Don't go there, Sarge. This is probably just some of the students playing silly buggers, lighting farts or something stupid like that.'

Joseph looked at the smouldering block that had once been a recording studio. 'Some fart!'

Cat nudged him. 'You know what I mean. Look, there's the fire investigator.'

They ducked under some cordoning and walked towards the wrecked building, careful not to slip in the puddles of dark greasy water that had pooled everywhere.

'DS Joseph Easter, isn't it? I'm Rebecca Lamont, fire and rescue investigator.' She held out her hand. 'We met briefly during the arson case six months ago.'

Joseph shook the hand and introduced Cat.

Rebecca Lamont was a heavily-built woman in her forties with short, dark brown, wavy hair and horn-rimmed glasses. She was one of the only female fire investigation officers in the country, and was highly respected.

'I'm here by chance today, Detectives. I came into town with my family for the festival, and found my colleagues hard at work here.'

'Lucky for us,' said Joseph. 'It wasn't an accident?'

'It would seem not. I didn't like the colour of the smoke right from when I first saw it. It indicated some highly inflammable materials and accelerants, and although I've only had a cursory look, I immediately noticed a very unusual fire spread pattern. The whole thing reeks of arson. As soon as it's safe, I'll get kitted up and give you a full report. And you'll need forensics down here.'

'What about the students involved?' asked Cat. 'Were they badly hurt?'

'That I can't tell you. Smoke affects people in different ways. If someone had asthma for instance, the effects could be very serious indeed. They've all been given oxygen and are being taken to Greenborough A&E for assessment.' She stared at the burnt building. 'There were six of them in the studio at the time, or so I'm told. None sustained burns, as it started in a storeroom attached to the main recording studio and they managed to get out before the fire really took hold, thank heavens.'

'Any idea of what we are looking at, Rebecca?' asked Joseph.

'I'm not even going to guess just yet. I need to know what was in that stockroom to cause such acrid smoke, and whether whatever it was actually belonged there, or was planted by someone.' She paused. 'And anyone who goes inside needs breathing equipment until I've ascertained whether we're looking at a hazardous material that could give off dangerous fumes even after the fire has died down. So have forensics ready, but no one enters until I say so.'

Joseph nodded.

'We need to get to the hospital, Sarge,' Cat said. 'We're useless here until we know more.'

She was right. Uniform had cordoned off a large area around the places where the firefighters were continuing to damp down and check for hotspots that could flare up again. Joseph thanked Rebecca and they hurried back towards their car.

Before they reached it, Cat stopped and pointed towards an ambulance. 'Hold up, Sarge! Something's wrong over there.'

Through the open doors they could see that the two paramedics were fighting to keep someone alive — or maybe bring them back from the dead, Joseph wasn't sure. Another first responder in motorcycle boots was standing by the steps of the vehicle, talking heatedly into his phone.

Joseph waited for the man to end the call and showed his warrant card.

'The last kid out took a turn for the worse,' the man said. 'She seemed fine, very few symptoms, just a bit of a cough, then suddenly she couldn't breathe. It looks like she has pulmonary oedema — fluid in the lungs. I've just called it in to A&E as a Code Red. She's the second one it's happened to.'

Joseph recalled Rebecca's words about hazardous materials and raced back to find her.

She glanced at her watch. 'Let me think. That girl must have been brought out maybe thirty minutes ago? And had very few symptoms?'

'That's what the technician told me. Just a bit of a cough. They gave her oxygen.'

'Now she's fighting for her life?' She began pacing up and down. 'I need to get in there, and fast. Something burnt that has given off a toxic gas. From the time delay, I'm guessing we're dealing with phosgene gas. It's an irritant and it's lethal.'

'Should we clear the area completely?' Joseph asked.

'Yes, get your guys on to it straightaway. If I'm right, that stuff can hang around for some time.' She turned away from him. 'I need to grab some safety gear and get inside that storeroom.'

Joseph handed her his card. 'Can you ring me immediately you know something concrete, so I can tell the doctors at the hospital?'

She took the card and hurried away.

Cat appeared at his side.

'Rebecca's talking about a toxic gas,' Joseph said.

'Shit! Okay, I'm on it!'

Cat ran off, and soon the onlookers were being herded back.

* * *

Nikki stared at Ben. 'Phosgene gas? I've never heard of it.'

'I have,' said Ben. 'There was a programme on the "Yesterday" channel a few weeks ago about the First World War. It was deployed in artillery shells and was responsible for a huge percentage of all the deaths caused by chemical weapons.'

'Chemical weapons? In the college of music?'

'What's happened here, ma'am, is an accident. Something has been burned and caused a gas to form, that's all. It's not weapons of mass destruction.'

Nikki wasn't convinced.

Greenborough will be a dangerous place . . . Could this possibly have a connection to the poisoner? Had their killer struck again, or was it just a terrible freak accident?

Ben had stood up and was pacing the room. 'I hate not being able to *do* something.'

'Look, as soon as we get the all-clear, get yourself down to the college and grab every bit of CCTV you can get your hands on for the hours leading up to the fire, and the night before too, just in case we get an image of the person who caused it.'

He flopped down into a chair. 'Half of me is still waiting for an emergency call telling us our killer has struck again, and the other half is wondering what on earth got burnt to cause such a lethal gas to escape? And was it deliberate?'

'I'm also wondering if it was the killer that started the fire,' Nikki added.

Ben stared at her. 'Really? That would be a major change of modus operandi, wouldn't it?'

'Not really,' Nikki said. 'We know he's some kind of science boffin, and it would take someone like that to know what to burn in order to produce this phosgene gas, wouldn't it?'

'It means he will have deviated from killing loners, but otherwise it's certainly insidious enough.'

Nikki nodded. 'That's what I thought.'

So now it was just a waiting game. After a lengthy silence, Ben said, 'Ma'am? This might be the worst time in the world to throw this at you, but could I ask you a personal question?'

Nikki knew that Ben had also lost a daughter many years ago, albeit to illness, and that this case would be extra tough on him too. Was this what was worrying him? She liked Ben Radley, had liked him from the moment they first met. 'Fire away. I won't promise to give you an answer, but you can ask.'

'It's about Cat. Well, Cat and me.'

'Ah.' Her two detectives had been living together for quite a while now. They were different in every way, but they complemented each other.

He sighed. 'We feel a bit trapped. Not by each other, you understand, but by the force.' He drew in a breath. 'The fact is, I want to marry her.'

'Ben, as you know, it's not advisable to work closely with your spouse, but officially they can't stop you. And if anyone could make it work, it's you two. If you were at a higher rank, then it couldn't happen.' Like her and Joseph. Get married, and the team would disintegrate. One or the other of them would be forced to move on.

Ben must have read her thoughts. 'Would you marry Joseph, if things were different?'

'Yes, I would, Ben. But things aren't different, so let's leave us out of it, shall we?'

'Do you think Cat would say yes if I asked?'

Nikki smiled. 'Since you came along, Cat has looked happier than I've ever seen her. She loves you. You know that, so why even ask me?'

'Scared, I guess.' For a moment Ben looked like a schoolboy, terrified of asking a pretty girl for a date.

'Why the feeling of being trapped?' asked Nikki.

'Because if we marry, it means that neither of us can be promoted, or else we'll have to move away from the station and the team. And that means we won't ever get a raise, and although we aren't struggling, we'd like a bit more.'

They were damned good detectives, and both were sergeant material. They loved their jobs, and were absolutely loyal. Nikki thought for a while. 'If I were in your shoes, I'd get married, stay as you are for maybe a year, then re-evaluate where you want to go. You might find that moving up the ladder and having different things to talk about when you get home is a good thing. Who knows?' Her smile widened. 'Although, of course, I'd never forgive either of you if you left my team.'

Ben smiled at this. 'Thank you for that, ma'am. I feel a whole lot better now.'

'Then get your clever brain refocused onto our killer. I'm not operating a lonely-hearts bureau here.'

CHAPTER SEVENTEEN

Joseph and Cat stood by the vending machine in the hospital waiting area and stared at the brown liquid pouring into the beaker. It was their second round of dreadful coffees, but they needed something to do other than just pace up and down. Three of the six students were now critical.

Just as Joseph was removing his drink from the machine, his phone rang. 'Rebecca. What have you got for us?'

'Confirmed. It is phosgene gas. Tell the doctors immediately. There's a good chance they haven't come across this before, so tell them that depending on the length of time a person's exposed to the gas, symptoms of even a fatal dose can take up to several hours or even days to show. Also tell them that once it's in the system, the gas reacts with the body's internal moisture and turns to hydrochloric acid, which damages the trachea and causes necrosis of the lungs. Got that?'

Joseph said that he had.

'I'll phone you again in ten minutes to tell you what I found in the storeroom. Speak then.'

Luckily one of the consultants on duty had recently attended a training course on dealing with emergency biohazard situations and immediately grasped what Joseph was saying.

'I never thought we'd see a poisonous gas like this in Greenborough. Even if we do manage to pull these poor kids through, they'll be damaged for life.'

Joseph's rage began to mount. His own girl, Tamsin, had been a student, and he knew what the parents would be going through. This had to be the work of the poisoner. His anger built and built.

The tipping point for him was the senselessness of these cruel acts.

He had thought his years as a special services soldier were over, but all at once he was back there again. Hard. That coldness. The willingness to kill if necessary.

He went back to where Cat was waiting by the vending machine.

'Sarge? What's the prognosis on those kids?' she asked, scrunching up her beaker and throwing it into a bin.

'Not good at all,' he said. 'And it's looking increasingly likely that this is the work of our killer. It's time we stopped him, Cat.'

Cat gave him a long look. She nodded slowly. 'You're right.'

The call from Rebecca came through. 'It's undoubtedly foul play, involving deliberate use of phosgene gas. I found some containers of dry cleaning fluids and solvents, items that had no place in a college stockroom. Plus, a very unusual and old-fashioned incendiary device. Would you believe a candle, a matchbook and a fuse made of highly inflammable wadding, leading to a plastic container of paraffin?'

'How much time would that have given him to get away after he set this device?' asked Joseph, thinking immediately of the CCTV.

'It would depend on how long the candle took to burn. Forensics will be able to work that out for you. At a guess, I'd say maybe around an hour?'

Joseph's brain went into overdrive. So, the killer could be placed in the vicinity of the College of Arts and Music at a pretty specific time. And if Rory could narrow it down even further, with the CCTV footage and thorough questioning of everyone who was in the area, they should be able to get a lead.

Call ended, he asked Cat if she would stay on at the hospital. 'I'll get someone down to free you up as soon as I get back to the nick. Right now, I have to go and inform Nikki about what we know.'

'Sure, Sarge. I'll ring you immediately there's any news. She looked at him ruefully. 'I was very wrong about lighting farts, wasn't I?'

'Rather.' He turned to go then stopped. 'Do kids still do that?'

'While there are boys on this earth, it will happen. Check out YouTube sometime, especially something called the Blue Angel.'

He hurried off, shaking his head.

* * *

'Interesting visit, wasn't it?' Eve and the others had gone back to Beech Lacey to have lunch. 'I can't begin to imagine the undercurrents between those two brothers over Oleander House and those paintings.'

'Long-term family feuds can be vicious,' said Wendy, pulling salads and cold meats from the fridge. 'Sometimes the original problem gets lost as the years go by, and it turns into a pointless vendetta. No one will give in, even though they can't remember what started it.'

'I'd love to meet Edward Richmond. I wonder if he's as charismatic as his brother Robert.' Eve arranged the salad. She admitted to herself that she had all but forgotten their mission of looking for suspicious people at the festival. Instead, her thoughts remained stuck in the dingy and mysterious Oleander House.

She opened the wine.

'I just heard on the radio that there was a fire in Greenborough,' announced Wendy. 'Must have happened just after we left. Part of the College Campus, apparently.'

'Good Lord! This town is really going through it this weekend,' exclaimed Rene. 'Was anyone hurt?'

'It was only a newsflash. It said reports were still coming in.'

Vinnie pulled out his phone. 'Yup, the music college. It says it's fully under control now and was contained to one studio area. Doesn't mention any casualties. Let's hope the kids were all at the festival.'

Eve set down her knife and fork. It would have caused chaos, which would be the perfect cover for the killer, wouldn't it? With the police deployed elsewhere, he could play havoc to his heart's content. She picked up her phone and texted Nikki. *Was the fire connected to the killer?*

She didn't have to wait long for an answer. *Unconfirmed, but I suspect it was. What do you know?*

Eve replied. *It was just a hunch, we know nothing . . . yet.*

For God's sake, be careful!

Always.

If Eve had needed something to bring her thoughts back to the search, she'd got it. 'Sorry to say this, gang, but we need to focus. I think it's time to ditch the attractions and do some serious work — the kind we're good at.'

She looked up to see all eyes on her.

'That fire — it could be connected to the killer. My daughter needs our help.'

At once, the atmosphere changed, almost as if a switch had been thrown. They were all immediately alert, and Eve welcomed it.

* * *

Dave made his way back to the police station. Before he left, he'd had an informal chat with Den Elliott but no warning bells had sounded. Den was intelligent and well-spoken, good at what he did, loved nature, but was certainly no academic. He also seemed to be totally stunned by what had happened to Norma. He admitted to never having been particularly keen on her, because, he said, he found her a bit intimidating.

To Dave's disappointment, all the people he really wanted to talk to — the residents of Cressy Old Hall's converted stable block — were out. It was one of the things that happened all the time in police work, but it still rankled. He'd left a message with the officers still on duty there to let him know if anyone returned, especially the two men that Clive Cressy-Lawson had told him about, Rufus Taylor and Anthony Laker.

As he drove away, he suddenly thought of someone else that he should possibly talk to, the leader of the History Society, Murray Kennington. He recalled the tall, imposing figure in that sweeping, cape-like coat. What was his background? Where had he worked prior to retiring?

Dave cursed himself. He'd missed another man off his list, the gamekeeper, Arthur Keats, though he considered him an unlikely suspect. He'd seen the shock on Keats's face when he saw what had happened to Norma. Even so, there was the fact that he'd worked in a research lab.

Dave hurried into the station. His list was growing by the minute, and their killer could be on it. He scribbled all the names on a blank sheet of paper: Murray Kennington. Arthur Keats. Den Elliott. Rufus Taylor. Anthony Laker.

He opened his computer and signed in. 'Now, who's first?'

* * *

'Okay, so why use such an antiquated technique to light a fire? A simple timer would have been easier and more accurate.' Connor tried to think. 'A candle and a matchbook? I didn't know you could still get matchbooks in this non-smoking era.'

'People collect them, or they did. There must be thousands still around,' answered Morgan Flint.

'Even so, it was such a hit and miss arrangement. Candles go out. Or it could have taken far too long to burn down and been discovered.'

'It was Saturday, and the festival was in full swing. Very few people were booked in to use the studio, so no one would have needed the storeroom until the following week. He would have done his homework first. It was a gamble, and it worked.'

'But why?' Connor was really bugged by the oddness of it. 'I'm sure it's significant.'

'Now you're talking sense,' Morgan said. 'I'm sure it is too. Until this happened I thought, as did DI Nikki Galena, that we had to find the motive first . . . but now I'm not so sure.'

'About what?'

'If he's insane, his reasoning could be too convoluted for us to understand. He is obviously a dangerous psychopath, so his motive could be so far detached from reality that we wouldn't understand it even if he told us.'

Connor let out a sigh. 'Back to the drawing board?'

'Kind of.' Morgan's smile was enigmatic. 'More a change of tack. Let's suppose that your candle and matchbook are of significance, shall we?'

Connor flopped into a chair. 'Okay, boss. Carry on.'

'Well, as I see it . . .'

* * *

From his voice down the line, Rory was a long way from being his usual self. 'I can't begin to tell you the extent of the horrible injuries that poor woman, Norma Warden, suffered. He had forced the acid down her throat — can you believe it? And he actually broke her jaw in doing so! I don't think I've ever come across such a monster in all my time in forensics.'

'Now he's gassed six innocent students,' Nikki added sombrely.

'I know. I've got my technicians standing by for the all-clear to get into that studio. Well, so much for toxicity ratings. We were way out with our guesses of plant material or strychnine.'

'I don't see how you could possibly second guess a psycho like this one,' said Nikki.

'I was wrong about something else too.' Rory sighed. 'Dear Spike was keeping an eye on the news from other departments around the country and he spotted something relevant to you and your deadly fake booze.'

Nikki sat up straighter. 'Oh?'

'There have been several other very recent cases of deaths caused by this highly sophisticated methanol-infused alcohol, all exactly the same formula. The thing is they are scattered halfway across the Midlands. Your man didn't produce this himself, he bought it in.'

'That means he's not necessarily a scientist at all?'

'Probably not. Sorry for the false leads. Out of character, I know, but I'm starting to think I should leave the detection to you guys.'

'Stuff that for a game of soldiers, Rory. You keep right on making guesses. We were thinking along exactly the same lines as you, and so was Morgan Flint, so you're in bloody good company. Detection is looking at all the information, then sorting the wheat from the chaff. We are always chasing dead ends, believe me!'

'I'm somewhat placated, dear heart. But only slightly.'

Nikki noted a little more humour in his voice. 'Perhaps I could ask one question and a favour, Rory?'

'Anything. But don't rely entirely upon the veracity of my answers until I'm a little more certain of myself again.'

'The incendiary device used in starting the fire. Morgan wants everything you can get on it as a priority, with special attention to the candle, its make, and the length of time it would take to burn. Is that possible?'

'No problem there. That's basic stuff.'

'And I'd like everything you can on the matchbook, if it's not too badly damaged.'

'Of course. Often the means of starting the fire is not totally obliterated, as the trail of accelerant takes the blaze away and in another direction. And then there's always trace evidence. Oh, and the new fire investigator is top notch, by the way. I'd go as far as to say hot stuff, only that sounds a bit dubious, doesn't it?' He laughed. 'Don't worry, we'll find out all we can for you.'

Nikki hung up and went to Morgan Flint's office to pass on the news. As she entered the room, she sensed a kind of energy, almost excitement, in the air.

Morgan looked up from her computer screen and beckoned to Nikki. 'Glad you're here, Nikki. I think we've finally got something for you. It's tenuous so far, but it is something.'

Nikki quickly told her what Rory had said. Morgan nodded. 'That fits in too.' She threw a knowing glance to Connor. 'I think we're on the right track here. Sit down, Nikki, and we'll run our thoughts past you. I'd welcome your opinion.'

Was light dawning at last? Might they be about to make some headway? Nikki had had enough of faceless monsters lurking in the shadows of the Greenborough alleyways.

'I think we can all agree that we are dealing with a psychopath. So maybe this is not some carefully planned revenge attack that is all about righting a perceived wrong. It's madness, pure and simple, a wish to destroy and cause pain and suffering. There might be a root cause somewhere in his past, and I'm sure there is, but that's not where we should be looking right now.' A spark shone in Morgan's ice-blue eyes. 'We believe that we should be looking only at his methods, analysing the ways he kills.'

'The venom, the acid and the poisonous gas?' said Nikki, not quite sure where this was going.

'Absolutely. There's a pattern here, and it's the odd choice of incendiary device he used at the college that put me onto this theory.'

Connor added, 'And I'm certain my boss is spot on! I've asked our people back at base to do some digging into whatever they can find on past murder sprees, and answers are just starting to come in.'

'What about the methanol in the bootleg alcohol? That's not particularly old-fashioned. In fact it's pretty hi-tech, if you consider the new underground labs and what they can produce.' Nikki hadn't yet grasped what was causing so much excitement.

'We think this man is very intelligent and really thought this terror attack through to the last detail,' said Morgan. 'He threw us the liquor as a cover story for the press, something to give to the public, knowing we won't want to cause a mass panic. He knew exactly how we would react, and although it was a gift to us, it was also a free ticket for him to keep killing.'

Nikki breathed out. 'Clever bastard!'

'Precisely! Very clever bastard!' Morgan Flint gave Nikki a rare smile. 'Now, don't laugh, but when I was a young rookie detective I became very interested in historical crime, and I don't mean the odd cold case, I mean Victorian stuff.'

'Jack the Ripper kind of thing?' asked Nikki.

'That era, yes. When I was a kid the story of Dr Jekyll and Mr Hyde really affected me, and I think it grew from that.' The smile vanished. 'And it would seem that nothing we read is ever truly wasted, because that candle and the matchbook stirred a memory from a Victorian crime I'd read about.'

Nikki was intrigued. 'It fits rather well with the Dark Greenborough Festival, doesn't it?' In her mind's eye, she saw the cloaked figures and the flickering torchlights down the town's cobbled alleyways.

'Doesn't it? And I think his choice of an archaic timer device is connected. In the 1900s an anonymous fire-starter set dozens of fires in the City using a similar method. Apparently a three-quarter inch thick candle would burn at one inch an hour, allowing him a couple of hours to get well away and always have a watertight alibi. He was never identified.'

'But matchbooks weren't around then, were they?' asked Nikki.

'Patented in the late 1800s, actually,' Connor read from a printout. 'An arsonist called Stackpole used them in the 1980s. He lit over two hundred fires in the States, using a lighted cigarette and a matchbook. Matchbooks are still around, but they're mainly curios now.' He grinned. 'Fictional detectives liked to use them to discover which sleazy cocktail bar the mysterious woman with the flaming red hair met her killer in!'

'Thanks for the history lesson, but where are we heading with this?' Nikki asked.

'I think he is fascinated by historical murderers,' Morgan stated flatly. 'So we've got our people scouring the archives for old material. There is something about his choice of methods that rings bells, but I can't recall where from.'

'So, if they can pinpoint some old case, or a particular historical criminal, we might have more of an idea about the man himself?' Nikki said.

'And if we find a suspect, I suggest the search history on his computer or smartphone could be very revealing indeed. It's where an awful lot of research is done these days, isn't it? Even a history buff reads papers and articles on line.'

So, more a history buff than a mad scientist.

'As I said, it's tenuous, but I swear we are heading in the right direction.'

'I agree,' said Nikki. 'I'm no history addict myself, but even I know that snake venom is one of the oldest methods of killing people, and I'm pretty sure phosphorus was used way back in time.'

'I'll let you know the minute we get anything that looks likely.'

'Thanks, Morgan. I appreciate it. Now I'd better get back on to the hospital for an update on those students. It makes me go cold to think that the heartless beast that did that to just some random kids is still out there, and planning his next atrocity.'

This needed no reply.

* * *

Cat's voice was sombre. 'The last student to be brought in died a few minutes ago.' She faltered for a moment. 'The doctor said it was respiratory and circulatory failure. She was seventeen, Sarge.'

Joseph gritted his teeth. He was certain that this would not be the last of the students to die. He'd looked up phosgene, and had been horrified to find that there might be no warning signs that dangerous levels of the gas had been breathed in until it was too late.

'Has anyone come to take over from you?' he asked.

'Yes, I've just handed over to uniform.'

'Then get yourself back here and I'll make you a strong coffee. You sound as if you've seen enough for one day.'

He heard a muffled sob. This wasn't like Cat. She was a tough woman who'd seen and suffered plenty during her time in CID. 'Come on, kid, home. Now!'

'Yes, Sarge. Sorry.' She sniffed. 'Just seems such a waste. And to see those other kids, all in terrible distress, gasping and coughing, it was horrible. The wicked son of a . . .'

'We'll get him. Even if we have to tear Greenborough apart to do it.'

'He's already doing that himself. Tearing our community apart.' She paused. 'Anyhow, I'm on my way.'

Joseph ended the call, thinking of Vinnie Silver. Despite his love and respect for his colleagues in the force, and above all Nikki, he needed something different right now. Something that only Vinnie could provide.

The old memories had begun to rise to the surface. Those violent, traumatic ones, combat situations and what they had made him do. He had spent long years shutting the lid on them and burying them somewhere deep in the recesses of his mind, so deep he thought they were forgotten. Now, like a horde of zombies, they were climbing out of the dark and re-emerging one by one. He thought about a dead seventeen-year-old, and let them come.

It was time to call Vinnie.

CHAPTER EIGHTEEN

The call ended and Vinnie stood in silence for a moment or two, frowning at his phone.

'That expression looks ominous,' Lou said.

'There were casualties from that fire. It was set deliberately. Six students inhaled toxic fumes from it, and one has since died.' Vinnie's face was taut. 'The rest aren't good, not good at all. Joseph fears for their lives.'

Rene crossed herself and Eve closed her eyes.

'But I do have something that we can work on at last. The perpetrator of these crimes appears to be a middle-aged or older man.'

'And that is something to work on?' Rene said. 'Do you know how many men in Greenborough fit that description?'

'There's more. He has an interest in history, especially old murder cases, historical ones that is. Apparently, he used a candle and a matchbook with a wick attached to give him time to disappear. They think it's significant.'

Eve stared at Vinnie. Why was Joseph divulging so much? It wasn't like him or Nikki, especially as she knew her daughter didn't want her mixed up in anything dangerous. So maybe Nikki didn't know? It would mean that Joseph was keeping things from her, and he didn't do that.

Eve glanced at Lou, and then at Vinnie. Lou read people, and she was reading something in Vinnie Silver right now. If asked to guess what it was, Eve would have said he was hiding something. What was going on?

'Right.' Rene narrowed her eyes. 'We need some kind of whiteboard, like they have in a CID room, something we can use to set down our thoughts in black and white so we can see them more clearly.'

Eve sent an enquiring look in Wendy's direction, and received a nod in return. 'As soon as this festival is over, we're going to be redecorating the study.' She went to one of the kitchen drawers and took out a couple of marker pens. 'Needs must. We'll sort out the mess after this is over.'

They followed her into the study and watched as she took down the pictures from the longest wall.

'This will serve as our operations room.'

Wendy placed a number of chairs in a semicircle, facing the blank wall. Without a word, they all sat down, leaving Eve standing.

'Okay, fire away. Who have we met or heard about recently who might fit the profile of late or middle-aged, of above-average intelligence, and with a knowledge or interest in historical matters or criminology?'

Lou was the first to make a suggestion. 'The guy who did the talk in the cemetery, Amos Fuller.'

Eve nodded, and wrote the name in large capital letters on the study wall.

'Your enigmatic owner of Oleander House, Robert Richmond,' added Wendy with a wry smile.

Eve set it down, if somewhat reluctantly, beneath that of Amos Fuller.

'And his brother, even though we haven't met him,' said Wendy. 'Edward Richmond would be the right age, and as he has a vested interest in the past as concerns his family, he could be a possibility.'

Eve nodded and added him. 'Not many names, is it? We need to get back out there.' She looked at the others. 'How should we play this?'

'I suggest two groups,' said Vinnie. 'One out there, mingling and listening to the word on the streets, and the other doing a few background checks on our three names.' He paused. 'I think Joseph would be prepared to help with that — you know, give us the thumbs-up if one of our men is known to them in some way.'

'Useful,' said Rene, 'and it will speed up the process.'

'Volunteers for spotters?' asked Vinnie. 'I'll go with that team.'

'I'll stick with background stuff, if that suits everyone?' said Eve.

'I'm happy to go mingle with the crowds,' said Rene.

'Me too, unless you want to do that, Wendy?' said Lou.

'No, I'm happy to do intel work with Eve. If we need them, I've still got some pretty influential contacts. You guys go and find us something more to work on. You're right, Eve, three suspects out of a town heaving with people isn't enough.'

Vinnie stood up. 'Our time is limited, so let's not waste a moment.'

Eve turned to the three names on the wall and looked at Wendy. 'Okay. Shall we start with Amos Fuller?'

'Do you know where he lives?'

'No, but I do know he's giving a different kind of talk today at the Wool Exchange building.' Eve looked at her watch. 'He's due to finish in thirty minutes, so if we hurry we'll just catch him.'

'Perfect. What's the talk about?' asked Wendy.

'Executioners and the history of hanging in this country.'

Wendy's expression said it all. 'Grab your coat, Eve.'

* * *

In the centre of the market square, a massive carousel had been installed and its distinctive music could be heard right across the town. This one, however, was nothing like the usual brightly painted fairground merry-go-round. There were no gilded, hand-carved horses, the lights were silver and purple and the horses were all black. The decorations depicted the Four Horsemen of the Apocalypse, and instead of the usual flowers, animals and pretty scenery, their subject matter was Conquest, War, Famine and Death. This macabre carousel was proving very popular indeed.

Vinnie looked at it with a mixture of incredulity and admiration. It was the antithesis of every childhood memory of the funfair, but it was perfect for Dark Greenborough.

'Little kiddies could suffer nightmares for years after seeing that,' Lou said.

Vinnie laughed. 'Don't you believe it. Look at that group there.' He indicated a gaggle of tiny skeletons, all jumping up and down and begging their werewolf "nanny" for a ride on the black horses. 'But to business, ladies. Where should we start?'

'Yesterday Eve mentioned someone we should go and talk to,' said Lou. 'Sheila Pearson, the landlady of the most popular pub in town. Eve knows her vaguely and reckons there's not much goes on that Sheila doesn't know about. The pub is called the Hanged Man and it's just a few minutes from here.'

'Sounds a good place to begin. Lead on.'

The Hanged Man was packed and the atmosphere cheerful, unlike Vinnie's thoughts. He knew the long, hard battle that his dear friend Joseph Easter had fought to bring himself to where he was now. He'd fought demons far more powerful than any terrorist, and he'd won. Vinnie had been shocked to hear the cold, hard edge in Joseph's voice when he'd called, and his consternation was even greater when Joseph asked if he'd be prepared to support him if he decided to take down this killer using "unconventional" means. From the way he spoke, Vinnie had taken that to mean the kind of thing Joseph had left behind in his beleaguered past. Naturally, he had said he would. He, Vinnie, had found his own ways of surviving and moving on, but he worried for Joseph — and for Nikki.

'That's her, I'm sure of it.' Lou's nudge brought him back to the present. She began to shoulder her way towards the crowded bar.

Having finally attracted the woman's attention, Lou introduced them. 'We are friends of Eve Anderson, she sometimes comes here for lunch.'

The landlady nodded, and what had been a rather suspicious expression softened into a smile. 'Ah yes, the lovely artist lady. She and her friends often call in after their class. So, what can I get you?'

'Three coffees, if it's not too much trouble?'

'Coming up.'

Fascinated, Vinnie watched her prepare the coffee. How attractive this woman was, but how sad! He had an almost overwhelming desire to get up and go to her, do what he could to dispel some of that awful gloom.

Vinnie was a womaniser. Not a predator, not at all. He just relished the company of women. He was fond of his "military ladies," for example, but he rarely felt such an intense attraction as he was feeling now.

He smiled at her almost shyly when she set down his cup in front of him. Was that the usual polite smile, or did her gaze linger just a little longer on him?

Lou leaned closer to the bar to address the landlady. 'We were wondering if you could help us. I know you are desperately busy, but would you have just a few moments? Is there somewhere private we could talk?'

Vinnie watched Sheila debate this with herself. She looked around at the crowds of people. 'Five minutes is all I can spare. Come around to the side of the bar.'

They herded into a small office just behind the main bar.

'I know this will seem a little strange,' Lou began, 'but did you know that Eve is Detective Inspector Nikki Galena's mother?'

Sheila nodded. 'She did mention it, and Nikki Galena and her sergeant, Joseph Easter, were here recently about the fake alcohol, so I've met them both.'

'Well, since the police are so hard-pressed, we have volunteered to help them during the festival,' Lou said.

'They need all the help they can get,' added Vinnie quietly. 'That's where we come in. We're looking for suspicious behaviour. Nothing in particular, just anything we think the police should know about. Can you help us?'

'I've been thinking about nothing but suspicious behaviour since someone chose *my* pub to murder two people in,' Sheila said.

Joseph hadn't mentioned that.

'I can't sleep for thinking about it!' Sheila went on, her voice shaking. 'I've been over and over the CCTV footage for that night, desperate to see some small thing that could indicate foul play, but there's nothing.'

Aware that the police would have done that too, Vinnie moved on. 'Sheila? Don't mention this to anyone, but do any of your regulars, possibly slightly older men, have an interest in history, as in old murders and dark deeds? You know the sort, they have a few bevvies and start spouting off to anyone who will listen.'

Sheila laughed. 'Plenty of locals are full of old tales and love to tell them to the incomers. I'd be hard pushed to name them all.' She looked up at an old wall clock. 'I have to get back, sorry.'

Vinnie handed her his card. 'If you think of anyone, or see someone in the pub who looks suspicious, this is my mobile number. Or ring the police of course.'

'I will.'

As they trooped out, Vinnie couldn't help looking back at Sheila. Now he knew the reason for her sadness, he wanted to help her even more. There must be a way he could get to know her better.

* * *

In her turn, Sheila watched them leave. They were the oddest group of amateur sleuths. That man, for example. What was he doing with those elderly ladies? Yet there was something about them that commanded respect.

She smiled to herself, remembering her father's favourite film. She'd watched *The Great Escape* with him countless times. Her favourite character had been Hilts, the Cooler King, played by Steve McQueen. Vinnie Silver had the same rugged, lived-in looks. It was the first time she had looked at a man with any kind of interest for . . . when exactly had she shut down that part of her life? She took his business card from her pocket. So, he was a security expert. A lot of people in security were ex-police or ex-military. She guessed military. The two women had that look.

Sheila was intrigued, and also lighter in spirits. Now she had someone to share her concerns with.

She turned back to the bar, her old smile back in place. 'Okay, folks, who's next?'

* * *

Nikki was talking to Cat in the CID room when Gill Mason turned up. A civilian brought the message that there was a "fortune teller" called Gill Mason asking for her. This was said with the hint of a smirk.

'Oh just perfect!' Nikki said. 'I wondered how long it would be before Madame Arcati came creeping out of the woodwork to tell us she'd had a vision of who the killer is.'

Ben looked up from his workstation. 'Gill Mason was the woman that Cat and I went to see for a friend of mine, boss.'

'And she's a flake, right?'

Nikki was surprised to hear the level-headed detective say, 'Well, no actually. I, that is, we were quite impressed. I'm not saying I believe in second sight or anything like that, but I thought she was a pretty astute woman.'

'So, you think I should go and listen to her?' she asked incredulously.

'I'll go if you like, and say you're tied up. I'm sure she'll talk to me.' Ben smiled broadly. 'And with respect, ma'am, maybe I'll be just a little more open-minded.'

Nikki pulled a face. 'A little? I don't mind saying that mine is shut tight where that kind of thing is concerned. Just don't be taken in.'

'As if!' With a wink at Cat, Ben hurried out.

Some fifteen minutes later he was back, smiling a little ruefully. 'Well, we both made rather an error of judgement there. We assumed Gill was here as a clairvoyant, but she simply came as a conscientious member of the public.'

Nikki frowned.

Ben went on, 'When we first heard from Saltern-le-Fen that the Harrison gang might be planning to work the area, Cat and I asked uniform to hand out some mug shots to local shopkeepers, landlords and stallholders. Gill Mason saw Harrison and another man in the covered market earlier today, and came to report it.'

'Really?'

'Yes, and they were arguing. Another of the stallholders thought he saw one of them brandishing one of our fliers, so maybe they've decided to cut their losses and get out before they are recognised.'

'Ah, well, that's good news at least. Smart thinking on your part, you two.'

'We've got enough to bloody well worry about without Harrison taking advantage of the situation and robbing people,' Cat added rather morosely.

'Gill also wanted us to know something else,' said Ben slowly. 'And this is possibly our first real lead.'

Nikki tensed. Wait for it! Was all to be revealed thanks to Mystic Meg and her crystal ball?

'It's about the young man who died from the snake venom — Peter Cash.' Ben was now looking serious, but excited. 'Of course, no one knows he was poisoned, everyone assumes it was fake booze . . . well, Gill has a vague connection to his family, at least, to his father.'

'And?'

'It appears that the father visited her for a reading after his wife died, and the son, Peter, went with him. They were both devastated at her death and were looking for consolation.'

Nikki swallowed her caustic comment.

'The crux of it is, she recognised Peter and spoke to him briefly, only hours before he died.'

This was serious. 'She spoke to him?' Nikki said. 'And was he sober, not acting funny in any way?'

'He was perfectly normal. Said he'd only just arrived, having come to town to have a look around and meet a friend.' Ben looked at her meaningfully. 'They chatted for a few minutes and he left, but,' Ben paused, 'he met someone at the entrance to the covered market, and they left together.'

Nikki's eyes opened wide. 'This is really important, Ben! It could have been his killer.'

'I think it was, boss.' He flipped open his notebook. 'Listen to this: a man, probably in his late forties, early fifties, tall, with a full head of long, greying hair and a long dark coat. He had his back to her, but she thinks she might recognise him if she saw him again.'

Nikki rubbed her hands together. A lead! At last. 'CCTV? Is there anything at the entrance to the covered market? Surely there is.'

'I asked uniform to check that out for me on my way up here. Niall's getting hold of the council's Public Space Surveillance control room and he'll notify you as soon as he knows exactly where the cameras are in that area.'

Greenborough was quite well covered after a recent upgrade of the control room and cameras. Some areas had digital wireless transmission and used high definition recordings. But not all. She wondered if they would get that lucky. She castigated herself for not going and speaking to the woman in person.

'Gill is going to keep her eyes open in case she sees him again, boss. And I gave her your direct number, hope that's okay?'

She nodded. 'Yes, of course. If she does spot him, we'd need to move fast, with all these visitors in town.' She smiled at Ben. 'Good work. Now let's just hope that a camera caught them together. I need to tell Joseph about this. Anyone seen him?'

Cat and Ben shook their heads. 'Sorry, boss, not for about half an hour.'

Nikki felt a tiny niggle of concern. Joseph had seemed distracted earlier, not himself somehow. It was nothing dramatic, in fact it was very subtle, but it still bothered her. And now where was he? It wasn't like him to simply disappear.

Partly annoyed and partly anxious, Nikki returned to her office and closed the door.

CHAPTER NINETEEN

'I've got four names, maybe five, Sarge.' Dave handed a memo sheet to Joseph. 'All have something that makes them possible suspects — apart from the last two that is. I really cannot believe that Clive's gamekeeper and groundsman could be involved.'

'The criteria have changed slightly, Dave. Forget the scientific background. We are now looking for an interest in history, especially of murder or criminology.' He stared at the names. 'Have you talked to any of them?'

'Not the tenants, they were all out, and I haven't managed to get hold of the guide from the History Society yet. His phone isn't being answered. I've left a message with uniform to contact me the moment either of the two guys who live at the Old Stables gets home and I'll go back.'

They made their way back to the CID room.

'Anyone strike you as being of particular interest, Dave?'

'Now you've told me about the history connection, the man called Anthony Laker is certainly number one. He's an academic of some kind. Clive thought he was writing papers or a book on something possibly historical. I'm looking forward very much to having a word with that one. And the other tenant, Rufus Taylor, is also an academic of some kind.'

'I'll come with you. Tell me the moment you hear they are back, okay?'

'Yes, Sarge. I'd welcome your company.'

Joseph grinned. 'Sounds like you are on first name terms with Cressy-Lawson.'

'Don't tell anyone, but I like him. I feel for him, Sarge. He's a good bloke deep down, he just has the weight of the world on his shoulders.'

Joseph pictured the magnificent Cressy Old Hall and grimaced. 'Not a bad weight to have to bear.'

'You'd think so, but it comes at a price.' Dave's face darkened. 'I thought I'd give my right arm to own a place like that, but listening to the catalogue of constant demands it sends raining down on him, I wouldn't want to be in his shoes for a minute.'

'The running costs must be astronomical.' Joseph left Dave with a parting reminder to call him before he returned to the Old Hall. He was determined to look every single suspect right in the eyes until he came face to face with their killer. And then? He just hoped he would be alone with him.

* * *

'Sorry. I was downstairs with Niall, checking on anything coming in from the streets.'

For half an hour? Nikki stared at him, suddenly aware of being shut out from his thoughts. Whatever was going on? Annoyed and unhappy, she didn't have the time to go into it right now.

'Did he give you an update about the security cameras at the covered market?' she asked.

Joseph looked blank. 'No, why?'

She filled him in on their latest information, courtesy of Gill Mason. His eyes brightened, then they seemed to set in a hard stare.

'That's massive! Want me to contact Niall again?' he said.

'He'll ring us.' She looked at him steadily. *What are you thinking, Joseph Easter?*

'Dave has several people out at the Old Hall that he needs to interview,' he was saying, 'one even has some kind of history degree. I've said I'll go with him, if that's alright?'

'Yes, of course. And now you have a vague idea of what to look for in terms of height, age and build — plus a long dark coat.' Nikki decided to give him free rein. 'You'll ring me if you have any immediate concerns?'

The old Joseph smiled back at her. 'Who else would I ring?'

For one fleeting second, Nikki didn't believe him. The smile was genuine enough, but there was something evasive in the way he spoke.

She was being paranoid. She smiled back. 'Now, why haven't we heard from Niall?'

The words had scarcely left her lips when her phone rang.

'Niall! What have you got for us?'

'Not just cameras, ma'am, but an image. Don't get your hopes up, though. It's a back view as they leave the market, and although they are picked up twice more, there are no shots from the front.'

'But we can place them together?'

'Absolutely, and less than ten minutes before Vonnie and I found him dying in that lane behind the shops.'

'So even though we haven't got his face, we have a picture of our killer,' she said.

'We believe so. By the way, the guys down here are calling him the "Coachman." It's that long coat — makes him look like a Victorian coach driver.'

Nikki had seen a hundred long coats over the last couple of days. Still, it was something.

'The images should be on your computer now, ma'am.'

'Thanks Niall, much appreciated.' Nikki hung up and turned to her screen. With Joseph leaning over her shoulder, they looked at the images. It might have been her imagination, but she thought she felt Joseph grow tense beside her. There was a kind of electric current flowing through him, an alertness that reminded her of something. Ah, yes. It was that state of adrenalin-fuelled excitement you experienced just before you went into a dangerous situation. But why should he feel like that now, when he was just looking at the back view of a possible suspect?

She glanced swiftly at him, and just caught a look of fierce intensity. Then it was gone.

'So, that's our man, is it?' he said softly.

'No proof yet, Joseph, but he is certainly very likely the last person to see Peter Cash alive.'

'And even more likely to be his killer.'

She nodded slowly. 'Very likely.'

Joseph went off to find Dave and show him the pictures, which could be invaluable when they interviewed the tenants of the Old Hall.

Nikki was left alone. She now knew without a doubt that Joseph had another agenda, one that she wasn't part of. The man she loved was keeping secrets from her, and she had no idea what to do about it.

* * *

Eve was standing outside the old Wool Exchange building, waiting while Wendy hunted for a parking space.

'Well, well! Eve Anderson, I do believe.'

Startled, she looked up to see Robert Richmond.

'Don't tell me you are interested in executions as well as fine art?' There was a glint of amusement in his eyes.

Eve stammered something about waiting for Wendy, and the awful parking. She wasn't quite sure what to do. The last thing she wanted was to let Amos Fuller go without talking to him, but she also wanted some information about Robert's brother, Edward, and this seemed like the perfect opportunity to do a little digging.

'Do you know,' she said, 'I keep thinking about those paintings, and how they shouldn't be locked away so people can't see them. They are so beautiful, they deserve to be seen.'

'I'm with you there, and no mistake.' Robert grimaced. 'One way or another, I have to defy my brother and make that possible.'

'Oh, your brother. Edward, wasn't it?' She looked at him enquiringly. 'Would he consider listening to a disinterested outsider? I'd be more than happy to talk to him, if you think it would help.'

Robert burst out laughing. 'Edward is practically a recluse, dear lady. He listens to no one, not even a lovely lady like you!'

'I could try,' Eve added hopefully. 'I feel quite passionate about those pictures. It's a travesty that they shouldn't be allowed to see the light of day.'

'Such enthusiasm!' Robert exclaimed. 'I admit I did hope for some sort of reaction when we decided to allow the public through the door, but you have exceeded my expectations.'

'I tend to get a bee in my bonnet about injustice, and that's how it seems to me.' Eve was choosing her words carefully. 'Tell me something about your brother. There may be some way I could gain access to him,' she tilted her head to one side, 'by fair means or foul.'

'You don't give up easily, do you?'

Eve smiled inwardly. *You have no idea.*

'But I still don't think it would be possible,' Robert said. 'He lives in a grim little basement flat in Ferry Street that he keeps closed up like a nuclear bunker. Even I haven't seen him in months.'

'He must shop, surely? Or visit the doctor? He has to go out sometimes, doesn't he?'

'Tesco delivers, and he won't allow the driver past the door. He's never sick, and if he were, he'd just suffer. No, Eve, he never goes out unless it's for something absolutely vital.'

With some relief, Eve saw Wendy approaching out of the corner of her eye. Amos's talk would be ending right now, and she needed her friend's support. She didn't expect to get too much more out of Robert regarding his brother. And anyway, if Edward really was a recluse, he was hardly likely to be roaming the streets of Greenborough searching for victims.

'Look, I'm sorry,' Robert said, 'I have an appointment in ten minutes, but I suppose I couldn't tempt you to come for a drink sometime soon, could I?' He looked at her expectantly. 'We could talk a bit more about art and the mysterious disappearance of my family's only famous member.'

'Why not?' Eve smiled, not wishing to pass up an opportunity to find out more about the Richmond brothers.

'You've got the house telephone number, it's on the flier about the open days. Ring me.' And before Wendy had even reached them, he was gone.

Wendy smiled. 'Two birds with one stone? I'm impressed.'

Eve watched people starting to straggle out from Amos Fuller's lecture. 'Don't think I'm any further ahead though. Edward appears to be some kind of hermit and rarely leaves his cave. As for Robert, he seems too . . . well, too sociable to be a cold-blooded killer. Let's go and see what sort of impression this next one makes on us.'

Amos Fuller was packing up his books and papers when they entered the hall. He squinted at them for a moment, and then smiled. 'Ah, two of my graveyard acolytes! Did you not fancy the history of hanging? Or are you just a little late?'

Wendy took the lead this time. 'Would you believe it, we got the time wrong! There's so much going on this weekend that we got a bit muddled up.' She gave a convincing sigh. 'Sorry, Mr Fuller.'

'No matter. It went down rather well, so I might give a repeat performance after the festival, possibly at the History Society.'

'Oh, good,' said Eve. 'We loved your talk about the Resurrection Men. You really do know your stuff, don't you? Am I right in thinking you studied history? You speak about it with such authority.'

'Only as a hobby. I'm no academic.' He gave a short laugh. 'The fine diction was the work of an over-possessive mother who believed her only son should be able to play the piano and speak well, even if neither his education nor his intellect was of the highest.'

'But you clearly love this kind of rather gruesome story,' said Eve.

'With a family like mine, it's hardly surprising. It was my ticket through school.' He grinned. '"Hey, Amos comes from a family of grave robbers! How cool is that?"' His smile widened. 'I was skinny, scrawny, wore glasses and had buck teeth. My infamous ancestry saved me a lot of pain.'

'I suppose this weekend is a blessing for your subject,' Wendy said thoughtfully. 'I mean, we love this sort of thing, but it isn't for everyone, is it?'

Amos snapped his briefcase shut. 'You'd be surprised. I'm booked up for the year, giving talks around the county. I'll bet you I'm busier than the flower arrangers, or those who give lectures on how to prune roses. Murder, mysteries and ghostly tales, people love it. It's in our blood.'

'Well, I'm sorry we missed you today, Amos, but we'll catch up another time, I'm sure.' Wendy nodded almost imperceptibly towards the door. Eve was happy to leave. Amos Fuller certainly looked the part, but wasn't quite what they'd expected in person.

'Take care, ladies.' He raised his top hat rather rakishly. 'There's some very scary goings on out there. Stay safe.'

Eve assumed he was referring to the festival, but she wasn't quite sure.

Following Wendy out, she glanced back. Amos Fuller was standing where they'd left him, watching them intently.

CHAPTER TWENTY

Morgan Flint hurried straight into Nikki's office, closed the door and dropped into the chair facing her.

'We've got something! The moment our guys mentioned it, I knew it was what I'd been trying to remember. We might not know who the killer is, Nikki, but I do know why he's killing!'

Nikki leaned forward. 'Tell me!'

Her eyes shone. 'As we suspected, it has to do with history, so prepare yourself for a lesson . . . Well, in the aftermath of the original Jack the Ripper killings, there was a spate of other terrible crimes. Some tried to implicate Jack in their own crimes, others to emulate him.' She pulled a face. 'And several wicked souls jumped onto the bandwagon, feeding off the widespread terror that the Ripper had caused, believing they could outdo him. One such individual, only ever referred to as Creep, made it his life's work to kill his victims in the most unpleasant ways possible.'

'The Ripper's victims were mutilated, cut open and eviscerated, weren't they? Wasn't that bad enough?' Nikki asked.

'Not as far as Creep was concerned. He searched out methods of dispatch that produced indescribable pain and suffering that would have the knock-on effect of striking fear into a population already reeling from the horrors inflicted by the Whitechapel Murderer.'

'Was he ever caught?' asked Nikki.

'No. There was plenty of speculation, but like the Ripper, he abruptly stopped and was never apprehended.' Morgan frowned. 'But listen, it's his methods that make his case so relevant to today's killer. It was said that he sent a message to a high-ranking police officer to warn him of his intentions, and he began his campaign by putting poison into a jug of ale in an old East End inn called the Gallows Tree.'

Nikki made the connection immediately. 'The Hanged Man. Methanol spiked drinks.'

Morgan nodded. 'Then he slipped more of the same into a woman's drink in another inn.'

Nikki breathed out. 'Shirley Campion, at the Coach and Horses.'

'After that, he began to get inventive. He experimented with whatever form of poison would cause maximum suffering, including snake venom, acid and poisonous gas.'

Nikki had to ask. 'How many deaths before he stopped?'

Morgan stared down at a printout. 'Four died from the poisoned ale, one from acid, one from venom, five asphyxiated from gas fumes after being locked inside a house that was set alight — and then two more.'

'Oh God. Two more?'

'And who's to say that he'll stick to the script?' Morgan said angrily. 'If the bastard's enjoying himself, he might feel like rewriting history.'

'Tell me, how did the last two die?' Nikki really didn't want to know, but had to ask.

'They were never able to analyse one of them, although the poison used was suspected to be plant-based, and one was cyanide.'

'So, Rory and Spike weren't wrong after all,' murmured Nikki to herself. Then, seeing Morgan's puzzled look, she said, 'Rory and his assistant guessed that he might use that sort of thing because of the intense pain they inflict on the victim.'

'You wonder how a human being, assuming he was once human, can turn into such a vicious, callous destroyer of life,' Morgan said softly.

'How come we've never heard of this Creep? Everyone and their grandmother knows about Jack the Ripper, and this guy killed far more than he ever did,' Nikki wondered.

'You have to remember that Whitechapel had some of the worst slums in London — poverty, crime, overcrowding . . . people died all the time, of disease, malnutrition, and were often beaten to death or stabbed and robbed for a few pennies. I read that it was so bad in Dorset Street that the police would only venture down it in groups of four! It must have been terrifying to live in that area when Jack the Ripper roamed the streets, with everyone suspecting everyone else and living in fear of the next attack.'

Nikki listened, fascinated. Morgan clearly knew what she was talking about.

'Even back then the police used strategies, so it was decided that it wasn't in the public interest to spread word of any of these new murders — the copycats, the chancers and the psychopathic egotists like Creep. Instead, the deaths were carefully logged and the reports buried in an archive. The bodies were quietly disposed of, recorded as sickness and accident. The truth of just how bad it was in the post-Ripper days didn't emerge for decades. It's only recently that cases have come to light, after the discovery of some old diaries kept by a police officer who lived through that era, and then the old records came to light.' Morgan shrugged. 'I never knew this killer had a name until intel dredged up an article on the diaries, even though I'd come across suggestions of a faceless killer who used horrific methods of murder. I had often wondered whether it was an urban myth.'

'So our man, the Coachman, has found access to these records and has followed in Creep's footsteps?' Nikki said.

'It can't be a coincidence, it just can't. I expect he got the details from the internet, like our guys.'

'But why? Why would the Coachman decide to emulate an obscure and unheard of murderer from, when, the nineteenth century?' asked Nikki.

'The Ripper's killings took place in 1888, and from what I can see,' Morgan pointed to her notes, 'Creep started work in 1889. It appeared to be something of a spree too. Death followed death in quick succession.'

'And then he stopped just like that?'

'Speculation has it that either he was enraged that his vile murders never made the press and gave him the notoriety he craved, or that he himself died. Maybe at another's hand, or possibly through illness or accident, like so many did in those days. Do you know that over a quarter of a million people lived in Whitechapel. Living conditions, working conditions and especially sanitation were horrendous! Since only half the children born there ever made it to the age of five, it was very possible he succumbed to disease.' Morgan smiled coldly. 'Although I've just read one supposition that he was arrested for something else altogether, and spent the rest of his life rotting in prison.'

Nikki had heard enough. While all of this was most interesting, it wasn't going to bring them in any new suspects. Still, as Morgan had said, once they had someone downstairs, this information would be vital. The search history on his devices should be very revealing indeed.

'Do we know anything concrete about this Creep bloke?' asked Nikki.

'I've got Connor working on that right now. Any detail we learn about him could help.' She exhaled. 'Like you, I cannot fathom why someone would want to emulate a figure from the past that no one has ever heard of.'

'I'll be sure to ask him when I catch him,' said Nikki dryly.

Morgan stood up. 'I'm relying on that.'

'You can. We'll get him. And right now, I'm off to tell the super what you've come up with — unless you'd prefer to tell him yourself?'

'No, I'll press on, and see if anything tasty has come in during my absence.' With a smile and a flash of those ice-blue eyes, Morgan Flint was gone.

* * *

Niall was taking a quick walk through the busiest hotspots, just to keep tabs on what was going on. The streets resounded with laughter and music, and streams of people in fancy dress and theatrical make-up flowed in and out of the various venues and public spaces. It was late afternoon, the pubs and bars were full and spilling over into the streets and it all seemed good-humoured.

'Niall!'

He looked towards the voice and his face broke into a smile. 'Tam!'

Tamsin, their dog Skipper at her heels, gave him a peck on the cheek. 'I came in to meet my friend Ellie, but I can't find her anywhere.'

'Not surprising in all this mayhem.' Niall ruffled Skipper's ears and gave him a reassuring pat. The dog was looking rather apprehensive. 'Isn't it all a bit much for Skip here? I'm just on my way back to the station. Want me to take him with me? He's still got a bed in the back office and there's plenty of dog biscuits.'

Tamsin nodded. 'Please, hon. I didn't dream it would be this busy.'

'The festival is a lot bigger this year than it has ever been before.' Niall paused. 'Er, Tam? Go careful, won't you? And if you don't find Ellie, don't hang around here on your own. Call in at the station and collect fur-face, and just go home.'

Tamsin rolled her eyes. 'I appreciate your loving concern, husband dearest, but this happens once a year. I'll be careful, I promise! Now go look after the people that need it.'

He felt another kiss brush his cheek and Tamsin blended back into the crowd. The dog stared up at him anxiously, and

Niall sighed. 'Yes, kiddo, I feel the same. But let's get you off these mean streets, shall we?'

* * *

The CID room was packed for the late afternoon meeting. Nikki took her time to relay everything they knew about the man they were now referring to as the "Coachman."

The whiteboard featured an enlarged still from the CCTV cameras outside the covered market place — the best shots of the last moments of Peter Cash and the man who had walked beside him. Normally this man would have cut an unusual figure in his long dark coat and boots, but during Dark Greenborough he was completely unremarkable.

'We are attempting to interview several men out at Cressy Old Hall. Joseph and Dave are dealing with those, but if any of you see someone who looks like that,' she jammed her finger at the photograph, 'alert me immediately. And that goes for anyone who seems to have an extensive knowledge of crimes from the Victorian era. Check out some of the speakers, and take note of their audiences too.'

Cat raised her hand. 'Ma'am? What if we take the picture of the Coachman and show it to the landlords of the town pubs? If he's a local man, maybe someone might recognise him?'

'Yes, do that. Take Ben, and start with the Hanged Man and the Coach and Horses, okay?' Nikki said. 'Good move.'

Dave looked up from his phone. 'Our two tenants from the stable block are home, ma'am. Can we get straight off, just in case they decide to go out for the evening?'

She nodded. 'Time to draw the meeting to a close anyway. Okay, everyone, go do your best.'

She beckoned to Joseph. 'Are you okay with going out to Cressy Old Hall?'

'Absolutely. And Dave said he could do with a second opinion. Whoever attacked Norma Warden knew their way around that old place, and as both men are apparently the right age and well-educated, they are definitely worth checking out.'

Nikki wanted to ask him more, not about the suspects but about what was going on in his head. He seemed to be there with her, but somewhere else at the same time. She shrugged. No use becoming paranoid over it. No doubt he would talk to her when he was ready. 'Okay, but keep in touch, Joseph.'

'Of course. I'll ring you as soon as we're through.'

She watched him hurry after Dave, who seemed anxious to get back to the Old Hall. She sensed that he felt responsible for what had happened to Norma Warden. She had been fatally attacked on his watch, and knowing Dave, he wouldn't be able to brush something like that off lightly, even if it wasn't his fault.

Her thoughts returned to the killer. According to Morgan Flint's intel, Creep had poisoned two more innocents before he stopped his killing spree. Was there any way they could find this animal before he killed again? Nikki reckoned it was almost impossible. All they had to go on was the back view of a middle-aged man in a dark coat, probably wearing a wig, who they believed had a fascination for a long-dead psychopath. Wonderful! Just wonderful!

An unusual feeling of depression threatened to engulf Nikki. Maybe it was the aftermath of Hannah's birthday? Anniversaries always made her feel her loss more acutely. Then again, it could be the thought of those young students who had been cut down in their teens, just like her daughter. Her heart ached for the parents.

Or maybe it was something subtler than that.

After she and Joseph teamed up in CID, it hadn't taken Nikki long to realise that they formed an almost perfect partnership. They worked as one, each understanding the other's reasoning. But something had changed over the past few days, something was off-kilter. Nikki felt hollow.

As she went through the door to her office, her phone rang. She looked at the display and saw that it was Eve.

'Mum. Everything okay?'

'Fine, sweetheart. I had hoped that I'd have something to give you, but so far, our "spotter" team is failing miserably.'

Nikki smiled. 'No more than the entire Fenland Constabulary, I can assure you.'

'I would just like to pass on a couple of names. I doubt anything will come of them and they'll turn out to be harmless, but they are rather eccentric characters. They might be worth adding to your list of "persons of interest."'

'At this point, I'd investigate Winnie the Pooh if someone told me he'd been acting out of character,' Nikki said dryly. She grabbed a pen. 'Fire away.'

'Edward Richmond. Lives in a basement flat in Ferry Street. Thought to be a recluse, but that could be a cover, I suppose.' There was a hint of amusement in Eve's voice. 'And Amos Fuller, public speaker on such delightful subjects as executioners and grave robbers.'

Nikki perked up on hearing that one. 'I'll run some checks. Anyone else?'

'Not at present, but I'll keep in contact.' There was a short pause. 'Are you alright, Nikki?'

For one moment, Nikki had an overwhelming urge to blurt out all her odd fears about Joseph, but she stopped herself. She was overtired, stressed and worried about what was going on in her town. Joseph had done nothing but seem a little extra preoccupied, probably for all the same reasons. How would she even put it? The whole thing would sound ridiculous. 'Yes, Mum, just desperate to catch our killer.'

'Mmm.' Her mother didn't sound convinced.

'I had hoped to get to meet up with you and the others, but as things are . . .'

'Forget it, darling, there will be other times. Lou and Rene are already talking about coming back again when it's quieter, and Vinnie too. Then we'll go and have a meal, and enjoy ourselves without all this noise.'

'You're right. Give them all my love, won't you?'

'Already have. Now, back to duty.'

'Watch your back, Mum, and don't forget, the slightest hint of danger from anyone, back off. Rory told me not to get within an arm's length of this killer, and I'm taking him at his word — and so must you.'

'Received and understood. Over and out, boss.'

Nikki heard a laugh and the line went dead. She looked at the two names. Well, everyone else was out at present, so she'd run a check herself. At least it would keep her mind off Joseph.

CHAPTER TWENTY-ONE

Tyrone grinned at his father. 'Epic, Dad! Tonight's a sell-out. It's almost a shame to close up shop on this little scam.'

'It is, isn't it? But there's no way you could carry it off while the town is quiet. It needs all the noise to work safely.' Reggie was having one of his sensible moments.

'I know, but it's just so sweet. Maybe do the odd one-off?'

Reggie was tempted, but knew it was too risky. 'Sorry, son. When Dark Greenborough comes to an end, the curtain comes down.'

Tyrone nodded. 'Ah well. Next year then?'

'Oh yeah! We won't allow a money-spinner like this to die.' He smiled at his son, relishing sharing a rare moment of warmth and closeness with the boy. 'We just need to move on and find something to do after the festival closes down.'

'Any more awesome ideas, Dad? Not that I'm expecting to ever top this.'

It was good to hear his son talk this way, after all the criticism he usually got. 'Not yet. I'm focusing on getting through tonight with no hitches. Once this is over, we'll put our heads together and make a plan. After all, we'll have a bit of money behind us this time. That means we have options and aren't scraping the barrel for crappy jobs.'

Tyrone nodded. 'Are we all set then? It's getting dark already, so we can get the first trip up and running soon.'

'Absolutely. And as long as it goes as smoothly as last night, we should be a couple of happy campers by close of play.' Reggie grinned wickedly.

Tyrone grinned back. 'Then bring it on!'

* * *

Before they left for Cressy Old Hall, Joseph rang Vinnie, needing to know where his friend was at any given moment. He had no hard and fast plan for taking down the Coachman, but the second he identified him, he would act. He'd phoned the hospital earlier, and had been told that another of the students was on the brink of losing his fight for life. The news had reinforced his resolve to stop this killer, no matter what.

Vinnie, though, seemed cautious, concerned about his friend.

'Listen, mate, I know exactly what it cost you to turn your life around and become a different Joseph Easter to the one that crossed enemy territory with a gun in his hand. Just don't compromise your new values because of this piece of shit. Do it the right way, unless all else fails, okay?'

Joseph wanted to agree. Something had happened to him when that first student died. He kept seeing his daughter Tamsin, Nikki's girl, Hannah, and every other child who had been unfairly torn from their parents. The Coachman had to be stopped, and if they couldn't get him by fair means, then foul was fine by him.

Vinnie was still speaking. 'You and I need to talk, mate. Can you get away for ten minutes?'

'I would, but I'm on my way to interview two possible suspects, so, sorry, but no. How about I ring you when we're through?'

'Okay. But if one of them sets off alarm bells, back off, right? No silly moves, Easter. Especially not without me.'

189

'Look, I'm not clinically insane. I'm not intending to go around topping people, just in case they turn out to be the murderer. All I'm saying is that he cannot be allowed to remain at large. These killings have to stop.'

'And does that sentence finish with "one way or another?"'

Joseph didn't answer.

He saw Dave waving to him from the corridor, so he muttered his apologies and rang off.

'Ready, Sarge?'

'Ready, Dave. Let's go see what the Tenants of Wildfell Hall have to offer. I'll drive, shall I?'

All the way there, he thought of Nikki, torn between wanting to talk to her and knowing she wouldn't understand. For the first time since they'd been together, their wordless rapport was just not there. Yet a few years back, she had been a hair's breadth away from doing just what he was about to do now. He had stopped her then, and that was why he couldn't speak to her now. To Nikki, he was the voice of reason, that voice that couldn't let her down. But reason had failed him, and he was back in the desert, toting a gun and far beyond her understanding. This was one journey they couldn't make together.

'You alright, Sarge?' Dave sounded concerned. 'I've never known you so quiet.'

'I'm fine, just frustrated that we have no leads to follow, and all the time the Coachman is stalking his next victim.'

'This one has really got to you, hasn't it?' Dave said softly. 'But then I can't talk. I feel . . .' he stopped, lost for the right words. 'I keep seeing that poor woman in the grounds of the Hall. Last night I dreamed about her. It should never have happened. I was there, Sarge, right there! It shouldn't have happened.'

If he hadn't been driving, Joseph would have given him a hug.

Dave had sounded so desolate. What was his home life like, now that his wife had passed away? No one to offload on, no one to listen, no one to hold him and keep the nightmares at bay. 'We'll get him, Dave.'

'We have to, Sarge. I want to be able to say sorry to Norma Warden, and the only way I know how is to catch the man who hurt her.'

'And that's why we'll do it, Dave. To make amends, and bring the victim's families some restitution.'

'To be honest, I don't think I could go through something like that again,' Dave said.

His words made Joseph even more determined to find the man who was causing such anguish. 'Hang on in there, Dave. You never know, we could be on our way to meet him right now.'

Dave shrugged. 'Could we really be that lucky?'

'At least they fit our criteria.' He glanced at Dave. 'Were they interviewed on the night of the incident?'

'No, Sarge. Uniform called, but they were both out.'

'Or they weren't answering the door.' A cold smile spread across Joseph's face. 'So, we are the first to talk to them. Good.'

Dave gave him a swift questioning glance.

'I've been checking out two others from the Old Hall, Sarge, but so far neither have given me much cause for concern. They are the game keeper, Arthur Keats, and the top banana at the History Society, a man called Murray Kennington who fits the bill physically, and obviously loves history.' Dave was looking at his notebook. 'When I saw that picture of the Coachman, I did think of Kennington, but it was just the long coat, and even that was different when I looked closer. Kennington's had a cape, the Coachman's didn't.' He scratched his head. 'And although he's well in with the society, he has no academic background, it's just a hobby. I think he's decided on local history as something to fill the days now he's retired. He was in the food industry, but had to retire early through ill health.'

'And the gamekeeper, er, Keats, did you say?' asked Joseph.

Dave huffed. 'Just can't see it, Sarge. I liked him. I know that's no reason to let him off the hook, but he looked really distraught when he recognised Norma. That was no act. It was real alright.'

The gates to Cressy Old Hall loomed before them in the twilight. 'Well, let's see what we make of Laker and Taylor,' Joseph said.

He pulled up outside the old house and stared up at the forbidding facade. He'd never seen it close up before. He knew that Dave loved this old place, but Joseph Easter just found it menacing. There was something about the place that was terribly wrong.

His unease was like in the old days, when he had advanced across enemy territory. Back then, he had always been able to smell danger. He was smelling it now.

Joseph followed Dave around the building towards the former stable block, his senses on high alert, every nerve screaming. He wished he had Vinnie Silver with him, rather than dear old Dave Harris.

* * *

Wendy looked up from her laptop. 'I'm beginning to wish I'd opted for tramping the streets with the spotters.'

'Then you are having as much luck with creepy Amos as I am with that hermit Edward Richmond.' Eve sighed. 'Let's hope the official police channels are a little more forthcoming.' She stood up. 'That man totally freaked me out, just standing there staring at us as we left. He had the oddest look on his face. Up to that moment I thought he was quite amenable, didn't you?'

'Yes. Amusing too, especially when he spoke about his dastardly family. Now I'm wondering if he's a letch.' Wendy grinned mischievously. 'I'm more interested in Robert Richmond asking you for a drink. And you saying yes! Goodness. I know he's charismatic, but that was fast work!'

'Shut up, Wendy! It's only so I can get to find out more about that recluse of a brother of his, as you well know.'

'So you told me. Several times.' Wendy chuckled.

'Tea?'

'Aha! Changing the subject, are we? But yes, please.'

Eve was also chuckling while she made their drinks. It was true, the man fascinated her, not that she was about to admit that to Wendy. Her friend was having enough fun teasing her already.

She took the tea to Wendy. 'No luck at all on Amos Fuller?'

'Just loads of stuff he's posted about his grave-robbing ancestors, and several notices advertising his talks and his "very reasonable" fees. He has a website, but again, it's all about the Resurrection Men. I even found an editorial from a local rag from about two years ago, but the journalist wasn't really interested in Amos, just his shady relatives.'

'Even so, you've done better than me. All I found on Edward was a news report on some row with his neighbour.' She pulled a face.

'Let's hope the others pick up something when they mingle with the natives.'

'I think they would have rung us if they had.' If the police had as few leads, they must be at their wits' end. Poor Nikki, she had sounded really low. Eve sank down into her chair. 'I think my daughter has something on her mind that she's not sharing.'

Wendy looked up sharply. 'She's heading up a major murder hunt, Eve. She's hardly likely to be all full of the joys of spring, is she?'

'I know that, but there's something else worrying her.' Eve shook her head. 'I never thought I'd be able to say this, but I know my daughter. Something's wrong.'

Wendy nodded slowly. 'I believe you. Is it something you want to follow up?'

Eve flexed her taut shoulders. 'I have a feeling that whatever it is, will show itself soon, so we'll just have to be there for her when it does.'

'We will. Of course.'

'Thank you, Wendy.'

It was good to have close friends. Eve wouldn't have wanted to be alone at this uncertain time.

* * *

Bliss had meant to go and see her friend Gill again, but the crowds bothered her and she was considering just going home. She felt almost weak, and she didn't like it at all.

Spooky had asked her not to go out unless it was urgent, but after taking Fox for a short walk, she had felt restless and claustrophobic in the flat, which, until a boy had died on the doorstep, had been her safe place. Now it seemed that even a short trip across the brightly lit part of town had been a bad idea.

From being a place of light-hearted fun, Greenborough had become shadowy, threatening, somewhere she no longer wanted to be. Where had this feeling come from?

At the entrance to the market, she allowed herself to relax a little. Talking to Gill would help, it always did. Bliss made her way through dozens of shoppers and browsers, to where Gill's brightly coloured "fortune teller's" tent called out a welcome. She was glad she hadn't just gone home.

She was taken aback to find the stall empty. She looked around, expecting to see Gill nearby, chatting with a fellow stallholder, but she was nowhere to be seen.

Bliss frowned. All her things were still there, the brightly coloured crystals, the books and the scented candles. So where was Gill?

Maybe she'd just gone off for a drink. Bliss was wondering whether to make her way back home when she saw something that really bothered her.

Inside the little gazebo, lying on the table, were Gill's tarot cards.

Bliss's frown deepened. Those cards were sacrosanct to Gill. After every consultation, she wrapped them in silk and replaced them in their box. Gill Mason would no more walk off and leave them than she would leave a new-born baby.

Bliss went to the stall next to Gill's, where a ruddy-faced woman was selling an assortment of macabre-looking Gothic jewellery. 'Has she been gone long?' she asked.

'Didn't see her go, duck! One minute she was there, and the next . . .' The woman shrugged.

'How long ago was that?' Bliss asked.

'Oh, maybe a quarter of an hour?' She pointed to another stall directly across from them. 'Ask Bill over there. He might have seen her go. She sometimes asks him to keep an eye open for her if she slips off for a wee.'

Bliss spoke to Bill and got the same story from him. What to do now?

She returned to her friend's stall and collected up the tarot cards, wrapped them in their silk, put them back in their box and tucked it away out of sight.

Bliss took out her phone and rang Gill's number, but it had been switched off.

As she was trying to decide what to do, a girl in a long flowing black witches' outfit offered her a couple of pounds for a crystal from the bowl on the counter. Distractedly, she took the money and reached under the table for Gill's cash box.

When she opened it, she found that it still contained a day's takings.

Bliss stared at it. Now she was really worried. She took out her phone and rang Spooky at the police station.

CHAPTER TWENTY-TWO

Show time at last! It was what Reggie loved to do. If he hadn't been tempted by the promise of easy money dealing in dodgy merchandise and staking his meagre resources on half-arsed gambles, he would still be a street trader of some repute. And like in the market, this current scheme allowed the showman in him to come to the fore. What's more, he had been pleasantly surprised at the way his son had performed. It made him think that if they put their heads together, father and son would make a pretty good team.

He looked at the people gathered around him. To think of it, all those excited and expectant faces just looking at him. Yeah, this was the life.

They had arranged to meet at the war memorial, since it had to be somewhere out in the open and away from anyone who might overhear what he said. Tyrone had selected two of the group to be torch carriers.

'Is everyone ready?'

There were murmurs of assent.

'You understand that this is dangerous and strictly unorthodox, and you are all prepared to take the risk, is that right?'

Everyone nodded.

'Then follow me. Let the journey into hell begin.' A ripple of anticipation ran through the little crowd.

They walked on in complete darkness for perhaps five minutes, the moon hidden behind a bank of clouds. Perfect. Just what Reggie wanted.

He led them off the main route and down a cobbled alley that led into a maze of backstreets. At first they encountered the occasional gaggle of people wandering around, and at one point they met a group on a ghost walk, but soon the group was making its way alone along a narrow, dimly lit pathway.

Soon Reggie had them gathered together outside the doors of a derelict warehouse. He pointed across the road. 'There you have it. That, my friends, is 11 Drakes Alley, scene of the brutal murder of Alan and Bernice Calder.' He paused for effect, and was rewarded by gasps and whispered comments. 'Now, I'll just tell you what happened to that unfortunate couple, and then . . . and then we'll take you inside, but . . .' another dramatic pause, 'you must prepare yourselves. As I said, this isn't for the faint-hearted, and you are about to hear why. Gather round.'

Reggie told the story of how Alan Calder, a local businessman, had returned home early one night to find his wife Bernice in bed with another man. He attacked the man, who fled, leaving Bernice to face her husband's fury. Alan had pursued her through the house, brandishing a large chef's knife, slashing and hacking at the unfortunate woman. Despite being terribly injured, Bernice had fought back. Finally, she had picked up a door stop and stunned her husband with a blow to the side of his head. Thinking she'd killed him, she crawled away to try and get help, but Alan was still very much alive. Realising what he had done, he rang the police and said he'd come home to find a man trying to murder his wife. He had managed to wrench the knife away from him, he said, but had been stunned and the man had made off into the night.

Reggie told the story with all the verve of an actor, finishing up with a description of Bernice's last moments, bleeding to death in a bedroom, and then Alan's sudden demise from a brain haemorrhage.

'Initially Alan's story was believed,' he said, 'because a man had been seen running from the property as if the hounds of hell were after him. It took the police a long time to piece together the facts and discover the truth.' From the corner of his eye, he saw his son giving him the thumbs-up from the side entrance to number eleven. 'And so, my friends, if you are quite ready to experience a real-life crime scene, let's go inside.'

He gestured to Tyrone and they crossed the deserted road to where his son was holding the door open for them. They were safe inside in a matter of moments, Reggie giving silent thanks that all the residential properties that five years ago had surrounded this one were now boarded up and awaiting redevelopment, and the few old businesses that kept warehouses on that back street were all closed up for the night.

'As I told you before we started on this adventure, this house has not been touched since the police and the forensic services left, some five years ago. What you see here is real, including the bloodstains. They belong to poor Bernice.' He gave a dry laugh. 'Incredible as it might seem, Alan's brother, who owns this property and lives abroad, hasn't allowed it to be touched, not even cleaned. It was locked up and left just as it was. No one knows about this except us. You are paying for the privilege of treading the boards of a real-life killing ground, which means you must never tell a soul. Don't forget that you are trespassing on private property, so when you leave, take with you only the memory of this terrible place, and never speak about what lies behind the door of 11 Drakes Alley.' He nodded to Tyrone.

'This way please,' said his son. 'Even though they are boarded up, the windows have blackout curtains, but as little light as possible, please. Don't shine the torches directly at the windows. And do be careful not to trip over anything. The search teams left a lot of mess behind.'

Tyrone led the way through the eerie property. In the moving beams of light dancing over the contents of the house, even Reggie couldn't help experiencing a shudder of fear.

The house was littered with shattered ornaments and broken furniture, with blood splatters on the walls and doors, and at one spot, even on the ceiling. Even though the bloodstains had blackened with the passing of time, there was no mistaking what they were.

As the voyeurs followed Tyrone from room to room, Reggie kept up his patter, until the grand finale, which was the master bedroom.

Reggie really built up the drama. 'Bernice, realising her husband was not dead, and knowing that she could not get past him to the front door, decided to use the last of her strength to get up the stairs to the master bedroom, where she had left her phone and there was a bolt on the door. It was here that she bled to death, unaware that Alan had died of a catastrophic brain haemorrhage as he mounted the stairs to finish her off.'

Tyrone opened the door.

'Bernice was found on the floor in the bay window, curled up in the foetal position in a pool of blood, her unused phone in her hand.' Reggie was about to go on when he heard one of his audience gasp, followed by a piercing scream.

Reggie pushed forward to where his son was standing, staring at something on the floor.

Then it moved, and uttered a strangled cry.

Everyone jumped back, and there were more screams. Someone yelled out, 'You sick bastards, you've really fucking overdone it! It was supposed to be a bit of fun.'

The shape moved again, causing a general panic. People shoved each other out of the way in their haste to get down the stairs and out of the house.

Reggie and Tyrone stood where they were, neither of them able to take this in. Initially Reggie thought a drug addict must have decided to use the abandoned property as a doss house, and accidentally overdosed. But that couldn't be right. Even in the torchlight, he noticed the man's good quality clothes, certainly not streetwear.

'Dad?' Tyrone's voice was trembling. 'What do we do?'

'You get an ambulance! That's what you do.'

They both turned, suddenly realising they were not alone.

An older man was watching from the doorway, a look of revulsion on his face. 'And quickly! He's really sick!'

Reggie pulled out his phone and dialled 999. He was a chancer and a wide-boy, but he wasn't a bad man, and the punter standing behind him was right, this man was probably dying right in front of his eyes. He snapped out the address and some directions, and begged them to hurry.

As soon as the call was made, he turned to Tyrone, grasped his shoulder and hissed, 'Get out of here, son! Now! This has nothing to do with you, alright? I'll wait for the ambulance while you disappear. This is my mess. I'll sort it.' He turned to the only one of his "customers" not to have run terrified from the house of death, and said, 'And you. Just go, please. I don't know what's happened here, but help is on its way. You don't wanna get caught up in this, so just beat it.'

The punter stared mesmerised at the helpless man on the floor, who was now barely moving, and then suddenly seemed to come to himself. He turned and hurried down the stairs.

'Get out, Tyrone! I mean it.' Reggie pushed his dumb-struck son after the retreating figure. 'I've got this, trust me!' He shoved the lad towards the door, and at last Tyrone stumbled away.

Reggie dropped to his knee and placed a hand on the dying man's shoulder, muttering words of comfort.

After what seemed forever, he heard the distant sound of sirens.

Reggie left his charge and went down to the street where he waited until he saw the blue lights threading through the narrow lanes towards him. Though desperately sorry for the sick man, whoever he was, he also felt distraught for his son.

Yet another dream shattered. He'd lose him now for sure. He'd had one last chance to prove himself in his son's eyes, and fate had stepped in, as it always did, and had blown it out of the water.

Utterly despondent, Reggie waved frantically at the green and yellow vehicle.

* * *

Spooky tapped on Nikki's door, stuck her head in and threw her an apologetic smile. 'I know you're up to your neck, but you remember that offer of hearing out a friend?'

Nikki beckoned her inside. 'What's the problem?'

'Might be nothing, but considering everything else that's going on . . . Bliss has just been to visit Gill Mason, you know, her friend the fortune teller in the covered market? And she's not there, but her day's takings and her precious tarot cards are.' Spooky drew in a breath. 'You don't walk off and leave a day's money sitting on your stall, do you?'

Nikki felt the slightest chill of concern. This woman had been at the station earlier, helping the police with their enquiries, and now she had disappeared? That didn't sound good. 'How long has she been gone?'

'Bliss thinks about an hour. She's hanging on there in the hope that Gill comes back soon.' Spooky frowned. 'I've a strong suspicion that all is not well.'

'I'll get someone down there.' Nikki lowered her voice. 'Listen, Spooks, Gill Mason might have seen the killer. It was just a back view, but she saw someone leaving the market with Peter Cash, the young man who died from snake venom poisoning.'

Spooky groaned. 'Oh no! Please, not Gill! That would just about finish Bliss off. She's so sensitive that she's still upset by the lad who died on our doorstep, and she didn't even know him.'

'Look, this could just be coincidence, Spooks. There wasn't the slightest indication that the man we suspect to be the killer saw Gill Mason, and if he did, she was just chatting to Peter as she would anyone else. There'd be no reason for him to hurt her.' Nikki wanted to sound reassuring, but she was as worried as her friend. 'Even so, I'll get onto uniform right now, and they can ask around the market. I suppose Bliss has tried to phone her?'

'Switched off. Although Gill does do that when she's giving readings or working. That's not unusual.'

'She's not doing a reading now though, is she?' Nikki murmured.

'No, she's not,' said Spooky. 'I know it will sound weird to you, Nik, but even if she did leave her money behind, Gill would never leave her tarot cards. In her eyes, they are more precious than money.'

'Then I'd better get straight onto this. You tell Bliss to hold on, if she doesn't mind, and I'll get some officers over to her, okay?'

Spooky nodded, pulling her phone from her pocket, 'And I won't be telling her about Gill seeing the killer either.' She glanced at her watch. 'I'm almost finished here anyway. I'll go down there myself. I don't want Bliss walking home in the dark.'

'Good idea, but don't forget, it's only an alleged killer, we don't know anything for certain . . . yet.' Nikki stood up and moved to the door. 'I'm going to talk to Niall.'

* * *

Sheila looked around the bar and exhaled. There had been no let up today. People had streamed through the doors, and as the evening drew on, it was getting even busier. She couldn't complain, the increased takings would be very welcome.

'Here, Sheila, what do you make of this?'

One of her regulars was waving a leaflet at her.

'What is it?' she asked, staring at the rather badly done pamphlet.

'Lord knows! Have a look at it and see what you reckon,' the man said with a puzzled expression. Sheila read it and felt equally puzzled. Unscrupulous people had been known to capitalise on events like the festival in the past, and she was pretty certain this was one of them. But she couldn't work out exactly what they were selling.

Come with us for the Ultimate Dark Greenborough Experience. We will take you to the darkest place imaginable, and it's not on the list of Tourist Attractions! This is not for the squeamish and we only consider serious applicants for this once in a lifetime tour.

At the bottom was a mobile number. No graphics and no other information. Sheila went to hand it back, then hesitated. 'Can I hang on to this, Fred?'

Fred grinned. 'Fancy the ultimate experience yourself, do you?'

'I get that every evening when I see you walk through the door, my lovely. But really, can I have it?'

'Be my guest, She. I don't think my old ticker would be up to anything too "ultimate," whatever that is!'

'Where did you find it?'

'Someone left it on that table over by the window. Probably the bloke who got shafted for a load of wonga and never got to see the *darkest place*.' Fred's face creased with laughter. 'Plonkers! If you're taken in by that twaddle, you deserve to be parted from your money, don't you think?'

She refilled his glass, then went through to the back room and picked up the phone. 'Vinnie? It's Sheila, from the Hanged Man.'

'Sheila! Are you okay? Nothing wrong, is there?'

Was that real concern in his voice? 'No, honestly, it's just that you said if something too small for the police should crop up, then . . .'

He didn't hesitate. 'Shall we come over?'

'Could you? As I say, it's probably nothing at all and I'll be wasting your time, but, well, you know how you get a feeling about something?'

'On our way, Sheila.' The line went dead.

She put her phone away with a thrill of excitement that had nothing to do with the weird pamphlet. The image of the Cooler King flashed across her mind, and she smiled.

Twenty minutes later, she was back in the small room, showing Vinnie and his two friends the flier.

'It's a scam for sure,' said Lou, 'but it has an undertone, doesn't it?'

Rene nodded. 'I was going to say the same thing myself. It's a lure, but I get the feeling that whoever produced this really does have something dark in mind.'

'But what, I wonder?' mused Vinnie.

Sheila shrugged. 'We've had this kind of thing in the past, and it's always been a way of conning tourists, but this felt different somehow. I hope you didn't mind me showing you? I can't think it has anything to do with those deaths, but you never know.'

Vinnie's disarming smile brought the warmth to her cheeks.

'We're glad you did, Sheila. We've discovered precious little else.'

'The police do seem to have some sort of lead though, don't they? Two detectives were in here a little while ago with a CCTV camera image, asking if I recognised the man in it.'

'I'm guessing you didn't?' said Lou.

Sheila sighed. 'Sadly, it could have been any one of a lot of people, what with the long coat, and it was taken from the back which didn't help at all. Still, I've got all of my staff keeping their eyes peeled for anyone who looks like that.'

Rene took out her phone. 'Oh well, nothing ventured . . . I'm ringing this number on the flier.'

Everyone waited.

'Switched off. Still, it was worth a try.' Rene pocketed her phone, then stared thoughtfully at the pamphlet. 'Could we take this with us, Sheila?'

'Of course. Do you think it means something?'

She saw the two women glance at each other. They both nodded.

'Not that we have a clue as to what that could be,' smiled Rene. 'As you say, the message in there has hints of something underhand, but,' she stopped for a moment, 'also something real.'

'The odd thing is,' said Sheila, 'you hear an awful lot, working behind a bar. People talk their heads off, especially after they've had a few, but I've heard no mention at all of any scary fringe event going on.'

'Well, if you do, ring me immediately, Sheila, and also if you find any more of these leaflets.' Vinnie looked directly at her.

'I will, of course. Now, can I get you all a drink? On the house.'

Vinnie stood up, 'We'd love to, but another time, if the offer still holds? We'd better get back out there.'

The two women left the room, but Vinnie held back. 'Do you ever take time off? Or do you work twenty-four seven?'

Sheila shrugged. 'I am a bit of a workaholic, I guess. But I can always leave it to my staff and go out if I need to.'

'Would you consider having dinner with me? When this festival is over, of course. I'm going home late Sunday afternoon, but only to sort some business out. I'll be back mid-week.' He looked at her hopefully.

She didn't give it a second thought. 'I'd love to. You've got my number. Ring me and I'll arrange cover for the evening.'

'It's a date.' That smile again. 'But don't forget, in the meantime, the slightest hint of anything that worries you, phone me immediately.'

Promising she would, she watched him go. Well, wonders would never cease. Sheila Pearson had just agreed to go on a date with a man she hardly knew. And she didn't have a single reservation about it.

CHAPTER TWENTY-THREE

Dave and Joseph went to the first of the two stable conversions and knocked loudly on the door.

Rufus Taylor answered almost at once. He stared at them suspiciously. 'Yes?'

Joseph showed his warrant card and introduced the two of them. 'Could we come in, sir? It won't take too long.'

Taylor was just as Clive Cressy-Lawson had described him — untidy, in an absent-minded kind of way, as if he had opened the wardrobe that morning and taken out the first things that came to hand. And that preoccupied manner, as if he had been interrupted in the middle of solving some deep and meaningful philosophical problem. He cast his eyes helplessly around the big living area, apparently in the hope of spotting some seating that wasn't piled high with books or papers. 'I, er, sorry, I don't get too many visitors.' He gathered up several heavy tomes and almost threw them on the floor. 'Please, sit.'

Dave looked at him. He was the right height, and probably around the right age, but they would need to know a lot more about Rufus Taylor if they were to add his name to the whiteboard in the CID room.

Joseph started by asking Taylor how well he had known Norma Warden.

'Oh dear, well, I hardly knew her at all. She interviewed me when I applied to rent this place, but apart from having to see her about a few small problems to do with the stable here, I didn't really talk to her.'

'You used to live on London Road, sir?' said Dave, using his friendly tone of voice, 'Such a shame they were taken under compulsory purchase. It always seems a sin to me to take beautiful old properties and pull them down in order to build something not nearly so lasting.'

'It suited me at the time.' Rufus Taylor ran a hand through his straggly hair. 'After my parents died, I wanted something smaller, and then I lost my brother as well, so,' he stared around him, 'this is perfect. It's quiet too, and I crave that above all.'

'You're a lecturer?' Joseph said.

'A tutor. I worked at a formal tutoring centre in Louth for some time, then started private academic tutoring in the students' own homes. Now I'm semi-retired, although I do still have a couple of private clients.'

'And your subject, sir?'

'English language and literature.' Taylor frowned. 'But why the questions about me? I'm assuming this is about Norma Warden, so why am I getting the third degree?'

Dave upped his smile. 'We have to talk to everyone living and working at the Old Hall, sir, no exceptions. We are looking to find out everything we can about her and we're starting by interviewing the tenants.'

'But I know nothing about her,' Taylor said.

'But she did work here, and she had a cottage on the estate. Did you never see her walk by? Did she have a regular routine of some kind? Or maybe a friend here that she spent time with? You don't have to know someone to notice their habits,' Joseph said crisply.

'I'm not the most observant man, Detective. I'm more comfortable with the characters in a book than real people.'

Dave thought Taylor was probably telling the truth, although he could of course be giving a sterling performance as the archetypal absent-minded academic. 'Were you at home on the evening that the attack took place, sir?' he asked.

'No, I wasn't. I'd gone to a talk in Wainfleet. When I got home, Arthur Keats told me that Norma had been attacked. I was aghast. I might not have known her well, but she seemed the last person you would expect to have been involved in something so horrific.' He looked thoughtful. 'I suppose you might get more from my neighbour, Anthony Laker. I think I've seen him talking to Norma sometimes. I'm sure he saw more of her than I did.' He gave them a somewhat rueful look. 'And he's more sociable than I am. I really don't do chat, sorry.'

Dave couldn't decide what he thought about this man, so while Joseph asked him to clarify exactly which talk he had attended, he watched his body language carefully. After a while he came to the conclusion that Rufus Taylor really wasn't comfortable with people, so he was probably telling the truth about not really noticing Norma. He clearly spent a lot of time in his own head, living alongside characters created by long-dead authors. To Dave it seemed odd to be happier doing that than talking to real people. After all, they also had exciting stories to tell.

After a few more questions, Joseph caught his eye. It was time to go.

Joseph seemed slightly rattled by Taylor. 'I didn't like him, did you? All that stuff about "I don't do small talk, I'm not observant." He was a tutor, wasn't he? He talked for a living. I'm not sure he adds up.'

'I didn't get that many bad vibes from him, Sarge, but I'm with you on not liking him much. He doesn't seem to have any sympathy for the living, does he? I mean, he said he was shocked to hear of Norma's injuries, but there was no feeling in it.'

They went to the next of Clive Cressy-Lawson's stable conversions, a much bigger apartment that had once been part of an old barn.

A smiling Anthony Laker opened the door. 'What can I do for you gentlemen?'

After Joseph had made the introductions, they were welcomed in immediately.

Dave looked around. This was more his cup of tea, neat and elegant with lots of exposed brickwork and original timbers. Clive might not have thrown a whole lot of money at these conversions, but they were nicely done.

Laker ushered them through to the living area and indicated two sofas. 'Please, do have a seat. So, how can I be of assistance?'

'How well did you know Norma Warden, sir?'

The smile left Laker's lips. 'Not as well as I should have, Officers. I feel terrible that I never made more of an effort to get to know her. After all, we were practically neighbours. Of course we spoke, but only pleasantries really. I can't say I knew much about her at all.'

'We are trying to understand why Mrs Warden was the target of such a terrible attack, sir, so we're talking to everyone who came in contact with her.' Dave looked steadily at Laker. 'And we have to know where everyone was on the evening she was attacked. I understand you were out?'

'I was. I'd spent the afternoon with an old college chum who was about to take off to join an archaeological dig in the Middle East.'

'We'll need to have that confirmed, I'm afraid,' said Joseph.

'Well, Hamish is now well off the radar, but we had a late lunch at the Vine Leaf in Peterborough. I booked it in my name and Costas the manager served us himself. He'll confirm we were there.' Laker got up and fetched a notepad. 'This is his number.'

Joseph thanked him. 'Was there anyone here that Mrs Warden spoke with regularly, a friend, or a close neighbour?'

Laker sat back down. 'I got the feeling that she liked her own company. I never saw her actually fraternise with anyone, and the nearest tied cottage to hers is empty at present. One of the groundsmen moved out recently to take a post at a National Trust property somewhere Norfolk way, I think.'

'You never heard of her being involved in any disagreements or arguments ?' asked Dave.

Laker shook his head. 'She was quite businesslike, you know? Kind of humourless, but there were never any cross words that I knew of.'

'And you, sir? Do you like living here?' Dave said.

'It's perfect for me. I love it. And it's good for my work, very quiet and peaceful. You could go all day without speaking to a soul if you so wished.'

Joseph asked, 'And what is your work, if you don't mind me asking?'

'Until recently I was a senior user researcher for a digital bank, but after five years, I decided I needed a change. So, at present I'm free-lancing, writing articles for professional journals and online academic sites. Stuffy and boring to most, I suppose.'

'And your subject, sir?' Dave enquired.

Laker smiled at him, 'Anthropology. As I said, boring to most people.'

'What field?' asked Joseph.

'Cognitive and Evolutionary Anthropology actually.'

'Did you study at Oxford, sir?'

The smile broadened. 'I did, Detective Sergeant, at Magdalen College. A great college.'

Dave felt a little out of his depth. It had been suggested that Laker went to Harrow, followed by Oxford — places the likes of which Dave Harris would never see the inside of. If he were honest, he had no idea what anthropology really involved. He looked at Laker as he chatted comfortably with Joseph. He was casually dressed in denim jeans, with a soft green check shirt and a Crew sweatshirt, but the man still managed to ooze class. His hair was greying at the temples but still full and wavy, and although Dave guessed he must now be in his late forties, he had a young face. He might be an academic, but Laker was no stuffy old fart.

Dave looked around the apartment, which was open-plan with a mezzanine floor above that constituted the bedroom area. The ground floor had been split into sections — an office, a kitchen with a dining area, and the lounge where they were now seated. The focal point was a big log burning stove that suited the "barn" design perfectly. Laker also had some very interesting artefacts and pictures that spoke of quality and money. His accommodation matched his character, and Dave could understand why he liked living there so much.

'How about your neighbour, Mr Taylor? Do you get on with him, sir? asked Joseph.

'Our paths rarely cross. He's not a mixer. In fact I doubt he has too many social skills.' He raised his eyebrows. 'I'm not meaning to be derogatory, but even though we are both university men, we have nothing in common. Actually, he can be quite rude.'

'How can he be a tutor, with no people skills?' Dave wondered aloud.

'Oh, get him on his chosen subject and he'll talk your head off. No, it's simple day to day stuff that he has no time for.' Laker shrugged. 'But, hey, you can't knock a man for being single-minded, can you?'

'I'm guessing it doesn't make him a very nice neighbour though,' said Dave.

'Indeed.'

Joseph stood up. 'We've taken up enough of your time, sir.' He handed Laker his card. 'If you think of anything that might help us, anything unusual, please ring me.'

Laker nodded. 'Of course. And I sincerely hope that you catch whoever did this. Norma didn't deserve to suffer in that way.'

'No one deserves to suffer like that. We'll find him alright.'

Dave noticed the hardness in his voice, a tone he didn't associate with the sarge. This case was really getting to Joseph.

Outside, Joseph was about to get into the car when he stopped. 'You said that gamekeeper guy fitted the criteria too? And what about the groundsman? I'd like to take a look at them while we're here.' He paused. 'Not that I'm doubting your opinion, Dave.'

'Okay, Sarge, no problem. But we'd better go down to the gamekeeper's cottage in the car. It's close to the lodge house at the bottom of the drive.'

There were no lights on in Arthur Keats's home, apart from one small lamp glowing dimly in the entrance porch. 'I think we're out of luck, Sarge. Do you want me to try his mobile phone?'

Joseph was staring at the small and rather tired-looking building set against a backdrop of high trees. 'Miserable place,' he muttered. 'But yeah, give him a ring, Dave, he might just be checking things round the estate.'

The phone went immediately to voicemail, but Dave didn't leave a message. A lot of Arthur's work took place at night. He had told Dave about a spate of poaching on the Old Hall estate, so he certainly wouldn't be checking his phone every five minutes if he were hiding in the undergrowth. 'No luck, Sarge. I'll just try Den Elliott's number while we are here.'

Once again there was no response, so there seemed little point in going to the man's cottage. Dave checked the time before putting his phone back in his pocket. Seven thirty, and Dave was hungry. 'Back to base, Sarge?'

Joseph was already in the driver's seat with the keys in the ignition. 'No use wasting time here, is there?' He gave a little grimace. 'I know you love this place, Dave, but it gives me the creeps. It's got a bad atmosphere.'

Dave climbed in beside Joseph. 'Maybe your impression is coloured by the awful thing that happened here. I have to say that prior to the attack, the Old Hall had quite a calming effect on me.'

Joseph didn't answer, but it was clear he felt far from calm.

Joseph was uncharacteristically quiet on the drive back to the station. Dave asked him what he thought about Anthony Laker.

'Confused. He's a bit of an anomaly. I've met a lot of academics, and a lot of well-heeled toffs, but you rarely get the two combined. Though he's puzzling, I can't see him as a serial killer. What do you think?'

Dave puffed out his cheeks. 'Can't see it either, Sarge. But then, I don't know a thing about the upper classes. Other than Clive Cressy-Lawson, I've never really understood what makes them tick.'

'Come on, Dave,' Joseph chided, 'you're so good at dealing with people. You're one of the best men I know!'

'Handling them is one thing, but understanding them is another. And what the dickens is that anthropology thing he studies?'

'It's really just the study of humans,' Joseph said. 'They look at language, culture, society, and how mankind evolved into what it is now.'

'And his particular branch?'

'Not totally sure. It's far too complex for me. I think it's more to do with the culture side, but don't quote me on that.'

Dave laughed. 'You sounded like you knew exactly what he was talking about, Sarge. You had me fooled.'

'Like you said, my friend, a big part of handling people is making the right noises.'

'Well, right now, my stomach is making all the wrong noises. I'm starving.'

'If you are up for working on, we can send out for something, although with the town this busy we might have a wait.' Joseph hesitated. 'Actually, it might be better if we got off home and started again tomorrow.'

Dave thought about his stock of emergency ready meals and the chilled beer in his fridge and thought that a very good idea indeed. 'If the boss is okay with it, I'm game for calling it a day.'

Though Joseph agreed, Dave had an idea he wasn't about to go home for a spot of relaxing culinary therapy. There was a determined look on his face.

CHAPTER TWENTY-FOUR

While Nikki waited for Joseph and Dave to return, she ran a check on the two names her mother had given her. The first one, Amos Fuller, was not known to them and she could find nothing on him at all. The second, Edward Richmond, cropped up a couple of times, but only regarding some skirmishes he'd had with his neighbours and a warning about keeping the peace. Other than that there was nothing.

She was just about to phone her mother and tell her, when Cat knocked on her door. 'Ma'am? We've got a sighting from the CCTV at the music college. Again it's not clear and not full face, but I'd swear it's the man who was seen with Peter Cash.'

'Show me!'

Cat led the way back to her desk, where they looked at the footage displayed on her screen. 'See? The time is an hour and a half prior to the fire, and here he is.' She froze a frame showing an open door at the back of the old building. Nikki saw a tall man in a long dark coat slipping out and closing the door behind him. He moved away, keeping his head down and away from the camera.

'He knows he's being watched,' whispered Nikki, 'and he doesn't care.'

'He's not showing his face, is he? Not even once,' growled Cat. 'The bastard! Look at him! He's so confident, meanwhile he's just deliberately laid a trap to kill or maim innocent kids.' There was a catch in her voice.

'You okay?' Nikki asked.

Cat didn't answer immediately. 'No, I'm not. This is inhuman what he's doing. How can anyone have such a callous disregard for precious life? It's just,' she held her hands up, 'beyond belief.'

Nikki spoke softly. 'We've been here before, Cat, haven't we? We've come across more than our fair share of monsters.'

'This one is different, boss. I'm not handling it very well, and if you ask me, the sarge isn't either.'

So, it wasn't just her who thought Joseph wasn't his normal self. 'It's a very bad business. I'm not surprised we are all strung out — and the festival isn't helping.'

'This bloody festival is why it's happening. It's the perfect cover for his hideous murders.' Cat had sunk into her chair, looking paler than she should. All of her usual vitality seemed to have gone.

'I think you should take some time out, Cat. I know it's not what you would want, but you are worrying me.' Nikki had seen breakdowns coming on before, and Cat was exhibiting all the warning signs.

'That's not going to happen, boss. Don't worry about me, I'll get through this, I promise. It was just seeing those students in such distress. We need to all work together to get the Coachman before he does more damage. I'll buckle down, I promise.'

Nikki was torn. Part of her wanted to pull rank and send Cat home but she also needed her here. Nikki was also conscious of how she would feel if she was told to stand down in the middle of a murder investigation.

'Okay, but you must keep talking to me, and I mean it. Come and see me, don't struggle or feel you have to put on a brave face. There are always cases that affect us more than the rest. After all, *we* are human — unlike the Coachman.'

Cat gave her a watery smile. 'Thanks, ma'am. I won't let you down.'

'You wouldn't know how. And that's not what's in question. I just don't want you cracking up — for your own sake.' She smiled. 'Or for Ben's.'

Cat sighed. 'Oh Lord! I don't want to worry him, but I know I do.'

Nikki thought about Joseph. 'Comes with the territory. It happens when you care about someone.'

Just then, a civilian hurried into the CID room. 'DI Galena, Sergeant Farrow asked if you have a moment. Something has come up that he thinks you should know about.'

Nikki threw a worried glance at Cat. 'We're on our way.'

They ran down the stairs to Niall's office.

'Ambulance Service has just rung in with what appears to be another one, Nikki. Will you attend?' Niall looked grey.

'Cat?'

'With you.'

'Okay, Niall. Where is it?'

'You're not going to like this, it's Eleven Drakes Alley.'

'Bloody hell!' she gasped. 'You're sure?' Graphic images seared through her mind. She had never forgotten those scenes of carnage.

'Absolutely. They have an IC1 male, too ill to move. They initially thought it was an overdose, but now they suspect it could be poison.'

'A squatter, I suppose? That place has been boarded up for years.'

'He's no squatter, ma'am. That's why they want you there.'

'Then show us attending.'

* * *

Bliss talked at some length with the two police officers who arrived at the covered market. They then went off to make more enquiries and she was left alone at the stall. Spooky had said to wait there and she would join her as soon as she had tied up a few loose ends, and, anyway, Bliss didn't want to go and leave all of Gill's precious things unattended. On festival days, the market stayed open till nine, and it was still heaving with people.

People dropped by to purchase the odd item, and she chatted to the other stallholders. Gill, it seemed, was generally very well liked, and Bliss began to see why her friend enjoyed this odd kind of work, it had a camaraderie about it.

If she hadn't been so worried about Gill, she would have enjoyed herself selling the brightly coloured crystals and aromatherapy oils. In her long flowing skirt and hand-knitted cardigan, she certainly looked the part.

'Am I too late for a reading?'

A rather dishevelled man was looking hopefully at her.

'Oh I'm so sorry, but Gill isn't here right now and she won't be back for a while.'

'Will she be long?' he asked, looking terribly disappointed.

'I'm afraid I don't know. I could take your name and number and get her to call you, if that would help?' she offered.

'I really wanted to talk to her today.'

The bleeding heart in Bliss felt for this man, who looked so desolate. Gill had often said that many of her clients really just wanted to talk, not to conjure up a deceased loved one but to share their memories with someone.

'Can I help?' Bliss heard herself say. 'I'm not a clairvoyant, but I could listen, if that's what you'd like.'

After a few moments of confusion, he nodded. 'If it's not asking too much. I'd be glad of someone to talk to, really I would.'

She pointed to the gazebo. 'Then come in and sit down.'

* * *

Cat drove the back-doubles to Drakes Alley, while, beside her, Nikki rang Joseph.

'Where? No! Surely not?' He sounded as shocked as she had been when Niall mentioned that address.

''Fraid so. I can hardly wait to see that dreadful place again.'

'Shall we meet you there?' he asked immediately.

'No, you get back to base, there's no one holding the fort at present. We'll keep you posted as to what we find.'

'Good luck then.' He hesitated. 'And be careful, won't you?'

'I don't expect the ghost of Alan Calder to come creeping up the staircase with a carving knife in his hand. I'll be fine.'

'You know what I mean,' Joseph said.

'We'll be careful, don't fret.' She grinned at Cat. 'We're big girls. We know how to look after ourselves.'

At least he was worried about her. It was a sign that the old Joseph was still there somewhere.

Two squad cars and an ambulance stood outside number eleven. Nikki and Cat went inside. It was too soon for protective coveralls — they weren't even sure that it was a crime scene yet, although her gut told her otherwise. She called back to the uniformed constable, 'I want access kept to a minimum. No one else inside until protective suits are available, okay?'

Then she became aware of her surroundings, and gasped in utter disbelief. 'My God! This place hasn't been touched since we left it! There's still bloodstains on the floor.'

'But why?' Cat said. 'Someone must own the place. Why leave it like this? Surely the first thing you'd do would be get it cleaned out? This is just gross!'

Nikki heard voices upstairs, so they went to see what the paramedics had found.

One of the paramedics shook her head. 'He's gone, ma'am. We were too late to save him. We've pronounced life extinct.'

Nikki stared down at the body, stark in the harsh light of a battery powered halogen lamp. She guessed him to be around thirty. He was dressed casually, and his clothes had been smart and clean — until he was taken ill. He had not had a peaceful passing.

'Any ideas about what happened to him?' she asked.

'Too soon to say for definite, but I'd guess he was poisoned. His heartbeat was all over the place, and we just couldn't get it to slow down. He arrested.' The woman looked up at Nikki. 'I had a similar case once before, although it wasn't fatal. It was an accidental overdose of digitalis.'

'Foxgloves?' Cat enquired.

'In processed form it's used to treat congestive heart failure, but the plant itself is deadly.' She looked down at her silent patient. 'Poor guy. And what on earth was he doing in a dump like this?'

Nikki would have dearly liked to know. She heard someone move behind them and spun around. 'Who the hell are you?'

'This is the guy who called the ambulance, DI Galena,' said the paramedic.

Nikki shone her torch at the figure, standing way back in the darkness and shuffling anxiously from foot to foot.

'Er, I'm Reggie Fisher, Officer. It was me who found him.'

Short and stocky, the man was dressed like some old street vendor out of Dickens.

'What were you doing in this hell-hole in the first place?' Nikki barked.

'I . . . I kind of look after it,' he stammered.

Nikki snorted. 'Well, you're not doing a particularly good job, are you? Look at it!'

'I don't mean look after in that sense. I just check that no one has broken in and that there's no squatters.'

Nikki frowned. 'Then we need to talk to you outside, Mr Fisher. This is now a crime scene. In fact, everyone out, please. We are contaminating it just by standing here. Cat, escort Mr Fisher to our car, please.'

Nikki stayed until the paramedics had gathered up all their equipment, and then followed them out of the house. It seemed disrespectful to leave the body alone in there, but there was nothing anyone could do for him now, except find out what had happened. To do that, they needed to clear the area and get forensics in.

Uniform were already setting up a log and taping off the area. Nikki impressed on them that no one should go inside until Rory Wilkinson and his cohorts arrived.

She went back to the car and took a proper look at the rather miserable looking Reggie Fisher. 'Okay, sir. From the beginning, please.'

'Well, see, the property is owned by Neville Calder, he's a developer with lots of properties. His brother was Alan Calder, who died here.'

'Alan Calder who murdered his wife here, you mean?' said Nikki.

'Um, yes, he did. But Neville, who now lives abroad, couldn't believe his brother had done it. He shut the place up and swore that no one would ever live in it again. All this street is destined for rebuilding anyway. He was just waiting for the wrecker's ball to wipe it out.'

'But to leave it like that, Mr Fisher, with his sister-in-law's blood all over it, it's unthinkable,' Cat said.

'I know, I know, and I told him that, but this is how he wanted it. Nothing to be touched, ever, was what he said.'

'So how did you know Neville Calder?' asked Nikki, eyes narrowed. 'Forgive me, but you don't look like a property tycoon.'

'I used to do odd jobs for him, and when he decided to go back to Spain for good, he hired me to keep an eye on it. And that's what I do. Just check it over every week, make sure no dossers have got in.'

Nikki frowned. 'And your visit just happened to coincide with a man dying in exactly the same spot as the unfortunate Mrs Calder?'

Reggie nodded vigorously. 'Absolutely. Except this was an extra visit. What with the festival and all these strangers in town, I've been checking it every day.'

It sounded feasible. After all, he had tried to get help for the dying man. So why did she feel that this odd little fellow was spinning her a yarn?

'Well, you'd better get off home, Mr Fisher. My detective constable here will take your details. We'd like you to come into the station tomorrow and make a formal statement. Oh, and I'd like the contact details for Neville Calder in Spain as well.'

'Of course, Inspector. He'll confirm everything, I know. He'll be furious that someone got in, let alone died there.'

Nikki began to feel sorry for Reggie Fisher. He looked pretty distraught. After this debacle, his easy little earner would no doubt dry up. Two murders in one house! Not exactly what any homeowner would want to hear.

After Cat had got all she needed, Nikki watched him walk slowly up the street and disappear round a corner. 'Cat, why do I feel there's more to this than meets the eye?'

'He's no murderer, that's for sure. But he's anxious about something, and for some reason I don't think it's the body in the bedroom.'

'He looked like he had all the worries of the world on his shoulders,' Nikki said.

'And I don't reckon he's being totally truthful with us,' Cat added.

'Well, that's your first job for tomorrow, Cat. Don't wait for him to come to us. Pay him a friendly visit and see what you can find.'

'Will do. And now we wait for forensics?'

'Yet again.' Nikki sighed.

'Do you mind if I ring Ben, boss?'

'Go ahead. I'm just about to report on this lot to Joseph, and then the super. Oh joy!' Nikki let out a loud sigh. 'This could well be the moment they pull the plug on us, and take the whole shebang to the bloody media.'

'Would they risk the chaos it would cause on the last day of Dark Greenborough?' asked Cat. 'It could turn into a bloodbath if people start to panic.'

'My only hope is that this death could be attributed to the fake booze . . . as long as no one at the hospital chooses to sell a scoop to the local rag, or worse still, one of the nationals.'

Cat suddenly brightened. 'Think positive, boss, because I've just seen something that might help.'

Nikki stared at her. 'What?'

'Look. Over that warehouse door. It's well concealed, but that's a private security camera, and there's another one, higher up and pointing down the street. That place is one of the few businesses that still run a storage facility down here, so I'm betting they work.'

'And they're right next door to number eleven, so anyone going there would have to walk right past them. Brilliant, Cat! Let the love of your life know that you are safe and well, then find out who owns that warehouse, and ask for the CCTV footage.' She grinned at Cat. 'I'm so pleased I didn't send you home!'

'Me too, ma'am. I have really good vibes about this one.'

Nikki smiled and crossed her fingers.

CHAPTER TWENTY-FIVE

'I'm back at the station and pretty well stuck here, Vinnie. Would you be able to call in?' Joseph said. He had told Nikki he'd stay put until she got back.

'Okay, be with you in ten. We aren't far away.' Vinnie ended the call, and in exactly ten minutes, the front desk sent word to say Joseph had a visitor.

'What have you done with your lady sleuths?' Joseph asked as he led Vinnie up the stairs to his office.

'Well, we've stumbled upon a scam, so Lou and Rene are out talking to people about it. We think it's just someone conning money from tourists, but it seems a bit suspicious. Then Eve and Wendy are trying to trace the history of a couple of oddballs that fit your description, but we don't know much about them.'

'Tread warily, won't you?' Joseph said. 'We have another CCTV shot of the Coachman. It shows him at the music college round about the time he must have set his timer to start the fire.'

'Any more news on those kids?' asked Vinnie.

'The remaining students are all critical,' Joseph said bluntly. 'Want a coffee?'

'No thanks. I shouldn't leave my two warriors out there on the streets for too long. I just needed to have a word with you about what you have in mind for the Coachman.' He looked long and hard at Joseph.

'I don't know, Vinnie, I really don't. I just want this finished, no more youngsters asphyxiated by poisonous gas, no innocent people dying in agony. This is a pleasant market town, not a war zone. At the moment it feels like something from the Vietnam War or the Nazi death camps. All orchestrated by one man.'

'And if that one man is terminated . . .'

'It will all be over.'

Vinnie continued to stare at him. 'But it won't, will it? For you, it will just be the start. If you exceed what's termed "reasonable force," then it's your career that will be over. Not only that, but your life with Nikki. Had you thought of that?'

Joseph didn't answer.

'Do you love Nikki?' Vinnie asked softly.

'More than anything.'

'But not more than stopping the Coachman.' Vinnie sighed. 'Listen, you are a good man, Joseph. You want this man stopped for all the right reasons, but you have to do it the right way. If not, you'll be crossing a line that you have no business crossing.'

'I don't trust the system. He cannot be allowed to slip through the net.' Joseph's jaw was set. 'He must not get away with this carnage.'

'You're a bloody good police officer, so make sure he doesn't. You know how it works. You get the right evidence. You make sure it sticks. Do your job, Joseph, and he'll go away for life. If you take matters into your own hands, it will destroy you.' Still, Vinnie stared. 'For years you've worked hard to get your head in a good place, the right place. Don't let this shit destroy you along with all those other innocents. Do it properly, Joseph Easter, or you will lose the woman you love and you'll regret it for the rest of your life.'

Joseph opened his mouth, but Vinnie was still speaking.

'You need to think carefully, Joseph. Get this wrong, and not only do you go down, but Nikki does too. And she will, because she's involved professionally and personally, and then the whole team will collapse. And what about your son-in-law? How will Niall take it, do you think? How many extra casualties do you want to add to the Coachman's headcount?'

'Stop it, Vinnie.' Joseph lowered his head into his hands. 'By the way, you left Tamsin off that list. My daughter would never, ever forgive me. Do you think I don't know all this?'

'Then think some more, mate. Weigh it all up.'

'So, I take it you won't be there for me if I need you?' Joseph whispered.

'Of course I will, you muppet. I'll make doubly sure because I'm going to do everything in my power to make Joseph Easter play by the rules.' Vinnie clapped him on the shoulder. 'You'll still get him, mate, but you'll do it properly.'

Vinnie's phone began to ring. He pulled it from his jacket pocket and stared at the display. 'It's Lou,' he murmured to Joseph, and switched on the loudspeaker.

'We've cracked it! We know about the scam — not the whole thing, but a fair bit.'

'How did you manage that?' Vinnie asked.

'We just hawked that flier around the tourists in a couple of pubs, and we got lucky.'

'Brilliant! I should leave you more often.' He grinned at Joseph. 'Where are you? I'll be finished here in a minute.'

'Heading back to the Hanged Man. We want to tell Sheila not to worry anymore. See you there?'

Vinnie ended the call. 'As soon as I see what they've uncovered, I'll pass it all on to you,' he told Joseph. 'I doubt it will be of any use to your investigation, but it might stop a few visitors getting fleeced.'

'Oh sure, getting even one shyster off the streets will be a help.'

Vinnie stood up. 'I'm on your side, Joseph, remember that. I don't want to see you flush your career and your relationship down the pan when there's another way to get the same result, okay?'

Joseph stood up and hugged Vinnie. 'I'm glad you're here.'

'Yeah, me too.' Vinnie suddenly smiled. 'Hey, I've met this great woman. She's agreed to have dinner with me next week.'

'You sly fox! Who is it? Do I know her?'

'You do, I think. She's the landlord of the Hanged Man.'

'Sheila Pearson? Wow! I'm impressed. But then what should I expect? Show you a gorgeous woman, and you're hooked.' Joseph laughed. 'You've always been the same.'

'Well, I think this one's different.' Vinnie had a faraway look in his eyes.

'I've heard that before too.'

'No, honestly. She's . . . well, different.' He grinned broadly. 'Anyway, time will tell. Catch you later.'

Vinnie went out, leaving Joseph feeling slightly more human than before. He thought of what was at stake. Vinnie had set it all out clearly, and it came down to everything he loved.

Even so, Joseph was not totally certain how he would react if he were to face the Coachman one to one. He hoped it would never come to that.

* * *

Lou and Rene looked pretty pleased with themselves.

'We put ourselves in the position of a couple of con artists out to get some takers for their "ultimate experience." Lou smiled smugly. 'So we decided to hit on the tourists, especially those who looked like they had a bit of cash to spend.'

'We were sure these people would be charging a lot for this once in a lifetime experience,' Rene added.

'And they were,' Lou chimed in. 'A fortune. The idea was to take the punters around a real crime scene. Remember the Calder murder?'

Vinnie shook his head. 'Means nothing to me.'

'The crux of it is,' said Rene, 'our con men have found an old crime scene left exactly as it was when the SOCOs moved out — bloodstains and all. The house was boarded up and no one has lived in it since.'

'The man we spoke to said his friend had done the tour and reckoned it was spooky as hell, and totally authentic,' Lou added. 'He'd expected fake blood and lots of window dressing, but it seemed to be the real thing. He thinks he'll have nightmares about it for months.'

'That's well worth telling Joseph about,' said Vinnie, grabbing his phone. 'Crafty sods! I wonder how they came up with that one?'

'Our informant's friend said that the older guy who guided them through the house, a funny little chap in Dickensian clothing, was very knowledgeable about the murder. He reckoned it was worth every penny.'

Vinnie laughed. 'Well, that's a first! A con trick that's value for money. Joseph will like that.'

As he talked, Vinnie's gaze strayed to Sheila, busy behind the bar. She saw him look, and gave him a smile. If only he could complete the sale of his business, then he'd have more time to spend in Greenborough.

There was a long silence.

'Joseph? We thought it was a bit of a rarity, you know, a scam the punters thought was worth the money. Bet you don't get many of those.'

More silence. Eventually Joseph said, 'The thing is, we've had another death, and it took place at an old untouched crime scene. I'm thinking it's the same place.'

'Oh shit! Well, we still have the flier, and there's a telephone number on it. We've tried ringing it with no luck, but you can trace the owner, can't you?'

'If it's registered, sure. Give me the number, Vinnie — oh, and tell the girls great work.'

Vinnie hung up, frowning. Another death. That wouldn't help Joseph to get out of his present frame of mind.

He rubbed thoughtfully at his chin. All he could do was stick close to his old comrade, watch his back, and if possible, take the flak for him. He and Joseph had been in some very dangerous situations, and survived. Hopefully that luck would hold out a little longer. He glanced across to the bar. It had better, for right now Vinnie Silver had plans.

* * *

The market square was a blaze of colour. In the midst of the funfair, a stage had been set up and various local singers and dancers were getting a chance to show what they could do. Barely audible beneath the thud of the bass, the singers belted out old favourites as if they were performing at a mammoth karaoke.

'My ears hurt,' shouted Eve. 'Let's get out of here.'

Having drawn a blank with Amos and Edward, they had decided to try and beard the lion in his den, and interview Edward Richmond in person.

It hadn't been difficult to locate the house, but after this propitious start their luck fizzled out. In stark contrast to the neat houses that flanked it, number thirteen was a dreary, unkempt place. It was also shrouded in darkness, and if Edward was in, he wasn't answering the door.

Almost relieved, they took to traipsing around the streets, watching and listening, and growing increasingly disheartened with every step they took.

'I think we should tie up with the others,' said Wendy morosely. 'We are getting nowhere roaming around aimlessly like this. I reckon this search needs some structure, don't you?'

'Dead right,' muttered Eve. 'I'll ring them and find out where they are.' She took out her phone. 'Should have known. They're in a pub, and they want us to join them.'

'Now I really wish I wasn't driving,' said Wendy.

Eve didn't feel like a drink. She didn't even feel like pushing her way into a crowded bar. She was beginning to understand what Nikki must be going through. Terrible things were happening right under their noses, but in the chaos of the festival they could find nothing to help them. And they were of no use to Nikki.

At least the others were in a more positive frame of mind, which lifted Eve's spirits a little. She also noticed the signals that Vinnie and Sheila were giving out, which was good news indeed. Vinnie wasn't the sort of person who would be content with living alone, and Eve knew how hard it was to make a new life after years of active duty.

'It's really weird though, isn't it?' Lou was saying. 'We uncover a scam, and the killer chooses that very place to commit another murder.'

Eve's eyes lit up. She'd had an idea. 'Guys! What if he took the tour?' She turned to Vinnie. 'How much do the police know about what was going on in that house?'

'Only what Lou and Rene discovered, I think. Do you want me to ring Joseph?'

'No, I'll ring Nikki.' Her mind buzzed. This could be important.

When Nikki answered, Eve told her what she suspected had happened. 'So, if you could get hold of whoever organised these tours, he might recall someone who resembled the Coachman.'

After a lengthy silence, Nikki said, 'Ah, that would explain it.'

'Explain what?'

'We know exactly who was organising those trips, and where he lives. Cat and I will be going straight round there to pay him a call. Thanks, Mum, that could be a real break.' She ended the call.

Vinnie nodded. 'Quick thinking, Eve. I think you've hit the nail on the head. The killer must have got hold of one of those fliers and decided to go and take a look.'

'It could be his first big mistake,' said Eve. 'I can't wait to hear what Nikki says.'

* * *

'Ben's chasing up the owners of that warehouse, boss, and then, if the CCTV system is working, he'll pick up the film straightaway.'

'Excellent. Meanwhile you and I will question Mr Reggie Fisher about his unofficial use of Neville Calder's ill-fated property. Now we know why he looked so bloody miserable.'

'His little money-spinner had just gone down the pan,' grinned Cat. 'Ah, shame.'

Reggie answered the door still wearing his old-fashioned street vendor's outfit. He took one look at them and sighed. 'You'd better come in.'

The living room was clean enough but it was tired, and everything in it had seen better days. Nikki and Cat seated themselves on an uncomfortable faded leather sofa while Reggie pulled up a dining chair.

'I don't think you've told us the whole story about Eleven Drakes Alley, have you, sir?'

Reggie closed his eyes for a second. 'What do you want to know?'

'Well, for starters, you weren't checking on the place for Mr Calder, were you? You were taking some bloodthirsty punters on the "Ultimate Dark Greenborough Experience" if I'm not mistaken. And charging a lot of money for it too.'

Reggie Fisher looked worn out. 'It's true. I had the idea that some of those thrill-seeking tourists would be keen to see a real crime scene, and would pay for the privilege.'

'So, would I be right in thinking you did a few tours last night?'

'I did. And they loved it. Not one complaint. They all said it was real value for money.'

'And you carried the whole thing off on your own, sir?' asked Cat. 'That's impressive.'

'Totally. All my idea. It was paying off, too, until someone decided to rain on my parade.'

Nikki looked at him thoughtfully. Who was he protecting? There was no way this little guy could have produced a flier like the one Eve had described to her, *and* touted for business, then gathered up his tour party, gained access, and done the tour, all single-handed.

'Okay, Reggie, I'm going to be straight with you. When you called that ambulance, you knew you'd be scuppered, didn't you? But you still did the right thing. Plenty of villains would have legged it out of there like greased lightning, but you tried to help that poor guy.' She looked at him seriously. 'It was no overdose, you know. We think he was murdered.'

Reggie's pale face bleached a shade whiter. 'Murdered?' He swallowed hard. 'I had nothing to do with that, I swear to God!'

'I don't think you did. But I do think that you took the murderer on your guided tour last night.'

'Jesus! Oh fuck!' He stared at her wide-eyed. 'Sorry, lady, I didn't mean to swear . . .'

'Forget it.' She leaned forward. 'But listen to me, Reggie. Frankly, your little scheme, and I have to be honest, it was a good 'un, is of no interest to me. There are far worse things going on in this town right now than a few idiots getting parted from their money by a local entrepreneur. You even had the owner's permission to be in that property, although admittedly not to use it for a freak show, but that's neither here nor there. What I want to know is, was there anyone on one of your trips last night that looked like this?'

Nikki thrust a photo at him, showing the Coachman, taken from the CCTV footage in the covered market.

'I, I'm not sure . . .'

Cat intervened. 'Come on, Reggie! Who was with you last night? You didn't pull this off alone. You had help, didn't you? Perhaps that person might recognise this man. We are talking murder, remember.'

'No, it was just me, really . . .'

'I helped him, officers.' A figure appeared in the doorway. 'We did it together. I'm Tyrone Fisher. Reggie is my dad.'

'Son! No!'

'It's all right, Dad, honestly. Thanks for wanting to keep me out of it. I appreciate what you are trying to do, but we were in it together. You're not taking the blame alone.'

Nikki looked at the young man and nodded. 'Thank you for coming forward.' She handed him the picture. 'Did you see this man in any of the groups, Tyrone?'

He looked at it. 'Yes, I did, on the last trip. I didn't like him.'

'Why?'

'He gave me the willies. Everyone else was, well, creeped out by the place, you know, lots of gasps and nervous laughs, quite a few questions and a lot of whispering. This bloke,' Tyrone scowled, 'he never said a word, but he hung about like he was drinking everything in. I practically had to force him out of the bedroom where Mrs Calder's body was found. He really was one spooky guy.'

'Would you recognise him again?'

'Oh yes, no doubt about that. He gave off something unpleasant. I'd know him anywhere.'

'And you, Reggie?' Cat asked.

Tyrone answered for him. 'My dad's not a bad man. He's made some bad decisions, but he's not a crook. He was a cockney barrow boy, then worked the street markets. He's a showman, Detective, bloody good at his spiel. When he gets into a part, he doesn't notice the audience. I'm sure he wouldn't have noticed if Elvis had turned up for the tour.'

Nikki smiled. 'Could you give us a description of the man, Tyrone? Maybe come to the station and work with one of our officers to make up an identikit likeness of him?'

'Yeah, of course. Now?'

'If you would? We need to act fast, and you're our best hope.' Nikki stood up.

Tyrone pulled on a jacket, and then turned to his white-faced father. 'Don't worry, Dad. We're okay. Understand? We're okay.'

Nikki thought the little figure in the old-fashioned clothes was going to cry. There were clearly issues between father and son, but right now she had a killer to catch, so she'd probably never know what they were.

As they left the little house, Cat's mobile rang. 'Ben's got the footage, and he says it's looking good. He and Dave are going through it now.'

'Then let's get a wriggle on. With that, and Tyrone here, we are getting somewhere at last.'

CHAPTER TWENTY-SIX

They got back to a station redolent with the aroma of pizza, reminding Nikki of how long it had been since she'd last eaten. But as soon as she saw Joseph, she forgot her hunger. He looked positively haunted.

She summoned him to her office. Hardly waiting for the door to close, she grabbed his arm. 'Talk to me, Joseph.'

She could see the shutters come down.

'It's just the frustration of still having no idea who or where he is. We are all feeling it, Nikki, not just me.' His tone was light and reasonable, but it was much too glib.

'But it's just you that I'm worried about right now, Joseph.'

'Then don't.' He lowered his voice. 'I'm fine, my darling, just worked up about what he's capable of, that's all.'

She wanted to believe him. They'd been through so much together that she knew him intimately, and she couldn't get past the fact that a barrier had arisen between them. It was as if he had stepped into another room and locked her out.

She let go of his arm. This was pointless. 'I'm hungry,' she said abruptly. 'If you're not going to be straight with me, we might as well eat.' She turned to leave, but he pulled her back.

'I love you, Nikki. You have to believe that.'

'I do. That's why I don't understand why you're being so . . .' She shrugged.

'Please, stop trying to analyse me. I promise that the moment he's off the streets, I'll be myself again. I just can't seem to focus on anything other than seeing his reign of terror brought to a close.'

Every copper in Greenborough felt like that, but with Joseph it went deeper.

Then it fell into place. He hadn't finished his last statement. What he meant to say was that he couldn't focus on anything other than seeing his reign of terror brought to a close *no matter how that conclusion was achieved.*

Nikki stared at him. His expression told her everything. She was right.

'Please, for all our sakes, don't do anything rash.' She knew she was begging, and she hated herself for it. It wasn't Nikki Galena's way. But she'd never loved anyone the way she loved Joseph Easter.

'He has to be neutralised.'

His tone was cold, and it sank into her like a shaft of ice.

'We *will* stop him. The way we always do. By the book.'

He shook his head. 'I hope so, I really do.'

'There's no other way, Joseph. You taught me that. I thought otherwise once, and it was you that showed me how wrong I was, remember?' Nikki had been there, in the place he was now, and had come through, with his strength to guide her. Now the roles were reversed. Could she be for him what he had been for her? That lodestar? She really didn't know.

Wordless, they faced each other. Then, still in silence, they opened the door and went out to the CID room.

She knew what to do now. It was the only thing possible. She must get to the Coachman before Joseph did. She must read him his rights and slap the cuffs on him.

She snatched up a slice of pizza from an open box, bit into it angrily and called out, 'Okay, guys, the CCTV from the warehouse — what have we got?'

* * *

As the mayhem intensified on the streets of Greenborough, the Coachman roamed restlessly in and out of bars, between sideshows and fairground attractions, trying to regain his earlier optimism. For some reason, perhaps because he knew he only had one more day before the festival ended, he felt unsettled and apprehensive. He should have been delighted with himself following his bonus performance in the house of horrors on Ferry Street. It hadn't been easy, particularly getting the timing right. It had been hard to get his chosen victim drunk enough to accompany him through what had been a barricaded window into the house. But he'd succeeded, and managed to administer the poison in perfect time for the arrival of the little cockney's group of tourist ghouls.

Now he must concentrate on his next planned death. As usual, he had already chosen the victim and was simply waiting for the appropriate time to make his move.

He padded on, his boots clicking on the cobbled streets, almost unaware of the tide of sinister characters dancing around him.

He should be exhilarated by now. This was usually the best part, the time when he came to exert his power. For that was what lay behind it all: control. It had been taken away from him once, and he intended never to lose it again. With absolute mastery, he had controlled every movement of his performance. Meanwhile, the police still had no idea who he was.

He walked down a narrow alleyway into a small square, lit up with fairy lights. There, in the central garden, a man wearing clothes very similar to his own was telling ghost stories with a Greenborough setting. His audience gazed up at him, spellbound.

The little tableau had the peaceful, distant air of a bedtime story, and so he tarried for a while before drifting off towards the river. He stood on the bank watching the coloured lights shimmer on the dark, oily waters, and came to a decision. There would be no more killing after this next one. He would stick to his original plan, carry out what he had planned for tomorrow, and then, as the firework display heralded the close of Dark Greenborough for another year, he would slip quietly away.

At some point the police would work out who had carried out the murders, but by then he would be gone, reinventing himself yet again.

Decision made, he focused his mind on the next killing. His victim should be a pretty woman, he supposed. But they were all, bar one, mere random choices, short straws in his deadly game of chance.

* * *

Rory Wilkinson was alone when he went into 11 Drakes Alley. He had been there years before, and the memories flooded back as he entered the hall and began to climb the stairs. At least this time he was prepared. On the last occasion he hadn't known what he'd find. He could still feel his horror upon realising that Alan Calder had been crawling up those same stairs, a knife in his bloodied hand, with the intention of finishing off his mortally wounded wife.

The malignant atmosphere of the place hadn't dissipated.

He found the man lying in the very spot where Nicole Calder had bled to death. What was the story behind this one?

Rory had brought two halogen lamps and more would arrive with the team. He surveyed the room. It was the crime scene from hell, a dumping ground for forensic evidence. Old stuff from the first two deaths, the rubbish left by the man who had been keeping an eye on the property, the visitors that in the past two days had stumbled up the stairs and into that room, all covered with the general filth and decay of neglect and the passing of time.

Sifting through it all would be a long job, keeping his technicians tied up for days, maybe weeks, so the only way to help the police find the perpetrator would be to concentrate on the body and a small area around it.

The victim was the most uncontaminated thing in the whole house. Rory had obtained the DNA of the paramedics who tried to save him, so anything else he found on the man could be of interest. Up to now their killer — what did they call him? The Coachman? — had been particularly clever, but as time went on even the most meticulous murderer got careless. Everyone left a trace eventually. Rory just had to find it.

He looked closely at the body. Another case of poisoning for sure, and from what he had been told on the way here, it had all the hallmarks of digitalis. The victim had been sweating profusely, he had vomited and showed signs of respiratory paralysis, and his heart rhythm had been in freefall.

He was inclined to agree. Digitalis, either in the form of a drug, or from the plant itself, the foxglove. But Rory trusted nothing until he had scientific evidence in front of him.

He stepped back. Time to call in the troops.

* * *

Niall had enjoyed having Skipper with him, but was nonetheless relieved that Tamsin had picked him up and taken him home with her. Having a loved one in the town while a killer stalked the streets was a constant worry. Tamsin was strong-willed, and insisted that she wouldn't be stopped from doing what she wanted to do because of some madman. If she cowered at home in fear of what might happen, he would have won, and she was having none of that. Niall admired her bravery, but he also feared for her. Anyway, she was home now, which was one less thing to worry about. He sent a quick text to his father-in-law, just to put Joseph's mind at rest, and then returned to what seemed like the longest shift in history. He should have gone home hours ago, but couldn't possibly walk out when they had another death to contend with.

Not only that, he was getting increasingly concerned about the missing clairvoyant. One of his officers had spoken to someone who had seen her hurrying away from the covered market as if the hounds of hell were after her, and then nothing. No one would run off and leave their day's takings sitting on their empty stand unless something serious had happened. While he was pondering this, he received a call from Tamsin. She sounded frightened.

'Niall, I need your help, I'm worried sick.'

'What's wrong? Tell me!'

'It's Ellie. She never got home. I've just had her partner on the phone asking if she's still with me.'

Okay it was selfish, but Niall couldn't help feeling relieved. 'Tell me what you did in the afternoon, and when you saw her last.'

'Well, we met up a bit late. As you know, I had trouble finding her, and the mobile signal is poor in some parts of the town. We went to several of the attractions like we'd planned, and then grabbed a snack at the Hanged Man. I came to collect Skip from you, and Ellie went back to get her car.'

'Where was it parked, Tam?' he asked, grabbing a notepad.

'West Street car park. She has a Ford Fiesta. I don't know the number, but it's bright red.'

'I'll check it out. What's her surname by the way?'

'Stevens.'

He scribbled it down. 'Tam, could you ring her partner and get the vehicle registration number for me?'

'I'll do it straightaway. Niall? You don't think—'

'Sweetheart, let's not jump to conclusions. She could easily have met another friend and forgotten to phone her partner. Or her car could have broken down.'

'But she's not answering her phone.'

'Get her reg number, Tam, and I'll get someone around to West Street, okay?'

He stared at his phone. Another woman missing? He didn't like the sound of this at all.

Niall hurried from his office. 'I want a car to West Street car park right away! Who's free?'

An older officer called Bill Brittain raised his hand. 'Show me attending, Sarge. What's up?'

'We're looking for a bright red Ford Fiesta. I'll radio you the registration as soon as I get it. Woman by the name of Ellie Stevens didn't arrive home.'

'On my way, Sarge.'

Niall watched him go, anxiety crawling slowly up his spine. Not another one, please.

* * *

There were now two whiteboards standing against the wall. One showed the victims — a gallery of lively, smiling faces, and below, forensics' graphic illustrations of the horrors perpetrated on them. The second board was decorated with a row of CCTV stills across the top, all showing their target, the Coachman, clad in his long dark coat and boots. Below these were pictures of men in their forties and fifties, all possible candidates for the role.

Morgan Flint read out the names in a murmur. Not being a local, none of them meant anything to her, yet there was a chance that one of them knew as much about Creep, the Victorian murderer, as she did, possibly a lot more. 'What about their alibis?' she asked Nikki.

'They've been hard to verify what with the chaos of the festival, plus some of the poisons could have been administered some time before they actually died. We have officers out talking to them and checking their movements, but although most were where they say they were, we can't pin the times down.' Nikki shook her head. 'Not one of them is watertight.'

'Connor is waiting for some more information on our historical murderer, Creep. I'm anxious to know if there was something specific about that man that brought him to the Coachman's attention.' Morgan couldn't shake the feeling that Creep was the key to this modern-day killing spree. 'I've got someone at HQ investigating all the major internet sites dealing with the post-Ripper era, and targeting Creep's murders in particular.' She looked at Nikki. 'I hope I'm not wasting time following the wrong track here, but my gut tells me there's a link, and it's an important one.'

Nikki nodded. 'Then you have to go with it. I would.' She stared at the suspects. 'It could be one of them, or someone we've not even considered. Right now, Dave and Ben are digging out more CCTV images from the warehouse in Drakes Alley. We should have something very soon.'

'And your young chancer is helping to produce an E-Fit picture? If he has a good memory and can convey what he recalls, that could be vital.' Though people's recall of faces and their ability to describe them was often vague, to say the least, they used a library of different physiognomies, and special software that adapted these to fit the witness's description. It took time and patience, but could be remarkably accurate. They had caught killers before thanks to an E-Fit image.

Nikki yawned. It was catching. They would have to call it a day before long. Even seasoned detectives needed food and sleep. 'I'm just waiting to see what kind of masterpiece Tyrone Fisher produces, then I'm off,' Nikki said. 'When we have an investigation like this running, I feel guilty every time I walk out of this place, but I also know the dangers of over-exhausting yourself.'

'Wise woman.' Morgan smiled at her fellow DI. She rather liked Nikki Galena, who had a reputation for being difficult to work with. Well, Morgan had found her most accommodating. She got the impression that even if Nikki Galena hated her guts, she'd keep a lid on it for the sake of taking the Coachman off the streets. That was professionalism, and Morgan Flint admired it in her.

She turned to go. 'I'll update you before I leave.'

Nikki smiled, 'Me too. And, Morgan? Thanks for all you're doing.'

Morgan shrugged. 'You're welcome, although it feels like naff all, as my son would say. But we'll get something on the bastard soon, I *know* it.'

'Good enough for me. See you later.'

* * *

PC Bill Brittain called Niall from West Street. 'Car's still here. Engine stone cold and the parking ticket ran out hours ago.'

Niall felt his stomach lurch. 'Thanks, Bill. I'm going to need you to go and talk to the owner's partner, but tactfully. Don't put the fear of God in him, just sound out her normal routines and stuff like does she often forget to ring him, or get home late. Okay with that?'

Bill confirmed that he was and asked for the address.

Next, Niall called Tamsin to ask her what she could tell him about her friend. The last thing he wanted was to see Ellie Stevens's face up on CID's whiteboard.

* * *

Dave squinted at the pictures from the warehouse cameras in Drakes Alley. Fisher and Son were clearly visible, ushering their little gaggle of tourists across the road and into number eleven.

'Dave?'

He looked up from the screen to see one of the uniformed constables who had been with him at Cressy Old Hall. 'Stewart. Hello, mate, how can I help you?'

'Not sure if this is important or not, but just before I left the Old Hall, the groundsman, that bloke called Den, he told me to tell you that he'd seen someone driving out of the grounds on three separate nights, after dark, and using the estate vehicle.'

'Estate vehicle?'

Stewart nodded. 'Yeah, it's a pickup. Anyone who needs it uses it to carry stuff around. Thing is, only his lordship, Arthur Keats and Den himself are insured to drive it.'

'So who did Den think was at the wheel?'

'He couldn't tell, just that it was a man. It was dark on each occasion. He reckoned it was odd, that's all. It's not the sort of truck you'd go out for a spin in, it's pretty well trashed from all the rough usage. Oh, and he said they turned out of the drive and went in the direction of the town, and it was always back by morning.' Stewart shrugged. 'He just thought you ought to know.'

'I suppose anyone could have borrowed it. Did he say where they keep the keys?' Dave asked.

'In the garage, on a hook just inside the door. Everyone knew apparently, so anyone there could have pinched it for a few hours.' Stewart turned to go. 'He said he'll keep an eye open tonight and tomorrow and ring you direct if he sees it being taken out again.'

'Thanks, Stewart. It might mean something.'

Dave turned back to his monitor. As soon as he'd finished here, he'd get onto Clive and see whether he'd given anyone permission to use the pickup. Or maybe he'd take this bit of information directly to the boss?

Dave desperately wanted to go home. He yawned, and flexed his tired shoulders. Staring at a screen like this was almost hypnotic, and he had to struggle to keep his eyes open. He was definitely too old for all this. Then he thought of Norma Warden, and shook himself awake. He paused the film. He mustn't let her down. He was being weak and selfish. All he needed was a night's kip and he'd be fine, but Norma would never wake up again. He stood up. A strong coffee was in order.

As he waited at the vending machine, he thought again about who might have been leaving Cressy Old Hall in the pickup after nightfall. Den was right, it was odd. Everyone who lived on the estate had their own car, you couldn't have coped without one.

He took his drink back to his desk and resumed the search. He had reached the point where Tyrone was checking Drakes Alley for passers-by. The young man looked both ways, then ducked back inside and ushered his punters out, a few at a time. The CCTV showed them scurrying away from the house of death and disappearing down the side streets.

He waited, holding his breath, for the Coachman to make his exit. And there he was, the last one to leave.

Dave froze the image and moved forward frame by frame, but the camera, angled to look down on the road, showed only his outline. Dave was certain it was him, but once again his features were obscured. He watched the man walk slowly out of camera range. He seemed to be deep in thought.

He heard a curse from Ben's side of the room. 'Sodding head down again. And I was so certain we'd get him on the way out!'

'No better on this camera, mate.' Dave sighed and his tiredness returned. 'Still, at least we know he was definitely there.'

'I guess,' growled Ben, 'but I'm not getting too much comfort from that right now.' He smacked the desk with his palm. 'Fuck it! No use even trying to follow him from now on because the moment he gets back onto the main drag, it's like sodding Mardi Gras and there'll be no hope of spotting him.'

'Then it's time to get home, boys.'

Neither of them had seen Nikki, looking surprisingly energised, enter the room.

'I mean it. Hop it. Grab some rest, and come back in early, okay?'

Dave threw her a rueful smile. 'There's nothing I'd rather do, ma'am, but I've just heard something that I think you need to know.' He told her about the pickup and its mysterious excursions. 'Should I contact Clive?'

She thought for a moment. 'Yes, Dave, please do, and get the licence number of that vehicle. If Cressy-Lawson didn't give his permission, then someone was using it illegally. It's more mind-numbing work for someone, but if we have the reg number and the time it headed into town, vehicle recognition could pick it up from the cameras on the main road into the centre of town.' She looked pensive. 'Ring him now, Dave.'

Clive answered after several rings. He didn't sound quite himself, and Dave wondered if he'd been drinking.

'The pickup? No, Dave. I certainly didn't give anyone permission to use it, and when I find out who it was I'll give them a piece of my mind. It's not there for all and sundry to use whenever they feel like it!'

'I suggest you don't leave the keys in the garage any more, Clive. Keep them with you and if anyone needs to use it, they'll have to ask.'

'Thanks for the heads-up, I'm going down there right now.' Clive sounded less angry. 'I can't imagine who would want to use that old gas guzzler. She's seen better days, and I really need to replace her, but . . .'

'I know, yet another expense,' finished off Dave. 'Anyway, could you give me the licence number? We're going to run a check and see if we can pick it up entering town.'

'Why go to all that bother just for—?' Clive stopped. 'Oh no. You think this has something to do with Norma's death, don't you, Dave?'

'It's possible. We have to check every little detail, no matter how insignificant it seems. I'll keep you updated, okay?'

Dave took the reg number to Nikki. 'Taken without the owner's consent, ma'am.'

'Right, I'll get on to the database. The only ANPR cameras are on the main A roads into town. If he came in by the back doubles, we won't catch him, but if he used the most direct route we might get lucky.'

Dave knew where the automated number plate recognition cameras were. He hoped Nikki was right and the driver had used the main road.

'Thank you, Dave. You can leave that with me, now out of here!'

CHAPTER TWENTY-SEVEN

'We've got a name!' Morgan Flint and Connor Hale burst into Nikki's office.

Nikki sat up straight. 'A name?'

Morgan's ice-blue eyes gleamed with excitement. 'We've just had the intel that we were waiting for. People doing multiple searches into Creep, the Victorian serial poisoner.'

Connor handed Nikki a file. 'Our intelligence officers have contacted internet sites, reference libraries, university libraries, Amazon and a whole lot of out-of-print book suppliers and asked them to provide us with the information we required. They all supplied it, apart from one that required a court order. We now know that, for a period of two years, one man was conducting exhaustive research into post-Ripper crime, including the history of the man called Creep.'

Nikki stared at the name — Dean Kennedy. It meant nothing to her.

'He was a local, Nikki,' added Morgan. 'Lived in the village of Cartoft, near Saltern-le-Fen. He finished his research and upped and moved out, but we don't know where. This has to be the connection.'

'Is he known to us? Is there anything on the PNC about him?' asked Nikki.

'Nothing. We are trying to find a photo, but so far we've come up with zilch.' Morgan exhaled. 'We'll take it further in the morning, when more people are available to take our calls. Time for food and sleep, I think.'

Nikki stared long and hard at the name. Was this Dean Kennedy the Coachman?

Joseph stuck his head around her door. 'Tyrone has completed the E-fit, ma'am. Can I show you?'

'Of course. Bring it in, Joseph.'

The facial composite was remarkably lifelike.

'I wouldn't say that was any of the suspects on the white-board, would you?' Nikki said. 'Shit.'

The others let out grunts of dismay.

Only Joseph didn't seem completely disheartened. 'People can alter their appearance quite easily,' he said thoughtfully, 'especially a middle-aged man attending a fes-tival where everyone is dressed up. The Coachman probably took great pains to disguise himself.'

'True,' agreed Connor. 'Hair colour, contact lenses, facial hair, clever make-up and wadding packed in the mouth can alter the features completely.'

'And even though Tyrone Fisher appears to have done a good job, he only saw the Coachman in torchlight,' Morgan added. 'He might not be good at description from memory, plenty are hopeless. We all know that.'

Nikki was still disappointed that they hadn't found a match with one of their suspects. 'I think Morgan's right. Time to go home. Tomorrow, we'll get Spooky to run one of her facial recognition software programmes to compare this guy's bone structure with the pictures we have of the main suspects. But right now, let's throw in the towel.'

As everyone traipsed out of her office, Nikki looked again at the name. Dean Kennedy. The fact that he was local and had shown particular interest in an historical murderer who had used the same methods as the Coachman made him a person of interest. And she was very interested indeed as to why he'd left so suddenly. She rubbed her eyes. This was one for tomorrow.

* * *

Spooky sat with Bliss inside Gill's gazebo tent. The market was closing down and packing up, and they were at a loss as to what to do.

'We'll take her cash tin and her tarot cards,' said Bliss. 'Everything else will have to stay here until tomorrow. Peggy, the lady on the stall next door, told me that the market is locked at night, and they have security guards on duty. Everything will be quite safe.'

'But where is Gill?' Spooky said helplessly. 'Should we start ringing round the hospitals?'

'The police have already done that, babe. That nice constable who saw me earlier told me.'

'Does Gill have our address?'

'Yes, and both our mobile numbers. I gave her yours as well as mine years ago, just in case she ever needed me and mine was switched off or had no signal.' Bliss stood up. 'We better get home. There's nothing more we can do here, and the police are still looking for her.'

Spooky picked up the cash tin. 'Is there a bag I can use? I don't fancy carrying this through the crowded streets.'

From her shoulder bag, Bliss produced a reusable supermarket bag covered in pictures of chilli peppers. 'This do?'

'Perfect.' Spooky put the tin and the box of tarot cards inside, 'Best not place temptation in someone's way.'

'We need to get back anyway. Poor Fox will be crossing his legs.' Bliss zipped up the gazebo.

'And he'll be hungry, poor little sod. He should have had his supper an hour ago. Come on, let's go.'

With a last backward glance at the empty stall, the two women made their way to the entrance gates. Along the road, Spooky glanced at Bliss. She was holding up well, considering how worried she was, but Spooky dreaded her reaction should the news about Gill be bad. Maybe she'd been working too long with the police, but it really wasn't looking good.

Bliss was smiling at her. 'I forgot to tell you. I did a bit of fortune-telling myself while I was waiting for you.'

'You what?'

'This guy was desperate to talk to Gill, and I remembered her telling me that a lot of people just need to talk rather than consult the cards, and he seemed so sad, I thought . . .'

'You didn't! Bliss! What were you thinking? There is a killer out there, and our friend is missing!' Spooky saw Bliss's hurt expression. 'I'm sorry. It's just that I love you and I'm frightened for you. You are such a bloody trusting soul!'

'Maybe I shouldn't have told you,' murmured Bliss.

'Of course you should. And I'm sorry I shouted at you, but, oh dear . . . you are exasperating sometimes.' Spooky took her arm and squeezed it.

'You wouldn't have me any other way though?' Bliss looked at her from beneath lowered eyelashes.

'No, I wouldn't, but, please, think before you talk to strange men!'

'You didn't see him. He was so distressed, and he really did just want to talk. He was no threat, honestly.' Bliss took hold of her hand. 'I'm a pretty good judge of character. Anyway, he was at a crossroads in his life, and he had no family member or close friend to offload to. I hope I helped, just a little bit.'

Spooky sighed and shook her head, 'I'm sure you did, sweetheart. But . . .'

'I know, I know. I'll leave it to Gill next time.' Her grip tightened. 'They will find her, won't they?'

Spooky had no idea what to say.

* * *

Before they left the station, Nikki asked the two detectives on night shift to see if they could find anything on a man named

Dean Kennedy, who had lived in Cedar Way, Cartoft. It was all she could do until the morning.

She and Joseph drove home in near silence. Two women unaccounted for, one who had approached them with information about the Coachman, and the other a friend of Tamsin, Joseph's daughter.

'With every hour that goes by with no news, it looks blacker,' Joseph muttered. 'And all we have is a picture of him that means sod bloody all.'

There was nothing more to say.

It was little better at home. For the first time since she'd known him, Joseph failed to produce a meal.

At around eleven, Vinnie rang. Normally, Joseph would have put the call on loudspeaker. Tonight he kept the conversation to himself.

'They did well with that flier,' Nikki said after he hung up, 'and trust Mum to wonder if the Coachman took the Fishers' tour. I think I'll give her a goodnight bell.'

'Then I'll go and grab a shower before bed.' And taking his wine glass with him, Joseph was gone.

Eve answered instantly. 'We've just got home. Not as productive a day as we'd hoped, but finding the "Ultimate Dark Greenborough Experience" was better than nothing.'

'It was brilliant, Mum. You haven't lost your touch, have you?'

'I hope I never will. I could cope with a bit of arthritis, but a slow brain would kill me.'

Nikki lowered her voice. 'Mum? Can I ask you something?'

'I was waiting for this. Is it Joseph? Or Vinnie?'

'Both. But what do you know that I don't?'

Eve laughed. 'Nothing, sweetheart, just a vague suspicion that they are keeping secrets from us. Vinnie is veering between euphoria whenever he sees Sheila Pearson, and deep anxiety, usually after talking to your Joseph.'

'I'm not surprised about the anxiety. I feel exactly the same.' Nikki wanted to tell her mother everything, but she was worried that Joseph would come back downstairs. So she made do with, 'He's shutting me out, Mum, and it's worrying me sick. He's always been so open with me.'

'When did it start?' asked her mother.

Nikki considered this. 'I think it was after the news of the fire at the college.'

Her mother said nothing for a while, then, 'That would coincide with his calls to Vinnie. Nikki, I think you need to cut him some slack. There always comes a time when we come across something that affects us so deeply that we don't know how to handle it. Maybe that fire was Joseph's emotional breaking point.'

Nikki thought about this. The first to die was a teenage girl. Hannah. Yes, Joseph had made connections, hadn't he? A young girl. And Tamsin. Nikki breathed out slowly. 'Mum, you're right.'

'I'm going to talk to Vinnie. Only he knows for certain, and I have an idea he might be relieved to share some of the burden.'

Her mother was a consummate diplomat, but Nikki couldn't help saying, 'For heaven's sake, don't let Joseph find out that I've spoken to you.'

'If there's one thing in this world that I know how to do, my love, it's watch my words. I won't need to mention you. Now, get some sleep, darling. And try to understand that sometimes the person we love most has obligations that even love cannot transcend.'

Nikki knew that Eve was thinking about her father, and the agonising decision he'd had to make.

'I love you, Mum.'

'I love you too. Try not to worry. It will come right in the end.'

Nikki hoped her mother would be proved right, but even though she now knew the probable reason for Joseph's reticence, she was scared. What might he be driven to do?

* * *

Vinnie and Eve sat in the kitchen. The others were all watching television in the lounge and having a nightcap.

'I'd better get back to the hotel,' said Vinnie. 'I need a shower and some sleep.'

'I just wish we had room for you here, but I'm afraid the chapel isn't geared for more than four people at a time, and I wouldn't insult you by making you sleep on the sofa.'

Vinnie grinned. 'I'm used to hotels, Eve. With all the travelling I've done, they're a second home to me.'

'All that will change if you sell the security business, won't it?'

'It's time for a change. I'm ready for one.'

Eve thought he looked rather wistful. 'I understand that feeling. It's hard to settle after the kind of life we had.'

'I can adapt. I've always been this way. I like fresh fields every so often, even if there are times when it's hard to get your head in the right place.'

'And Joseph?' She threw in, 'Is his head in the right place?'

Vinnie seemed to grow tense. Then he sagged. 'I'm worried sick about him.'

'You aren't alone. My daughter is far from unobservant, you know. Joseph is causing her a lot of anguish at a time when she needs him to be supporting her, not shutting her out.' She took another sip of her drink. 'I love him to bits, but Nikki should be focusing on catching the poisoner, not worrying about Joseph. That kind of distraction could be very dangerous. And what is happening to the gentle, reasonable peacemaker anyway?' She stared at him. 'I know he's talked to you, Vinnie. Should we be really concerned about his state of mind?'

Vinnie fiddled with a coaster. 'He's afraid that even if they catch the Coachman, the system will let them down and he'll either walk, or finish up in a psychiatric hospital, rather than the Cat A prison where he belongs.'

'And he's willing to risk everything he's done with his life and all the people who love him to see this man, well, terminated?'

'That's how it seems to me. I've told him how crazy it is, but, Eve, he's my comrade, my brother, my friend. Whatever I think of his decision, I cannot walk away from him.'

'I understand, but if that time comes, don't ruin your own life. Just help him make the right choice, if you can.'

'That's the plan. Although I'm hoping that someone else gets to the Coachman first.'

You and me both, thought Eve. Because the aftermath of Joseph doing something rash was almost too much to consider.

CHAPTER TWENTY-EIGHT

At around three in the morning, Spooky and Bliss were woken by the sound of the phone ringing.

Spooky answered, and was astonished to hear Gill's voice.

She sounded shaky. 'I'm so sorry. I hate to ask at this hour, but could you come and fetch me? I'm in the A&E department at Saltern-le-Fen Hospital.'

Bliss took the phone from Spooky. 'Are you alright, Gill? What happened? We've been worried sick about you.'

'I had a bit of an accident. I'll explain when I see you.'

'We're on our way. It'll take about half an hour, but we'll be there, just sit tight.' Bliss ended the call and hurried to find some clothes.

'What shall I do with Fox? He's used to sleeping on the bed. He'll probably bark the place down if we leave him shut in the kitchen.' Spooky was pulling on jeans and a hoodie.

'We'll bring him. Gill loves dogs, she won't mind.' Bliss laughed. 'She's safe! Even if she's hurt in some way, it can't be serious or they wouldn't let her out. And at least that monster hasn't got her.'

Five minutes later, having bundled a bemused collie into their car, they set off for Saltern.

'I thought the police checked the hospitals,' said Spooky.

'That's what that constable said. I've no idea what happened there.' Bliss took her mobile out. 'I'm ringing the station to let them know we've heard from her.'

'Good idea. Tell them we'll update them when we know what happened.' Spooky could hardly believe this was happening. All along, she had secretly believed that the Coachman had chosen Gill for his next victim.

A&E was overflowing. Apparently they were mopping up for Greenborough General, which was at crisis point, overloaded with casualties from the festival — mostly drink related.

They found Gill in a corridor lying fully clothed on a trolley bed. She looked pale and uncomfortable. 'This has been a nightmare,' she whispered, 'a real nightmare.'

'Can we take you home now? Have you been discharged?' asked Spooky, anxious to get her away from the mayhem and to find out what had happened to her.

'Yes. I just need to speak to one of the nurses and then I can go.' She beckoned to one of the nurses. 'My friends are here now, they've come to take me home.'

'Okay, just remember the head injury observations, won't you, and any problems, come back immediately.' The nurse gave her arm a squeeze. 'So sorry for the mix up, Mrs Mason. You take care.'

Thanking her, Gill struggled to get up. 'Let's get out of here.'

With Spooky and Bliss supporting her on either side, they made their way slowly towards the car.

They put Gill in the front, and Bliss shared the back seat with Fox. As soon as they were out of the car park, Gill began to explain.

'I was stupid, I know, really stupid, but the thing was, I saw him. I saw the man who went off with that nice lad, Peter — the boy who was murdered.'

'Oh my God!' Bliss exclaimed. 'Please don't tell us you went after him.'

'Well, yes, I did. He was heading out of the market and I just dropped everything and followed him. My idea was to get a really good look at him, close up, then ring the police and tell them where he was, but,' she shivered, 'he was faster than I expected. I had to almost run to keep up, and it was so crowded! I didn't dare stop and find the number I'd been given because I'd have lost him completely.'

Bliss handed her a bottle of water from her voluminous bag. 'Have a drink, Gill, and take your time.'

After a few moments, Gill continued. 'Well, we finished up close to the river. There was this dance thing going on — a competition, I think, all fancy dress and people leaping around like mad things. He stopped to watch for a few moments and I managed to get closer, then he was off again. I gave chase but I tripped over some wires from a sound system, and fell down. I hit my head on something.' She rubbed gingerly at the back of her head and winced. 'I woke up in the back of an ambulance.'

Bliss leaned over and squeezed her shoulder. 'Oh, my poor Gill. How awful!'

'I think I frightened them,' she added ruefully. 'But the worst thing was that I couldn't remember a thing for a good hour or so, and because I'd run off so quickly, I had no identification on me.'

Spooky sighed. 'So that's why the police couldn't trace you.'

'Even worse, I had one of my client's business cards in my pocket and they thought it was me. I couldn't understand why they kept calling me Louise, and I was too woozy to put them right.' She groaned. 'And I must have dropped my phone when I fell, because that's gone too, so they couldn't get my name from that either.'

'That's a long time to have amnesia, Gill. Are you sure you should have left the hospital?' Spooky asked.

'I had an X-ray and a scan, and they checked me out every few minutes. When I did begin to remember, it all came flooding back to me, with no gaps or lost moments. It's a mild concussion and they've told me what to be aware of.'

'Well, no way are you going back to your hotel. You're coming to our place. The guest room is always made up, so that's that!'

Gill said, 'Bless you. I'd love to, if it's not too much trouble.'

'We are just so glad you're safe,' Spooky said. 'You have no idea what we were imagining.'

'I think I probably do, and I'm so sorry to have worried you. God knows what I was thinking of, tearing off like that. I'm not exactly Jason Bourne, am I?'

'We've got your cash tin and your tarot cards safe at home,' Bliss said. 'The other stallholders said the rest of your things would be okay overnight.'

'Oh thank you so much. You two have been real heroes.' Gill burst into tears. 'What an idiot I've been!'

Spooky let her cry for a while, knowing it was the shock catching up with her, then she said, 'Gill? Did you get a really good look at him when he stopped to watch the dancers?'

Gill blew her nose. 'Oh yes. And if anyone hands my phone in, there's a photograph of him there. Everyone was taking pictures, so I did too, only not of the dancers — of him.'

'We have to get that phone back.' Spooky drew up at the kerb and pulled her own phone from her pocket.

'Duty Sergeant, please, it's urgent.' She waited impatiently for a minute or two. 'Sergeant Smith, it's Spooky here — er, Sarah Dukes from IT. A phone was dropped in an area close by the river where a dance competition was being held. I believe it has a photograph of the Coachman on it.'

The sergeant swore, making Spooky smile. He said he knew where the competition was, and would get a crew down there immediately.

She told him as precisely as possible where Gill believed she had fallen, and added, 'Could you let me know if you locate it, as I have the owner with me?'

The sergeant assured her he would, and ended the call.

Soon they were home. Spooky felt drained. She'd been riding a roller-coaster of emotions. First her fear that Gill had been abducted, then the relief of hearing her voice, and now the realisation that she had taken a photograph of the murderer.

Bliss took charge. 'Spooky, you take Fox outside, I'll get Gill comfortable in the spare bedroom, then it's hot drinks and sleep, alright?'

'Sounds like heaven,' whispered Gill.

Bliss beamed at her friend. 'Oh, it's so good to know you're safe!'

* * *

The call came an hour later, when only Spooky and Fox were still awake.

'Sergeant Smith? You found it?'

'We've got it, Spooky. It was found in some bushes behind the dance venue. We need the owner's permission and password to access it.'

'Got it here, Smithy. The owner is Gill Mason, the woman reported missing earlier. She dropped it when she had the fall and is now sleeping, but she's left me her pass code and says to tell you to go into the gallery. It's the last picture she took before she went down.'

Spooky waited in anticipation.

'Got it! Yep, we have a side view of our man, and it's a pretty good one too. That's ace, Spooky!'

'Look, I'll be in around eight o'clock. Let me have it and I'll enhance it as much as I can, then you can hit the town with it, or whatever DI Galena wants to do.' Spooky was elated. Then she had a thought. 'Do you recognise him, Smithy?'

'It's weird. I think I do, but I can't place him. It's going to bug the hell out of me for the rest of the night.'

'Keep thinking, and I'll see you later.' She ended the call and looked at the time. Five o'clock. She could grab an hour or two, then it would be back to work. At least she wouldn't be leaving Bliss on her own. No way would Gill be up to working the market later on.

She slipped into bed, snuggling down between the collie and Bliss.

* * *

Five o'clock. Rory's racing thoughts put paid to further sleep. He hated John Does, they bothered him more than all his other cases. He always felt the need to give them back their identity. The man from Drakes Alley was still without a name, so Rory was calling him Francis.

He lay nestled close to David, warmed by his body and luxuriating in its touch. Meanwhile, the questions were rattling around in his mind. Why, though the signs all pointed to digitalis, was he not totally happy with that conclusion? He listed the symptoms that had led to the man's eventual death: sweating, vomiting, diarrhoea, unconsciousness and a heart that beat so arhythmically, it had led to cardiac arrest. What else could it be?

He squeezed his eyes shut and tried to push away the thoughts. Why go over it now, when he would have the results of the tests on his desk tomorrow?

He moved a little closer to David. Enjoy the moment, Wilkinson. He closed his eyes and listened to his breathing, but the doubt would not go. If not digitalis, what else could it be?

CHAPTER TWENTY-NINE

Five o'clock. Having struggled to sleep, Eve got up early and as soon as it started to grow light, went for a walk in the garden of remembrance that was attached to the chapel. She and Wendy, with help from various local volunteers, had made an overgrown plot of land into a peaceful place for the inhabitants of Beech Lacey to enjoy. Today she was pleased to have it to herself. She wanted some time alone to try and make sense of what was happening to the two most important people in her life.

All she could do was draw upon her own sadness for comparison. She had loved Nikki's father, Frank Reed. Even though he felt the same about her, he was married, and she had always known they could never be together. Now, just as she had always known that she would lose Frank, simply because he was an honourable man, she knew that one day Nikki and Joseph would find the job they both loved so passionately driving a wedge between them.

Until now, she had believed that the rift, should it happen, would come about through Nikki's doing. She certainly hadn't considered a scenario in which Joseph reverted to being the person he had hated so much and had moved heaven and earth to leave behind. It was ironic that his reason for doing so was entirely altruistic. He wanted justice for the innocents who had suffered and died, yet he was prepared to deliver it without benefit of trial or jury. Had he calculated the price? And how?

Eve sat down on one of the benches.

She hadn't known her daughter for very long, but having lived close to her over the last couple of years, she had come to understand what made her tick. Nikki Galena was sensitive. She had been damaged, partly by the job she did and the terrible things she had seen, but mostly by having her precious daughter taken from her. Hence the tough exterior.

The awful thing was that she could do nothing to help her daughter. All she could do was be there, provide some solace, but she couldn't intervene. She just had to trust that fate would step in and avert the looming tragedy.

* * *

Nikki stood in the CID room, ready to head up daily orders. At least there was something positive to tell the troops today.

'Okay everyone, settle down. We have a lot to discuss today, so listen up.' She stood in front of the whiteboards and looked around the crowded room. 'Today is the last day of the festival, and it's also the busiest. We have one day in which to catch the Coachman, and then it goes public. Believe me, if you are looking forward to fireworks tonight, they will go up under us if we don't get this killer behind bars by midnight.'

A low murmur rumbled around the room, and Nikki held up her hand. 'However, we are now in a better place, thanks to Gill Mason, a trader in the covered market who identified him as the man who went off with Peter Cash. She managed to take a much clearer photograph than the ones we've had so far. He is the same man seen on CCTV leaving the music and art college prior to it being set on fire, and a dead ringer for a man who took a trip around the old crime scene in Drakes Alley.' She pointed to the new photo pinned centre stage on the board. 'Anyone know him?'

Several officers said they thought they had met the individual, but they couldn't put a name to him.

'We are sure he has disguised himself in some way. That long hair, for example, may not be natural, so try to see through all that. But we'll leave his identity for the moment. Does the name Dean Kennedy mean anything to any of you? He lived in Cartoft Village, and almost three years ago he suddenly packed up and left.' Receiving no response, she continued. 'Some time ago this man did detailed research into a Victorian murderer who used identical methods of dispatch to the Coachman. It's vital we find him and talk to him. He could well be our killer, or if he isn't, he might know who he is, since it's his research that is the connection to the present day murderer.'

'Ma'am?' Cat raised her hand. 'Cartoft is a very small village. DI Jackman of Saltern-le-Fen lives there. Should we ask him if he knows anything about this Dean Kennedy?'

'Good point. I'll phone him when we're through. Thanks, Cat. The night shift were going to do some ferreting for us, but they got caught up on other calls, so it's down to us. Cat, do you think you and Ben could make Dean Kennedy your priority today?'

'Certainly,' they replied.

'We also have someone who's taking a pickup from the Cressy Old Hall estate. On two or three evenings recently, it's been seen heading towards Greenborough town after dark. We should have a picture from the ANPR cameras available later this morning. We are looking at the driver of that vehicle in connection with the murder of Norma Warden, so once again, it could be the Coachman.'

She waited while people scribbled quickly in their notebooks, then continued, 'And finally, and most importantly, we have a young woman by the name of Ellie Stevens who's missing. Her partner says it's totally out of character for her to stay out and not contact him, so we are taking this very seriously indeed. She was last seen leaving the Hanged Man after a late lunch. The details that we do have about her are in this.' She got Dave to pass around copies of a typed memo.

Nikki looked around at the gathered officers. 'This is a big day. We have more than enough to cope with, but we *have* to find the Coachman, and we *have* to find that young woman. I cannot emphasise enough just how much is riding on this. I'd like to say that all I can ask of you is that you do your best, but today I want more than that. I want you to work your arses off with no thought for anything else. Just get that girl back safely, and find the bastard who is terrorising this town. Now, go!'

As the room emptied, her head started to pound. Every word she'd said was true. They had one day to catch the killer. There was no leeway.

As she was about to go back to her office, she saw Joseph and Dave both staring at the picture from Gill Mason's phone.

Dave looked totally perplexed, Joseph as if he was planning a funeral. The thought made her shiver. 'I'm guessing you are in the "I know him but I can't think who he is" camp, right, Dave?'

'Very true, He looks a bit like . . . but no. Oh, that's so annoying.'

'I think we can agree that he's wearing some kind of disguise,' said Joseph shortly. 'Or someone would have put a name to him by now.'

'I've thrown that one into Spooky's playpen,' said Nikki. 'She's going to change his hair style and colour, facial dimensions, whatever she thinks, and send us all the results. Even if we ended up with a mildly reasonable facsimile of someone we know, it would give us someone to pull in and interview.' She stared at the picture and shook her head. They were so close . . .

'Joseph, will you concentrate on the Ellie Stevens case, please. Dave, ring Cressy Old Hall and see if anyone tried to hijack the pickup last night, and watch out for those pictures from the cameras on the main road. I'm going to ring DI Jackman at Saltern-le-Fen and see if he's ever heard of Dean Kennedy.'

Had Joseph looked put out at being asked to take on the missing woman investigation? She knew he wanted to be hunting down the Coachman, but that was tough. She would have to keep a lot of balls in the air today and no one was going to question her orders, not even Joseph.

DI Rowan Jackman greeted her warmly, and commiserated with her about what she was having to deal with. 'I've never liked that festival, and to have some psycho choose it to stage a kill-fest — it's unthinkable. If we can offer any assistance, Nikki, just shout. We'll do all we can to help.'

'Appreciated, Jackman. We've actually got a whole load of your uniforms with us already. Right now, I need some info on a man who used to live in Cartoft.'

'Okay, fire away.'

'His name is Dean Kennedy, and we think he lived in Cedar Way.'

Jackman remained silent for a while. 'I didn't know him personally, but the Maynards, the couple who look after my house, told me a bit about him a while ago. What do you want to know exactly?'

'Anything. Anything at all. We believe he is linked to what's going on in Greenborough at the moment. There is a strong connection between something he was working on for several years and our killer.'

'Then sorry to pull the rug from under you, Nikki, but Dean Kennedy is dead. Has been for years.'

Nikki cursed.

'Really sorry. He hanged himself apparently. According to Mrs Maynard, he was always an odd boy. Intelligent and very good looking, but a real loner. The little house in Cedar Way belonged to his mother, but she went off with some man and left him there alone.'

'We were told that he just upped and walked out of his home. Do you have any idea where he went?'

Jackman grunted. 'Sorry, no, but if you tell me what info you need, I'll happily give Hetty Maynard a ring and see if she can help. I'm sure she will. She was born and bred in Cartoft, and there's nothing goes on here that she doesn't know about.'

'Brilliant. I need his background, as detailed as possible, and anything about where he might have gone, and now I suppose, why he killed himself.'

'I'll ring you back directly.' Jackman hung up.

'Dead? Double damn it! He was my best bloody lead!' Nikki sounded off to an empty office.

It seemed to take forever for Jackman to get back to her.

'Got a pen? Right. Here goes. He was an only child. Father died when he was young, mother did her best with him, but there was little doubt he was a strange boy — Hetty's words, not mine. Went to local schools but although he was very bright, didn't want to learn. This changed when he reached secondary school and he showed signs of having a fairly high IQ. He went to college, but gave up before he'd completed his course. Worked for a printing company for several years, and she thinks he also worked from home on a computer, but doesn't know what he did.'

'Hold on, let me just get all that,' Nikki scribbled hastily. 'Okay, what's next?'

'Well, this is hearsay, but I'll give it to you anyway, his neighbours said that he took to going out in the late evening, and sometimes didn't come home for perhaps two or three days. Then he suddenly acted friendly to them, which was unusual. They said he was on something of a high for several months, and then he suddenly packed up his stuff, shut up the house, and moved out. Never even said goodbye. No one ever knew where he went. All anyone knew about his death was what they read in the papers — that he hung himself, somewhere over your way I think. Hetty wasn't sure about that.'

'That's a real bummer, Jackman. We have so much evidence linking his research work to the killer that we were certain there was a close connection. There *had* to be, it was so precise.'

'There still may be,' said Jackman thoughtfully. 'Someone else must have got hold of this work of his. You need to find out where he went when he left home, and who he spent his time with, and I reckon you'll be back on track.' He paused. 'Oh, and Hetty reckoned he was a beautiful looking lad, and she had heard rumours that he was, well, probably not interested in girls — again her words, not mine.'

Nikki considered that. 'If he was gay, that could account for a lot of his not wanting to socialise. These small villages were, and sometimes still are, rather narrow minded.'

'Downright bigoted!' said Jackman. 'Some of the old rural spots are still living in the dark ages, and I really mean that. I've only owned my house at Mill Corner for about seven years, but Hetty and Len can tell some real horror stories about the old-uns — believing in folklore, and half of them being married to cousins and the like. You wouldn't believe it was the twenty-first century. It's quite scary.'

Nikki knew that to be true. 'Thank you, Jackman. If you come across any other little snippets about Dean Kennedy, can you give me a ring?'

'Of course, and the very best of luck getting through today.'

Amen to that. She was certainly going to need it.

Nikki went out to break the news to Cat and Ben and found they had just discovered about Dean's death for themselves.

'He made the headlines in the local news, boss,' said Cat, 'although there was very little useful information about him — nothing we hadn't already worked out.'

'Did you work out that he was gay?' Nikki asked.

Cat and Ben looked at her blankly.

'Ah, well. There was a picture of him in the paper, and he was certainly very beautiful, so that doesn't surprise me,' said Cat.

'It's as yet unconfirmed, but the locals were sure that was the case.'

'That could answer why he moved out so suddenly,' added Ben. 'To go and live with another guy,'

'And months later he kills himself?' Nikki wondered about that. If he had been so happy just before moving, how come things suddenly got bad enough for him to top himself? We need to find who he went to stay with, as a matter of urgency. I don't like the way this is going. I've got a gut feeling that the person he moved in with is the Coachman.'

'We're on it!' Cat looked at Ben expectantly. 'We can do this, can't we?'

'Dead right we can. Leave it with us, boss.'

Nikki smiled, happy that she had done the right thing by keeping Cat working and not signing her off.

Dave called over. 'Photos are in, ma'am! We've got the pickup entering the town by the main road.' He hurried across and placed the sheet of photos in front of her. 'This one.' He pointed to a shot of the front of the big vehicle.

Nikki looked at it closely. 'The truck is clear enough, but we need to see the driver. Spooky will have to try and clean this up and magnify it. Take it to IT, Dave, and ask her what she can do.'

Joseph appeared from his office, looking excited. 'Niall has just picked up a report from early last evening, a couple having what everyone thought was a domestic in the car park in West Street. Now the woman who reported it is worried that the young woman involved may not have known the man and was actually being abducted.' His eyes flashed. 'The witness described the man as tall and wearing a long dark coat. And Niall has just been assured that all the cameras in West Street car park are operational.'

'Go check that out, Joseph. If he used his own vehicle, and we can make out the reg, we've got him.'

'On my way.'

The adrenalin began to pulse through her veins. Things were moving at last. They would catch him, but would it be in time to save Ellie Stevens from a horrible death?

* * *

'I knew it!'

'Nice dance moves, Prof.' Spike stared at Rory with interest. 'Not seen on the dance floor for the last twenty years, but nice all the same.'

Rory smiled benignly at his young acolyte. 'I once won the area jive championship, I'll have you know.'

'Well yes, you have mentioned it, Prof, many times, but why the excitement?'

'I've just had the reports back. Our lovely Francis here didn't die of digitalis poisoning.'

'You're joshing me!' Spike's eyes were wide. 'But he has all the symptoms.'

'He does, but there is another beautiful deadly plant that imitates all the same symptoms and effects — the Jericho Rose, Spike. Nerium oleander.'

'Oleander! Of course. Every part of it is poisonous, isn't it? Flowers, seeds, branches, leaves, roots . . .'

'And even the pollen. If bees feed on the nectar, the honey produced is also poisonous. And it has such a pretty flower. Glorious pink stars on dark evergreen leaves.'

'But they are all over the Mediterranean, and here too. My auntie has some in pots in her garden. How come the wildlife isn't dropping like flies?' asked Spike.

'Wildlife tend to avoid it. Mind you, I wouldn't have one in the garden if I had a puppy or a dog who chewed things. Or a child, come to that. I'm sure I used to eat plants.'

Spike shook his head. 'I wouldn't be surprised.'

Rory turned his attention back to his charge. 'Now, Francis my good friend, all we need to do is find your real name, and slap handcuffs on the sick sack of shit that did this to you, then maybe you can rest in peace.'

'Poor sod,' muttered Spike. 'Out on the town for a bit of fun, and he has the misfortune to run into a poison-loving psycho.'

'Indeed. Now, I'd better let Nikki know what killed him. I'm not sure it will help her find the killer, but she still needs all the details. Would you care to place Francis back in the chiller, dear boy?'

* * *

Nikki wrote the word oleander on a memo pad. For once she knew exactly what that particular plant looked like, but she'd had no idea it was deadly poisonous.

She stared at the word for a moment, and then decided to pass it on to Morgan Flint, just in case it tied in with the poisons used by the Victorian murderer Creep.

She found Morgan alone.

'Connor has gone with your Yvonne to see a snout of hers. This fellow professes to have some info for her on a source that will apparently get anything you want, including lethal chemicals.'

'Sounds promising. Yvonne has some very good snouts, she's been tending them for decades.' Nikki handed Morgan the sheet of paper. 'It's been confirmed that our John Doe found in Drakes Alley died from poison extracted from that.'

'Ah, oleander. That was definitely one of Creep's botanical poisons. The Coachman really is sticking to the hymn sheet, isn't he?'

Nikki told her that she suspected Dean Kennedy had been gay, and that whoever he went to live with when he walked out of his home could be the Coachman.

Morgan narrowed her eyes. 'I'm still at a loss to know why this young man did such a lot of research on Creep. Was it for a paper? Research for a thesis or a doctorate or something like that?'

'Or a book maybe?'

'Maybe. But I've never come across one that dealt solely with the post-Ripper killers.' Morgan grunted. 'And believe me, I've looked.'

'You wouldn't work for two years on something without there being a purpose, would you?' asked Nikki.

'Absolutely not. Where oh where did that lad go when he moved out of Cartoft?' Morgan mused. 'Did anyone ever ask the mother, I wonder?'

'Cat said she was going to. If she can find her.' Nikki frowned. 'Hopefully she'll be able to track her down through the household bills.'

Nikki's mobile rang. 'Joseph? Any news?'

Joseph sounded despondent. 'The possible abduction in West Street car park was a false alarm. I got the vehicle reg off the CCTV, and then an address, so I took a couple of uniforms straight there. He's not the Coachman, and the woman really was his wife. She'd had too much to drink but wanted to stay in town and party. He wanted to get her home. Simple as that, I'm afraid. He bundled her into their car and she objected. They are kosher, Nikki.'

'Damn and blast! Okay, well, better get back here, Joseph.'

'On my way already. See you in ten.'

'Another dead end?' Morgan sighed. 'Wouldn't it be nice to have a proper lead for once?'

'And we might just have one, guv'nor!' Connor Hale strode in through the door, closely followed by Yvonne Collins.

'This woman is amazing!' Connor said admiringly. 'Got some really ace snouts — and listen to this.' He held out his arm and Yvonne took over.

'My snout has been hunting down info on which dealer you might go to if you wanted to get hold of dangerous substances. I dropped him some cash and he found a name for me. We met this guy and leaned on him a bit — well, Connor did.' Yvonne grinned. 'We struck a deal. If he gave me a lead on who'd been asking for illegal chemicals or poisons, we'd back off and forget him. Then Connor offered him a few more unpleasant alternatives. Although he wouldn't say too much, this dealer said that he'd had a couple of requests over the last six months, and they both came from the office at Cressy Old Hall. He knew it was the Hall because, as he said, he rang the number back later and some toffee-nosed woman answered, saying "Cressy Old Hall, how may I help?"'

Nobody spoke for a full minute while that sank in.

'Good grief!' Nikki said. 'Add that to the pickup truck sneaking out under the cover of night, and it being the place where Norma Warden was attacked, and it looks very much like our man is based on that estate.'

'Rufus Taylor, Anthony Laker and Arthur Keats.' Morgan listed the possible suspects from the whiteboard.

'And one other,' said Nikki, 'although I'm sure Dave Harris won't agree. His lordship himself, Clive Cressy-Lawson.'

'And that other guy who spends a whole lot of time there, the History Society bloke who organises the hall's ghost walks, what's his name?' Connor asked.

'Murray Kennington. And don't forget the groundsman, Den Elliott,' Nikki added. 'Any one of them could have used the phone in the main office.'

'I think we should go back to the Old Hall, and this time with a whole lot of uniforms and a sheaf of warrants.' She turned to Yvonne. 'Your favourite job, my friend. Go find a friendly magistrate. We need access to the hall itself, and every dwelling on that estate that houses one of our suspects. Will you organise that, Vonnie?'

'With pleasure. The court is open, so hopefully I'll find someone who won't put up too many objections.' Yvonne looked at Morgan Flint. 'Okay with you, ma'am?'

'Oh yes, and well done, you two.'

Nikki felt a small thrill of excitement. She couldn't wait to go through that stately pile. She meant to pick it apart until she found some evidence of who the killer was. 'You coming?' she asked Morgan Flint.

'Try and stop us.'

'Yeah, just try,' echoed Connor with a big grin.

'I'm off to see the duty sergeant and organise as many uniforms as he can muster. It's a big place and I don't want whoever it is seeing us coming and legging it.'

'Excellent,' Morgan said. 'No offence, but I can't wait to get out of this office for a while.'

'None taken. I'm going stir crazy myself.'

Nikki was aware that she would need to keep very close to Joseph. This could be the raid that flushed out the killer, the very thing Joseph was waiting for. She needed to have her eyes wide open so as to make sure he didn't get an opportunity to do anything unlawful.

CHAPTER THIRTY

Just as they were about to go out, Eve received a phone call.

'Robert Richmond?' she said.

'Don't sound so surprised, Eve Anderson. I said I'd be in touch.' There was a hint of amusement in his voice.

'But I didn't give you my number.'

'Ah, true, but you left a contact number when you phoned up about the tour, didn't you?'

Eve laughed. 'Yes, I did, didn't I? So how can I help you?'

'By calling round to the house in about an hour's time. I have something interesting to tell you.' Robert sounded excited.

'Oh dear. My friends and I have plans for today.'

'Just for half an hour? I hate to beg, but I will if necessary. And it's not that coffee and a chat that I mentioned. This is something different.'

Now he had her attention. 'Okay, but I really can't stay any longer than that. I don't have too many chances to spend time with my friends, and they leave tomorrow.'

'Appreciated, dear lady. I'll not detain you any longer than necessary, I promise.'

Eve ended the call, intrigued. What could have prompted that call? He certainly sounded keen to tell her something.

Wendy was staring at her with a shrewd expression. 'Okay, you. What are you planning now? I know that look.'

Eve told her about her extraordinary conversation.

'I wouldn't advise going alone, Eve. He's still a name on our whiteboard, remember. If you go, I go too. And don't tell me I wasn't invited because I know that, but I'll happily play the gooseberry if your safety is at stake. Besides, your daughter would kill me if I let you waltz off alone.'

'Now there's a point,' Eve said. 'Okay, you come. He'll probably expect it anyway, and if there's nothing devious about him, he'll understand.'

'Sensible decision. It could just have saved you a serious tongue-lashing from a certain detective inspector.'

'That's certainly worth avoiding, I agree.' Eve had experienced one of those in the past, and wasn't anxious to relive the experience. 'Let's go tell the others. I'm dying to know what this is about.'

'Okay, I suggest we all drive in together this morning, just in case we need transport in a hurry.'

Eve nodded, 'Okay, I'll rally the troops and we'll move out.'

* * *

While Lou and Rene went off to meet Vinnie, Eve and Wendy knocked on Robert Richmond's door. They had arrived half an hour before the house was due to open to the public, and the family were hurriedly making last-minute arrangements to their makeshift café.

Robert, who showed no sign of being bothered by Wendy's presence, took them through to a small study. 'Sit down, ladies. This won't take long, but I think it might have something to do with you, Eve Anderson.'

Eve smiled at the way he always used her full name. It seemed to give them a kind of bond, as if they were sharing a private joke.

She and Wendy sat next to each other on a small two-seater sofa, and Robert sank into an armchair close to the unlit fire. Like the rest of the place, where it should have been cosy and warm, the room felt chilly and neglected.

'I'll not waste any time. Last night, I had an unexpected call from my brother, Edward. He informed me that he'd be going away for a few days.' He raised his eyebrows. 'Edward *never* goes away. Even odder than that was the fact that he was talking to me quite civilly. He hinted that when he returned, he wanted to talk to me privately, here in Oleander House.'

Eve began to wonder why this should concern her. It seemed to be a private family matter, not something to share with a comparative stranger.

'Ladies, I cannot recall a single occasion in the past decade when my brother has addressed me politely, or expressed the slightest wish to discuss anything at all. Last night he was subdued and reasonable, to a point where I feared for his sanity. It was as though a different man was on the end of the line.'

Eve felt Wendy nudge her in the ribs. Edward Richmond was one of their prime suspects for the Coachman. What had caused this abrupt change? Nikki needed to hear about this.

'I'm not sure what to make of that, Robert,' said Eve thoughtfully.

'Don't you?' He smiled enigmatically.

'No. Why?' She felt totally perplexed at why she should understand the behaviour of Robert's recluse of a brother when she'd never even met him.

'Is this you being modest? Or am I barking up a wrong tree?' For the first time, Robert too looked puzzled.

'A very wrong tree,' said Wendy. 'We have no idea what you are talking about.'

Robert closed his eyes. 'Oh dear, and I really thought . . .' He looked at them apologetically. 'I'm sorry, I obviously got this all wrong, but even so, it's something I still have to tell you.'

Eve leaned forward. 'Tell us, Robert, before my brain starts to overheat.'

'It's . . . Edward has given me the impression that he's going to give up his claim to this place, and the art work.'

'That's amazing! We're delighted for you after all this time, but where do we come in?' Eve asked.

'All he would tell me was that he had spoken to someone who had changed his whole way of thinking about everything. That's why he's going away. He wants to think things through, away from Greenborough. I believed that person was you, Eve Anderson.'

'I hate to disappoint, and we did try to speak to him. We found his address and called round, but either he wasn't there or he was just not answering the door.' Eve felt quite sorry that it hadn't been her who had made such an impression on him . . . unless? What if he really was the Coachman, and he knew that the net was closing in? He would have to move on quickly, and wouldn't want to draw any suspicion to his sudden exit from the house he'd imprisoned himself inside for years. What better way to set up an alibi than to throw his brother a story that would fill the poor man so full of hope that he wouldn't ask him any questions. And that house? If no one was ever allowed inside . . . what did it hide? Oh yes, Nikki really did need to hear this!

Eve stood up. 'Robert, forgive us, we have to go, but if this is for real, I cannot tell you how delighted I am. If that coffee is still on offer, you'll ring me?'

Robert got to his feet. 'You can rely on it, and I'm sorry to drag you over here. That'll teach me to make assumptions, won't it?'

Outside, Eve poured out her suspicions to Wendy.

'I confess I'm following a similar train of thought,' her friend said. 'I think you should call your daughter right now.'

Eve's phone was already in her hand.

'Mum?' Nikki said. 'Can't talk. We have a lead at last.'

'So do we, or we suspect we do,' Eve said.

'Does it concern Cressy Old Hall?' Nikki said.

Eve frowned. 'No, it's that guy Edward Richmond I told you about.'

'Then I think you could be off the mark this time, Mum. Our intel is pointing us in a different direction, with a lot of evidence building up.' She called out to someone. 'Really sorry, Mum, but I'm pretty tied up. I'll get back to you ASAP — but listen, if you have real concerns, don't involve yourself, you hear? It could still be a dangerous situation to walk into. Observation, remember? Just observation.' There was more shouting in the background, then, 'Love you, Mum. Must go.'

Eve ended the call. Well, one of them was wrong. What if Nikki was chasing shadows at Cressy Old Hall?

Wendy had picked up the gist of the conversation. 'Oh dear, it's down to us, is it? The old team again?'

Eve considered the options. 'Looks like it. We'd better get back to Vinnie and the girls.'

Wendy's eyes lit up. 'I hoped you'd say that. Let's go.'

* * *

Dave hurried back to the CID room to find everyone pulling on protective vests. This moment, just before an action, had always given him a thrill.

Not today, however. When Cat rang and told him where they were heading, his heart sank. He felt as if he had betrayed Clive, so much so that for a moment he was tempted to call him and warn him of the surprise visit. This raid would destroy all the goodwill between them, and it saddened him deeply.

For the first time since he had joined the force, Dave believed he had made some friends that had nothing to do with Greenborough nick or the Fenland Constabulary. Real friends, not just workmates who thought he was a good copper. Now all that would be gone.

With a heavy heart, he handed Nikki the enhanced picture from the vehicle recognition camera.

'It's the Coachman alright, you can tell from the hair and the shape of his face and the collar of the coat he's wearing, but Spooky said it's not the right angle to get a proper picture of his features. It's no more use than any of the other CCTV pictures.'

Nikki stared at it. 'The one from Gill Mason's phone is still the best by far. Has Spooky sent those modified images yet?'

'Ready in half an hour, she thought.' He sighed. 'I'll stay here and look after things this end if you like, ma'am, and then I'll collect the images when they're ready.'

He saw the look she gave him. She understood perfectly why he didn't want to go.

'That would be a great help, Dave. Thank you.' She tightened her vest and secured it. 'I'm sorry, Dave, but everything points that way, you know?'

He nodded. 'Has to be done, but I don't have to watch it, do I?'

She patted his arm. 'No, you don't. Just keep me up to date with anything new. I'll be on my mobile or the radio.'

He assured her he would, and watched them go.

Soon he was alone in the big room. He put his arms on his desk and rested his forehead on them. He didn't want to be a part of this anymore, any of it. It was as if his career, the mainstay of his whole life, had suddenly evaporated, like a Fen mist when the sun rose.

He'd see this one through, wait until everyone in the custody suite was talking about their new guest, the Coachman. And while the back-slapping and the cheers faded away, he'd fade too.

His short time at Cressy Old Hall had taught him that there was a world outside the force, one that he could enjoy while he still had the physical and mental capacity to do so.

* * *

Outside in the corridor, Nikki took Cat to one side. 'Look, no way would I make you stop. If you want to get your hands dirty, that's fine, but I think your old partner needs a good mate right now.'

Cat stopped in her tracks. 'Davey? What's wrong?'

'He built up a bloody good relationship at the Old Hall, and he's about to see all his work shattered. When we tear through Clive Cressy's precious stately home, we'll be taking a wrecking ball to everything Dave's built up.'

'Oh fuck! Er, sorry, ma'am, but that's a bummer.'

'It is. He's looking tired and pretty low, so . . . ?'

'No contest.' Cat began to undo her protective vest. 'I can beat up bad guys anytime I want, can't I? But I can't always be there for my mate. Thanks for the heads-up, boss.'

Nikki gave her arm a squeeze. 'No, Cat, my thanks to you. I owe you one.'

She watched Cat go back through the doors of the CID room yelling, 'So why isn't the coffee machine bubbling, old man? Don't think you're going to stick your size tens on the desk and have a nap, 'cause your little Catkin and you have got work to do!'

Nikki smiled. Cat Cullen had come a long, long way.

CHAPTER THIRTY-ONE

Gill Mason felt pretty awful, but still a lot better than she had the night before. The fact that she had clients waiting was already worrying her. She knew she wasn't up to working but, Coachman or no Coachman, she was reluctant to let them down. Luckily, it didn't take long to convince Bliss to go with her to the covered market to collect her appointment book and tell the other stallholders that she was safe, but not up to working.

Bliss agreed quite happily, the only stipulation being that they ask a police constable to accompany them, just in case. For once, Gill made no objection. It terrified her to think that this unspeakably evil man was still at large.

* * *

Vinnie was split in two, he who was never indecisive. Joseph had texted him, telling him where they were heading and what he expected to find, and at the same time Eve and her warriors had turned up with a plan for the siege and possible extraction of a murder suspect somewhere else. Both scenarios were potentially lethal.

The women were so involved in strategy and tactics that they hardly noticed his silence, until he saw Lou watching him.

'Joseph has contacted you, hasn't he?' she said.

'Okay, where've you hidden the crystal ball?'

She shook her head. 'I just know you, and that look can mean only one thing — acute indecision. You're plagued by a sense of loyalty and a feeling of guilt.'

'As I said. Crystal ball.'

'So, what are you going to do?'

'Fuck knows! Oh, sorry Lou. But I really haven't a clue.'

'Tell us your problem. We women are way better at sorting emotional stuff than you guys. We have to do it on a daily basis, especially if we have men in our lives.'

'Offer accepted.'

Lou called for quiet. 'Vinnie wants our help with something.'

The three turned expectant looks in his direction.

'Er, well . . . The thing is . . .'

'Oh, for heaven's sake! You men.' Lou addressed the others. 'Vinnie is torn between chaperoning us and looking out for Joseph's back. He doesn't believe Joseph is thinking all that straight at the moment. Show of hands, please. Those for sticking here with our squadron?'

No hands went up.

'And for supporting his old comrade?' Lou looked around. 'Carried unanimously. Now bugger off.'

Vinnie stood with his mouth open. 'But—'

'But nothing, soldier,' said Rene. 'It's sorted. Ring us with a situation report when you're free.'

Eve was pointing to the door. 'There are four of us, Vinnie. We are very capable and we have no intention of doing anything reckless, I promise. Go help your friend. He needs you more than we do.'

Vinnie went through the door, still undecided as to whether he had made the right decision.

* * *

A convoy of police vehicles streamed through the gates to Cressy Old Hall. Leaving Tail End Charlie to man the entrance, the rest split up, some going directly to the main house, others to the tied cottages and the converted stable block.

Nikki Galena took the main house, sending Joseph and Ben to the stables.

As she had foreseen, Clive Cressy-Lawson was incensed by the intrusion, and, as she had also foreseen, tried to bar their entrance. She shook the warrant in his face.

'I'm surprised it isn't good old Dave Harris handing me this,' he spat out angrily. 'Deceitful sod! After all the hospitality I offered him. What an absolute—'

Nikki pushed him roughly back against the door. 'This has nothing to do with Dave Harris. He isn't even here.'

'Not surprised. Too ashamed show his face, I suppose. Now, get your hands off me.'

Nikki moved closer. 'Dave isn't here because for some unknown reason, he likes you. He stayed away out of respect for you, and as far as I can see, he's totally misguided. Now, let us in before I book you for obstruction.'

Clive raised himself to his full height but then, apparently thinking better of it, stood aside. The search team officers filed into the hallway.

'Thank you, *sir.*'

Nikki followed them in, suddenly almost certain that Clive Cressy-Lawson wasn't involved. He was a pompous prat, but he wasn't the Coachman. They'd give every room a brief once-over, and proceed to the other areas of the estate.

Having made sure everyone knew what they were doing, she went to find Joseph.

She found him seated amidst heaps of books and papers, trying to placate an irate Rufus Taylor.

'This is abominable, an invasion of privacy. I've cooperated, I've told you all I know, and you treat me like this. It's like some ghastly scene from a film.'

'Sir, we have to check everyone, I've told you already. This is a murder enquiry, and no one is exempt. I'm sorry, but that's how it is.' Joseph was speaking through gritted teeth, emanating waves of frustration.

Nikki took it all in. This was not the way he normally worked. Joseph could calm the highest sea and charm the birds from the topmost branches. He never showed anger unless the situation really warranted it.

Looking at Rufus Taylor properly, she saw someone possibly a little strange, distraught and angry at this incursion into his private space. His distress was too real for him to be hiding something.

She beckoned to Joseph, who followed her outside. 'Is there anything particularly damning about this one?' she asked

'Not really. We've found no long coat, and no boots other than a pair of Wellingtons. His alibi for the night Norma Warden was attacked is vaguely confirmed by people who attended the lecture he says he went to. No one actually knew him, though, so their recollection of seeing him there wasn't particularly reliable.' He frowned. 'All the people who rent these conversions have a small storage space at the end of the block — used to be tack rooms I think — somewhere to store stuff that isn't wanted in the apartment. We are checking those for evidence of poisons and the like.'

'So, no need to terrorise him any more than necessary, eh?' She threw him a grin, to which he didn't respond. 'He's not the killer, Joseph, unless he's taken acting lessons from the Mad Hatter. He's too neurotic to have conducted such a well-planned killing spree.'

Joseph exhaled. 'I know. He just bugged me to the point of exasperation. And he's so bloody rude.'

'Cressy-Lawson wasn't all sweetness and light either. He blamed Dave Harris.'

'Bad move on his part.' Joseph reverted to his old self for a moment. 'Hope you hit him where the bruises won't show?'

'I was close, believe me. But it's not him, I'm sure of it.'

'Shall we join the troops next door? The next one is at least polite. Mr Antony Laker has class and intelligence.'

'Which is something we are looking for. Lead on, Joseph.'

* * *

With Cat's company, plus that of the few pool detectives now in the CID room, Dave began to regain some of his usual composure. Nevertheless, he was still upset about what he knew to be the end of his trips to the Old Hall. He had honestly liked Clive, and cared about what was happening there.

Cat had expressed the opinion that if Clive Big-Nob wasn't understanding enough to know that Dave had been perfectly straight with him, then he wasn't worth knowing, so sod him. She was right, but even so, Dave knew that on top of all his other worries, having his precious home raided would seem like the end of the world. He was pretty sure that if he had been in Clive's situation, with his manager murdered and his wife having danced off to the smoke with no return ticket, he'd probably feel the same.

'I'm just off to see if Spooky has finished those modified e-fits, Cat. Won't be long.'

When she didn't respond, he saw that she was deeply engrossed in a lengthy report on her screen. He patted her shoulder and whispered, 'Back in ten.'

Spooky greeted him with a tired smile. 'All ready, mate, but I warn you, there are dozens of them. I've given the brute every hair colour and style imaginable, plus no hair at all, of course. Plus fatter faces, thinner faces and variations of skin tone. In the picture he seems very pale, which could be make-up. He's obviously Caucasian, but I've tanned him up a bit in some of the images. Every little helps, as they say.'

'Appreciated, Spooks. I'll look through them, then text the boss to say they're here. She has great hopes for these.' Spooky didn't look convinced.

He took them back to the CID room.

Before he could show Cat, she jumped up from her desk and ran over to him. 'I've got something on Dean Kennedy at last!'

'Well done! Tell Uncle Dave, then.'

'I've tracked his mother down. She refused to talk, but I finally convinced her to "chat" to me on Messenger, and she really opened up. She confirmed that he was homosexual and very hung up about it.'

'So, not out and proud?'

'Far from it. She tried to make him understand that it meant nothing to her, that she loved him no matter what, but it seems that he didn't only have problems declaring his sexuality to others, he couldn't confront it in himself.'

'Poor little devil. So that's why he became a loner. But if she cared so much, why did the mother leave him?'

'She reckoned it got so bad that she could hardly bear to be in the house with him. Apparently it got worse when he began researching for his, as she put it, 'precious bloody manuscript.'

'A book?'

'She told me he believed it would be the definitive volume on some particular aspect of the Victorian era, finally bringing him the recognition he deserved, and he would no longer be a freak. She said that a year into this "research," she met a man, fell in love with him and moved out. She doesn't think Dean even noticed she'd gone.'

Dave began to understand. At some point self-preservation always kicks in and gives you the courage to step away from a hopeless situation.

Cat's eyes shone. 'And here's the best bit. She kept in touch, and just when she thought he was a completely lost cause, her son changed. He sounded happy for the first time since he was a little kid. He said he'd told an older guy he worked with at the printers about his book, and this individual was really enthusiastic. He was reading it for Dean, helping to make it as good as possible, and they had become friends.'

'Very good friends?'

'Well, his mother suspected that it was a close relationship. He told her they wanted to move in together, ostensibly to work on this magnum opus and save all the travel to and fro. She told him she was fine with his friend staying with him in Cartoft, but he wouldn't have it. He was afraid people would talk.'

'So he moved in with his friend, who is . . . ?'

Cat made a face. 'Not quite there yet, but feelers are out. All his mother knew was that he intended to close the house up for a while. He promised to look in regularly and make sure there were no problems, and off he went. As far as she knows, he never went back. Then he stopped phoning, and the next thing she heard, he was dead.'

'Oh my! I wonder what happened?' Dave said.

'I've asked the printing works for a list of the staff that were there at the same time as Dean. I also got the manager to try to find out if anyone remembers him and who he was particularly friendly with.'

'You can't do any more than that, kiddo. Well done. The boss is going to be well pleased with you.'

Cat almost purred. 'Don't you love it when something comes together?'

'Glad you stayed to look out for your old fossil of a partner?' Dave grinned at her.

'Fossil indeed. Now, let's have a look at your rogue's gallery.'

* * *

'He told his brother he was going away, so there's a good chance he won't be there,' Rene said.

'So we get inside and check it out anyway,' said Wendy.

The four women sat in Eve's car and looked down the road at number thirteen, Ferry Street.

'We are lucky it's a basement flat. We're less likely to be seen while we break in,' said Eve. 'No sign of life in the whole property.'

'So, Plan A?' asked Lou.

Eve nodded. 'Plan A. All ready?'

It worked perfectly. Eve drove as close as she dared to the house and she and Wendy got out.

While Eve waited on the pavement, Wendy hurried down the basement steps and knocked on the door.

As expected, there was no answer. This didn't necessarily mean that Edward wasn't there, but it was their cue to get inside.

Wendy, having acquired a number of dubious skills during her years in the field, had the lock open in minutes. The other two women joined Eve outside the house and when the door swung open, they all hurried down the steps, Lou saying in a loud voice, 'Cousin Edward! Surprise, surprise! We haven't seen you in eons, darling! Can we come in?'

All that remained of their presence was a hint of perfume and a parked car.

* * *

'Okay, what's *he* doing here?' As if she didn't know. 'I love him to bits, Joseph, but this is an organised police raid, not a free for all.'

Vinnie was loping towards them, an apologetic look on his face. 'I was going to hide in the bushes and wait to see if I was needed, but then I thought, hey, there's that gorgeous Nikki Galena, so—'

'Cut the crap, Silver! I'm assuming my sergeant here decided that forty seasoned coppers were not up to arresting one single man?'

'I do come highly recommended.' He grinned at her, 'Good to see you, Nikki.'

She couldn't keep it up. She had no intention of melting where Joseph was concerned though. 'Good to see you too, Vinnie — at least it would have been if we were not in the middle of a raid.' She glared at Joseph. 'So I'm assuming my mother and the rest of her coven are not doing anything too illegal right now, or you wouldn't have left them. Would you?'

'Reconnaissance and observation. As per orders.' Vinnie tried hard to look innocent.

'I bloody well hope so. But as you're here, you'd better stick with this officer. He called you in, so you are all his. And no silly stuff, either of you. If any part of this operation goes tits up and you are even remotely connected to it, you will not find me very pleasant, or the way I deal with you. Got it!'

'You've made yourself perfectly clear, thank you.' Joseph gave Vinnie a resigned look.

'And you too, Vinnie. You have no right to be here, so observation only.'

Vinnie saluted. 'Understood, ma'am.'

'Oh, bollocks to the both of you! Finish up here with Mr Town and Country Laker. I'm going to see how Morgan and Connor are getting on with the gamekeeper.'

Nikki was actually relieved that Vinnie had turned up. It was unorthodox, but she knew she could justify his presence to Cameron Walker if need be. Most importantly, Vinnie would do everything he could to keep Joseph from stepping out of line.

All they needed now was to bloody well find something, because so far, forty coppers, now with the additional presence of an ex-army veteran, had found sod all.

CHAPTER THIRTY-TWO

Rage coursed through him. Just when the whole thing was almost done, it was starting to go wrong. They were searching his home. They wouldn't find anything of course, but still, nothing must stop him completing his mission. He had to do it for Dean. If he failed, neither of them would rest.

What was this? Tears? He hadn't cried since the day he found Dean. He tried to push the image from his mind — the terrible creaking of the rope as Dean's body swung gently back and forth like a pendulum.

He would just have to improvise. There was no alternative. It wasn't what he wanted, but it would still work. At least he had left nothing incriminating in the place he called home. By tonight, it would all be over, and he would have kept his promise to Dean.

* * *

'What a disappointment,' Eve said.

'Disgusting,' added Wendy.

'Ugh. I can't wait to get out of here. This is not the lair of a cunning killer,' concluded Lou.

'More like an annexe to the local tip.' Rene's nose was wrinkled in distaste. 'Look at all these old papers! And all these bags of shredded documents. It's a nightmare.'

It was the home of an obsessive. Eve recalled the home of a hoarder she had once visited, and this was certainly heading that way. The odd thing was that the kitchen and bathroom were both moderately tidy, and the sinks and toilet were spotlessly clean.

She opened a wardrobe and peered inside. Ordinary clothes, rather uncared for. Clean shirts, un-ironed but certainly not filthy rags. It seemed that Edward Richmond had let his campaign take over his life, but had held onto some vestiges of sanity.

Well, however mad or sane he was, Edward wasn't stockpiling archaic poisons or keeping young women imprisoned in his spare room. It was time to go.

'Come on, girls. We've seen enough. I was wrong about this man, he's just got a very sad life.'

Soon they were back in Eve's car and driving away from Ferry Street.

'Knowing what we do now, do you think Edward really has had a change of heart?' asked Wendy. 'Could someone who has spent so long fighting for a cause suddenly turn their back on it?'

'Yes,' said Lou. 'Absolutely. Tipping point. Everything builds up until one day someone says one small thing, or you come to a decision about a very minor issue, and everything changes.'

'Almost beyond your control?' queried Rene. 'I can understand that.'

'So, do we think he might just allow Robert and the family to do the right thing, and show those amazing pictures to the world?' Eve felt a tiny shiver of anticipation. One of the reasons she had agreed to meet Robert again was to get another look at those paintings.

'I'm just glad I didn't damage the lock,' Wendy said. 'He'll never know we were there.'

'Unless someone tells him,' said Lou. 'Although I doubt that would happen. Apparently he doesn't get on with any of the neighbours, so he'll hardly be chatting to them.'

'I feel really guilty,' admitted Eve. 'I allowed my imagination to run away with me, and now we could all be charged for breaking and entering, probably by my own daughter.'

'For some reason I don't think Neighbourhood Watch has a branch in Ferry Street, and if they do, I reckon they'll turn a blind eye where Mr Richmond is concerned.' Rene chuckled. 'Relax, Eve. No harm done. And on the positive side, we helped Vinnie make the right choice, didn't we?'

'As I recall, the poor fellow didn't *have* a choice,' laughed Lou.

'And no police time was wasted chasing down a dead end,' Wendy added. 'We've done Nikki a favour, Eve, she should actually be pleased with us.'

'If she ever hears of this, you are all dead meat,' Eve said.

Lou ran a finger across her lips. 'Your secret is safe with us.'

Rene chortled. 'And on the plus side, we now have something to blackmail you with.'

Eve drove to the rarely used car park they had been told about, wondering what might have happened if she had been right about Edward being the Coachman.

'You okay, Eve?' Rene patted her shoulder.

'I'm fine. Who's going to text Vinnie and tell him it was a big, fat zero but we are all safe?'

'Me, please.' Lou already had her phone in her hand. 'He's been gone so long, I'm having withdrawal symptoms.'

Rene shook her head. 'Hopeless cause.'

'So,' Eve said, 'let's decide what to do next. I'm up for anything that doesn't involve breaking and entering.'

* * *

As morning turned into afternoon, Nikki grew anxious. Neither of the men from the tied cottages could be located, although the other workers were adamant that they were in the grounds somewhere.

Joseph had become increasingly tense as the day progressed, and Vinnie was far from being his normal, ebullient self. Nikki recalled Joseph telling her that Vinnie reacted badly to fireworks. Was that all it was?

And who was this Edward Richmond her mother had been talking about? He had flagged up concerns. Had Eve been right that he was the Coachman, and he wasn't here at all?

Nikki strode over to where Vinnie and Joseph were deep in conversation. 'Any news from my mother, Vinnie?'

'Oh yes. That Richmond guy was a false lead, or so they reckon. They are now wondering what to try next.'

What a relief. One less worry. 'Good, well, I suggest that until Morgan and Connor, or Ben, eventually tracks down the gamekeeper and the groundsman, you two help out with checking the top floor of the Hall. That's the final area to be searched.'

She watched the two men move off and sank down onto a low wall that surrounded the old stable yard. Everything had pointed to the Old Hall. Poisons had been sourced from the phone in the office. The Coachman had to be here. She turned her mind to one other possible suspect. No one had been able to find Murray Kennington today. He came and went as he wished, and had access to all areas of the Old Hall. He didn't live here but was accepted like part of the furniture. And from what Dave said, he knew more about the place than even Cressy-Lawson himself. Because of his enthusiasm for the old building and its history, Clive trusted him implicitly and thought nothing of letting him roam the halls and investigate the unused areas.

Nikki looked back at the rambling old mansion. There was no way her officers would be able to cover every nook and cranny in a single day. It was the perfect place to hide things away — or people. Was Ellie Stevens concealed somewhere in this labyrinth of attic rooms, basements and outbuildings?

Or had she, Nikki, made a costly mistake in bringing her officers here?

This was no good. They had three men, all suspects, still to track down. Nikki Galena refused to give up until they were accounted for. She stood up and marched towards the front door of the Old Hall.

She found Joseph wandering around a big attic room with a very high ceiling that had a kind of minstrel gallery across one end.

'This place is massive. It could be a flat conversion in its own right.' He opened a heavy wooden cupboard door and peered inside.

Nikki gazed out of a high window, 'Tell me, Joseph, what did you think of the gamekeeper and the groundsman?'

'Never met them. They were both out that day I visited with Dave. He doesn't reckon either of them is a murderer, and they are definitely very loyal to the Cressy-Lawsons. Dave also said that they were working with him when Norma was attacked. Apparently Keats, the gamekeeper, was pretty devastated when he saw her — Dave had a feeling he may even have had a crush on her. Neither of them would have had an opportunity to hurt her in that way.'

'What about their history? Are either of them skilled in something other than estate work?'

'I can only go by what Dave told me, which was that Den Elliott worked in some kind of factory before coming here. Apparently he has a real love for the garden, especially the conservation and management of the woodland areas. Arthur Keats was in the Navy, and did a short stint in a research lab, something to do with food testing, I believe. Then he finally followed in his father and grandfather's footsteps and became a Cressy gamekeeper.'

'Dave doesn't want to believe it's anyone from here, I know that, but confronted with the evidence, I had no choice,' Nikki said.

Joseph nodded. 'Absolutely. Well, we haven't finished here yet, not nearly.'

Nikki ran her hand over a carved wooden panel. 'We mustn't forget that it was the groundsman, Den Elliott, who noticed that truck being used without permission and reported it to Dave, so that doesn't put him too high up the list of possibilities, does it?'

'I keep thinking that we must have overlooked someone, but no one else fits the description.' Joseph opened the lid of an old carved oak window seat, and let out a startled whoop of surprise. 'Oh! Look, Nikki!' He held his arm across her to stop her getting too close. 'But be careful!'

'What the f . . . ?'

Nikki was staring at heaps of phials, syringes, boxes of tablets and powders and several glass bottles, all lying on a thick bed of bubble wrap and some kind of soft wadding, in one of those shallow boxes used to pack bananas for a supermarket. 'Is this his stash of poisons?' she whispered.

'I can't think it's anything else. Shall I ring for forensics?'

'Too right. I want to know exactly what all that stuff is, and fast.' Nikki narrowed her eyes. 'And I think a word in the ear of the lord of the manor is in order.' She turned around to see a uniformed officer passing the door. 'Constable! Get this room sealed off please, quick as you can.'

As the PC hurried off, Nikki peered closer at the paraphernalia in the chest. 'No labels that I can see, can you, Joseph?'

'No, but there are different liquids in them. I'm guessing he knows exactly what is what.' Joseph looked around the big room, 'But why hide them up here? I mean, people like the gamekeeper or the groundsman wouldn't be happily traipsing around in the main house, would they?'

'I'm thinking that too. I reckon they've been placed here for us to find, don't you?' Nikki said.

Joseph nodded. 'Looks that way. But why?'

'To throw us off the scent and stop us from looking elsewhere. To keep us well away from his real lair, and possibly from where he's hiding Ellie Stevens.' Nikki felt as if her mind were about to explode, so many odd thoughts were pouring in. 'And that puzzles me too. He's always taken random victims and dealt with them at once. Why suddenly snatch a woman off the streets, and, well, do nothing? She's been missing since yesterday. It just doesn't fit.'

'Abduction is risky, and hiding someone even riskier.' Joseph nodded thoughtfully. 'I'm with you on that. It doesn't fit at all.'

'Bloody conundrums. I could do without them right now. Joseph, stay here. I need to go down and talk to his lordship, and I don't think he'll be too happy when he hears that we are bringing forensics in on top of everyone else.'

'Rather you than me.'

Nikki found Clive Cressy-Lawson in the main office, but before she could utter a word, he began to apologise. 'I'm sorry, Inspector. I behaved appallingly. What I said about Dave Harris was unforgivable. I didn't mean it in the slightest. He's a fine fellow and, well, all this, I mean I never realised how much I relied on Norma, and to think of how she died . . .' There was a catch in his voice. 'It's beyond reason. Then, when I saw the police cars and all those men and women trampling over my home, it was all just too much . . .' He threw up his hands. 'My behaviour was inexcusable, I know, but I hope you accept my sincere apologies. I really am sorry.'

Nikki was so taken aback that she hardly knew what to say. 'Er, well, I don't think I was exactly at my best either, so let's forget it, shall we, sir? But I have something to ask you. There's an attic room with a high ceiling and a sort of gallery — you know which one I mean? Is it used much?'

'Oh, that room. No, pretty well never. Why?'

'Certain items have been found in an old window seat there, sir, and we believe they are connected to the killer.'

'What?' Cressy-Lawson was clearly shocked. 'But no one goes up there, especially as that area is one of the places that is haunted. Murray Kennington set up a ghost watch in that room and the corridor outside not too long ago, and our visitors were taken along that way during the ghost walk, but other than that it's left untouched.'

'Ghost? What sort of ghost?' Nikki asked. *How convenient.*

'The Cressy Wraith, an ethereal young man in dark clothing who roams the roof and that area of the attic space.'

'And have you seen him, sir?'

'Not personally, but some of the staff have, and one of Murray Kennington's history buffs apparently.' He raised his eyebrows. 'I don't believe in ghosts, Detective Inspector, but this is a very old house and sometimes I do wonder if . . .' He stopped. 'No matter. This is no time for a discussion on the paranormal. How can I help?'

Nikki was mildly stunned by his complete change of attitude. She guessed that his original outburst had been the result of shock, and now he was himself again — the person that Dave had come to like. 'We have to secure the room, get the items taken away for analysis and check it for forensic evidence like fingerprints and DNA. I just wanted you to know that no one can go up there for a while.'

'Can I ask what you found, Inspector?'

'I'm sorry, I can't say at present, sir, and in truth, I have very little idea of exactly what we have found.' She smiled. 'I'm not trying to be deliberately obtuse, and I promise we'll tell you as soon as we can.'

'Then I'll make sure everyone knows not to go up to the top floor until you're finished.'

Nikki left, still quietly amazed at his sudden transformation. So, Dave wasn't such a plonker after all. She'd seen a side to Cressy-Lawson that she, and most others, never knew existed.

* * *

Dave put the phone down and cursed under his breath. He wanted to check out the modified photos that Spooky had done for them, but ever since he collected them, the office phones hadn't stopped ringing. Even Cat, who was keeping one eye out for the staff list from Dean Kennedy's printing company, was fielding calls right left and centre.

Finally, the phones fell silent and he was able to pull the sheaf of images towards him.

Face after face stared back at him. All of them had that tiny something, a kind of half recognition that he couldn't put a name to.

He was halfway through the pile when Cat let out a gasp. He leaned over her shoulder and stared in amazement. 'It can't be! But . . .'

Cat leapt from her chair and snatched the printout from the machine. 'That's it, Davey! We know who the Coachman is!'

Dave held up the E-Fit, his mouth ajar.

'Get the boss, Dave! She's there right now.'

Dave snatched up his phone.

The moment she answered, he blurted out, 'It's Den, boss, Den Elliott, the groundsman! Spooky has managed to get an image that is clearly him, and Cat's just found that he worked with Dean Kennedy at the printers. Dean was his only close friend there.'

'And he's missing. Shit! Morgan, Connor and Ben have been calling at his cottage on and off all morning. He must have seen us coming and done a runner.'

'Or hidden somewhere, ma'am. It's a big estate. There are outhouses, sheds, stores, even an old air raid shelter where they keep potting compost and weed killer.'

'Okay, I've got enough bodies here. We'll concentrate on places he would know about, and we'll strip his house down to the floorboards. Go tell the super about this, Dave, and tell him to put out an attention drawn in case he got off the estate, okay? Oh, and Dave, you and Cat are due as many rounds of drinks as you like! You are diamonds, both of you.'

'Pleased, is she?' asked Cat.

'Delirious, Catkin — except for the fact that he's not there.'

'What a bummer. Still, at least we finally know who the bastard is.'

'I'm finding it very hard to get my head around that. He was such a . . . a gentle guy. Loved the woods and knew all about the plants and—'

'*Poisonous* plants?' Cat said. 'Like oleanders?'

Dave suddenly recalled a big greenhouse with rows of terracotta pots all planted with tall, spiky, evergreen plants. 'You could well be right. I'm still not sure how he managed to get to Norma when he was helping Arthur and me on security when she was attacked.'

'I'd take a closer look at your timings there,' said Cat. 'Prof Wilkinson said it was a pretty violent attack. It probably only took minutes.'

Dave nodded. 'Now we need to go fill the super in. Coming?'

Cat shook her head. 'I'll hold the fort here, Davey. You can claim this particular scalp.'

'I'm claiming it for both of us, Cat. You did the clever bit. I just looked at the pictures.'

'Sod off and give Cameron the good news. He could do with something to get him off the hook with the ACC.'

Smiling, Dave climbed the stairs to the superintendent's office. Maybe the job wasn't so bad after all.

CHAPTER THIRTY-THREE

Morgan Flint was first inside Den Elliott's cottage, with Connor Hale hot on her heels.

It was unexpectedly clean, very neat, and full of house-plants. The walls were covered with nature photographs of trees, many showing weird bark formations, moss and lichen and dewy leaves.

'Not quite what I expected,' muttered Nikki.

'Me neither,' said Morgan.

Connor returned from a search of the upstairs rooms. 'All clear, ma'am, nothing incriminating. The only thing that stood out was this.' He held up a photograph in an elegant carved wooden frame, a close-up portrait of a star-tlingly good-looking young man whose androgynous beauty had something timeless and classical about it, like a Greek sculpture in a museum. 'The picture in the local paper didn't do Dean Kennedy justice, did it?' said Connor.

'Hard to think that such beauty should be the cause of so much pain and death.'

'And what a waste that he should take his own life,' mused Nikki.

'It was most likely the catalyst for what followed,' Morgan said.

'I'm sure it was.' Nikki stared at the picture for a moment. They were wasting time. Den Elliott had vanished, and they had no idea what he was carrying with him. If it was something deadly, anyone who crossed his path was in mortal danger.

'Shut this place up. We'll get uniform to cordon it off and restrict access, although I'm pretty sure he won't be coming back here.'

'I'm sure you're right,' said Morgan. 'Let's join the search. It'll be sunset at around seven pm, and it's a huge area to cover.'

Leaving some constables to secure the cottage, they all moved off to find the uniformed officer in charge of what was now a manhunt. Whatever happened, they mustn't let him escape.

* * *

Dave saw Cat pulling her jacket from the back of her office chair. 'I've just had a call from the sarge. He says it's all hands on deck out at the Old Hall. We are to leave the pool detectives here and get out there pronto.'

Dave didn't move. 'Maybe I'll sit this one out. They have half the county's force out there, so one less won't make too much difference.'

'He also said, if you'd let me finish, that Clive Big-Nob keeps asking if you will please go and see him.' She pulled a face at him. 'So there. You are not persona non grata after all.'

'Oh, is that so? Well, in that case . . . I'll drive.'

* * *

Eve and her friends sat in her car, staring gloomily through the windscreen. They had got it all wrong, and it hurt. Vinnie had called to say the killer had been identified as Den Elliott, who was most likely holed up somewhere at the Old Hall. A patrol car had found his vehicle concealed off the road outside the main gates, no doubt left there in the event of him getting a chance to slip out.

'I really goofed this time,' said Eve.

'Well, we all thought the same, so it wasn't just you.' Wendy grinned at her. 'You don't always win, do you? There were times when we took some heavy knocks.'

'At least we didn't sustain any casualties,' Rene said.

'Unless you count Eve's ego,' giggled Lou. 'That's pretty bruised.'

'I keep thinking of your room at Monks Lantern. We buggered up a perfectly good wall for nothing.'

Wendy shrugged. 'Oh, I don't know. It was fun having a command centre again, wasn't it?'

A faint smile crept slowly over Eve's face. 'It was, wasn't it? One thing I do know is that I'm going to need a new challenge, otherwise I'm going to turn into a cabbage.'

Wendy laughed. 'One enquiry that didn't come off does not imply that you're in danger of becoming a vegetable. So, what shall we do with the rest of the day? We daren't go out to join the manhunt. Even I realise that would be going a step too far.'

'How about we hit the festival? This time we can just enjoy the fun. The Coachman is miles away, so why not join the party? That's what we originally came here to do.' Lou looked at the others.

'Why not?' Wendy opened the car door. 'I could do with a bit of light relief.'

* * *

Nikki was almost beside herself. 'Just an hour of bloody daylight left. He has to have legged it across the fields.'

'The super doesn't think so, Nikki.' Morgan stood beside her. 'When we arrived, Elliott was working in one of the wildflower gardens on the other side of the house. A member of the estate staff saw him there. We came in from the opposite direction without blues and twos. As soon as Dave told the super what was happening, he called in every spare man and woman from across the county and set up a perimeter patrol. With that many police watching the estate boundaries, Cam is certain he went to ground right here.'

'Well, if he is still here, where the hell is he?' Nikki stared across the acres of gardens.

In growing desperation, they moved on.

* * *

Having moved into one of the estate's woodland areas, Joseph and Vinnie were looking at a tiny structure built like a log cabin set in a small clearing. In front of it rested a big circular metal drum with a lid, and beside it, stacks of neatly cut wood.

'Charcoal production,' said Vinnie. 'Look — hardwood. There's hazel, chestnut, apple, all dried and ready for burning. He certainly took his woodland management seriously, didn't he?'

'This isn't how a killer operates, surely?' muttered Joseph.

'Shall we take the cabin now?' Without thinking, they took up their old army positions. 'Pincer movement?'

'You right, me left.' Joseph glanced at his comrade. 'Go.'

They slipped into the treeline and approached the cabin, one from each side. They peered through the two grubby windows, and then checked the door, which swung open to reveal an empty room. The place was nothing but a store to keep all the things Elliott needed for making his charcoal and bagging it up. No cupboards. No place to hide anything. Just a chair, some tools, a folded pile of sacks and an empty packing box used as a table.

On their way out, Vinnie ran his fingers over the makeshift kiln. 'Still warm. Nevertheless . . .' He picked up a pair of heat-resistant gauntlets that were resting on the log pile and carefully lifted the lid.

'Surprise, surprise,' he muttered. 'Charcoal.'

He replaced the lid and gloves, and they moved out of the wood and into an area that looked like an allotment.

The small shed wasn't really big enough to conceal a person for too long but it had to be checked.

As they cautiously approached it, Vinnie suddenly held up a hand. Joseph froze.

He knew no other police officers were in the vicinity, but he could hear something.

They crept forward silently.

The sound was clearer now, a rustling, like dried autumn leaves. Then he heard something else. Someone in distress.

'Here!' Vinnie ran forward and knelt down. 'Joseph! Call the medics!'

Joseph was already on his phone. One look at the black stab-proof vest had told him everything he needed to know. 'Man down!' He barked out their position and dropped to his knees beside the young police constable.

'Quick. Get him on his side. We don't want him choking.' Vinnie was easing the lad over.

His voice was little more than a whisper. 'Elliott. He . . . he stuck me with a needle.' His eyes rolled upward and his breathing became laboured. 'The house. He went towards the house.'

'Rest easy, lad, help is coming.' Joseph clasped the young policeman's hand. 'You hang on in there, and that's an order.'

Joseph didn't like the way the kid's pupils were contracting. He just hoped that this time it was a poison they had an antidote for.

The paramedics were with them in minutes.

'I think I know what this is,' one of the paramedics exclaimed. 'It's an overdose of morphine.'

'Morphine?' Joseph had been thinking of exotic poisons.

'I'm sure it is. If we can give him Narcan pre-hospital, and blue light him to resus, he might have a chance.' She looked at Joseph anxiously. 'If it's been injected, he's in trouble. We have to do something fast or he'll slip into a coma and die.'

Joseph nodded, recognising the slang for Naloxone, a drug that was administered for opiate overdoses. 'Go with your hunch. Do it.'

In moments, her partner was offloading the necessary equipment, and had radioed for another crew or an emergency doctor to help them.

When they saw that there was no more they could do, Joseph and Vinnie stepped aside.

'The house then. Are you ready?' Joseph asked Vinnie.

Vinnie hesitated. It was a fraction of a second, but Joseph had noticed. 'Vinnie?'

'Nothing. Let's go. But you must notify Nikki.'

'No time! He'll get away!' Joseph threw back. 'Come on! He's just one guy, and he'll be frightened.' He turned and started running towards the Old Hall. As he ran, he heard Vinnie's footsteps close behind him.

* * *

The light was fading. The day had been overcast and the night clouds were rolling in early. The news that an officer had been attacked and injured had spread like wildfire through those involved in the manhunt.

Dave sat in the library with Clive, glad he wasn't tramping the gardens and the woodlands like the others, although he hadn't enjoyed being the one to break the news about Den Elliott.

'Another attack, right here at my home. I just can't believe that Den, *Den* of all people, is responsible for it all. He's not capable of violence of any sort, let alone what was done to Norma, I swear he's not.'

Clive leaned forward and put his head in his hands.

'We believe that someone he cared a great deal about killed themselves, and it pushed him over the edge,' Dave said.

'But Norma, a woman he knew so well. How is that even feasible?'

'Anything is possible, Clive. I've seen stranger things in my job, believe me.' As a matter of fact, Dave had never seen anything as horrific as the suffering Elliott inflicted on Norma Warden.

'Then I don't know how you do it, I really don't.'

'Nor do I sometimes. Actually, I'm thinking that this could be my last case,' Dave confessed. 'But don't tell my boss.'

'It would be enough to finish me, that's for sure.' Clive looked up. 'Talking about your boss, maybe I should tell her that there is another way up to that attic room where they found some evidence.'

Dave straightened up. 'Tell me, I'll go pass it on.'

'It's called the Wraith's Route. It's the way our lonely ghost is supposed to gain access to the roof. There's a second staircase that runs from the outside down to the old kitchens, then right up to the attics and the roof. The below stairs maids used it in times gone by, to get to the rooms on the other floors without being seen by their masters.'

'Can you show me, Clive?'

In the fading light, they made their way around to the far end of the building. Clive pointed to an old wooden door set in the wall. 'We do lock it, but since it's rarely used except for maintenance, it does sometimes get forgotten.'

He tried the door, and it swung open. He made a face. 'As I said.'

Dave peered in. The one small ceiling lamp did little to dispel the shadows. There was a short flight of steps down to the kitchens, and then a curving stone staircase led up into darkness.

'There are other lights as you go up, unless the bulbs have blown, and a door giving access to each floor.' Clive gazed upwards. 'I've been told to stay away from the areas that forensics are working in, so if you want to go up, you'd better go alone.'

'I'll report back to the boss first, then we'll check it out.'

'I'll go back indoors.' Clive gripped his upper arm. 'Go careful, Dave, the steps are steep and worn. Make sure you have a torch.'

Dave watched him leave, pulled out his phone and put it away again. He'd better go and find her and explain properly.

As he exited the door, something moved further along the path. He backed into the tiny hallway and watched.

Someone was making their way towards him, keeping close to the house and in the shadows. Dave swallowed. He was not exactly in the peak of condition, and if this was the Coachman, he didn't rate his chances.

Heart hammering in his chest, he looked again. 'Sarge! Thank heavens it's you! I thought it might be Elliott.'

If Joseph was surprised to see Dave there, he didn't show it. Rather, he looked annoyed.

'What on earth are you wandering around on your own for, Dave? No one goes anywhere alone with this guy loose, you know that.'

'I was with Clive. He's only just gone back inside. But listen to this.'

Joseph was being unusually curt. 'Hurry up then. What is it?'

'He called it the Wraith's Route. Look.' He pushed the door open. 'It leads to all the floors and the roof. It also leads to the room with the evidence you discovered. Convenient, huh?'

Joseph glanced at Vinnie Silver, who had just then emerged from the shadows. A silent message passed between them, to which Dave was not privy.

'Don't worry, we'll check it out, Dave.' Joseph's voice had softened but it still didn't sound like him. 'Don't you come. You go back to Cressy-Lawson. He could probably do with some support right now.'

About to object, Dave considered the steep steps and capitulated. 'Okay, but I'll go and tell the boss first.'

'No need. I'll ring as soon as we see if there's anything worth telling her.'

Then the two men were gone, up the circular staircase and into the darkness.

Bemused by the sarge's odd attitude, Dave went back to find Clive. Maybe it was the stress making him oversensitive. Joseph was more than likely just worried about him.

* * *

Joseph raced ahead, certain they would find Elliott somewhere in the maze of chimney stacks and gables. After some time, he had a feeling that Vinnie was holding back.

'He's up there, I know it,' he whispered back over his shoulder.

'So do I,' Vinnie said. 'Look, Joseph, this really isn't something we should be tackling alone.'

'Come on. We understand how to do this better than anyone here. You know that. We take him down, game over.'

Vinnie didn't answer.

By now they were up at roof level.

Joseph opened the door and was immediately buffeted by a chill wind. 'Remember,' he whispered, 'he'll most likely have a syringe in his pocket, or even something worse, something like a spray? No way can we let him reach into his pockets.'

Vinnie was standing in the doorway, gazing up at the darkening sky. There was little light left now, but Joseph could just make out the expression on his friend's face. It looked very much like fear.

Suddenly Vinnie moved forward and gripped Joseph's arm, so hard it hurt. 'Joseph, if he's here, we do this quickly, and we do it right. I will not let you ruin your life, or that of any of the people you love, understand? We do it by the book.'

'He's a ruthless murderer, Vin. If he resists, I'll do whatever's necessary.'

'You will use reasonable force. Now let's get this over with.'

These words caused Joseph to hesitate for a moment, but then he thought of the dying student.

All at once and as if on cue for the performance to begin, the place became bathed in light. Joseph had forgotten that on special occasions, the entire building, along with the gardens, was lit up at night. The Old Hall took on an ethereal glow. Clive Cressy-Lawson must have decided that it would help the searchers. It would certainly help them, even if the place wasn't exactly floodlit.

They moved off in opposite directions, keeping each other in sight. Joseph moved stealthily, eyes peeled for the slightest movement. So far nothing indicated the presence of anyone else on the roof, but that didn't mean they weren't there. Most of the roof area was flat, but there were deep pools of shadow caused by giant chimney stacks and dark gullies where one angle of roof met another, all places where a man could easily hide. But was Vinnie with him? There was something odd about the way he was behaving, hesitating and occasionally glancing upwards.

Vinnie saw him first. He held up a hand and pointed to where the Coachman stood, still as a statue. Unaware of Joseph and Vinnie, he was standing at the very edge of one of the crenelated towers, looking down at the dozens of police officers now returning to the house in the encroaching darkness.

Joseph and Vinnie slipped back into the shadows and crept towards Elliott, one from each side, keeping their distance, waiting until he stepped away from the edge of the roof.

Just as Joseph thought he would never move, Elliott stepped back a few paces and leaned on a stretch of decorative balustrading about two metres from the edge. It didn't allow much room for manoeuvre but it would suffice to take him down. Joseph began to calculate the best way to reach him in order to take him by surprise.

Just as he was about to lunge forward, he heard a series of small explosions, and a massive firework lit up the night sky.

Vinnie froze, a look of horror on his face, and Joseph realised why his friend had been looking upwards. He had been on the point of leaving Greenborough early, so as to be miles away before the fireworks began, but he had stayed to protect Joseph, who hadn't given Vinnie's deep-seated fear of pyrotechnics a single thought. In his all-consuming obsession with getting to the Coachman, he had completely forgotten about the fireworks that accompanied the last evening of the festival.

Trying not to alert Den Elliott to their presence, he went to Vinnie and took his arm. 'It's okay, mate. Look, you get back to the staircase. I'll bring him in alone, you just get off this roof and down to ground level.'

Vinnie was already sweating profusely and his hands were shaking. 'No way. I'm not going anywhere,' he whispered hoarsely.

His expression told Joseph that it would be useless arguing. He was steps away from their killer. He should end this now.

He squeezed Vinnie's arm.

Elliott was still standing by the balustrade, seemingly deep in thought. Joseph grabbed him from behind and pinned one arm behind his back.

'I should throw you over the edge,' he growled. 'It would be better for everyone. In fact, I think I will. No one will know that you didn't slip and fall.'

He wrenched Elliott's head around to face him, and to his surprise, Elliott was laughing. 'Please do! Why do you think I'm up here? To watch the fireworks?'

Joseph shoved him slightly closer to the edge. Elliott didn't resist.

'Joseph! By the book! Think of Nikki!' Vinnie was screaming at him.

Another firework tore its way up into the sky, and exploded into dozens of whining, crackling fireballs.

Joseph saw Vinnie crouch, head down and hands clasped over his ears, desperately trying to block out the horror. He had to go to him!

Joseph looked from Elliott to Vinnie, undecided. He gripped Elliott tighter. Just a shove, and it would all be over.

'Help me! Bunny! Help me!'

Vinnie was calling out his old army nickname, derived from the Easter Bunny. As Joseph turned to look at him, he caught sight of a group of armed officers creeping stealthily across the roof from the direction of the stairwell.

He closed his eyes for a second, and then pulled Elliott away from the edge. It took an instant to have him cuffed and lying face down. 'Take it from here, please!' he called out to the advancing team, 'And do not, I repeat, do not touch his pockets. We don't know what he's carrying, and it could be lethal.'

As soon as the firearms unit had the man covered, Joseph ran over to Vinnie, now curled up in a tight ball. Overhead, colours blazed and the screeching, whooshing, thunderous sounds of the fireworks resounded through the dark.

Joseph picked up his friend, put him over his shoulder and carried him back toward the stairs.

Nikki stood, waiting, Morgan Flint on one side, Dave on the other. Now he knew who had raised the alarm and called in a tactical squad.

'Help me! I've got to get him into the stairwell and away from all this noise.'

Nikki flung the door open. Joseph and Dave dragged the big man inside and slammed the door shut, cutting out the worst of the noise.

'PTSD?' asked Dave softly.

'Yeah.' Joseph had known for years, and yet tonight he hadn't given it a thought. Hating himself, he sat Vinnie on the top step and sank down beside him. 'I'll get you away from here, man, right now, okay?'

Vinnie was taking deep, rasping breaths. 'Panic attack,' he gasped.

'Don't talk, Vin, just concentrate on your breathing.'

Joseph turned to Dave. 'I have to get him away from here, but I'm not sure where to go. You can see these bloody things for miles.'

'What about Beech Lacey? Why not ask Eve if you can take him there?' Dave suggested.

'Good man!' He pulled out his phone.

'Get him here immediately,' Eve said. 'We are too far out to even hear them clearly. We are all here. We'll look after him, don't worry.'

'Tell Nikki what I'm doing, Dave. Okay?'

Dave nodded. 'Go careful, Sarge, you're both strung out. Oh, and well done for getting the Coachman away from that ledge. It could have been very nasty, couldn't it?' Joseph didn't reply.

With Joseph supporting Vinnie, they made their way down the stairs, one step at a time. Joseph wondered about the way Dave had spoken those last few words. Had he seen something? Had Nikki seen it?

He turned his attention back to Vinnie. 'I'm so sorry, Vinnie. It was unforgivable of me.'

'But he's in police custody, isn't he?' Vinnie breathed.

'Yes, he is. By the book.'

'And what if you had been up there alone?'

Joseph didn't answer.

'Then it was worth it. Now get me the hell out of here.'

CHAPTER THIRTY-FOUR

Nikki and Morgan waited in the interview room for Den Elliott to be brought up from the custody suite. He had been on suicide watch all night, but was now considered fit to interview.

Nikki thought it appropriate for Morgan Flint to be with her, rather than Joseph, considering the circumstances.

She read out the introductions for the tape, sat back and looked long and hard at Den Elliott. The Coachman. It was hard to believe that this gentle-looking man could have even imagined those atrocities, let alone carried them out. He appeared shorter than the Coachman, until it was found that the boots he had worn had elevated soles. And his hair was not long. They had been correct when they suspected a wig. He had also applied a little wadding along his upper jaw, and used a very pale make-up, resulting in a subtle but remarkable alteration to his features.

'You admit to all of the charges against you, Mr Elliott?'

'I do.' He said it reverently like a marriage vow.

'Can you tell us why you did those things? The deaths you caused and the terrible injuries you inflicted.'

'Not yet, but I will.' It was an odd thing to say.

'Can you clarify that, Mr Elliott?' asked Morgan Flint.

'You will need to send an officer to my other address. He must collect something and bring it here. Then I'll talk to you.'

'Other address?' asked Nikki.

'I have a rented flat in town. I'll give you the address.' He narrowed his eyes. 'On reflection, perhaps you should go in person?'

Neither Nikki nor Morgan responded. Nikki wrote down the address. 'Alright, sir, but before we do that, are you aware that there is a young woman missing?'

Den Elliott shook his head. 'No, I haven't heard anything about that.'

'Where have you hidden her, Mr Elliott?' Morgan stared at him unblinking.

'Hidden her? I don't understand. I haven't hidden anyone. Why would I?'

'You seem capable of quite a lot as far as we can see. Abducting someone would be nothing to a man like you,' Nikki stated bluntly.

His face seemed to crumple, as if he were about to cry. 'I don't know what you're talking about. I've never abducted anyone in my life! I've admitted to the things I did, so why would I deny that?'

'Ellie Stevens. Pretty young woman. Goes missing in Greenborough while you are roaming the streets killing people. You can't blame us for thinking you might be involved, can you?' Morgan's eyes never left him. 'Perhaps she was your next victim. Was there some sort of hitch? Did you have to postpone killing her?'

'Or is she already dead, Mr Elliott?' demanded Nikki, her voice as cold as Morgan's. 'Will you tell us where she is? The people who love her are worried sick, they want her back.'

'Where is she, Mr Elliott?' Morgan barked.

'Stop! This has nothing to do with me, I swear!' Den Elliott was clearly distressed by the accusation, and Nikki was inclined to believe him. Suddenly she switched the conversation back to his flat.

'So, if we go to your other address, what are we looking for?'

Elliott took a few seconds to respond. 'A manuscript. It's in a purple box file, with a couple of letters inside.'

'And that's all?'

'All? It's everything!'

Nikki stood up. 'Don't go away,' she said brightly. 'We'll be back.'

Outside the room they were met by Superintendent Cam Walker, who had been listening in to the interview. 'No one must walk into that flat, Nikki. Given his history, there could be a booby trap on the other side of the front door. We have to let a special unit check it out first.'

'Not a HazMat team, sir. That will take forever.'

'Would you prefer that someone got a face full of sarin gas? Nothing would surprise me about that man.'

'Of course not, Cam, but the clock is ticking on this guy, and he could well be using delaying tactics.'

'Even so, Nikki, it would be irresponsible of me to let you enter that place unprotected. All I'm suggesting is that you get advice from one of the Fire Service's scientific specialist managers.'

Nikki knew she wasn't going to win this one, so she threw up her hands. 'Then as fast as they can, please. Since he's refused to talk further until we have this bloody manuscript, we're snookered.'

As the super hurried off, Morgan asked, 'What was your take on the Ellie Stevens question?'

'Frankly? He didn't know what the hell we were talking about.'

Morgan nodded. 'My impression too. And he was right, wasn't he? If he's admitting to multiple murders, why deny abduction?'

'So where is Ellie Stevens?' Nikki inhaled. 'Look, while we are waiting for the go-ahead to enter his flat, I'm going to have a word with Niall about her.'

'Okay, I'll see you back in the CID room.'

Nikki found Niall in the back office, going through a heap of reports. He smiled at her. 'So, the Coachman's in our custody suite. Another great team effort. Congratulations, ma'am.'

Nikki didn't feel that it had been anything like a team effort, but she couldn't tell Niall that. 'The bastard's off the streets, that's what counts.' She flopped into a chair. 'Niall? Your Tamsin knows Ellie Stevens, doesn't she?'

Niall nodded. 'They're good buddies. They go to the gym together, shopping, they get on really well.'

'Would you ask her if Ellie was acting out of character in any way before she went missing? Morgan Flint and I are pretty certain that the Coachman knows nothing about her.'

'Tamsin's calling in this morning. I'll talk to her. What are you thinking?' Niall said.

'I'm wondering if there's another explanation for her disappearance.'

'I'll call you after I've spoken to Tam, Nikki.' He peered at her anxiously. 'Are you okay? You look kind of . . .'

Was he hesitating because he really didn't know how she looked, or because he didn't like to tell her? She raised an eyebrow.

'Well, I guess you look distracted,' he said.

Nikki would have liked to unburden herself, but this was between her and Joseph. 'I think tired and overworked is more accurate. Oh, and maybe a bit of reaction, knowing that the Coachman's reign is at an end. Don't you worry, I'm fine.'

He seemed satisfied with that, so she stood up. 'Speak later, Niall.'

She returned to her office, went inside and closed the door. Niall was pretty astute. She was indeed distracted. She kept picturing the scene on the roof of Cressy Old Hall. It could have been taken from a thriller movie: the dark chimney stacks of the old house, the fireworks illuminating the black sky with dramatic colour and explosive sound, two men locked in a struggle on the roof edge, and one other cowering on the floor.

Alerted by Dave, she and Morgan had arrived with the firearms unit just in time to hear Vinnie call out to Joseph, begging for his help. She had seen Joseph immediately look to his friend. She knew he wouldn't abandon him, but what haunted her was the few seconds that followed. Joseph seemed to be pushing his captor *towards* the edge, not away from it. Or was it a trick of the light?

Clearly, they had a lot of talking to do.

* * *

It was an hour before they received the okay to enter the Coachman's other address. It was a small one-bed flat in a complex of reasonably priced apartments close to the river. Thankfully, there had been no lethal welcoming gift when the door was opened.

Whereas his home on the estate was an attractive shrine to nature, this was more like a busy office. No home comforts in the living area, just a desk and chair, a computer, printer, shredder, filing cabinets, high bookshelves and a massive stationery cupboard. There were no pictures on the walls. Instead there was a clock, a large wipe-clean magnetic message board and a large-scale street map of Greenborough.

While keeping her eyes open for the precious purple box file, Morgan wondered exactly what Elliott had been doing here.

She had assumed that the bedroom would be as serviceable, just a room to sleep in. Nikki opened the door and gasped. 'Oh hell! Come here, Morgan.'

Morgan looked over her shoulder. 'What the . . . ?'

It was a good sized double bedroom, but it had been kitted out like a laboratory, and a pretty hi-tech one at that. Well, half of it was. The room was divided down the centre. One side was all stainless steel with modern lab equipment and some electronics that Morgan couldn't put a name to.

The other side of the room was from another era altogether.

An old scrubbed wooden table housed an ancient set of scales and dozens of coloured bottles, a pestle and mortar, and some vintage laboratory equipment that belonged in a museum. Brass Bunsen burners were set beneath a series of bulbous glass test tubes held in place by more brass fittings and narrow coils of tubing. Above the table, suspended from an old ceiling mounted Victorian clothes drying rack, were dozens of bunches of herbs and dried flowers.

'Well, I think we've found what we came for.' Morgan indicated to the far wall of the room where, placed exactly halfway between old and new, stood a small crescent shaped table. On it was the purple box file and a small spray of fresh wildflowers, and above that, on the wall, a larger copy of the framed photograph they had found at Elliott's cottage on the estate. Dean Kennedy smiled down at them graciously, forever beautiful.

'It feels almost disrespectful to take it away,' said Morgan.

'Bugger that!' Nikki pulled on her latex gloves, marched over and picked it up. 'Back to Jekyll and Hyde.'

Smiling, Morgan followed her to the car. The more time she spent with DI Nikki Galena, the more she liked her.

* * *

Assured that they no longer suspected him of abduction, Den Elliott began to talk. The interview was one of the most bizarre Nikki had ever conducted.

'Of course it wasn't meant to be like this at all.' Den Elliott shrugged. 'Not that it matters now. I accomplished what I set out to do, except for the final one. I had planned to leave the manuscript with the last victim, with a letter of explanation, and as the fireworks lit up the heavens, I was going to leave forever. You wouldn't know who or where I was, and I'd be long gone.' He smiled benignly. 'But this is good too, because now I can actually tell you why it had to happen, and then you'll understand.'

Like fuck I will, thought Nikki.

'Could you take us back to the beginning, Mr Elliott?' Morgan asked.

'Den, please. We were the two Ds see — Dean and Den, the Dream Duo.'

'From the beginning?' Nikki urged, trying not to picture them in matching anoraks.

Den settled back in his chair. 'Dean was a brilliant writer, Officers, and a lovely person, once you got him to open up.' He gave a gentle laugh. 'It took time, but was worth every second.' Tears filled his eyes. 'He was so beautiful, and so terribly sensitive.'

Morgan pushed a box of tissues towards him. 'Tell us about the manuscript.'

Den took a deep breath. 'He spent two years working on it, every spare minute he had. He worked all night sometimes, and the research he did . . . he contacted every source imaginable.' He sniffed. 'I helped as much as I could, but mainly I just read what he'd written and commented on structure and continuity, that kind of thing. I've always been a bit of a wordsmith.'

Nikki recalled the letter to the ACC, with its precise, careful wording.

Den was continuing. 'He was obsessed with Victorian era crime, which was odd considering his age. He spent a long time searching for some aspect of it that had not been done to death,' he gave a taut little laugh, 'if you'll excuse the pun. Then he chanced upon Creep, who was the perfect subject. It turned out to be an excellent piece of original work.'

'So why didn't he ever publish?' asked Nikki.

Den Elliott's eyes hardened. 'Because he was destroyed before the manuscript ever saw the light of day.'

'He was destroyed?' Morgan looked puzzled. 'By what?'

'Don't you mean whom?' His voice rose.

'Do I? Explain, please.'

Den Elliott fought to compose himself. 'It was my mistake. I was so sure that if given to the right publishing house, it would be snapped up, that I forgot about Dean's profound insecurity and self-doubt.'

Nikki was beginning to see where this was going, but couldn't believe that the source of all this carnage was a rejection letter. 'So . . . he did submit the manuscript?'

'I submitted it, Inspector Galena. I made a list of the very best non-fiction publishing houses that specialised in history and historical crime, and then sent them letters requesting permission to submit the manuscript. Several responded, and I chose a major London publisher.' He stared down at the table. 'I wish to God I hadn't.'

His guilt at causing Dean Kennedy's death was palpable. A well-meaning act of kindness had gone horribly wrong. Was that the start of Den Elliott's madness? Or had he always been this way?

'We waited a long time for a response. I knew it happened in publishing, sometimes they never replied, so you moved on to someone else. But a reply did come. It arrived when I was working an early shift, and Dean was alone.' He pointed to the purple box. 'The letter is in there.'

Morgan opened the file and removed a letter emblazoned with a fancy logo and a copperplate header. She read through it and passed it across to Nikki.

It was addressed to Dean Kennedy and started with the usual apology for rejecting the manuscript. The writer of the letter then went on to say that they felt the author should be aware of their thoughts on his book before sending it elsewhere. They then proceeded to slate the entire thing, citing the appalling standard of writing and research. According to them, the subject matter was a "*farcical sequence of impossible events that belonged in a fantasy world.*"

'But I thought you said it was good?' Nikki asked, shocked at the savagery of the attack on the manuscript.

'It was!' He exclaimed bitterly. 'That,' he pointed to the letter, 'that disgusting piece of filth was a mistake! It was meant for another author and a different book. A secretary had mixed it up with Dean's manuscript. Much later, recently in fact, when I challenged them, they told me that they would have been more than happy to accept it and welcome him to their catalogue. But Dean was dead by then, wasn't he?'

Nikki still didn't understand why this had led Den Elliott to become the Coachman, and commit those terrible crimes.

'Mr Elliott, sorry, Den,' Morgan sounded reasonable, even if she was as puzzled as Nikki, 'Den, I understand your grief, because I assume Dean killed himself immediately he read this letter, but I don't understand why you waited, and then began killing people in this horrific manner.'

He closed his eyes. 'It's simple. Think about it.' Apparently exasperated, he glared at Morgan. 'Like he did, I believed the letter was meant for Dean. They had called the subject an impossible fantasy, and I wanted to prove them wrong. That's all. I learnt about all the kinds of poisons Creep employed, and as I've always been interested in chemistry and botany, I decided to recreate them, and prove that Dean's work was based on fact.'

Nikki frowned. 'But you've just told us they admitted the letter was a mistake. They weren't even talking about his book.'

'Oh yes, but by that time I'd prepared my plan. Everything was in place. I realised it was the perfect way to make someone pay for Dean's unnecessary death. I owed it to him. I needed to make his book live on.'

'You could have had the damn thing printed posthumously, given it to the world to appreciate, and saved a lot of lives,' Nikki spat out. She was getting tired of Den Elliott and his lack of remorse. 'All those poor people, random victims you've either killed or maimed. How is that a fitting memorial for a talented dead boy?'

'Random?' His eyes had narrowed to slits.

Morgan drew in a breath, nudged Nikki and pointed to the publisher's letter. 'Look.'

She hadn't read to the very bottom. Now she saw it. The name of the publishing house employee who had made the error was Norma Warden.

Nikki swallowed hard. Norma had been the one most viciously attacked, the one who was mutilated and died in agony. 'And the others?'

'Characters from the book, Creep's victims. The snake venom character, the oleander character, nothing more. They were bit parts. Norma Warden had the leading role.'

Bit parts? Nikki remembered Jim Fortune, a heroic paramedic, and all the others who had died. For a second, she wished Joseph had pushed him off that roof.

'So, years later, you tracked Norma Warden down, took a job in the place where she was then working, and put your plan into action?' Morgan asked incredulously.

'Exactly. And Dark Greenborough was the perfect backdrop to the production.' He looked at them with wide, innocent eyes. 'You do see now why it had to happen, don't you? That woman's actions took the most beautiful thing in my world and destroyed it. You can't do things like that to decent people! It's not fair and it's not right. You *have* to pay.'

Decent? Nikki thought. Decent people don't commit murder.

Morgan stared at him, her icy gaze unwavering. 'We saw your home, Den. You are capable of appreciating the beauty in nature. You tend the gardens with a great deal of care, and yet on the streets of Greenborough, and on the estate, you have committed the most horrific crimes against human beings. How do you explain it?'

He stared back, equally steadily. 'I am Dennis Elliott, who loves and cherishes beautiful things. I still do. In order to avenge Dean's death, I had to become Creep. As Creep, I could do anything, anything at all. As Creep, I made her pay.'

Neither she nor Morgan answered him for a while, then Nikki said coldly, 'It wasn't for you to play prosecutor and executioner, Mr Elliott. After all, it was just a terrible mistake, not a deliberate act. Only God could judge Norma Warden, not you.' She stood up. 'We'll talk again later. I've heard enough for now. Interview terminated at eleven twenty.'

Outside, the two detectives stared at each other. 'He'll never go to jail, will he?' Nikki said. 'It will be a secure psychiatric unit somewhere.'

Morgan looked dubious. 'If he goes anywhere. I'm not sure he'll even make the trial. When he said he had planned to go away forever after this was over, maybe he was planning on joining the other member of the Dream Duo.'

'Maybe. Joseph did say that when he accosted him on the roof of Cressy Old Hall, he announced he was going to throw himself off.' Nikki didn't want to think about that rooftop scene right now, so she quickly moved on. 'And if he loves nature and the woods so much, being banged up in a psych ward would probably finish him off. So, you could be right, Morgan.'

Morgan stretched and leaned back against the wall. 'He really is a Jekyll and Hyde, isn't he? I don't think I'll ever get my head around someone who's capable of making charcoal in a woodland clearing, photographing trees and picking wild flowers, and then breaking a woman's jaw as he forces phosphorus down her throat.' She shuddered. 'I think I need an antidote to the last half an hour.'

'A strong coffee?'

Morgan grinned. 'I was thinking more of a bar of chocolate.'

'Now you're talking! Come on, my treat.'

* * *

An hour later most of the team were gathered in the CID room for an impromptu catch up on what had happened over the last few hours.

'I've been trying to work out the times on the afternoon when Norma was attacked,' said Dave. 'I remember noticing Den accept a cup of tea from one of the caterers, but before then there was a period of around ten minutes when he was unaccounted for. That would have given him time to assault Norma. Forensics have found splashes of phosphorus in one of the sheds, which tells us where he first accosted her.' He ran a hand through his hair. 'What then bothered me was where he put the acid container and the gloves he had to have worn. But,' he grinned, 'although uniform had done a search after the incident, no one looked inside all of the big watering cans stored in the shed.'

'You found them?' asked Nikki.

'We did. Acid container in one and gloves in another. The cans were both full of water which made spotting them difficult. Oh, and contrary to what we were told about Norma not having regular habits, she always walked the same way back to her cottage. The route took her right past the shed where the phosphorus was found. Elliott would have known that.'

'And we've discovered that both he and Arthur Keats regularly used the main office phone for ordering garden supplies and other equipment for their work,' said Ben.

'So when he tried to source the stuff he couldn't make himself in his creepy laboratory, it wouldn't have raised any eyebrows,' added Cat.

'I've been thinking,' Ben said. 'It's odd, isn't it, that everyone, including Dave here, thought Norma Warden was one of the most efficient people ever. And yet she was killed because she made a sloppy error.'

Morgan said, 'We talked about that. Nikki and I think she became so competent *because* of the terrible mistake she made that caused a young man to take his life. We think her guilt at what she'd done made her into a solitary.'

Ben nodded. 'That makes sense, I guess.'

Yvonne raised her hand. 'I've spoken to Sheila Pearson at the Hanged Man, and she's confirmed that Den Elliott was in the pub the night that Jim Fortune died. He often dropped in after work, had a single glass of lager and then went home. He never stayed for long. She said he was so inoffensive and quiet that she never gave him a second thought.' Yvonne paused. 'I was wondering why he would drive from Cressy Old Hall to the Hanged Man for one drink, then leave again and go back, but I'm guessing he was scouting for suitable victims.'

'Good point, Vonnie. Did the CCTV of that evening show anything?' asked Nikki.

'We've examined it minutely,' Yvonne said. 'There is no actual footage of him tampering with Jim's drink, but he did stand right next to him on two occasions. It was just that the camera angles were wrong. I would say he was certainly close enough to have spiked a drink.'

'And forensics have suggested that he was producing something in his laboratory that contained methanol,' Connor Hale told them. 'It looks like he never bought that refined stuff after all, but manufactured it himself. He had some pretty hi-tech equipment and he admitted that he enjoyed chemistry. They'll confirm that when they've finished their tests. And Prof Wilkinson said to say thank you very much for finally getting your fingers out and putting an end to all this, as he was having sleepless nights worrying about finding accommodation in his mortuary for so many new guests. And he said to remind you what he gets like when the worry lines start to show.'

Nikki smiled. She needed something to lift the mood that kept descending upon her. She still hadn't spoken to Joseph. She would have to do it tonight, when they were alone. She needed to hear from his own lips exactly what his intentions had been regarding the Coachman, and also why Vinnie had still been there with him when, knowing there were going to be fireworks, he had expressed the clear wish to head off before dark.

Vinnie had left for home that morning. Eve had rung her to say that she and her friends, plus a couple of glasses of malt whisky, had soon restored him to his old self, and after some sleep and a good breakfast, he had been fine. She had ferried him back to his hotel early in the morning to pick up his car and his things before he drove back to Kent. He had not, to her knowledge, seen or spoken to Joseph before he left, but he had phoned Sheila Pearson and promised to be back later in the week to take her out to dinner. Eve reckoned that was by far the best thing to come out of Dark Greenborough. She ended the call.

Nikki noticed that Morgan was looking at her with a slightly concerned expression. 'We'll be off in a day or so, Nikki. We can get the paperwork underway back at base, but anything you need or want to talk over, just ring me, okay?'

Nikki said she would. 'You've been a great help. All that stuff about Creep you found was invaluable.'

'Talking about that, I've had a swift look at Dean Kennedy's manuscript. It really was good, you know. He was talented.'

'I'm not sure I want to know that.' Nikki felt terribly sorry for the dead young man. 'He spent his whole life feeling insecure, not allowing himself to be honest and admit who he really was. Then, the moment he found something he was really good at, as well as someone who believed in him, a clerical error left him hanging from a tree. And his dearest friend goes from being a gentle naturalist to a psychotic killer. It's unbelievable.'

'Next time something crops up around the time of Dark Greenborough,' muttered Connor Hale, 'I may well be on holiday, or sick leave.'

'Rubbish! You loved it,' said Yvonne, who had developed rather a soft spot for their "guest" detective. 'You'll miss us like crazy after you've gone.'

Connor held his hands up. 'Very true, PC Collins. You've been great, all of you.'

Nikki recalled something she meant to tell Dave. 'You're going to like this one. Den Elliott has admitted to using the back stairs to the attic and the roof regularly over the years, often wearing dark clothing so as not to be noticed. I'm thinking that those occasional sightings of your ghostly Wraith at the Old Hall were actually him!'

Dave laughed. 'I don't think I'll tell the ghost hunters that one. It would really spoil their show!'

Ben raised a hand. 'I forgot to mention, I've finally got a name for the man Rory calls Francis. He was a rep who decided to stay on after work and enjoy the festival, poor guy.'

'As you say, poor guy.' Nikki shook her head. 'But now we are left with one rather big outstanding worry. Ellie Stevens.'

'You totally believe that Barking Den hasn't squirrelled her away somewhere?' asked Cat.

'He knows nothing about her, I'll guarantee it,' said Nikki.

'So will I,' added Morgan.

'Tamsin Farrow, who is a good friend of Ellie's, has gone over the time she spent at the festival with her, and come to the conclusion that there was something not quite right about her friend. For starters, Ellie wasn't where they had agreed to meet. She finally found Tamsin over half an hour later, and was quite cagey about where she'd been. They had a fun few hours together, but on reflection, Tamsin thinks she was unusually hyped up, and seemed eager to get away. So, what does that tell us?' Nikki asked.

'She was meeting someone?' chanced Cat. 'She's done a runner with some other guy, and didn't have the bottle to tell her partner.'

'It's going to be an ongoing investigation. Joseph is working on it right now and we'll all join him tomorrow, but that's what my gut tells me too,' Nikki said.

The door opened and Superintendent Cam Walker walked in. 'So, Dark Greenborough is finally over. What a festival! Thank God it's done with for another year. And somehow, although I have no idea how, we got away without having a media frenzy and a mass panic on our hands. We survived the weekend. Well done all of you.'

'And well done to you, sir, for keeping a lid on it for us,' Nikki said. 'Have you ever considered a career in politics? Maybe you're just the right person to steer us through Brexit.'

Everyone laughed at Cam's look of total horror.

'Perish the thought! You lot give me enough sleepless nights and nightmares, thanks all the same.'

* * *

Later that evening.
Monks Lantern, Beech Lacey.

When the phone rang, Eve had been expecting the caller to be Lou or Rene, to say they'd arrived safely, so she was surprised to hear the voice of Robert Richmond.

'I'm ringing for several reasons, Eve, but mainly to invite you to a small celebratory dinner here tomorrow night. It'll just be my nephew and his wife, but I thought you and Wendy might like to join us?'

'That would be lovely,' said Eve, 'but what's the celebration for?'

'I heard from Edward earlier. My brother has confirmed that he no longer wishes to oppose the family's wishes. When I pressed him as to the change of heart, he said that I must not ridicule him, but during the festival he had paid a visit to a fortune teller. She wasn't there, but he had spoken to a most intuitive and lovely lady. Somehow she managed to open his eyes to the fact that he was wasting his precious life and making everyone else's miserable in the process. I've no idea who she was, but this family owes her a great debt of gratitude.'

'Oh, that's wonderful, Robert! I'm so pleased for you.'

'The other thing is more of a business project. I'm not sure how you would feel about this, but I'm going to be tackling a complete renovation of Robert Matthew Richmond's studio, and I wondered, considering your genuine interest . . . would you, and perhaps Wendy, be interested in helping me?'

Eve recalled the feeling of dreadful waste and disrespect of the artist that big abandoned workroom had aroused in her. It had felt as if his soul had been buried under layers of dust and decay.

She had wanted a new project, hadn't she? And what better project than this?

'It will be a pleasure, Robert. I can't speak for Wendy, but you can count me in.'

'Excellent! I did so hope you'd agree. So, I'll see you tomorrow evening at seven thirty, here at Oleander House?'

'You will. And thank you.'

After she had hung up, Eve sat for a while, thinking. She had felt low in the aftermath of that ill-fated festival, but now she began to see some good coming out of it after all.

She would never know who Edward Richmond's "wise woman" had been, but her counsel would benefit hundreds of people. Finally the world would see and appreciate the most beautiful botanical studies it had ever been her privilege to set eyes on.

That woman's kind words would affect her too. Eve smiled to herself. A new chapter was about to open in the life of Eve Anderson, and she welcomed its advent with open arms.

* * *

The Hanged Man.

It was possibly an odd choice, given the case they had just been working, but Ben and Cat had decided that the old pub would be the perfect place to unwind. One of Sheila's legendary steak and ale pies and a couple of beers would be the perfect end to an extraordinary investigation.

Cat was shaking her head. 'I'm still trying to match up that gardener guy, Den Elliott, with the Coachman. It's too weird for words.'

After downing a good quarter of his beer, Ben agreed with her. 'I keep wondering if he was always predisposed to murder, or whether his guilt and grief just unhinged him.'

'I guess we'll never know the answer to that one.'

'I bumped into Spooky just before we left,' said Ben. 'Gill Mason is recovering well from her accident. She is staying with them for another day or two.'

'That woman's contribution to the investigation, especially that photo she took, really made a difference. And she's pretty brave too, to charge off after a killer like that.' She giggled. 'Even if she did go arse over tit and concuss herself in the process.'

Ben grinned. 'Dare I say, clairvoyant or not, she didn't see that coming!'

Cat groaned and rolled her eyes. 'Shut up, Ben! Jeez, I'm going to be so glad to say goodbye to ghoulies and ghosties for another year. All I want is ordinary crimes, and good solid, proper stuff.'

'Me too,' said Ben, 'and, well, is this the kind of proper stuff you mean?' He took a deep breath. 'Cat Cullen, will you marry me?'

Cat's face broke into a wide smile. 'If you're willing to take the risk, Ben Radley, so am I! I think that's the best suggestion I've heard for weeks.' She reached across the table and took his hand in hers. 'Yes, I will.'

'And we'll deal with everything that decision throws at us as we go along?'

'We'll deal with it together, Ben.'

'Champagne? To celebrate?'

'Nah, let's just go home.' Cat stood up and winked at him. 'I can think of a far better way to celebrate.'

* * *

Cressy Old Hall.

Dave sat across from Clive Cressy-Lawson in front of the open fire, and stared into the flames. In his hand was a small glass of Glenmorangie. He wasn't sure why he had been summoned here, but he sipped his drink appreciatively and cursed the fact that he had to drive home.

Having talked for nearly an hour, they had fallen into a comfortable silence. After a while, Clive said, 'I've been giving some of the things you mentioned a great deal of thought, Dave, and I think that the only way to come back from what happened is to face it head on.' He smiled. 'I've decided to open the Old Hall to the public. I shall keep parts of it private, of course, but talking to you has made me appreciate that I've been totally selfish about the place. Seeing your appreciation for the things I take for granted has been an eye opener. It really is time for a change.'

Dave looked delighted. 'That's excellent news, Clive. And if I might say so, a really sensible one from a business point of view.'

'Don't think I'm trying to cash in on the terrible things that have happened here, but I have no doubt the notoriety will attract plenty of visitors.'

Dave nodded. 'Indeed, many people will want to take a look at the most haunted house in the county.'

'Murray Kennington has offered to help with that side of it.' He paused, looking enquiringly at Dave. 'Er, Dave, you mentioned at one point that you were thinking about retiring from the force. If you were serious, I'd be delighted if you would consider working with me. If I'm going to have tourists here on a regular basis, I'm going to need some form of security, and I can think of no one better. Will you give it some thought?'

All his previous doubts came back to Dave. He'd seen too many deaths, met too many evil people — liars and cheats and bullies and thieves, and he was tired. Maybe this was just what he had been waiting for. Nowhere was perfect, and Old Cressy Hall had certainly seen its full share of horrific events of late, but it was still magnificent. Not only that, the majority of visitors would be decent people, coming to see and appreciate its beauty.

'Thank you, Clive. I will certainly give it some serious thought. It would be a wrench to leave the team — it's become my family over the last few years — but it feels like the right time to move on.'

Clive lifted his glass. 'I am very glad you'll consider it, Dave.'

They touched glasses. 'New beginnings for you,' Dave said, 'and I'm certain it will be for the best. Will Cilla join you, do you think?'

Clive raised his eyebrows. 'I've left it with her. I'm hoping she'll come home, but if she decides she can never be happy here, then we'll need to consider a different path for her. I'll not force her to come back. She must come because she wants to.' Clive sat back in his chair, looking relaxed for once. 'Oh, and tell your astronomer friend Spooky that there's a meteor shower expected early next week. If she's interested, the observatory is all hers.'

'I'll do that, Clive. And I won't keep you waiting for an answer, I promise.' Dave took another sip of his whisky. *So. New beginnings?*

* * *

Cloud Cottage Farmhouse, Cloud Fen.

Nikki had lit the fire, and was sitting warming herself at the flames, waiting for Joseph to come home.

He arrived half an hour later, with a bottle of wine, or was it champagne? He also carried a large brown paper bag.

'I took a gamble on Chinese, as I'd nothing to cook for tonight. All right with you?'

Nikki nodded. She was never at her best when she was hungry. It made her irritable, and she wanted their conversation to be amicable, but above all, honest. Snapping at him wouldn't help. At the back of her mind were her mother's words, her advice to cut him some slack. She loved him, and was prepared to give him the benefit of the doubt, but that scene on the roof would need a lot of explaining.

'Before we say anything else.' Joseph gave her an animated look. 'Tamsin just phoned me. She's had a text from Ellie Stevens. Our suspicions were correct. She's gone off with another man. She apologised to Tam for any worry she'd caused, etc., etc., and Tam rang me immediately.'

'So, we can put that one to bed, thank heavens!' Relief flooded through her. One less worry to deal with.

They ate at the kitchen table, and then took their drinks into the lounge. It had been wine that Joseph had bought, but it was her favourite Sancerre, and not cheap. She sipped it appreciatively and let out a long sigh. 'We had a second interview with Elliott, but it wasn't easy. It's hard to remain calm when someone is as disturbed as he is.'

'You are sure it isn't a front? An act to make you believe he's totally insane, when he's really a cold-blooded killer?' There was an edge to Joseph's voice that Nikki didn't like.

'I do know the difference, Joseph. He's as screwed up as anyone I've ever met.'

Joseph looked far from convinced, but then he hadn't met Elliott, other than to wrestle him to the ground and cuff him. Nikki took another sip of wine and decided that there would never be a better time to have it out with him.

'This case has really been hard on you, hasn't it, sweetheart? It's affected you more than any of our other investigations — apart from the one that almost saw you killed, of course.'

Joseph slowly swirled the wine around in his glass. 'It's his callous disregard for life — and young life at that. Now, because you believe he's mentally ill, he'll be treated like a sick man, not a murderer. He should be hanged for what he's done, though I know I'm not supposed to say that in these enlightened times.'

'It's not what I personally believe, it's what he is, Joseph. Morgan Flint will confirm it, and that's what the jury and the judge will see too.' Nikki tried to keep her voice from trembling. 'Den Elliott is damaged. You are the most reasonable and non-judgemental policeman I've ever met, so forgive me for not understanding the change in you over this. We've confronted terrible things before, you and I, and you have always seen all sides and been prepared to try to understand. Why is the Coachman so different?'

Joseph closed his eyes for a moment. 'It was the student. Another one died today, did you know that?'

She said that she did.

'I saw *my* daughter, *your* daughter, their lives extinguished with no regard whatsoever for who they were. Tossed into the flames, like discarded, unwanted toys. How can anyone be generous and forgiving with someone who does that?' Joseph asked bitterly.

'No one is asking you to be either of those things, Joseph. It's just that in the past, you've always looked at the reasons behind someone's behaviour. And you've always, always trusted the judicial system to do the right thing.'

'Ha! The CPS? You're joking! How many times have they thrown a perfectly good case out for lack of evidence? How many villains have walked because of them? I wouldn't know where to start.'

'He won't walk, that's for sure.' This was not going the way Nikki had hoped it would, but she needed to keep digging. She set down her glass. 'Joseph. Why didn't you tell me how you were feeling? Why did you shut me out? You've never done that before.'

Joseph put his own glass down. 'I didn't want to, Nikki. All I wanted was to talk to you, but I couldn't.' He leant forward and put his head in his hands. 'Something took over my thinking, and all I knew was that the Coachman had to be stopped before any more daughters, or sons, died horribly.' He looked up at her. 'For a while, I would have done anything to prevent another death.'

'Anything? Even if it meant losing your job, and losing the team, *our* team?' Nikki's mouth went dry. 'Is that why you brought Vinnie over to the Old Hall, to help you "stop" the Coachman?'

'Yes.' Joseph looked thoroughly miserable. 'But Vinnie wanted it done by the book. No other way. And that's how it happened, didn't it? You saw that yourself. By the book.'

'And if he hadn't had that panic attack? Which should never have happened, by the way, because he shouldn't have been up on that roof in the first place.'

Again, he put his head in his hands. 'I'll never forgive myself for that.'

Nikki persisted. She had to get to the end of this. 'And if that hadn't happened, and if you hadn't noticed that a firearms unit was up there with you, what would you have done, Joseph?'

'For a moment, I believed I was a soldier again, and Elliott was the enemy. I wanted to . . . to finish it. But I'm not that soldier, not now, and I won't be ever again.'

They both fell silent.

Nikki kept thinking of the life they had built together. That life, along with their precious team, had been on the verge of destruction.

Suddenly, it was all too much for Nikki to take in. She stood up and looked at him coolly. 'I think maybe you should go home tonight, Joseph.'

'I thought I was home,' he said quietly.

'So did I.' She swallowed back a sob, 'Now I'm not so sure.'

After a moment, Joseph slowly got up and walked out of the room.

As she heard her front door close, she had a sudden flashback. Once more she was alone in a room with the woman who had condemned her daughter Hannah to death. She had been a split second away from handing her over to a man who would certainly have killed her, but she had heard Joseph in her head, begging her to do the right thing. She had listened to him then, but what if she'd chosen not to? Did she have any right to judge him? Were they so different?

Nikki ran out of the house and into the night. 'Joseph! Joseph! Come back!'

But his car was moving out onto the marsh lane and accelerating away from her.

Still calling out his name, she chased after him until she saw his brake lights glow red in the darkness.

Joseph stepped out of his car and stood stock still, hardly visible against the black sky.

Nikki ran up to him, then stopped, breathless and unsure of what to say or do. Suddenly tears flooded her eyes, and she threw her arms around him. 'Come home, Joseph.

I know there's a lot more we need to say to make this right again, but right now, just come home.'

Joseph looked down at her and she saw he was crying too. 'Home? With you?'

She pushed him to arm's length and held him there. 'Yes, home, Sergeant! But only after you've moved this badly parked vehicle to a place of safety, or I'll see it's towed away!'

Nikki turned around, roughly wiped the tears from her eyes and marched back towards Cloud Cottage Farm. After a few seconds, she heard the purr of an engine behind her, and she breathed a sigh of relief.

THE END

THE JOFFE BOOKS STORY

We began in 2014 when Jasper agreed to publish his mum's much-rejected romance novel and it became a bestseller.

Since then we've grown into the largest independent publisher in the UK. We're extremely proud to publish some of the very best writers in the world, including Joy Ellis, Faith Martin, Caro Ramsay, Helen Forrester, Simon Brett and Robert Goddard. Everyone at Joffe Books loves reading and we never forget that it all begins with the magic of an author telling a story.

We are proud to publish talented first-time authors, as well as established writers whose books we love introducing to a new generation of readers.

We won Trade Publisher of the Year at the Independent Publishing Awards in 2023. We have been shortlisted for Independent Publisher of the Year at the British Book Awards for the last four years, and were shortlisted for the Diversity and Inclusivity Award at the 2022 Independent Publishing Awards. In 2023 we were shortlisted for Publisher of the Year at the RNA Industry Awards.

We built this company with your help, and we love to hear from you, so please email us about absolutely anything bookish at feedback@joffebooks.com

If you want to receive free books every Friday and hear about all our new releases, join our mailing list: www.joffebooks.com/contact

And when you tell your friends about us, just remember: it's pronounced Joffe as in coffee or toffee!

Milton Keynes UK
Ingram Content Group UK Ltd.
UKHW012331100724
445430UK00010B/156

9 781835 266113